## Praise for the Novels of Devon Monk

### *Magic on the Hunt*

"This is a really action-packed story with tons going on.... Once you get involved with these characters, you don't want to stop reading. They come alive and you begin to see Portland in a whole new way.... This is an absolutely awesome series with a complex world set in familiar surroundings. With action and characters that can't help but draw you into the drama and the dilemmas, you'll find yourself ignoring everything as you travel along with Allie, Zay, and their friends." —Night Owl Reviews

"The most exciting of the series yet."
—Dangerous Romance

"Get ready for another nonstop adventure in *Magic on the Hunt*." —Romance Reviews Today

"Superb." —Genre Go Round Reviews

"Congratulations to Ms. Monk for yet another great installment in the fantastic Allie Beckstrom series."
—A Book Obsession

"Oh, how much I love Devon Monk's Allie Beckstrom series. I have never missed a beat with her amazing urban fantasy.... This is one series that I can't get enough of and I really love how kick-butt Allie is."
—Seeing Night Book Reviews

### *Magic at the Gate*

"The action-packed fifth Allie Beckstrom novel amps up the magical mayhem.... Allie's adventures are gripping and engrossing, with an even, clever mix of humor, love, and brutality." —*Publishers Weekly*

"Devon Monk takes her story to places I couldn't have dreamed of. Each twist and turn was completely surprising for me. *Magic at the Gate* truly stands out."
—Reading on the Dark Side

*continued ...*

"A spellbinding story that will keep readers on the edge of their seats." —Romance Reviews Today

"Suspense is the name of the game. . . . I'm really enjoying this series. . . . Each book brings you a little bit further into it and leaves you wanting more." —Night Owl Reviews

### Magic on the Storm

"The latest Allie Beckstrom urban fantasy is a terrific entry. . . . This is a strong tale." —Genre Go Round Reviews

"First-rate urban fantasy entertainment."
—Lurv a la Mode

### Magic in the Shadows

"Snappy dialogue, a brisk pace, and plenty of magic keep the pages turning to the end. Allie's relationship with Zayvion, her friend Nola, and the other Hounds adds credible depth to this gritty, original urban fantasy that packs a punch." —Monsters and Critics

"This is a wonderful read full of different types of magic, fascinating characters, an intriguing plot. . . . Devon Monk is an excellent storyteller. . . . This book will keep everyone turning the pages to see what happens next and salivating for more." —Fresh Fiction

"Monk sweeps readers up in the drama and dangers of the heroine's life as it steadily changes and grows . . . an intriguing read with fascinating characters and new magical elements introduced to the mix." —Darque Reviews

"The writing moves at a fast pace with plenty of exciting action. . . . This series just gets better and better with each new book." —Night Owl Reviews

### Magic in the Blood

"Tight, fast, and vividly drawn, Monk's second Allison Beckstrom novel features fresh interpretations of the paranormal, strong characters dealing with their share of faults and flaws, [and] ghoulish plot twists. Fans of Patricia Briggs or Jim Butcher will want to check out this inventive new voice." —Monsters and Critics

# Magic Without Mercy

## An Allie Beckstrom Novel

## Devon Monk

A ROC BOOK

ROC
Published by New American Library, a division of
Penguin Group (USA) Inc., 375 Hudson Street,
New York, New York 10014, USA
Penguin Group (Canada), 90 Eglinton Avenue East, Suite 700, Toronto,
Ontario M4P 2Y3, Canada (a division of Pearson Penguin Canada Inc.)
Penguin Books Ltd., 80 Strand, London WC2R 0RL, England
Penguin Ireland, 25 St. Stephen's Green, Dublin 2,
Ireland (a division of Penguin Books Ltd.)
Penguin Group (Australia), 250 Camberwell Road, Camberwell, Victoria 3124,
Australia (a division of Pearson Australia Group Pty. Ltd.)
Penguin Books India Pvt. Ltd., 11 Community Centre, Panchsheel Park,
New Delhi - 110 017, India
Penguin Group (NZ), 67 Apollo Drive, Rosedale, Auckland 0632,
New Zealand (a division of Pearson New Zealand Ltd.)
Penguin Books (South Africa) (Pty.) Ltd., 24 Sturdee Avenue,
Rosebank, Johannesburg 2196, South Africa

Penguin Books Ltd., Registered Offices:
80 Strand, London WC2R 0RL, England

First published by Roc, an imprint of New American Library,
a division of Penguin Group (USA) Inc.

First Printing, April 2012
10  9  8  7  6  5  4  3  2  1

 REGISTERED TRADEMARK—MARCA REGISTRADA

Printed in the United States of America

PUBLISHER'S NOTE
This is a work of fiction. Names, characters, places, and incidents either are the product of the author's imagination or are used fictitiously, and any resemblance to actual persons, living or dead, business establishments, events, or locales is entirely coincidental.
    The publisher does not have any control over and does not assume any responsibility for author or third-party Web sites or their content.

*For my family*

# *Acknowledgments*

Without the many people who have contributed time and energy along the way, this book would not have come to fruition. I'd like to give a much-deserved thank-you to my agent, Miriam Kriss, and my editor, Anne Sowards, two consummate professionals and all-around awesome people who make my job easy.

My love and endless gratitude go out to my fantastic first readers and brainstormers, Dean Woods and Dejsha Knight, whose loving support and brilliant insights not only make the story stronger, but also make me a better writer. Thank you also to my family, one and all, who have been there for me every step of the way, offering unfailing encouragement and sharing in the joy. To my husband, Russ, and sons, Kameron and Konner—if I haven't said it lately, thank you for believing in me. You are the very best part of my life. I love you.

Lastly, but certainly not leastly, thank you, dear readers, for letting me share this story, these people, and this world with you.

# Chapter One

I had a headache. That headache's name was Shamus Flynn.

"Allie, my love," he said, "you're wrong." That got him a quick glare from Zayvion, who was sitting cross-legged on the floor in front of the fireplace. Zay dragged a whetstone along the edge of his katana and caught my gaze.

"Would you like me to make him shut up?" Zay asked with a little more excitement than I liked to hear.

Terric, who was rummaging through a stack of knives on the shelf, just snorted. "Good fucking luck with that."

"No, it's fine," I said. "It's just—"

"You're wrong," Shame said again, flipping off Terric. "I'm telling you, you'd do best with a projectile weapon. You can't use magic anymore, so you'll have to keep a certain distance from the fight. Get in too close and magic will eat you alive. Then it will eat you dead just for good measure."

Shame was right. I couldn't use magic. Ever since we'd fought Leander and Isabelle at the Life well and nearly gotten killed, magic had been making me sick. It had only gotten worse the more I used it, and when I'd tried to use a Tracking spell on a Veiled—an undead magic user I'd seen step out of a living person—I'd passed out and hit my head on the concrete.

Now if I so much as breathed an abracadabra, I was

on the floor puking. I had no idea why I was the only one suddenly allergic to magic. Maybe because I was the only possessed person I knew? Maybe because I could literally pull magic up through my body, whereas other people just drew it into the air and directed it into spells. Whatever the reason, it was seriously cramping my style.

"I don't want a gun," I repeated.

"Come, now," Shame coaxed. "Look at all the pretty options."

"Options" was an understatement. When Shame had told us he had a small stash of weapons that the Authority didn't know about, his only omission was how damn many blades, cudgels, whips, sticks, pointed things, explosive devices, and guns he had squirreled away in the rickety three-story town house bolted into the cliff side.

Seriously. I flinched every time he lit a cigarette.

"Shamus," his mother, Maeve, said from where she was resting on the couch in what might have been a comfortable modern living room before Shame had covered the walls, bookshelves, and entertainment center with both magical and nonmagical killing devices. "If she doesn't want a gun, don't trouble her so about it. What weapon would you rather carry, Allison?" she asked.

I glanced over at Maeve. She was drinking a cup of tea, her bare feet up on an overturned crate that said EXPLOSIVES across the side. She looked a little more rested after her short nap. Victor still had his eyes closed and was resting in the reclining chair by the window.

Shame had had the sense to keep most of the house in working order. There were beds, a surprisingly nice kitchen, and a fairly well-stocked pantry that Hayden was off investigating.

I rubbed my palms down the sides of my jeans, wiping away sweat. Staring at the guns Shame had laid out on the coffee table made my skin crawl. I wasn't sure I could touch a gun, much less use one.

I didn't want to kill again. Not like that.

*Bartholomew gave you little choice,* my dad, who was still dead and still possessing a corner of my brain, said quietly. *Whatever advantage we have now, it is because of you. Of what you did to him.*

It was strange hearing my father talk about us—me, Zayvion, Shame, Terric, Hayden, Maeve, and Victor—like he was a part of our group, wanting the same things we wanted, fighting for the same things we were fighting for. Or maybe it wasn't so strange anymore. He'd helped us—helped me—more in the past few days than he had in my entire life.

And now that we had mutinied from the Authority, gone against Authority law—and, oh, yeah, did I mention I shot the man who had assigned himself as head of Portland's Authority?—we needed all the help we could get.

Even if that meant listening to the dead guy.

"I don't know," I said, answering Maeve's question. "Maybe I'll stick to a blade."

Shame made a *tsk* sound. "Don't want to shoot a man, nice and clean," he said, "but you're more than happy to carve him up? You sure about that? Swords can be messy business."

"It's all messy business," I said. "And the only thing I'm sure about is that I'm not going to decide this right now."

"Better sooner than later."

"I'll do it in the morning."

Zay stopped running his thumb along the edge of his katana and sheathed it. He gave me a steady look. The same kind of measuring look Victor, who I had thought was half asleep, and Terric, who was finished digging through the things on Shame's shelf, were giving me.

"What?" I asked.

"It is morning," Shame said. "Has been for hours now."

I closed my eyes and tipped my face up to the ceiling. Hells, I was tired. I didn't remember the last time I'd slept, didn't remember the last time I'd eaten. I smelled like old magic, death, and blood. And I was not going to pick up a gun, make another decision, or do another damn thing until I got clean and fed.

"Someone make breakfast, okay?" I lowered my gaze from the ceiling. "I'm going to take a shower."

I strode down the hall, past the open kitchen area — where Hayden was whistling a song from *Phantom of the Opera* — and past the two guest bedrooms where everyone had slept . . . except for me. I'd spent my downtime sweating off nightmares and staring at the darkness while listening to make sure whoever was on watch was still awake and watching.

The last door on the right was the guest bathroom. I walked in and flicked on the lights.

I didn't know why Shamus had decided to buy a house. When we'd asked, he had used an unconvincing innocent-eyes look on his mother and told her he hadn't bought it — he'd won it in a poker game.

Most likely he'd stolen it.

Whoever had built the thing was either a genius or a madman. It really was bolted into the cliff, the roofline beneath the road above, which snaked the hill in hairpin curves, and the hill around it was covered in sword fern and vine maple among the fir trees. If you weren't trying really hard to look for it, you wouldn't see the house at all. Not because of magic. No, nothing other than a perverse sense of architectural humor kept it hidden.

But for all that, it was decorated in a clean, modern style with just enough nice touches to show that whoever had lived here liked luxury and knew which luxuries mattered most.

And one of those luxuries was the shower. The thing took up half of the huge bathroom, and had more sprays, mists, and other watery onslaughts than a November storm front. Dark marble and chrome hinted toward a man's aesthetic, but didn't make the room feel cold or uninviting.

I shucked out of every stitch I had on, hoped Dad would do me the favor of not paying attention to me for the next twenty minutes or so, and turned on the shower.

The entire ceiling above the shower sprayed water as if someone had nailed a rain cloud to the rafters. I stepped into that steady stream and closed my eyes, letting the water sluice away my aches.

But when I closed my eyes, all I saw were images of the Veiled—far too strong now, and growing stronger. The Veiled had always wandered the city, not that most people believed in them.

It didn't used to be a problem to share the city with dead magic users. But something had gone wrong with the Veiled and with magic itself. Somehow magic had been poisoned, and the Veiled had been changed in some way. The Veiled were carriers of the poison now, biting, possessing, and killing people.

Sure, I got sick when I tried to use magic, but other people could use it just fine. However if a Veiled touched or bit them, they came down with a sickness. The Veiled were roaming this city, hurting people like my friend Davy Silvers, or, worse, killing people like Anthony Bell.

The news outlets had reported it as a fast-spreading virus. Nothing magical. But we knew differently. And the one person in a position to stop the sickness and death had been the head of the Authority, Bartholomew Wray.

He hadn't wanted to stop it. He had wanted the disaster to reach massive proportions. Because he had a grudge against my father and wanted Dad's technology that made magic accessible for the common magic user deemed not only unsafe but deadly. Once the technology was destroyed and outlawed, magic would once again be under the singular control of the Authority. His control.

Bartholomew Wray had planned to destroy more than just my dad's technology. He wanted to ruin his business, his wife, and me.

And he didn't care how many deaths it took for him to get his way. All of Portland could fall and he wouldn't care.

So I'd shot him. Killed him. In cold blood.

My thoughts skittered away from that—away from his death. The back of my throat tasted sour. I'd stared him straight in the eyes and pulled the trigger.

I wasn't a killer.

No, that was a lie now.

I'd changed. I had killed. More than once. I didn't know what I was anymore.

*Alive,* Dad whispered from the back of my mind. Then, *Strong.*

Nothing like a dead man talking in my head while I was showering to remind me that I had plenty of current problems that needed taking care of. One thing was for sure: I didn't want to talk morality with my father. I didn't agree with Bartholomew, but Dad's opinions of right and wrong weren't mine. I didn't like what I'd done. I wasn't sure I ever could.

I got busy with the shampoo and soap and used a scrubby cloth over every inch of my skin.

Dad gave me the decency of privacy, or at least the

sense of it, since he didn't say anything more, and pulled far enough away in my mind that I couldn't feel him.

Problems. I had them. It was time to make a list:

One, I didn't know what was going to happen to the Authority now that Bartholomew was dead. Two, we had to find a way to cleanse magic of the poison or whatever it was, stop the Veiled from biting and spreading the poison, and find a cure to end the epidemic. Maybe that was really two through four. So, five, I needed to find a way to cure Davy before he got any worse. And six, we were running out of options and allies to do anything.

In short, we were screwed.

I reached over to turn off the shower. Before my hands touched the handles, a flash of light filled the room, bringing with it the stink of hot copper and concrete. I squinted against the glare and pressed my back against the wall, tracing Block before I remembered I couldn't use magic without barfing.

My left palm stabbed with cold and pain.

Shit.

I shook the spell free, breaking it and waving off the cold and pain, then pushed away from the wall and opened the shower door.

The flash of light was now a concentrated bolt of magic frozen midstrike at a ragged angle from the ceiling to the floor. The air tasted of salt and concrete and hot copper.

In the three seconds it took for that to register, I knew what the spell was.

Gate.

Something, or someone, was about to join me in the bathroom.

And here I was all naked. Again.

Go, me.

The lightning bolt burned black, then split in half,

opening a space, or doorway, wide enough I could see the arc of a distant blue sky where the ceiling lamps should be.

A man stepped through the gate.

Tall, rugged, world-worn Roman Grimshaw, the ex-con, ex–Guardian of the gates, strode into the room. With a flick of his hand, the gate slammed shut behind him, leaving gray ashes of the already dying spell to drift down and cling to his long leather jacket. I blinked and the bolt of lightning was a faded afterimage in the steamy room.

For a moment, there was no sound other than our breathing and water raining against tiles.

Roman held very still, his hands away from his body, not using magic. His frown slowly shifted to surprise as he focused on the slightly damp, exceedingly naked me standing in front of him with my hands on my hips.

"You going to hand me a towel or what?" I asked.

That seemed to snap him out of his shock. He quickly turned and picked up the towel folded on the edge of the sink.

The bathroom door burst open.

Hey, just what I needed. More people in the bathroom with me and my birthday suit.

Roman spun to face Zayvion, who had a fistful of Impact spell that snapped like a ball of red fire. His blood dagger in the other hand was already halfway through a Cleave spell.

"Peace," Roman said, with the slightest hint of his Scottish accent. He threw his hands out to the sides, dropping my towel on the floor.

Neat. Who knew when that floor had last been swept?

Zay stopped drawing the Cleave and flicked a gaze at me. I gave him what I hoped to be a bored look and he went back to glaring at the ex–Guardian of the gates. He did not, I noted, drop the Impact spell.

While they were sizing up each other and the situation, all the warm copper-tasting steam was cooling on my bare skin. I shivered and turned off the water. Then I bent and got my own damn towel, shaking it once before wrapping it tightly around me.

No one said anything. No one moved.

Until Shame strode up to the door, a mug of coffee in his hand. "For Christsake, Grimshaw, use the frickin' front door. Is it some kind of requirement that all Guardians of the gates have to do that creepy stalker thing?"

"What are you doing here?" Zayvion asked.

"I have been hunting Leander and Isabelle," Roman said.

"And?" Zay asked.

"They are no longer in Portland."

That was a problem. Leander and Isabelle were Soul Complements who had lived hundreds of years ago and found a way to cheat death. They were here among the living, and though they didn't have physical bodies, they were capable of possessing people, and drawing on incredible amounts of magic together. Soul Complements can make magic break its own rules. If they figured out how to use the tainted magic to their advantage, it might not be just an epidemic we were fighting. It might be an apocalypse.

"Super interesting," I interrupted. "Really, just. But I'd rather hear it clothed. Take it outside, gentlemen."

"You're naked?" Shame said, trying to get a better look around Zayvion and Roman.

Zayvion canceled the Impact spell, and motioned Grimshaw out into the hall with his blood blade.

"She's naked?" Shame asked again as Zayvion shoved his shoulder to make him turn around. "Aw, give a man a break. What's a little accidental nakedness between friends?"

"Not happening." Zay gave Shame a harder shove and closed the door so that only he could see into the room. "Are you all right?" he asked me.

"Peachy. I don't think Roman expected to show up in a bathroom. It's hard to predict where Gates will open, right?"

Zay paused. "For normal people. Roman can open a Gate on the head of a pin. I'll talk to him." He gave me a not-entirely-tolerant look and then shut the door behind him.

Fantastic. So Roman had intended to show up in the bathroom, alone, with me. Or maybe he just wanted to show up in the bathroom. I wondered how he even knew there would be a room here. He'd been in jail for years before Shame had wheedled his way into home ownership.

More questions that needed answers. And how Roman knew we'd be here, now, was just the beginning. We needed to know everything he had found out about Leander and Isabelle too.

I dressed, then rubbed the towel through my hair so my shoulders wouldn't get wet. Took me all of a few seconds. Then I walked out into the living room.

Roman had been given the guest interloper seat of honor—a chair in the middle of the room with everyone else standing in a circle around him. No one was casting magic, but everyone had a weapon in one hand and a spell in the other. Well, everyone except Roman.

"Sounds like good news to me," Hayden said, his shotgun resting casually across his shoulder. "The farther away Leander and Isabelle run, the better. Now tell me how you knew we'd be here, and who sent you to find us."

Roman looked up at the big man. "I came here of my own accord. My days of serving anyone's agenda are long gone."

"You do know you're a criminal?" Hayden asked. "And I have every right to take you down and take you in."

Okay, so these two were not friends.

"We're all criminals," Zayvion said. "We've broken our vows with the Authority. We've gone against their direct orders."

"I haven't." Hayden gave Zayvion a hard look. "And neither has Terric."

Terric had taken his place beside Shame behind Roman's back.

"Is there some reason we need to go over this again?" Terric asked. "If you want out of this, Hayden," he said calmly, "then you should leave now. I'm in this to the end."

Hayden scowled. "I didn't mean—"

"It doesn't matter," I said, flat, hard, in the voice that always stops the Hounds from bickering. Everyone looked over at me. Good.

"Roman," I said, "we've broken with the Authority and no longer follow their rule or orders. You should know that before you say anything else."

"And who's running the Authority now?" he asked.

"We're not sure," I said. "Maybe Jingo Jingo. I killed Bartholomew Wray."

Roman's eyebrows shot up, and then he looked me up from foot to face. His expression when his gaze finally met my eyes was one of deep respect and maybe just a little fear.

Good. Respect and fear went a long way when doing business.

"Why?" he asked.

"The Veiled are on the streets possessing people and killing them. Hundreds are falling ill from the tainted magic they're carrying. Hundreds are dying. He knew it. He wouldn't stop it. So I stopped him."

My voice was even, but I broke out in a sweat saying those words. I didn't think I'd ever get used to the reality of what I'd done.

"I see." He looked at each of the magic users in turn. Then nodded. "I have only one goal—to see that Leander and Isabelle die. I have no grudge with any of you, and do not care who controls the Authority. I broke with it long ago."

"See, we'd just love to take you on your word, mate," Shame said, "but I say we should Truth on it." He pulled a switchblade out of his belt and grinned as he strolled around in front of Roman. "Worth a little blood to you?"

"It is." Roman held out his left hand, palm up.

"Shame," Maeve said.

"Not to worry, Mum." Shame flicked the blade free. "Sweet and easy."

He sliced the side of Roman's hand, then pricked his own finger. With the blood caught and mingled on the blade, he drew the glyph for Truth in the air between them. The room filled with the overpowering smell of sweet, sweet cherries. Blood magic.

"Who are you working for?" Shame asked.

"No one but myself."

"Why did you come here?"

"To tell you that Leander and Isabelle have left Portland and I don't know why. To see if you have information I can use to track them."

"How did you know we'd be here?" Shame asked.

"Allison has a piece of death in her palm. Given to her in death by Mikhail. It's easy enough to find if you're looking for it."

I glanced down at my left hand. The dark circle in the center of my palm was still there, and still cold, though it wasn't hurting anymore like it had in the shower the moment before the Gate had opened. It hadn't been much trouble lately, so I'd taken to ignoring it. Pike had said it was something the dead could see like a beacon. Maybe it was something ex–Guardians of the gates could see like a beacon too.

I'd traded away the small flicker of magic that I'd always carried inside me for that black blessing from Mikhail. It was the only way I could get myself and Zayvion back from death. Dad had helped me use the mark to cast magic against the Veiled, but that was about all the good it'd done me.

I lifted my hand in case anyone in the room didn't have the complete scorecard on all the weird things that had happened to me in the last year.

"Are you here to betray us?" Shame asked.

"No."

"Is that accent of yours fake?" Shame asked.

"No. Is yours?"

"I don't have an accent," Shame said.

"Shamus," Maeve sighed. "Blood magic isn't a toy."

Shame grinned. "Everything's a toy," he said, "if you mess with it enough. Anyone else have any questions for our man Roman here?"

"I think it's enough," I said.

But Zayvion spoke up. "What are you going to do to Leander and Isabelle if you find them?"

"Kill them. Send them through a gate to death. Remove them from this living world. Anything I have to do to stop them."

Zayvion nodded.

Shame broke the Truth spell and the scent of sweet cherries was so thick it made my eyes sting.

I pinched at the bridge of my nose, trying to ease the headache hovering behind my skull. Magic and me were not a good mix lately.

Maeve broke whatever spell she'd kept poised on the

tips of her fingers. I think it was Hold. "Well, then," she said. "Roman, we were just going to have something to eat. Would you care to join us?"

The other magic users dropped their spells. It was like watching stained-glass windows shatter into liquid drops of color that turned to mist and were gone.

Magic, sometimes, can be a very beautiful thing.

Roman gazed at Maeve and gave her a smile. I'd never seen him smile and suddenly wished I'd known him in better times. Man was handsome, but that smile carved a decade off his looks and brought to him a humanity that imprisonment and a hard life running hard magic had not afforded.

I noted his smile was not lost on Maeve.

Or Hayden.

Ah, suddenly the tension between Hayden and Roman made some sense.

"Thank you, Maeve," Roman said as he stood. "I would."

# *Chapter Two*

That settled, we all got busy divvying up the food Hayden had cooked: potato hash, scrambled eggs, sausage, and toast.

None of us sat. We stood around the kitchen island so we could reload our plates more easily. Well, that, and from the feeling of restlessness in the air, we were all a little twitchy, wanting to get moving before we were found out, tracked down, or forced to run.

"How do you know Leander and Isabelle aren't in Portland?" Zayvion asked after he demolished half a plate of potatoes.

"I saw them open a Gate and step through," Roman said.

"Were they solid?" I asked. Last time I'd seen Leander and Isabelle, they were ghostly, no more solid than the Veiled. They'd been looking for a body to possess, but needed one that was caught between life and death in some manner. There's just not enough room in a body for more than one soul for very long, so Leander and Isabelle needed a person who was only part of a soul, or partly dead, if they wanted to be physical.

And yes, it made me wonder how Dad and I both managed to survive in my body. He'd asked me about it briefly when we were in Death, but I hadn't had much time to contemplate the logistics of it. Zay once said it had something to do with us being blood related. I didn't know if that was true or not.

"They were not solid," Roman said. "They possessed two young people for a few hours." He frowned at his plate, pushing at the eggs with his fork. "Neither of them survived. They were discarded like candy wrappers after Leander and Isabelle opened the Gate. I didn't see where the gate opened onto."

"Horizon?" Zayvion asked.

"Trees. Out of doors," Roman said. "But that was all. No building, no landmark, no body of water."

"Time zone?"

"It was night when they opened the Gate. Before midnight." He frowned, sifting through his memories. He nodded slowly. "I saw daylight. I'm sure it was daylight on the other side. Early morning."

"So the other side of the world," Zayvion said. "Maybe England? Russia?"

"Nowhere in the Western hemisphere." He straightened, and ran his finger and thumb down from the corners of his mouth. "Half a world to hunt."

"What kind of Gate were they using?" Victor asked.

Roman shook his head. "Ezekiel's Hands."

Terric whistled in appreciation. "I've read about it," he said. "Never seen it. Zay?"

"No. I attempted it. Once."

Shame laughed. "I remember that. You couldn't pronounce your name for a week."

"Why is that Gate so difficult?" I asked.

"It's old," Victor said. "Ancient. And it's based on both light and dark magic being used together in large quantities. The price to pay for it is . . . extreme."

Which meant those young people they had been possessing and discarded like candy wrappers had paid the price to open that Gate.

"Why did they choose that Gate?" I asked.

"Distance," Roman said. "And precision. The man who can open Ezekiel's Hands has the world at his beck and call."

"Can you cast it?" I asked.

Everyone else in the kitchen got a little quieter, pausing with their forks, waiting.

"I've done it," he said. "Years ago. When I was younger. And stronger." He took a drink of his coffee. "But today? Today it would be my death."

"So what do you use?" Zayvion asked. "For distance and precision?"

"Trigemina," he said.

Zayvion's eyebrows shot up and he smiled. "I never got the hang of that one. Three spells at once?"

"You have to hold them at once," Roman said, "but you don't have to cast them simultaneously."

Zay leaned forward. "Really? Is there a preferred order?"

Like a kid in a candy shop. Zayvion had just found someone he could learn from, a man who had held the same position in the Authority as Zayvion. A man who had stood as the guardian between this world and any other place the gates could open upon.

"I find it easiest to begin with the most inward spell," Roman said. "That sets your focus, grounds your will, holds magic to your direction. If you can hold it in your mind's eye, then the companion spells flow easily from hand and voice. If not"—he gave Zay a quick smile—"well, there's always a plane ticket."

Zay actually laughed. "I suppose there is."

It was great to see them talking shop and all that, but we still had an issue at hand. Several issues.

"Are you going to hunt Leander and Isabelle?" I asked.

"I am," Roman said, the smile gone now. "But it may take me time to find them."

"They'll make themselves known," Zayvion said. "Trip some trigger, open another Gate. You'll know."

"With a Gate shift at that distance, they'll have to rest," Roman said. "It could be a while before they do anything."

"Then maybe you could help us," I said.

He looked at me. Correction, everyone looked at me. "We are limited on manpower," I said. "And there's every chance we won't succeed in what we're doing. If we fail—"

"As if," Shame said.

"If," I continued, "we fail, the information we have needs to fall into the hands of someone who can do something to stop this plague."

"What plague?" Roman shifted his gaze between me, Victor, and Maeve.

"Bartholomew Wray had Maeve and me Closed," Victor said. "My memory's spotty on some of the recent events."

"As is mine, I'm afraid," Maeve said. "Allie, would you tell him what you know?"

"We think magic has been poisoned," I said. "We know the cisterns are tainted, and that the tainted magic is mutating the Veiled, who are in turn spreading the tainted magic by biting and possibly possessing people, which is causing people to become sick."

"Magic can't be poisoned," he said. Even though it was a statement, his eyes questioned each of us.

"So we've always assumed," Zayvion agreed.

"Roman," I said. "You were there when we fought Leander and Isabelle at the Life well. Shame was possessed by Mikhail, and Sedra was possessed by Leander and Isabelle. Do you remember seeing Leander and Isabelle using a spell, or something else that could have poisoned the magic in the well?"

He shook his head. "They were using a lot of magic. Old spells. Mixed disciplines. Did things with magic that only Soul Complements can do. I can't be sure of every spell they cast."

"We have to be sure," I said. "We have to find out if all magic has been tainted, or if it's only the magic filtered through the cisterns. We have to find out how magic has been poisoned if we're going to stop it. If we fail, we will need someone, someone we trust in a position of power, to know what's going on here. I want someone to have a fighting chance against this if the poison spreads outside Portland and infects the rest of the world."

That was the big problem we weren't addressing. That was the long-range worst-case scenario. All magic in the world was connected in some manner. Something that had gone this bad this quickly had every indication of picking up speed as it spread. People dying from tainted magic could become the first magical pandemic we'd have to face.

"Who do we trust?" I asked.

Shame just scoffed. "You're looking at us. Mostly."

"What kind of person do you have in mind?" Terric asked, giving Shame a shut-up look.

"Someone in the Authority, high up, who can give orders people will listen to," I said. "The Ward, maybe?"

"No," Victor said. "He is only the power over the region. If we want this information in the best hands possible, it should be given to the Overseer."

"What's that?" I asked.

Roman raised his eyebrows, stunned. "It's not a what. It's a who. You don't know who the Overseer is?"

"Should I?" I looked at Zay.

"The Overseer is the highest head of the Authority," Zayvion said with the kind of rhythm that made it sound like he'd memorized and recited this years ago. "The final Voice. The end Watch, the last Ward. The Overseer guides the world of magic and all who use it." He paused, then: "The position rotates between countries every four years. It is the highest rule, the highest position in the Authority. Right now, Margaret Stafford is the Overseer. She will be for three more years."

"Will she believe us?" I asked.

Victor rubbed at the bridge of his nose, then sighed. He was tired. We were all tired. "I suppose it depends on what we have to tell her. And which of us attempts to reach her."

"She needs to know that magic may be tainted and that the Veiled are mutating and possessing and killing people," I said. "That as far as we can tell, the spread of poison here in Portland isn't caused by a failure in the technology and magic integrations systems—"

*Thank you,* Dad said.

I ignored him.

"—which is what Bartholomew Wray may have told her, but that it may be the wells that are poisoned," I said. "Is there any way to reach her?"

Terric shook his head. "Not with Bartholomew's men still in town."

"And out for blood," Shame noted cheerfully.

"If Jingo Jingo is taking over the position of head of the Authority," Terric said, "he'll have every member of the Authority gunning for us."

"And our blood," Shame noted.

"They'll monitor gates," Hayden said. "Hell, they'll monitor the airports, bus terminals, highways, trains."

"And they'll be looking for blood," Shame said.

"Shamus," Maeve said. "Please. Shut it."

Shame rolled his eyes, but had the sense to seal his yap.

"Who will the Overseer listen to?" I asked.

We all looked at Victor.

He crossed his arms over his chest. "I've been removed from my position and Closed. She won't listen to me or Maeve. Zayvion has walked away from his vows, Shamus has never been considered one hundred percent reliable—"

"Watch it, mate," Shame said.

"—and neither have you, Allie. Which leaves either Hayden or Roman. With Roman's past, I am certain he would be quickly detained. That leaves Hayden."

"You want me to go to England to tell the Overseer that Bartholomew was killed because he didn't stop the spread of tainted magic?" Hayden asked. "I hate to break it to you, Victor, but there was a reason I've spent the last decade in Alaska. More than a few black eyes on my record. The Overseer wouldn't believe me."

"I'll go," Roman said. "Though I don't know if she'll listen to me. What proof do we have to offer her?"

*The box,* Dad said.

*What box?* I asked.

*The one I told you to pick up when you were in Bartholomew's office,* Dad said.

I frowned, wondering where I'd put it.

*On the bedside table,* Dad said.

Which meant he'd been paying close attention to what I'd been doing, so, ew, in the shower department, and that he was interested enough in the box to keep track of where I'd left it.

*What's in the box?* I asked as I walked out of the room, leaving everyone else to discuss the situation.

*Evidence.*

*Uh-huh. Want to give me a little more to go on?*

"Allie?"

I turned around. I was in the hall in front of the bedroom door. Zayvion was following me.

"What?"

"Are you all right?"

I frowned. "So far. Why?"

"You left right in the middle of the plan you were making."

"Oh. Right. Plan." I flicked on the bedroom light and walked in. "This is a part of it. Or might be." I walked over to the bedside table and picked up the metal box. Heavier than it looked. My dad had told me to take it after I'd shot Bartholomew. Somehow I'd kept ahold of it through our fight with the Veiled, closing the cistern, and then loading into Terric's van to come here.

Frankly, if he hadn't mentioned it, I probably would have left it behind.

"This," I said, hefting the lead box, "is something Dad says might help us."

"What is it?"

"He says it's evidence." *How is it evidence?*

"How?" Zayvion said at the same time.

*It is a recording device. Very subtle magic. It's been in that office, recording whenever it senses the vibration of speech.*

"You're kidding me," I said out loud.

"What did he say?" Zayvion, luckily, was getting used to me losing track of who was talking with their outside voice and who was talking with their dead-guy-in-my-brain voice.

"That it is a recording device." I handed him the box. "Can you make out what any of those spells are?"

Zayvion turned it in his hand and looked at all sides. He shook his head. "If I'd seen this any other time, I'd think it was some kind of decorative sculpture. I don't see any spells on it."

I could feel Dad smile in my mind. It was weird.

*There are no spells on it,* he said. *But the magic within it is shaped into spells that record onto a disk. What you see is just a decorative sculpture.*

"He said the recording is on a disk inside it."

*How do we open it?* I asked.

"Ah," Zayvion said.

*Like that,* Dad answered.

I looked over. Zay had slid one of the panels to the side and then pivoted it outward so that it was connected only by one corner.

Inside the box was a stack of a dozen disks suspended by copper, which surprised me, since copper is an inferior material when it comes to magic use.

Zayvion flicked a latch with his thumbnail, and the disks slid forward and then fanned out like, well, a fan. He tipped the box so he could read the spells on the disks. "I'll be damned," he said. "They must be pure silver and glass."

He gently drew the first disk out from the others. It was thin glass with grooves etched into it and a swirling webwork of silver painted through it. It looked more like art, or a very expensive brooch, than a recording device.

I was once again, if a little reluctantly, impressed by my father's genius.

"How much do you think that can record?" I asked Zayvion.

He shook his head, hard curiosity lighting his features as he tipped the disk to the light. "Hours at least."

*Days,* Dad said. *Months. Years.*

"Holy shit," I said quietly. "Dad says it can record for years."

"Looks like it will play on a computer. Am I right about that?" Zay asked.

Dad sort of nodded inside my head—another weird feeling. *The Overseer will have the correct equipment to extract the information.*

"So this was running while I was in the office with him?" I asked, finally catching on to why this might be a helpful thing.

"Hey, you two," Shame said from the doorway. "Enough snogging. Let's get this party on the road."

*Yes,* Dad said. *It was running while you were there, and when anyone was in the room.*

Bartholomew had held a lot of meetings in his office. That was where Melissa Whit had used that painful Truth spell on me. That was where Zayvion, Terric, and Shame had all testified on what had happened when we were fighting Leander and Isabelle out at the Life well. That was where Bartholomew had met with each of the people he had assigned as Voices of the Authority. It stood to reason there were a lot of interesting meetings held in that room. Plenty of information that could be used to clear our names, or at least get other people on our side to try to keep the poison from spreading.

If there was proof that Bartholomew was acting in his own interest instead of in the interest of the Authority, it was on those pretty, shiny disks.

"He said yes, Zay," I said. "Our evidence of what Bartholomew had been doing is on those disks. Anything that happened in his office is on those disks."

"Very nice," Zayvion murmured as he very carefully replaced the disk inside the copper webbing and pressed another lever. The disks retracted back into the box and Zayvion set the locking latch.

"That's a beaut," Shame said. "Your da put it together?"

I nodded. "And we're going to get this to the Overseer. Did that get settled? Is Hayden up for it?"

"Hell no," Shame said with a grin. "Arguing like it's buy-one-get-one-free doomsday out there. All I know is I'm not going to be the one who flies off to England to get audience with Stafford. I'd like my internal organs, and my memories, to stay right where they are, thank you very much."

"Someone needs to go," I said.

"Not me," Shame said. "Unreliable, remember? So sad."

"I'll go," Zayvion said.

It felt like a punch to the stomach. "You can't."

He raised one eyebrow. "Why not?"

*Because I don't want you to* didn't seem like a very logical thing to say. It wasn't even a very convincing thing to say. So instead I just held my hand out for the box. "Because you are needed here."

"Hmm." Zayvion placed the box in my palm, holding eye contact. I knew what he was thinking. We were close enough, his thoughts would have been easy to read even if we weren't Soul Complements. He thought I was being overly protective of him. He thought I was going to make decisions with my heart instead of my head.

Wasn't he going to be surprised?

"We do this right, and we do this smart," I said. "No one's going to martyr on my watch. That's just a dumb way to waste manpower. Understand, Flynn?" I asked.

Shame was leaning in the doorway, his arms crossed over his chest. "Glare at some other sucker, Beckstrom," he said. "I don't throw myself in front of bullets. That's your gig."

"It's not a gig if you've done it only once," I said.

Shame held up three fingers. "I think you're a little off on your bullet count."

"Fine. Three times. But only twice to save someone."

"You mean Zay," he said. "Only twice to save Zay. Maybe you ought to get him out of town for a bit. Could make for a bullet-free day or two. Good for the staying-breathing portion of your plan."

"Not talking about it anymore," I said. "Going to go figure out who can get this info to England instead." I pointed down the hall, and Shame turned and walked ahead of me.

"Who do *you* want to do this, Allie?" Zayvion asked as we followed Shame back to the living room, where everyone was waiting.

Correction—not waiting. More like strapping on weapons and preparing to leave.

# Chapter Three

"Did someone make a plan?" I asked.

Roman shrugged. He had a sword lying across his back, the hilt rising just above his left shoulder. He was picking up and putting down several long knives spread out across what used to be a dining room sideboard.

"I'll take the message to the Overseer," he said.

"Why you?" I asked. "You're just as guilty as the rest of us for breaking Authority rule."

"No, I am not." He turned. "It was Isabelle possessing Sedra who trumped up the charges to lock me away. Isabelle has never been the head of the Authority, though she has possessed Sedra for years. I was wrongly imprisoned. The Overseer will hear my case."

He sounded pretty certain about that.

"And I can get there in two gates," he said. "I think even Zayvion would have to use more than five." He looked at Zayvion.

"I could do it in two," Zay said.

"Aye, but I'll be conscious by the end of it." Roman gave him a hard smile.

Zayvion strode over and Roman squared to meet him.

Zay was wider in the shoulder than Roman but just as tall. Where Roman had the long lean lines that spoke of height and his age and maybe too much imprisonment, it didn't give him the fuck-you-up bruiser build Zayvion carried so smoothly.

If I had to put money down on a fight between the two of them, I'd side with Zayvion every time.

"How about we do this?" Zayvion said in that low rumble that usually resulted in someone getting his nose broken. "You and me. See who can punch holes through reality and come out smiling on the other side."

"How about we do?" Roman agreed.

"How about we do not?" Victor said in the stern teacher tone I hadn't heard for weeks. "This is not a contest of which of you is a better Guardian of the gates. This is a mission that will save lives. Let us remember our vows, gentlemen."

"To keep magic safe," Roman said.

"And the lives of the innocent," Zayvion said.

"Even if we have broken with the Authority," Victor said, "we have not broken with our honor."

Zay paused, then listened to the man who had always been his teacher. "Safe journey, Roman."

"And to you," he replied.

Zayvion turned toward me. "Allie, he'll need the box." He gave me a quick smile. He liked Roman, liked a man he could compete with, prove himself up to. I was suddenly glad Roman was taking the mission. Otherwise I had a feeling I'd be spending the next several days trying to keep the two of them from daring each other into ever-increasing stupid contests.

I walked past Zay and handed Roman the box.

"This contains a dozen disks of glass and silver. On them is all the proof the Overseer will need to know that there is a magical plague spreading in the city. It contains our statements about the fight with Isabelle and Leander out at the Life well, and it probably has a lot of other information. It's been in Bartholomew's office, recording conversations since Bartholomew came back to town."

*Before then,* Dad said.

"And before then," I added. "The Overseer should have the equipment needed to access the information."

Roman stashed the box in the innermost pocket of his long coat. "I'll put it in her hands myself."

"Thank you," I said. "Safe journey."

"Keep tight hold on him, girl," he said, quietly. "We're all counting on the two of you in this. Have been for some time now."

I nodded, not having the faintest clue what he was talking about. Keep tight hold on whom? Zayvion? My dad? And who was this "we" he was talking about?

But he had already walked off to the center of the room. "When I open the Gate, they'll see the spike in magic for miles around," he said. "You'll want to be on your way shortly after."

"Here, Allie." Shame straightened from where he'd been kneeling by a shelf and pressed a holster into my hand. "This is a gun. Not the one Collins made, since you're all cootified about that one. This is metal, and the clip?" He pulled the gun out of the holster and slapped the clip free. "Bullets worked with magic."

"I don't—"

"You damn well do." He shoved the clip back in the gun, the gun in the holster, and put it all in my hand, holding his hand over it so I couldn't let it go. "I want you to get out of this alive. That means you will use any weapon necessary to see that you survive. Zay won't force you to do it, but I will. You'll carry a gun, and you'll use it to keep yourself and us alive. Got that?"

No joking, no bullshit. This was Shame stripped down to the stark darkness that curled like death and violence in his soul. He knew as soon as we stepped out on those streets, we were walking blind into a war. All of us were going to have to bear the pain for the magic we called upon. And I was going to have to bear the pain for carrying a weapon that made me face what I had become. A killer.

"I hate you," I said quietly.

"Better to hate than to be dead, love." He let go of the gun and turned his back on me. "Plenty of blades, bombs, and bludgeons to go around, people," he said. "Let's get on with it, shall we?"

I hesitated a moment. Didn't matter what Shame said. This was my life, my choice. I didn't have to carry a gun just because he told me to.

But he was right. And I'd known it all along. I needed to use any weapon I had at my disposal to get through this. I slipped the holster over my shoulders, my hands steady and sure.

"Roman's taking the evidence to the Overseer," I said to keep my mouth busy doing something while Zayvion handed me spare clips that I slid into my pockets.

"Terric, I want you to find out if the Authority and Bartholomew's men have discovered you're with us. If they haven't, I need you to gather information on who's running the Authority now. If you can find out what resources they're using to find us, to stop us, and whether they're guarding the wells, that would be more than useful.

"Also see if they've changed their stance on the technology-is-poisoning-magic theory by some damn miracle. If someone running the Authority is suddenly working on a cure for this magical infection, that would be good news."

"How do you want me to contact you?" he asked. Terric was going with more subtle weaponry. And by subtle I meant two axes he tucked in the belt at his hips, and several throwing knives he was snicking into place on the bolero across his chest. I assumed he also had a gun stashed somewhere on his body.

The trench coat/loose coat look that Terric, Zayvion, and Shamus always seemed to favor suddenly made sense to me. I wondered if there was a coat here I could borrow.

"I tossed my phone. So did Zayvion," I said. "So we can't keep in contact that way. Any ideas, people?"

"Did you happen to steal any of the message beads, Shame?" Maeve asked.

"Steal? Please, Mum. Give me some credit." Shame paused, hands on his hips. He tipped his head as if going through a list of things.

"Might have something in the master bedroom. Just a tick." He strode off down the hall.

"So," I said, "we need to get to the wells and see if magic has been tainted at those source points.

"Zayvion and I will go to the Life well. Maeve, do you think you could get to the inn without anyone noticing and check the Blood well?"

"Unless there were cameras at the cistern," she said, "or someone following Zayvion, no one knows I have been Unclosed. And since I live there, I can't imagine they would expect me to be anywhere else right now. So, yes. I think I can check. If I run into trouble, I can take care of that too."

Maeve was a Blood magic user. A very good Blood magic user. She might seem like a gentle soul, but she was fury in a fight.

"I'll go with you," Hayden said.

She smiled. "I'd hoped so."

"Where do you want me, Allie?" Victor asked.

That was the strangest thing. Victor was my teacher, and I guess I'd sort of expected him to stay in the fatherly mentor position in my life. I'd never had him ask me what he should do before. It was strange to be taking the lead position. But not entirely unfamiliar. I'd been coordinating the Hounds for months now.

"Two things," I said. "Can you get in to the Faith well and see if it's clean?"

"I should be able to. What's the second thing?"

"I'd like to get information to Violet, to warn her and Kevin about the poison."

He thought about it a second. "I think I could contact Kevin fairly easily. Zayvion, did you Close all the years he and I have worked together?"

"No. Just the last fifteen or so."

He set his shoulders, like bearing an unfamiliar weight. "Well, then. I imagine I might want to have coffee with him just to catch up on our chess game. It shouldn't be a problem, and shouldn't take long. What is the plan afterward?"

"We'll contact each other once we have information," I said. "Find out if the wells are tainted, who's running the Authority, what they're sending out to stop us, and whether Violet is at a safe distance from all this. I'll need to contact Collins to see if Davy's doing all right, but that can wait until after we check on the wells.

"Where should we meet up?" I asked. "Should we decide that now?"

"Better not," Roman said. He was still standing in the center of the room, looking relaxed, instead of like someone who was about to open a Gate halfway across the world and march straight up to the very people who could lock him away again. Or kill him.

"The less that any of us know where we're all going," he said, "the less chance there is someone will Truth it out of us."

That made sense. "So we'll contact each other with the information and a meeting place when the time comes," I said. "Works for me."

Shame strolled in with a shoe box. "Here we are."

"You put them in a shoe box?" Maeve asked. "Shamus, these are invaluable. Heirlooms."

"Which is why I stuck them in a shoe box. Safekeeping."

He placed the box on the coffee table and lifted the lid. The soft scent of roses filled the room.

"I didn't know you'd kept these, Maeve," Victor said. "Hugh did fine work."

"Yes, he did," she said wistfully. "But as you can see, I didn't keep them. Shamus did. So then, do they still work?"

"I think so." Shame reached into the box and pulled out a long string with square black metal beads strung on it. "We have enough for" — he quickly counted — "six of us. So one of us will go without and buddy up. Draw straws?"

"Let's see if they work first," Hayden said.

Shame unstrung the beads and handed each person twelve beads and a silver bracelet with a channel carved into it so that the beads could slide into the channel.

Everyone got busy slipping the beads, apparently in a specific order, into their bracelet. Shame looked at Zayvion and me. "Which of you wants to wear it?"

"Allie," Zayvion said quickly.

"No," I said, "not Allie. If it's got magic in it, I'll probably break out in a rash or worse. And even if it doesn't, I have no idea how it works. Is it like a phone?"

"Not at all," Shame said with a grin.

"It's a code," Zayvion said. He stepped over so that he was right in front of me, head bent, the bracelet he was threading the beads into between us. "The beads represent numbers and the numbers represent letters or sentences in a book."

"What book?" I asked.

"*Winnie-the-Pooh.*"

"And you're not joking," I said.

His lips quirked into a smile. "This isn't magic, Allie. This is a little trick Shame's dad put together when Shame was a kid. They actually run on batteries." He tipped the bracelet so I could see the inside of the band, where a little watch battery was inserted. "And the signal is on a frequency that gets boosted by magic. If you can recite *Winnie-the-Pooh*, you can decipher the coded messages sent and received."

"Can you recite *Winnie-the-Pooh*?"

"In my sleep."

I couldn't help but smile. "You know I'll find every way possible to tease you about that, right?"

"I have no doubt."

"So what if you don't know the works of Pooh word for word?"

Zay bent, reached into the shoe box, and pulled out a palm-sized book. "Have Pooh. Will travel."

I shook my head. "Maybe I should carry that."

"Maybe you should wear the bracelet," he said.

"No, I wouldn't know how to read it. And I'm not going off on my own anytime soon. If I need to, you can give me your bracelet then."

He hesitated a moment, then put the bracelet on. "You do know by me wearing this, I will demand that you stay beside me at all times."

"It had crossed my mind, yes."

He handed me the book, which I stuffed into my back pocket. "Thanks. I think I'll need a coat too."

"I'm sure Shame has something you can use. Shame?"

Shame was handing out copies of the book to the other people in the room. "What?"

"Got a coat Allie can wear?"

"Sure, but a coat isn't going to make you look different to the police cameras." He turned, gave me a look. "I'd recommend a haircut."

"Or a hat," I said.

"Or both."

I didn't want to cut my hair. I didn't want to do a lot of things I needed to do right now. And hair would grow back. If I lived long enough. "Where are the scissors?"

Zayvion frowned. "I don't think you have to—"

"No, Shame's right. Anything I can do to change my look is a good idea right now. It's not just magic users after me, Zay. The police are looking for me too."

Maeve walked across the room. "Why don't you let me help you out?" she said. "I hate cutting my own hair, but I'm quite good at someone else's. Promise I'll make it cute."

"I don't care if it's cute. I'd shave it right now if it would make me stand out less."

"No, dear. I think a bald-headed woman might draw more attention."

We headed off to the guest bathroom, and Maeve found a set of barber scissors in the drawer. "You'll need to sit, since you're so tall," she said.

I walked into the adjoining bedroom and dragged a chair back to the bathroom, plunking it down in front of the mirror. There was just enough room for Maeve to walk around me, and she started by standing behind me, the mirror at her back. She wrapped a towel around my shoulders, tucking it into my collar.

"I'm going to take it quite short, something like a pixie cut, I think," she said cheerfully. "It will look darling on you."

"Go as short as you want," I said. "I've been meaning to cut it for a while."

She brushed out my hair, then began cutting, the scissors making that silky metal-against-metal sound.

"How are you feeling?" she asked.

"Worried and angry and tired. I didn't sleep much last night."

"I don't think any of us did. Nightmares?"

"Yes."

She was quiet for a bit, then, "I've been a member of the Authority for many, many years. Most of my life, really. I've seen so many people pass away. Friends, family." She pulled a comb through my hair, and I could feel the plastic teeth on the back of my bare neck before the cold edge of the scissors replaced them and cut again.

"But I've never once seen magic take such a terrible turn. The Authority has always been strong, Allie. No matter what happened or who decided to throw a coup, the Authority has remained true to its purpose. There have always been more of us with good intentions, logic, common sense, and conviction to see that the laws of the Authority are upheld."

She placed the scissors on the countertop behind her and pulled out a razor blade. She ran the blade in quick, short strokes through my hair.

"And while I can only hope that this time everything will return to normal, that the good of the Authority will stand, it is also true that I have never once in my life seen magic damaged. Changed into something that could mutate the Veiled, changed into a disease. Poisoned.

"So," she said a little more firmly. "I wanted a chance to say that I am so very fond of you, Allie. I've watched Zayvion grow from a very serious boy to a very serious man, and I have never seen him as happy as when he's been with you."

"Not even with Chase?" I asked before I could stop myself.

It was a stupid thing to ask. Chase was dead, and she had dumped Zayvion long before he and I started seeing each other. But he and Chase had been together for a long time, had fought together side by side. Had trained together and fallen in love. A small, insecure part of me wondered if I'd ever fully have his heart.

"Not even with Chase," Maeve said. "I know he's a quiet man. But if he ever lost you, if you died, I don't know how he would go on. You're more a part of him than anyone he's let into his life." She stopped cutting my hair and walked around in front of me so she could begin on my bangs.

"I want you to be very careful. There isn't a person in Portland who won't be looking for you. Most of them to do you harm. If you were my daughter, I'd pack you up and send you out of town. Overseas. But I know you won't leave town and won't back down from this fight."

"Would you?" I asked.

She stopped cutting and I looked up at her. She smiled. "No. I'd stay right here and fight until they kicked my cold body into the grave."

"You and I are a lot alike that way," I said. "And I love you too, Maeve."

"Ah, Allie." She shook her head, the corners of her eyes glittering with tears. "There's a reason I never had a daughter. It's so there'd be room in my heart for you."

She reached down and gave me a quick hug, which I returned.

"Now, that's enough of that nonsense," she said as she pointed to the mirror over my shoulder. "Let's take a look at the new you."

I turned in the chair so I could see my reflection in the mirror.

It was like a different woman was looking back at me. Somehow, she'd managed to cut it so that all the white streaks seemed stronger against my natural brunette. Short, spiky, but longer in the bangs, it made my pale green eyes look twice as wide and gave my cheeks and chin a sharper edge. Surprisingly, it did not look bad on me.

"Um, wow?" I said.

"Yes, wow. Maybe a little too wow." She frowned, and gave me a critical look. "How do you feel about glasses?"

"I don't need them, but sure."

"Shamus?" she called as she pulled the towel off my shoulders and dropped it in the sink.

"What?" he yelled from the hallway.

"Bring me a broom, son."

He walked in a few seconds later. "Here's your broom."

I turned and looked at him. He grinned. "Well, well. Look at you."

I raised one eyebrow. "It was your idea."

"Proof that I am a brilliant man." He held the broom out for his mother. "But I thought you were going to try to draw attention away from her, Mum, not have every man on the street following her."

"Hush," she said. "Do you have a pair of glasses? Not sunglasses. Just a pair of frames?"

"What do you think I am? A one-stop shopping center?"

"You can tell me no," she said, "and I'll send Terric out to get her a pair. He's usually so reliable."

Shame scowled. "No need to be like that. I might have something around here. For Allie, right?"

"Yes." She finished sweeping and dumped enough hair to make a wig into the wastebasket.

"I don't think glasses will make that much of a difference," I said, helping with the cleanup by getting the chair out of the way. "Maybe if I dyed my hair, but we don't have time for that."

"It will help. So will changing out your clothes. Let's see what Shame has."

We headed into the master bedroom, where Shame was already looking through several pairs of glasses he had spread out on top of the dresser.

The room was nice, tastefully decorated. Except for the one wall, across which was written *$41,000.00* in huge strokes of black paint.

"Nice decor." I pointed at the graffiti. "Gangtastic."

"That's what I was going for—thanks."

"Why the dollar amount?"

"Don't know. Didn't write it."

"I didn't know you wore glasses."

"These aren't mine," he said.

"Then why do you have them?"

"I told you. I won the house in a poker game. And everything inside it." His smile spread to a wolfish grin. "Maybe a few other perks as well."

I picked up a pair of plain black frames and put them on. "These?" I asked.

He shook his head. "Not unless you and Zay are going to be spending the rest of whatever time you have left sexing it up. Maybe these."

I switched the black out for a pair of thin wire-rimmed oval glasses. "Yes?"

He tipped his head, finally nodded. "Yes. Mum?"

She was going through the closet and glanced over her shoulder. "Those will do nicely," she said. "Now leave us, Shamus. We're taking your clothes."

"The very shirt off my back." He shook his head. "I'd say that's worth at least one hundred percent of reliable, wouldn't you? Far more reliable than Terric."

"The clothes aren't yours, are they?" I asked.

"Nope. So help yourself." He left the room and Maeve pulled out pieces for me.

"Keep your jeans; they'll be the most comfortable for you. But you'll need to do something other than that tank top. No hats, no sunglasses, no gloves. No one wears those things day and night unless they're trying to hide. And that's what the police, and the Authority, will be looking for. You'll be best to hide in plain sight. That means departing from your regular style, but not covering up so much that people try to see the person behind the disguise."

"But I like sweaters and jeans."

She pulled out a man's button-down shirt that looked like it would fit Zayvion, not Shame, and then a tailored jacket.

"Kind of masculine," I noted.

"Which might be a good idea," she said. "Try this on." She handed the ensemble to me—and I took off the gun holster, then pulled the shirt over my tank top and buttoned it up.

"Not the jacket, unless I'm not wearing a coat, and I want a coat," I said as I shrugged back into the holster.

"All right, how about this?" She pulled a long camel-colored wool trench out of the closet. Built for a man, it didn't look too long for me, which was good. But I spotted something in the closet I liked even more. "How about the other coat?"

Maeve reached back in the closet. "You mean this?"

She retrieved a black leather jacket. It was meant to sit on the waist, and when I shrugged into it, it hit me right above my belt line. It was zippered from cuff to elbow, wide at the collar with nickel-colored studs punching a line down one side and around the waistband. I zipped the jacket and ruffed up my hair a little.

Maeve handed me a long, bloodred scarf that I wrapped around my neck a couple times.

A different person stared back at me from the full-length mirror beside the closet. Still tall, but the biker's jacket made me look heavier and wider-shouldered than I really was. The bulk of the coat squared off any womanly curves I might possess, yet wasn't so huge that it looked like I was wearing my big brother's clothes.

But it was the short, spiky hair and glasses that made the biggest change. I looked a little harder edged, tough, maybe just a bit mannish. Looked like maybe I should take up smoking, get into brawls, and carry a gun.

Right. I already did two of those things.

"This is good, I think," I said. "Thanks. Are you going to change what you're wearing?"

"No. If any of the rest of us changes our looks—well, except perhaps Zayvion—we would just tip them off that we're trying to hide or run. This will help you fade on the streets in case the police are out there. And you'll need to do something about the marks on your hands."

I glanced at my right hand and the whorls of magic that flowed there like multicolored strands of ribbon, and my left, which was ringed at the knuckles and wrist with black. "You said no gloves."

"Maybe cover makeup?" Maeve suggested.

"No," I said. "The sleeves are long enough to hide most of my hands anyway. This is enough." I stared at my reflection that did not look like me. "This is more than enough."

"Wait," Maeve said. "Here." She tugged something out of a shoe box. "Now, *this* is enough."

She handed me a pair of fingerless driving gloves. Black leather to match the coat. Very nice. I smiled and slipped them on.

"Perfect," she said.

And I agreed.

We walked back out into the living room.

Roman was still standing in the center of the room. Terric was pacing. I didn't know what everyone was waiting around for.

"Are we ready?" I asked.

They all looked over at me. And just kept staring.

"I think everyone remembers what they need to do," I said, heading for the weapons out on the coffee table. I wanted at least a few long knives to go with the bullets in my pockets.

"And when we get our jobs done," I continued as I looked through the available blades, "we'll check back in with the Pooh Bear code."

No one said anything. Finally Zayvion spoke. "Allie?"

I glanced up. The expression on his face wasn't quite shock. It wasn't confusion either. More like a startled wonderment.

"Yes?"

"You look . . . different."

"That's the idea," I said, not sure quite how to take that. "So are you ready, Roman?" I asked.

"Have been so for many, many years."

I finished looking through knives and just took the closest ones I could reach. Truth was, I was so rattled about everything we were about to try, all the things we were about to do, separate from one another, that I didn't even care which knife I was sticking in my belt.

I loaded up with blades, then walked back toward the kitchen, putting as much space between me and Roman's magic casting as I could.

Roman paced the room in a circle and everyone else took a clue from me and moved back to give him space. He was chanting a string of words over and over, and when he had finished hitting the four compass points, he spread his stance, and began tracing the spell with wide, Tai Chi–type movements for whichever Gate he was going to use.

Zayvion had strolled over to stand so close his shoulder pressed against mine. "This new look," he said quietly.

"Mmm?"

He shifted so he could run his fingers through the back of my hair and gently brush my bare neck. He slid his thumb over the curve of my jaw and edge of my ear. The warmth of his fingers lingered and sent shivers across my skin.

"Hot," he murmured.

It had been a long time since he and I had been alone together. I suddenly wished I'd spent last night doing something other than sweating through nightmares.

"You think?" I asked quietly.

"I think." His hand slipped down across my back and then rested on my butt, tugging me closer to him.

I smiled and leaned into him for a moment. But as soon as Roman stopped chanting, Zayvion pulled away so both of his hands were free to cast magic, if needed. He traced a basic Shield spell but didn't pour any magic into it. I could feel concern roll off him like a wave of heat.

"Don't worry," I said. "I'm not going to pass out from that." I nodded toward Roman. Magic was making me sick, but being this far away from the massive spell Roman was casting should be enough for me not to feel the effects.

"Didn't think you were," Zay said. "I just know that Gates open on both ends. Two-way door."

It took me a second to think that through. Then I got it. Even if Roman managed to open the Gate exactly where he wanted it to open, there was still a chance something on the other side could use it to step through to this side.

And if I were the Authority, I'd have my goons ready to jump at any possibly suspicious Gate opening in the world.

Magic rose to Roman's call, spears of light that flashed inward from the frame worked in the building's walls and ceiling. I'd lived in a lot of apartments that were poorly plumbed for magic flow, but this place looked like the walls and ceiling—the entire building—had been designed to channel magic.

Maybe that was why it was bolted to the side of a cliff.

*It was,* Dad said quietly in my mind. *For a time, it was de rigueur to have your home as a focal and channel for magic. Then it was outlawed.*

The stench of rot filled the room, but I was the only one who smelled magic like that. I covered my nose and mouth with the sleeve of the jacket and smelled the slightly sagey scent of the soap used to clean it.

Roman coaxed the spears of light into a single wrapped column that stretched from the ceiling to the floor and sent out runners of silver and white light.

But he wasn't done yet. He took the stance that I'd seen Zayvion and Victor use so often, a sort of bent-knee thing, and then painted the glyphs in the air to shape the magic he had called, like a blacksmith bending magic to shape on an anvil.

It was not the way magic was usually cast. Everyone cast glyph first, magic second, but not, apparently, Roman.

"Which Gate is it?" I asked Zayvion, who managed to hear me through the muffle of the sleeve.

He flexed his hands in a quick pattern—Sight, I realized. Oh, right. I was the only one who could see magic with my bare eyes.

"Salaria," he said as he dropped the Sight spell.

Roman finished casting the Gate and a flash of light—this time magic crossing over to the visible spectrum—filled the room. I could see a sandstone wall on the other side, and cobblestones. Wherever he had decided to open the Gate, it appeared to be an alley in shadows.

Without a backward glance, Roman stepped through, and the Gate closed behind him in a rush of hot air and salt and rot.

I coughed and tried hard not to gag up breakfast. "Let's go, people," I said.

We gathered our things, and headed down two flights of stairs to the bottom floor of the house. This floor had a separate address, and didn't look nearly as well furnished as the upper floor. Which was smart since this was the only floor people could possibly look into.

It was built facing the back side of a small gas station. Which reminded me.

We had a problem—transportation.

"How are we going to swing this?" I asked as we walked toward Terric's van.

"I'll loan you my car," Terric said. "You won't want to use Shame's or Zayvion's right now. Then I'll take Maeve and Hayden off to the inn. Hayden, your car's there, right?"

"It is," he said.

"Leave me at the inn," Victor said. "I'll take a cab to my house, and get my car there."

I thought that over for a minute, wondering if we were doing the smart thing to split up like this. What I really wanted to do was to rent some cars, or steal some cars, but neither of those ideas was good either.

"Just be careful, okay?"

"Allie," Victor said, climbing into the van, "we will." That was his stop-worrying voice. Since there was no chance I'd stop worrying, I did the next best thing. I closed my mouth and got into the car.

# *Chapter Four*

Terric dropped Zayvion, Shame, and me off at his car first, which was conveniently parked and covered by an Illusion on the north side of town. One thing I'd noticed during the drive was the lack of people out on the street. Usually any ray of sunny weather brought everyone outside. But not today. The epidemic had people spooked. They were staying inside, staying home, if they could. But the walls of buildings couldn't keep the Veiled from finding them, eventually. And I'd seen a lot of Veiled wandering the empty streets.

"Wait," I said as Shame got out of the van. "You're not coming with us, are you?"

"Of course I am," he said. "Where did you think I'd go? With Terric?"

"With your mother maybe?" I said.

"Hayden's with her. They know how to stay out of danger. I don't want to send you two all the way out to Multnomah Falls to the Life well without . . . firepower." He shut the van door. Zayvion walked around the vehicle and took a minute to talk to Terric.

"Excuse me?" I asked.

"You can't use magic, Beckstrom. That means it's Zayvion, and you and your weapons—which you don't want to use—against whatever the Authority has set up at the Life well to protect their interests."

I rubbed my eyes and ran into the glasses there, leaving a nice fat fingerprint smudge in the middle of the lens. I was so not used to the new me.

The van pulled away, and Zayvion strolled toward Terric's car.

"We don't even know if the Authority has someone calling the shots yet," I said. "Much less if they are putting protection around the wells."

"We don't know they aren't," Zay said.

He was already opening the car doors. He wasn't wearing the beanie anymore, and had put on a pair of sunglasses and a very nice leather trench coat that I wish I would have noticed before Maeve gave me the biker jacket.

Since Zayvion made a point of looking homeless most of the time, this sort of classy urban style was probably the best disguise for him, though I thought all that leather made him look a little too good.

"Let's go," he said, getting into the driver's seat.

I took front. Shame slid into the back. "Stinks in here," he said.

I took a careful sniff. It didn't smell like magic, which was fine by me. But it did have the slight scent of Terric's cologne.

"Are you sure we should use Terric's car?" I asked. "Won't the Authority be looking for it?"

"We switched the plates," Shame said.

"When?"

"Last night when you were not sleeping." He stretched out in the backseat and rested the back of his head against the window. "I'm closing my eyes for the drive. Wake me up if we're going to die."

Zayvion drove, keeping to the speed limit, and using his blinkers, which I was happy about. Didn't want a random traffic infraction to tip us off. This neighborhood was as noticeably unpeopled as the others we'd driven through, but that didn't mean there weren't police still on duty.

About five minutes into the drive, before we'd even managed to head east toward the falls, Shame was softly snoring.

So much for firepower. He still hadn't recovered from the last few days. None of us had. But Shame had been forcibly possessed by Mikhail and nearly killed. If we weren't running for our lives, I'd suggest he get about a month of bed rest.

"Do you think he'll be okay?" I asked softly so as not to wake Shame.

Zayvion drove for a bit, not answering me.

"Zay?"

He sighed. "I don't know, Allie. He's stubborn. But he can be stupid about . . . everything, really. The odds of all of us surviving aren't good. His odds?" He drove for a bit, the muscle at the edge of his jaw tight.

"We'll find a way," I said. "We'll fix this, make magic right again, make Portland safe again. It's not too late to turn this mess around."

He glanced at me, and even through the dark tint of his sunglasses I could see the burn of gold in his eyes. "Who are you trying to convince? Me or you?"

"Me," I said honestly. "I want things right again. I want Shame to get well. I want to watch my baby brother grow up. Hell, I want to have enough damn time to eat popcorn and watch a movie with you on the couch, or cook a dinner together, or argue over who gets to use the best pillow in bed." I stopped, worried I'd say more. Worried I'd tell how much I really wanted, needed, to think he and I might have a life—a normal life— together.

"We'll find a way to make things right," he said. "But

we won't argue over the best pillow. That bad boy's mine."

I leaned my head on the headrest and looked over at him. That bittersweet longing filled me and I wondered how I just kept falling deeper in love with the man.

"Pillow hog," I said.

"A man has needs."

"Do you think they'll have guards on the well?" I asked.

"I would."

"What if we don't make it to the well?" I asked quietly. "What if we can't tell whether it's poisoned—what if we don't know how to clean the magic in the cisterns and the network? What if the Veiled take over the city and kill everyone? Davy, Violet, my baby brother? What if we fail, Zay?"

"Roman will get word to the Overseer. And hands, better hands than ours, will take up weapons and take up the fight. We'll win this, Allie. Whether or not we're standing by the end of it."

I reached over, put my hand on his thigh. "I'd like to be standing by the end of this."

"You will be," he said. "Popcorn and a movie, remember?"

"Are you saying that for me or for you?"

A very small smile ghosted his lips. "Both. But I get to pick the movie. Also, I promised I'd keep this city safe. And that's exactly what I intend to do. Starting with you, starting right now."

"What? Safe driving and me whining is going to save the city?"

"No. You're going to get some sleep. We have about a half hour before we get there."

"I can't sleep," I said. But a yawn broke my oh-so-convincing lie.

"You'd sleep if I cast a Sleep spell on you."

"Yes, and then I'd be barfing in your car."

"It's not mine; it's Terric's."

"All right. Barfing in Terric's car."

"Not going to sing you a lullaby," he said.

"No? Not even a Winnie-the-Pooh song?"

"Look at you with the funny," he said. "Wonder what movie I'm going to pick now. *Rollerball*? *RoboCop*? *Platoon*?"

"Okay, fine, fine." I shifted in my seat and leaned against the car door, tucking up one of my legs, and pillowing my head with the scarf. "I liked *RoboCop*." Then, a minute or so later, "Does my hair look stupid?"

"No. It looks like I should strip you naked and ravage your body until you beg me for mercy."

"You always say the sweetest things," I murmured. "Zay?"

"Mmm?"

"In case this all goes to hell . . . I love you."

"Even if things don't go to hell, I love you too."


"Allie?" Zayvion said. "We're almost there."

I took a deeper breath and realized I'd been asleep. The dreamless kind of sleep, which was my favorite. I sat up and rubbed at the kink in my neck, trying to get my bearings. "Everything quiet?"

"You mean Shame?"

"I mean your Pooh News. Any rumblies in the tumblies?" I gave him a big grin.

He shook his head. "You just can't let that go, can you? And all's quiet on that front. Shame too."

I glanced back at Shame. I might have been sleeping, but Shame looked like he'd fallen into a coma.

"Shame?" I said. "Time to wake up."

He jerked, then started coughing. When he finally got

a couple decent lungfuls of air, he pointed a finger at me. "Do not sneak up on me like that ever again."

"Shame, we're in a car. I can't sneak up on you if I tried."

"Bullshit. You're a Beckstrom. You're made of sneaky."

"Hey," Zayvion said. "Watch it, Flynn."

"Like it's not true. Nothing personal, Al, but you know it's true."

"No," I said. "My dad might have been sneaky, but I am aboveboard. Way aboveboard."

Shame scowled and dug in his coat pocket for his cigarettes. "Which is why you cut your hair, put on glasses, and decked yourself out in some ex-biker's idea of the latest in men's fashion. Totally aboveboard move."

"Look who woke up under a little black rain cloud," I said.

"That's two," Zayvion murmured.

I flashed him another smile, but to Shame, I said, "Maybe we should have left you with Terric."

Shame lit his cigarette and rolled the window down enough that he could exhale the smoke out. "That's just cold. Wouldn't be in a bad mood if I hadn't been snuck up on by a Beckstrom."

"Shame?" Zayvion said. "Shut the hell up."

And, wonders of wonders, Shame did just that.

By the end of his cigarette, he was in an obviously better mood, and we were pulling into the parking area just past Multnomah Falls. It was middle of the afternoon, a nice May day, and the place was crawling with tourists. Apparently, even news of a quickly spreading virus couldn't stop people from driving out to see the falls. I had no idea how we were going to get up the trail to the doorway hidden in the hillside and down to the well without being spotted.

Zay parked the car and we sat there for a bit.

"Plan?" Shame asked. "Storm the castle?"

"Walk in nice and slow," Zayvion said. "Maybe buy a cup of coffee."

"I'd kill for a cup of coffee," I said.

"What, like use a gun on someone? The horror." Shame swung out of the car.

"Maybe I'll start with him," I mused.

"You'd have to get behind me," Zayvion said.

I would have asked what had really put Shame in such a prickly mood, but it wasn't hard to extrapolate why he was wound up so tight. There just was nothing fun about strolling off to your own death. And that was pretty much what we might be doing.

We got out of the car, the sound of the highway behind us as we walked the narrow parking lot toward the crosswalk to the falls. We let a car cruising for parking roll past, and then we were crossing the pavement toward the wide ribbon of water that fell six hundred or so feet off the tree-lined cliffs, the arched stone bridge crossing at the lower drop.

Waterfall ahead and slightly to the left, gift shop and restaurant to our right, and coffee stand between the two.

There were plenty of people here, which suddenly seemed like a good thing. If we'd been the only three to come strolling along, there would be more of a chance people would notice us and maybe be able to tell the police they'd seen us if they were asked. As it was, we seemed to blend in pretty well with our fellow waterfall gawkers, and we did indeed stop for an espresso before taking a leisurely walk up to the lower falls, then up the steeper concrete pathway that led to the footbridge over the lower falls.

"Bloody hell," Shame said. "I hate hiking."

"But it's the great outdoors," I said sweetly. "It's not only good—it's great."

"Don't care if it's the sodding magnificent outdoors. Still hate the hiking."

Zayvion paused once we reached the bridge, and we did what all tourists did: stopped and stared at the upper falls. It was slightly cooler here, the spray from the falls making the air taste like spring rain. Several groups of people stopped to take pictures, but luckily didn't ask any of us to put our very fingerprinty fingers on their cameras.

Since I had on gloves, a scarf, and a jacket, I was sweating like a hog.

Zayvion looked how Zay always looked. Cool. Calm. Collected. And Shame just looked annoyed by the world, which was pretty much standard for him too.

After enough time for Shame to catch his breath, we headed up the hill again. Being out in the forest, or at least away from the city, was like a soothing balm on my magic-jangled senses. There weren't very many spells out here—a few on the restaurant, the bridge, and any other man-made structure, mostly for stability and safety. And the lack of spells made me a very happy girl.

"What are you smiling about?" Zay asked as we chugged up the incline, old tree snags and mossy lichens and ferns adding to the lush, moist green of the place.

"No magic." I moved to walk behind him to let a group going downhill pass us.

He paused so I could catch up with him again and took my hand. "I don't think it's the best idea for you to go down to the well with us," he said quietly.

"Oh, I am so not letting you and Shame down there alone."

"You might have to," he said.

"No."

"Magic makes you sick."

"No."

"We'll see."

"We'll see nothing," I said. "I'm going down to the well with you."

"It's a long way," Zay noted. "I'd hate to have to carry your unconscious body back up all those damn stairs."

"Did you just threaten to knock me out?"

"No. Magic can knock you out all by itself."

Crap. I hadn't thought about that. Going down to the well, to one of the deepest, purest, and strongest concentrations of magic, might not be a good idea for someone who broke out in hives before hocus got all the way to pocus.

"I won't get in your way," I said.

"That's not what I'm worried about."

We kept walking. Zay might not be worried about it, but I was worried not only that I would go unconscious, but also that seeing might be a problem for me, since the place was likely swarming with spells. I dug in my memory for what the well was like. I seemed to recall the stairs that led downward were lit by electricity, not magic, and were made of wood. That shouldn't be a problem.

No, the problem would be once we hit those double doors that led to the Life well, and stepped through them into that big underground chamber.

That was, if we didn't run into Authority goons and have to deal with them first.

One thing was for sure. I'd forgotten how long and steep this stupid climb to the stupid hidden door to the well was.

And where was the hidden door anyway?

Zayvion stopped in the middle of the path. "This is it."

He pointed at the rocks and moss and fern. Not a lot

else. But he knew exactly where the door was, even though I didn't see any magic marking it, didn't feel any magic marking it, and there wasn't any other sign I could see.

"About damn time," Shame huffed. He stood there, breathing heavily, and looking a little pale and nauseous.

"Ever think about giving up the smokes?" Zayvion asked.

"Sure. I've thought about killing you too. Guess which would happen first?"

Zay didn't answer. He was setting a Disbursement—which formed in front of him like a gray mist, and disappeared into him when he inhaled. It was weird to see every magical step of what he was doing, also weird to see him setting his own price for working magic. Most of the people I knew in the Authority used Proxies for their price of casting magic. Including Zay.

Looked like my lover picked a long, easy pain. He'd feel a slight muscle stiffness over the next few weeks probably. I always went for the short, hard pains, so I could stay on top of my game.

Then he drew the spell that would unlock the door.

I heard footsteps coming up the path behind us, and a child's voice. "People are coming," I said.

Zay flicked the spell at the wall of green, and a doorway opened. "In," he said. "Shame?"

"Got it."

Shame drew a nice, solid Illusion, a Disbursement spell biting at his wrist. I covered my mouth as the Illusion settled around me in rotted stink. Magic didn't usually smell so bad. Yes, magic had been making me sick since we fought Leander and Isabelle. But seeing it with my bare eyes had only really started after I cast that spell on the Veiled, passed out, and hit my head. I didn't know why that had changed things so I could see magic and smell it as if it had gone rotten.

Maybe my other senses were making up for the fact that I couldn't use magic. Maybe it had something to do with the poison in magic. Or maybe it was because I had a dead magic user sharing a corner of my brain.

Whatever it was that had changed magic, or me, to this level, it was getting annoying.

I walked through the darkened doorway to the platform at the top of the stairs, Zay right behind me and Shame right behind him.

Shame broke the spell, closing the door.

"Did they see us?" Zayvion asked quietly.

"No," Shame said. He flicked on the light switch. "They were still far enough off, they couldn't have seen us."

In the low glow of the single lightbulb above us and smaller lights scattered beneath the stairs that spilled out below us, we each unpacked weapons. I went for sword and knives. Zay chose sword, and Shame opted for two guns.

"Let's do it," Shame said quietly. "Z, you taking point?"

"Yes. Allie, I want you to stay behind us."

He stared at me for a long time until I finally said, "What?"

"I thought you'd argue about it."

"I'll stay behind you as we walk into the room. After that, all bets are off."

He nodded. Shame tapped the tiles on his bracelet, then cast the softest Light spell I'd ever seen. Zayvion's bracelet glowed slightly in the dark.

"What did you say?" I asked.

"Three, one, five," he said.

"Which is?"

"Third page," Zayvion said, "first sentence, fifth word: 'coming downstairs now.'"

"Seriously?"

"Look it up," Shame said.

"No, I'll take your word for it. The others will know what you meant?"

"They should," Shame said. "They knew we were going to the Life well, and they have the books if they need to check. But they won't have to with that simple code. There are a few we use a lot. That's one of them."

I had severely underestimated how good this code system was. Of course, if anyone from the Authority captured one of us, or all of us, and found the books, it wouldn't take much to figure it out.

"How many people have it memorized?" I asked quietly as we started down the stairs.

"Me, Zay, Terric, Mum," Shame said. "Probably not Victor or Hayden. But they have the book. They can look it up."

Walking down the stairs took more time than I remembered, and my legs were already tired from our climb. Another indication that we were not at our best. I didn't used to be this out of shape—or this worn down.

I didn't know how Shame was managing.

We got to the bottom of the stairs. No goons. We'd been quiet enough, our soft-soled shoes on the wooden steps making no echoes against the walls, that I was pretty sure if there were people actually in the well chamber, they wouldn't have heard us coming.

Zayvion stopped in front of the big double doors, and Shame stood shoulder to shoulder with him.

I stayed behind them, like I'd promised. And since I couldn't throw magic, I resheathed my long knife, and pulled out the gun instead. I slapped a clip into it, and

Shame gave me half a glance over his shoulder. He was smiling.

Bastard.

Zay drew the spell to open and unlock the door. It looked like brass ribbons of magic spun out from his fingertips and clicked into five different places in the carvings on the doors.

The doors opened.

Magic lashed out, and wrapped us in an inferno of pain.

# *Chapter Five*

Zayvion broke the attack with a clean slice of his ka-tana, chanting a spell for Impact that grew like a wall of bullets in front of him.

He pulled magic into the spell and sent it singing into the room.

Shame went with a more direct attack and unloaded his gun into the room while Zayvion pulled a Block out of the ground like a liquid net of energy around Shame, me, and him.

Yes, it smelled like hot hell. But since whoever in there casting couldn't break the barrier, I didn't care what it smelled like.

We strode into the room. No use hiding. Whoever was in there had already seen us, had already decided we were dangerous and worth the fry-by-magic, ask-questions-later treatment.

Screw that.

Shame dropped the clip and reloaded without breaking stride. He might have looked sick and exhausted before, but he looked like someone you would not want to fuck with now.

I caught the movement to the far left of the room. "Two men, left," I said. "Three right."

"Shame, left," Zay said. "Allie, right."

Zay heaved back and cleaved the spell he was holding with his sword, catching the magic of the Block in the black and silver glyphs that swirled down the blade. He yelled and swung again, this time throwing all that magic, like a spray of hot bullets, out to both sides of the room, where they struck and burned.

He ran to the right—so did I.

Not being able to cast magic was seriously pissing me off. But the anger was good. Anger, I could use.

I took the first man. Shorter than me, built like a brick shit house, he met my sword with an ax, and a handful of magic. The impact of both set my bones on fire.

Yes, I had the gun in my left hand. No, I couldn't make myself raise it and shoot him.

Zayvion didn't hesitate. He threw enough magic to kill an elephant. All three men dropped, and were still.

"Are you all right?" he asked.

I was pretty much not all right. I was dizzy, nauseous, and in a lot of pain from that last attack I'd cleverly blocked with every bone in my body. I thought about listing my pains, but decided it would take too much lung power.

All I got out was, "Swell."

He strode over to Shame. Not that he needed to. Shame had both men on the floor, flat on their backs unconscious, one of them, at least, bleeding heavily.

Shame stood over them, lighting a cigarette.

"Bartholomew's," he said. "Likely. Might be it's time for a change of guards down here or for them to check in. We don't know how much time we have left."

Zayvion glared at the men. "One way to find out." He crouched down next to the man who was very unconscious but very not bleeding. He moved his sword into his left hand—not a handicap for him, I knew for a fact;

I'd been on the sparring mats with him plenty—and placed the palm and fingers of his right hand against the guy's forehead.

He spoke a word, and even though I didn't know that word, I knew it was a Disbursement spell. From the glyph that flared in the air in front of Zay, and just as quickly flashed out, I knew it was a short, brutal pain he was going to pay for this magic.

Then he began whispering. Soft, sibilant, the words slipped out like a hush of rain. Zay said one last word. A glyph blazed bloodred in his hand, between his palm and the man's forehead, and then sank into the man.

Even unconscious, the man stiffened. Even unconscious, he screamed.

Zayvion was still whispering, a rush of words, half-caught phrases, like someone had hard jacked an information stream into his head.

No, not information—Zayvion was reading, whispering, ripping through the man's memories. Zay's voice grew louder and he straightened his elbow, somehow pressing the spell deeper into the man's brain, then twisting it like a knife.

The man yelled out again and went still. Unbreathing. Dead.

Zayvion drew his hand away. Inhaled, exhaled, and stood. He was sweating.

"So dead guy have anything interesting to tell us?" Shame asked.

"They were sent here by Bartholomew. Have been here for three days. Don't know that he's dead."

"Well, that's good news for us," Shame said. "Did he know when his replacements were coming?"

"No."

"And there's the bad news, right on schedule."

"You killed him," I said a bit belatedly.

Zayvion arched a look at me as he knelt next to the bleeding man. "Yes."

"You took his memories and killed him." I felt like I was stuck in a loop. I mean, I'd seen Zayvion kill things, beasts that crossed through the gate of death, the Veiled, who were not really people anymore. But he'd put his bare hands on an unconscious man, sucked out his brains, and left him dead.

"Yes," he said again.

"Why aren't you paying the price?" I finally asked. "Death for a death, that's what magic makes you pay. If you kill someone with magic, you have to pay the same price: death. Unless you have some weird Proxy setup I can't see?"

Get enough Proxies linked up and you could spread the price of a death across enough people that everyone except the target would walk away. Hurt, but still walking.

"No," he said. "No Proxies."

He put his hand on the next man, and whispered a spell. I saw the harsh Disbursement flare again and Zayvion's shoulders jerked back and down like he'd just stuck his finger in a light socket. He was breathing a little heavier now, but began whispering again.

"Shame?" I said quietly.

Shame was in mid-inhale on the cig. "Mmm?"

"Is he going to kill him?"

I didn't know why it bothered me. It shouldn't. Bartholomew's men would have killed me in a second. Killed Zay. Killed Shame. Done more than that. They would have turned us inside out if they got the chance. They had just tried to kill me, all of us, as we walked in here, as a matter of fact.

Shame exhaled and threw the cigarette to the ground. "Likely, yes. He's in a mood, that one."

I kept my mouth shut while Zayvion dug through the man's mind. He took his hand off his forehead and then pulled his knife. One quick stroke and the man wasn't breathing anymore.

Zay stood, stalked over to the three men on the other side of the room. One was dead already—gunshot. He put his hand on the other two men's foreheads, digging through their brains with magic. Then snapped their necks with brutal efficiency.

"Check the well," Zay said, a rough edge to his voice, as if he'd just been yelling his lungs out instead of whispering the brains out of people.

"Crazed rogue Closers," Shame said. "Gotta love them. All business, no manners." He clapped his hands together once. "Let's get to this, shall we?"

I just stood there, staring at Zayvion. His eyes were hammered gold, no pupil at all, his jaw set as if trying to hold back a scream. It wasn't fury that boiled beneath that expression—it was madness.

*Too many minds,* Dad said softly.

*What? You mean he Closed too many minds?*

*It wasn't just Closing,* he said. *He was sorting through their memories, their knowledge, their lives. Four lives in just a few minutes is like trying to suck the ocean down in one gulp. He would have caused himself less pain if he'd just Closed them.*

"Zay?" I said, walking toward him.

He locked his jaw, his nostrils flared, and he shook his head once, as if just hearing his name hurt. He managed to take a step away from me.

"Ah-ah, leave him a bit," Shame said. "He's got some sorting to do."

Shame had knelt and taken off his boots and was stuffing his socks into them.

"What the hell are you doing?" I asked, glad to have

something else to focus on, but also wondering if he had gone as crazy as Zayvion.

"Checking the wells," he said. "What the hell do you think I'm doing?"

"Getting naked for no reason?"

"While that is always a pleasant option," Shame said as he stood, "there's no time for naked. Yet." He tipped his head down, inhaled, then exhaled, as if setting himself to a heavy weight. He paced across the floor, working a very slow counterclockwise circle toward the center of the room where the patterned woodwork flowed into the symbol that marked where the well of magic swelled far below.

I'd seen him walk this way once before, back at the Blood well, moving as if he were walking on rice paper and trying not to tear it, as if there was a far-off sound that he could hear. It was meditative, a pure focus on magic that didn't flare and move like most magic. No, this was more like Shame attuning to magic, making himself a grounding rod, a tuning fork.

But every step he took drew something from the floor, leaving behind black scorch marks. Death magic. He was drawing energy from the floor. Maybe even from the well or the earth around and above us.

Was he tasting the magic? With his feet?

Shame inhaled a quick breath in a soft *ah* as if he had just figured a lock. And then he strode straight to the center of the symbol, faced the door we'd come in through, and lifted his arms above his head, shaking his wrists a little so that his coat sleeves settled comfortably.

"Step back a bit," he said.

I did so.

Shame called magic from the carvings in the ceiling, drawing it down around him like a very light rain. Except the rain didn't fall all the way to the ground. It got to about shoulder level, and then a pulse of light in the center of his chest—the stone that Terric had accidentally embedded in Shame to keep him alive—absorbed the magic.

After a couple seconds, Shame drew his hands down and traced a Disbursement glyph. He was going with a short, quick pain. The Disbursement glyph flared and wrapped up his arm, hugging there like a purple leech and digging deep. I figured it was muscle aches.

He drew a glyph for Open, which hovered about three feet in front of him. He poured just a small bit of magic into it, and before the glyph was completely closed, he pulled a line of it with him as he turned to face the wall. He repeated the Open glyph, caught the edge, keeping it open as he turned, connecting it with the next glyph, turned to the next wall, did the same, and repeated the process on the last wall.

A circle of glyphwork, of spells, hung midair around him, glowing a soft yellow, each glyph connected to another. A very intricate and beautiful Open spell.

Shame was facing the door again. The Disbursement on his arm had grown to three times the size, each spell he cast bloating it and adding to the price of his pain.

He didn't seem to notice. No one really noticed Disbursements. If I couldn't see magic with my bare eyes, I wouldn't even give it a second thought.

Then Shame tipped his left palm open and up, and used his right hand to trace a new spell over the top of it. This spell was black fire. He blew across his palm like blowing a kiss, and the black spell caught on the edge of the Open spell and burned through it, consuming it faster than a lit line of gunpowder. It crackled from one Open spell to the next, gaining speed.

Shame was breathing hard, holding his concentration

on that black burning spell while the purple Disbursement sent out shocks of pain through his body.

The black spell zinged through the last Open, and exploded in a lash of black smoke tentacles in front of Shame's face.

"Fuck it all." Shame took a deep breath, got about halfway through a lungful, and wiped his face with the bend of his elbow.

"Shame?" I said.

"Minute."

"No. Now."

"I said wait," Shame said.

"The floor's opening," I said.

"Oh." He glanced down. "That's right. Open up, you cranky bastard." With what appeared to be a lot of effort, Shame walked toward me, away from the wooden floor that swirled like a lotus opening.

The Life well was beautiful, a glowing pool of magic that seemed bigger than the room we were standing in. It was the opposite of the Rift—that slice of dark magic between life and death. In death, the Rift was a black stream with flecks of opal rainbows glinting in the flow. The Life well was opal silver, white, with crystal slices that sparked with dark black rainbow fire.

I expected it to reek like hell, since every time anyone used magic, it stank to high heaven. But it didn't smell bad. As a matter of fact, it didn't smell like anything at all.

It was beautiful, raw power. I stared at it like I'd never seen magic with my bare eyes before. Truth was, until this moment, I felt like I never had.

Even the best Sight spell hadn't been this clear.

"Oh," I breathed. I suddenly understood why people would want it, would covet it. Why my father's goal was to have magic in the right hands. The things that could be done with it, the possibilities of how the world could be shaped and formed, flickered in that light, with tempting, tempting promises.

This was what Leander and Isabelle wanted. This was what they wanted to control.

*No,* Dad said quietly. *This is only half of what they wanted. When light magic and dark magic are joined, it is even more powerful, even more pure, even more deadly.*

*You think they want light and dark magic joined?* I said. *But it was broken to keep them apart. And now that they're both in life together, they won't want magic to go back together, will they?*

*They want power. They want control of life and death. Only magic can give that to them. Only dark and light magic joined can give that to them.*

*But you said there would need to be a Focal to join light and dark magic. A person who could hold it long enough to heal it. And everyone who's tried has died.*

*Leander and Isabelle don't care who they kill. They'll look for a Focal, for a body strong enough they can possess it and then use it to bring dark and light magic back together into their hands.*

*Are you sure?*

He hesitated. Then, *I would do that if I wanted to rule magic. And the world.*

"Might want to come back now," Shame was saying.

Whoa.

"What did I miss?" I asked. The well wasn't any more open than it had been; the pretty colors were just as pretty. Zayvion paced between the two piles of dead people on the far side of the room.

"You missed that." Shame pointed. I followed his finger and had to squint against the crystalline brightness of magic.

"I can see the well," I said. "Blindingly, actually."

"Not the well; there at the edges where the magic is curling inward?"

I glanced at Shame. He wasn't holding a Sight spell.

"Can you see the magic in the well?" I asked.

"Sure, let's go off topic," he said sunnily. "I cast Sight when you were doing your impression of a hypnotist's assistant. I know how the magic is flowing. Satisfied? Now look."

"Fine." I looked at the edge of the pool that seemed to flow and curl back in on itself like a wisp of candle smoke hitting a glass bell.

"What am I looking at?"

"Do you see smoke?"

"Yes."

"And where the smoke is touching?"

I held very still and stared. The well seemed to be getting smaller, the magic not reaching out as far. "The well's shrinking?" I asked.

"The well's not shrinking," Shame said. "The magic is turning solid."

And as soon as he said it, I could see it. It was like watching mud get deposited against a stone at the side of a river. As the magic flowed to the edge of the well, it left behind a thick sludge, tar that looked exactly like the black tar that had consumed Anthony and killed him. Tar that looked exactly like the poisoned magic that was killing Davy. And as that tar was building, the smoke was growing thicker too, pushing questing dark tongues into the crystal-hard shine of the magic.

"The poison," I said. "The well is tainted."

"That's my guess," Shame said.

"Shouldn't we sample it?" I asked.

"Well, it's not like we can just reach in and dip our hands in it, now, is it?" he asked.

"I guess not," I said doubtfully.

"Christ, Beckstrom. No," Shame said. "Sure we throw magic in spells, we twist glyphs like frickin' balloon animals and fill them with magic. And you are a freak and can actually carry some magic inside your body. But the main word there is 'some.' This is the pure stuff, the endless stuff. Tapped straight to the roots that spread throughout the world. You touch it, it eats you."

"Sounds like a story to keep kids from dipping their toes in," I said.

"It's not," Shame said. "I've seen it happen."

I looked away from the well to Shame. He was standing a respectful distance away from the well, his hands very carefully at his sides and in fists so that he didn't draw on the magic at all, though I could see the steady stream that lifted in a gentle mist and filled the stone in his chest.

"Ex-friend of yours?" I asked.

"Dead friend of mine."

"You do know that crystal in your chest is pulling on the magic," I said.

He raised his eyebrows. "You can see that?"

"Yes. It's been pulling magic from anything it can. And it's been pulling on your life energy when there isn't any magic nearby. Did you know that?"

He held his breath a moment, his dark green gaze steady. "It's not like I've brought it up at the dinner table."

"Have you had a doctor, a doctor who understands magic, look at you . . . at what the crystal is doing to you?"

"What do you think it's doing to me?"

"It's drawing on magic, I think to feed or charge itself. There were glyphs carved in that crystal. Glyphs my dad put there to hold magic and help it recharge."

"That's what the doctors said about it."

"Is that all they said?" I asked.

"That, and they had never seen anything like it before."

"It's draining your life, Shame. I know Terric somehow used magic to bind this crystal to you when you were wounded during the wild magic storm, and I think he saved your life."

"Please. I save my own life."

"But," I said over his grumbling, "the crystal was never meant to be fused into someone's body."

"Oh, you think?"

"What I think is it's hurting you. Taking your life energy when it doesn't have enough magic to fill it. It might be killing you, Shame."

"I know."

"That's it? That's all you have to say?"

"We're all dying, Beckstrom," he said with a steady kind of sobriety, as if he'd been so long staring into the face of death, he'd become accustomed to it. "Use magic, it uses you back. Until you're dead. That's the way it is."

"It's not how it has to be," I said.

He gave me half a smile, his bangs falling over his eyes. "You are such a dreamer. Listen, Terric did what he thought he had to do. I thought . . . last time we were here and Mikhail possessed me . . . I thought that would be the end." He shrugged. "Yet, here I stand. I'm not going to go easy, or quietly, crystal or no bloody crystal. But I'd appreciate it if you didn't bring it up to my mum, okay?"

I nodded. "Is there someone in the Authority who might be able to remove it, or cancel the glyphs?"

"Not like I've had time to ask around."

"Maybe Violet?" I said. "She invented the disks, and those hold magic a lot like the crystal. We could ask her if she has any ideas of how to negate its effects."

"How about we unpoison magic, stop the spread of the plague that's killing everyone, and convince the Authority that we got screwed by Bartholomew? Survival first, doctors later."

I didn't want to let it go, but he was right. If we called Violet and met with her, it would put her in incredible danger right now, since the Authority wanted us dead. Until we cleansed magic and cleared our names, it was better for the people we cared about to not be involved.

"All right," I said, rubbing at my eyes underneath my glasses. "So magic's been poisoned. Does it feel any different to you?" I asked.

"What's magic supposed to feel like?"

"Just tell me if right now, while the crystal is drawing magic directly from the well into your chest, if magic feels any different from any other time you've pulled on it."

"I thought we'd just agreed we were done with crystal talk."

"We're done with the doctor talk. Not the crystal talk."

He rolled his head back to stare at the ceiling. "I do not know how you put up with her, Z."

Zayvion didn't say anything, but his pacing was slower now, his breathing calm. Whatever overload of information he was dealing with, it seemed to be easing some.

"If you can't tell the difference in the magic, say so," I said. "I just wondered if it hurt."

"It hurts," he said quietly. "It always hurts." He lowered his gaze from the ceiling to look instead at me. "Since the minute Terric shoved this thing in my chest, nothing's felt the same. Not my body, not my head, and for damn sure not magic. Death magic . . . It comes to me easier than before the crystal. That desire to consume and destroy, something a user always has to manage when casting Death magic, is"—he exhaled—"much, much stronger."

"And now?" I asked. "Right now?"

"It's not any worse than it ever is. Why?" he asked with darkness hooding his eyes. "You think I'm going to go evil?"

"Can't go somewhere you've already arrived," I said.

Shame laughed. "Fuck you. Just for that, you get to help me close the well."

"We came all the way out here," I said, "killed people, almost got killed, got the well open, and you want to close it? No. I want proof of the poison that I can shove in someone's face if I have to. We need proof that the well is tainted."

"Which would be what, exactly?" Shame crossed his arms over his chest and waited for an answer.

Holy hells, I didn't know. I didn't have a camera, or a cup, or a balloon animal. "When you pulled on magic from the well, it didn't stink like the rot. It still doesn't smell bad."

"I think the taint is just beginning to take root," he said.

"So it might not have started here," I said.

Shame shrugged. "Or it's been self-purifying."

"Is that possible?"

"This has never happened before. Anything is possible."

"Which means it might have started somewhere else," I said. "A different well. Maybe the Death well?" A memory of the Veiled pulling up out of the crypt in the Lone Fir Cemetery came to me, along with the memory of the Veiled stepping into one another, possessing one another. Had this all started there?

Leander had been there too, and one of his Veiled had nearly killed Shame, Terric, and me. He must have been there for a reason.

But then, Leander had been a lot of places doing a lot of harm. Including in Maeve's inn, over the Blood well.

Maybe Leander didn't have anything to do with it and the contamination was coming from a cistern. Bleeding out, or bleeding back into the wells. Hell, I wouldn't put it past Bartholomew to have planted a poison, just to tear apart the network lines and conduits of magic my father had made.

"Where does your head go when you frown like that?" Shame asked. "Is it your dad in there kicking around?"

"No, I was just thinking that we need to check the other wells. Blood and Death, at least. Places Leander has been. Places the Veiled have shown up en masse lately. And we should check the other cisterns too. We have a lot of ground to cover."

"You make too many plans," he said. "Right now, the only thing that needs to be done is to close this well. That, and maybe see if Zayvion's found a way to un-scramble his brains."

"They're not scrambled," Zayvion said in a raspy voice.

Shame didn't look at him, but smiled. "He's getting there. This—" He pointed at the floor. "Closed. Before someone calls to check on Bartholomew's buddies over there and finds out they've finally kicked their nasty breathing habit."

"I want a sample from the well."

"Not going to happen." Shame cracked his knuckles

and shook out his hands. "Looks like I'll be closing this on my own. Thanks a lot, Beckstrom."

"Wait," I said, running through possibilities. What did I have on me that might be able to hold a sample from the well? A gun, bullets, a knife, a pair of glasses, and a classic children's book. Not a lot of help there.

*Stone,* Dad said.

*What?*

*He might be able to carry some of the magic. He is a construct, an Animate. The very nature of an Animate is to contain magic.*

Huh. I hadn't really thought about that. I mean, I knew he ran on magic somehow, but I'd never thought about storing magic in him. *I don't want to poison him with tainted magic. And besides, he's not here.*

*He may have a filter built into him like the cisterns. We can check for that. And I think we will need a sample from this well—from all the wells—if we are to make an antidote for the poison, or a cure to cleanse the well. Summon him.*

*He doesn't even sit on command. What makes you think he'll answer a Summon?*

*You are running out of time, Allison. Is it worth the risk?*

"Shame, Dad thinks we should summon Stone," I said.

"Not listening to that man."

"Stone might be able to contain some of this magic and we can use it for proof, or for comparison to other samples in other wells, and maybe for a cure. I can't use magic to summon Stone. You need to do it."

Shame tipped his head to the side and the muscle of his jaw tightened. "Bad idea. And we don't have any time to wait for him to get here. For all we know, killing these men, or opening the well, set off alarms. The Authority could be on their way right now."

"No," Zayvion said from across the room. Then, a little louder, "No. It's a good idea." He walked our way. His pace was off a little, too stiff, as if his spine hurt, or like he had the world's worst migraine balancing on top of his skull. His eyes had faded to a hot bronze with flecks of brown instead of the pure, hard gold.

"Call the gargoyle, Shamus," Zay said, "or I will."

# *Chapter Six*

Shame studied Zayvion for long enough, I thought he might fight him for it. But then he nodded. "If for no other reason than to get the two of you off my bloody back."

He strode away from the well, standing as close to the doors as he could. Then he set the Disbursement again and the purple leech spell slipped through his fingers and attached to his left shoulder, biting in deep, ready to exact the pain for the magic.

This time he drew a very soft, very small Summon spell. I always thought the glyph was shaped something like a butterfly, and when Shame poured magic into it, it was like watching a butterfly come to life and lift off his hand. As it did so, wicked tendrils of lightning snapped out from it to the Disbursement spell. The Disbursement absorbed the magical backlash, and doled it out as pain into Shame's muscles.

The Disbursement wasn't a shield. It was a focus for how and where magic would hurt. I knew it worked that way, but it was still weird to watch it with my bare eyes.

Shame flicked his wrist, and the butterfly took flight — a blur of sapphire and fuchsia that shot up to the ceiling, and then disappeared through it.

"There. One gargoyle summoned. In the meantime, let's get this damn well closed before someone notices it's open." He tapped a cigarette out, stuffed the pack back into his pocket, and dug for his lighter.

"No. We wait," Zayvion said.

Shame lit the cig. "You gonna go with two-syllable man here, Beckstrom, or listen to reason?"

"Two-syllable man," I said.

Shame just shook his head. "Fine." He walked off to the corner of the room and put his shoulders against the wall, leaned his head back, and closed his eyes.

The Disbursement was still stuck to his shoulder. It stretched out to bite at his neck and crawl up the side of his face. The boy had a hell of a headache for throwing that spell. Since he'd just pulled on a ton of magic to open the well, I wasn't surprised.

I didn't know how long it would take for Stone to find us. I wasn't even sure Stone would know how to find us. I'd never brought him to the wells.

Zayvion was on the opposite side of the well from me. The hard white and silver of magic played across his dark features. He stood with both hands out to his sides, sword unsheathed in his right hand, head bent so he could stare into the depth of the well as if he were ready to dive into it at any sign of trouble.

I couldn't tell what he was thinking, what he was feeling. Though whether that was because there was enough magic to power the sun between us, or if Closing those men had done something, done too much to his mind for me to hear his thoughts, I didn't know.

I walked around the edge of the well until I was standing next to his right hand, so I could grab that sword if I needed to.

"Hey," I said quietly.

He didn't say anything.

I slipped my hand down, and gently touched the back of his hand clenched around the sword's hilt.

"No hurry," I said, staring into the shifting light of the well with him. "You've still got time."

It took some time for Zayvion to work his way through the pain he was in. Maybe half an hour. I didn't say anything. Neither did Zayvion. Shame smoked three cigarettes down, while the Disbursement on his face and neck faded to lavender, then pink, then was gone, leaving nothing but the magical ashes of the spell dusting his skin.

Finally the set in Zayvion's shoulders eased, the clench of his hand eased, and then he shifted the sword into his left hand and put his arm around me.

I slipped my arm around his waist, and leaned my head against his shoulder. He smelled of pine, and, beneath that, pain and sweat.

He inhaled, holding his breath and centering himself, eyes closed. I wasn't any good at Grounding—it made my claustrophobia kick into high gear. But I held still, trying to stay calm, relaxed, easy, so that Zayvion might pick up on my mood and find his footing again.

More time passed. Maybe fifteen minutes.

Then there was a scratch on the door, and a bump. I opened my eyes. The bump turned into a slam, and then a pause while something snuffled at the crack at the bottom of the doors. That something tried the handles.

Sounded like my gargoyle to me.

Shame hadn't moved. He leaned against the wall, one boot flat against it, his head still back, eyes still closed. The cigarette in his hand had burned down to ashes between his fingers. Several cigarette butts scattered the floor at his feet.

Looked like I was the most conscious in the room.

Go, me.

I pulled away from Zayvion carefully, and he stirred, opened his eyes.

More brown than gold, thank goodness. I gave him a small smile and strode around the well to the double doors.

"Stone?" I whispered.

He gurgled and wiggled the door handle.

That was my boy.

I opened the doors and a whole lot of rock carved in the shape of a living, breathing gargoyle the size of a Saint Bernard tromped up to me. He bumped his head on my leg before doing a full circle around me, sniffing and clacking as if looking for something, his wings lifted to their full height.

I dragged my hand down his back. "Good to see you too, Stoney." He felt like warm, silky marble under my fingertips as he slid past me toward the well.

"Don't touch," I said. "Don't touch the magic."

"Wasn't going to," Shame said blearily.

Stone burbled, his ears flicking back, then forward. He turned toward Shame and trotted over to him, sniffing at his fingers.

"Hey," Shame said, swatting at him without actually opening his eyes. "Give a man some privacy."

But Stone, apparently satisfied that he'd found what he was looking for, cozied up to Shame and rested his head on Shame's boot.

Gotta love a good Summon spell.

Zayvion sheathed his sword and looked around the room, as if gathering his memories of why we were here, and what we were trying to do.

"Why is Stone here?" he asked.

"Bloody hell," Shame muttered. "Last time I listen to a scramble-headed Closer."

"Shut up, Shame," I said. "He's here because I need to gather some of the magic out of the well to use it as proof that there seems to be some contamination happening to it, and maybe to help us find a way to cleanse it."

"How is Stone going to help with that?" Zayvion asked.

"Dad said he contains magic. He thinks he can hold some of this magic, store a little of it."

"Interesting that your father thought of it," Zayvion noted.

There was my logical, suspicious man.

"What?" he said.

"What what?" I asked.

"Why are you grinning at me?"

I shrugged. "Just happy to have you back. I don't care why my dad thought of it. Let's just see if we can get Stone to take in a little of the magic and hold it. Ideas?"

Shame chuckled, a sort of dry cough. "Ask the madman."

"Love you too, buddy," Zayvion said.

Shame finally rolled his head forward, opened his eyes, and gave us one laconic blink. "I meant her father, you nit."

*Do you know how he can hold it?* I asked Dad.

*In theory.*

*That's more than I have.*

*I'd suggest Shame use Death magic to cast a Transference spell. Something that will pick up the magic, keep it in its native state, and deposit it in Stone. There are glyphs, or I think there may be glyphs, on Stone's chest that indicate which Transference spell would work best.*

*And you know this how?* I asked.

*I see what you see, Allison.*

"Dad says Shame might be able to use Death magic and a Transference spell to move magic in its native form, into the glyphs on Stone's chest."

"Love being dragged into this," Shame said. "Be sure to tell your da that. And you," he said to Stone. "Good gargoyle. You came when I called. I'll buy you a cookie. But get your head off my foot, mate. You're killing me."

Stone did as he was told and, after pushing his nose into Shame's hands, trotted back over to me.

Shame stretched and strode over to us. The rest had done him some good. And from the white pulse of magic glowing from the crystal in his chest, the passive recharge of magic straight from the well had done him some good too. Maybe our delay came with added benefits.

"Come here, you big rock," Shame said. "Let's see your scribbles."

Stone had been staring at the well, tipping his head from side to side, as if he'd never seen anything like it before. And he hadn't. I'd been afraid he'd just jump in like a stupid lug, but he was staying a cautious distance away, one hand lifted, his finger and thumb held up as if trying to feel the warmth of the magic roiling within it.

"Stone," Shame tried. "Come here, Stoney."

Stone backed away from the well, watching it as if it would leap up and bite him. He was growling, a low, constant rumble that almost sounded like a purr. His ears were still up, though, and he wasn't showing any teeth. He wasn't in attack mode, but I didn't think he was far from it.

Shame got around in front of him and knelt so Stone could still see the well over his shoulder.

"Need to look at your chest, big guy."

Stone held still, and Shame traced a glyph on Stone's chest. "Passage," he said. "That's an odd one to carve on a gargoyle."

He glanced over at Zayvion. "Are you sure Cody carved all the gargoyle statues for the restaurant?" Shame asked.

Zayvion nodded. "As far as I know. It was a large commission."

"Why would he carve Passage on something that should have remained a statue?"

Stone growled.

Shame rubbed his ears. "Don't blame me, Stoney. If Allie over there hadn't triggered whatever spell started your engine, you'd just be a big dumb yard decoration sitting in front of a restaurant."

"Maybe Cody didn't carve him," Zay said. "He looks like the other gargoyles out there, though."

"Who knows?" Shame said. "Cody was always in trouble with someone and always hedging his bets. He might have thought he could use Stone for something other than art. Or maybe he just liked the lines of that spell. It looks quite smart on you, boy."

Shame rocked back on his heels, then pressed his hands into his thighs and stood. "I can pull on magic, I can use Passage to place some of that magic in Stone, but I want you to think about it, Allie. You're trusting your father here, and you're putting Stone at risk."

"We need a sample of the magic. I don't think we'll be able to come back here once the Authority finds out we offed Bartholomew's men. Get the sample while we have the chance. Stone can handle it. I can handle my dad."

"Didn't think you'd change your mind. Still think it's a bad idea to do this to him, but hell, it's not the worst thing I've done. Not even the worst thing I've done today." Shame turned to the well, set the Disbursement, and this time the purple spell wasn't a leech—it was a flickering fire that settled in the hollow of his neck.

Fever. And a strong one, by how deep the color was.

"How hard of a spell is Passage?" I asked Zay.

"Depends on what you want to give it to," Zayvion said. "Inanimate objects are easier. Living beings are incredibly difficult. Ghosts, fairly easy. I don't know about magic. From that look in Shame's eyes, it's going to hurt."

Shame exhaled a thin stream of words that sounded more like a soft prayer. He drew on magic to cast the spell, and the wooden floor darkened around his feet, the scorch moving outward and going ash gray as he drew magic from the glyphs and walls around the well, but not the well itself.

Very tricky move.

Then he poured that magic into the spell—a spell that had an oddly hollow center, the outside woven and intricate, like a frame of Celtic knot work.

Shame pointed his left hand at the well, and a ball of magic, no bigger than his fist, bright as liquid diamonds, pushed up out of the well and drifted as if pulled on a string straight into the spell that Shame held very steady with his right hand.

The ball settled in the center of the spell, hovering there, and spinning, but not touching the framework of the glyph.

Shame inhaled, held his breath, then exhaled that soft prayer again. He cupped his hands on either side of the glyph and pressed inward. Hard. The muscles down his neck strained as he forced the spell to compress. He crushed it until it was the size of an amulet. Then, with the spell still in both hands, he turned to Stone.

Stone didn't need any coaxing. He lifted up on his hind legs, resting his hands on Shame's shoulders.

Shame fastened the spell into the glyph on Stone's chest, where it flashed a soft blue, then sank and faded into the charcoal gray of Stone's skin.

Stone dropped down on all fours and sneezed. He shook his head and sneezed again. Then he looked up at Shame, grumbled and clacked, then trotted over to me and sneezed. He didn't look any different, didn't smell or act any different. And when I rubbed behind his pointy ears, he didn't feel any different.

"Can we get that magic out of him again?" I asked.

Zayvion nodded. "The spell will hold it separate of any other magic. It can't be opened by anyone except the caster, so Shame can get to it when we need to."

"Not that it's going to prove a damn thing." Shame wiped sweat off his forehead with the back of his hand. He flipped up his coat collar to cover his neck and stuffed his hands in his pockets, hunching as if the room had suddenly frozen over.

"We might be wrong, you know," he said. "That smoke and tar in the well might just be a temporary muddying up because of the cisterns being fouled."

"Which is why we need a sample from each well," I said. "Shame, can you send a message to your mom? Tell her we need a sample from the Blood well if she can get it. And Victor too. Ask if he can get a sample from the Faith well."

"How many of the damn things do you intend to dip into, Beckstrom?" he asked.

"All of them should do it."

"Do what, exactly?" Shame asked. "Besides get us caught or killed?"

"Dad said the combination of magic from each well might be enough to help us find an antidote to the poison, or a way to cleanse magic."

"And who are we going to take this antidote to once we prove our theory?"

"I don't know yet."

"You don't know yet."

"You're the one who doesn't like planning too far ahead. Just tell your mom and Victor. We'll figure it out as we go."

I turned to Zay. "Can you close the well?"

I hated asking him, but I couldn't use magic, so I was out. Shame had just handled three large spells in a really short space of time right on the heels of a fight. He was currently rocking a hell of a fever from that last spell.

Maybe it would be better to ask Shame to do it since he hadn't just dragged himself back from the edge of insanity.

Shame tapped the bracelet at his wrist, though I noticed he was shivering. "Sure, ask the crazy guy," he said. "This ought to be interesting."

Zayvion didn't say anything. He simply drew a Disbursement, a short hard pain that snapped a thick black line down his spine. Zay stepped forward to the edge of the well and drew a Lock spell.

The glyph for Lock hovered in front of him, stretched to touch the ceiling and all four walls. Then it speared straight down into the well.

Zayvion threw his arms wide, then pulled his hands together, palm to palm. He said one word and the Lock spell set lines of bronze fire through the floor under our feet. The wood rolled and spiraled like gears flowing in oil. Magic, stone, and wood closed over the well.

The floor was just a floor again. Locked tight.

In the sudden un-magicness of the room, things seemed too quiet. "I think we should be going," I said.

"I've been saying that for an hour," Shame said, "and you get twitchy only now?"

We started across the floor, Stone trotting along behind, then ahead of us. Shame opened the door for him.

"Did you contact the others?" I asked.

"Yes. But that's not going to do us a lot of good if we don't know where to meet."

Stone sniffed at the bottom step of the staircase back up to the outer world, then took off up it, half climbing, half winging and clawing. If anyone was coming down those stairs, they were about to get a face full of gargoyle.

We started up after him, listening for sounds of people above.

I thought through possibilities of where we could meet up. The den was out. Not only did the Authority know that I owned it, but so did everyone else, including the police. We could return to Shame's place, but after that Gate Roman opened I was pretty sure it would be under observation, or wrapped in yellow tape by now. Not Maeve's place at the inn, not Zay's place, not my place. Maybe Grant's under Get Mugged. No, I'd already used him as a cover once. Twice felt like pushing it.

*Collins,* Dad suggested.

There's someone I wasn't sure could be trusted. Sure, I'd hired him to take care of Davy after Davy had been bitten and infected. I knew Collins had no love for the Authority, for how they had Closed him, and nearly destroyed his ability to use magic.

But he had business dealings with my dad back in the day, and even though he'd said he was a doctor, Shame told me they had a fun little nickname for him: Collins the Cutter.

He was currently in hiding, trying to keep Davy alive. Maybe going to Collins would be a very good idea.

*Why Collins?* I asked. It wasn't that I didn't trust my dad. Okay, I wasn't sure if I trusted him or not. He'd been really great recently, saved my life, maybe saved all our lives with that recorded box Roman had taken with him to England. Still, old habits were hard to break. And I had a long-standing habit of being suspicious. *Not that I don't think it's a good idea,* I added.

*He has access to tech devices that may be far better equipped than Stone to contain the magics from the wells. He's tending Davy. You want to check on Davy. And,* he said, a little hesitantly, *Davy's condition may give us more clues as to how magic is tainted and what can be done about it.*

And that was my practical-nigh-unto-coldhearted father. Let's go study the guy fighting for his life to see what this epidemic could do to someone up close.

Still, it was the best plan we had.

"What about us meeting wherever Collins is?" I said. We'd gotten about halfway up the stairs, Zay in front, then Shame, then me, Stone ahead of us all making gurgling sounds like he was talking to the walls. Which he probably was.

Zayvion was still moving stiffly, as if his left hip hurt with each step. He covered it pretty well, but I knew him enough to know when he was trying to bull through an injury.

"Where is old Cutter?" Shame asked.

"Bea told me he was in the warehouses under the water tower," I said.

"Anyone who trusts Collins the Cutter, do a cartwheel," Shame said, his voice slightly slurred. That fever must be a special sort of fun while climbing the stairs. "No?" he continued. "Well, there's your answer, Allie."

"He has Davy," I said. "And we need a place to meet."

"He's gonna rat us out," Shame said. "And if he rats us out, I get dibs on killing him."

"I don't think—," I started.

"You get first blood," Zayvion countered. "I get to break his neck."

"But that's what we did with the last rat bastard," Shame whined.

"And how well did that go?" Zay asked.

"Grand," Shame said. Then, "Fine, be that way. You get to break his neck."

"Excuse me?" I asked. "He's a doctor. He's looking after Davy. We don't kill him."

"We?" Shame said. "*I* never took an oath not to hurt him."

"No one hurts him until we know for sure that Davy's okay," I said. "We just don't go in there guns a-blazing."

"Us? Guns a-blazing?" Shame said. "No, never that."

# *Chapter Seven*

No one was on the hiking trail when we stepped through the door back into daylight. We must have been down there for longer than I realized. The light of afternoon was headed toward that hard gold of presunset, and the temperature had taken an uptick. It was at least in the high seventies, the kind of weather that made me want to go to the coast and put my bare feet in the sand.

Or used to make me want to do that. All it did today was make me sweat as we clomped down the trail back toward the bridge.

I'd told Stone to hide and find me tonight. I wasn't sure how much of that he actually understood, but he got the hide part at least. He clattered up the hillside, disappearing in the greenery. He was fast and he was smart. He looked like a rock if he held completely still. I was pretty sure no one would spot him. He'd find me again.

On the downhill side of the bridge that crossed the bottom of the falls, Shame lifted his wrist and glanced at it, like he was checking the time. Only I knew he didn't wear a watch.

One of the Pooh Sleuths must be checking in.

He glanced at Zay and nodded. They didn't clue me in, and I didn't ask until we'd gone across the walk and over to the parking area again, where the highway traffic covered the sound of the falls.

"How about I drive?" Shame asked.

"No," Zay said.

Shame turned to me. "Allie, he needs time. I'm not being a dick about it, but I do not want to be in the car if he hits a flashback of something he pulled out of someone else's head and suddenly can't feel his own extremities."

"That can happen?" I asked.

"Yes."

I looked over at Zayvion. He had his sunglasses on and looked every inch the cool, urban tough customer.

"Let me see your eyes," I said.

He tipped his sunglasses down. Gold and brown. Gorgeous. He didn't look out of his mind. But he didn't argue with Shame. Which meant what Shame was saying was true and he knew it too.

"I think I should," I said. "I've been doing the least heavy lifting. It's my turn to pitch in."

I held out my hand. After a slight hesitation, Zay dropped the keys into my palm. I unlocked the car and we all piled in, Zay in the front next to me, and Shame in the back.

"So who sent the message?" I asked.

"Victor," Shame said.

"What was it?"

"He said Violet's safe with Kevin and out of danger."

"Uh-huh," I said. "That's in the book?"

"Forty-two, three, four, and forty-two, three, eleven: 'quite safe with him' and 'out of all danger.'"

I just shook my head. "I still can't believe you use that book."

"You know I like to keep things simple."

"Well, until I hear straight from Victor that Violet's

not only okay but cleared the hell out of this town with my baby brother, I'm not going to stop worrying."

"Of course not," Shame said. "Worrying is what you do best."

Zayvion reached over and put his hand on my thigh. Even through my jeans, his palm was hot, heavy, welcome.

I was careful to drive under the speed limit as we headed back to town. I didn't know exactly where Collins was, and didn't want to have to use a Tracking spell to find him. There were several old warehouses under several water towers in Portland. I wished I'd asked for specifics when Bea told me where Collins was hiding out with Davy.

"Do you know which warehouse?" Zayvion asked.

"Sort of in process-of-elimination mode," I said. We were rolling down streets, trying not to look too suspicious as I scanned the buildings for any hint of where Davy might be. If I could use magic, I'd just flick out a Tracking spell. But I couldn't do that. The few spells I could see clinging to the buildings weren't exactly big neon signs telling me my dying friend was behind the burger joint.

"Careful," Zay warned.

A car cut in front of me and then slowed to almost a complete stop.

"What the hell?" I muttered. Then I realized it was Jack Quinn's car. Jack was a Hound and Bea's boyfriend. The left blinker flashed on for just a second, and then Jack drove at speed again.

"Zayvion, I'm sorry to tell you I think I have a crush on another man."

"Who is this unfortunate and soon-to-be-dead fool?" he asked.

"Jack. That's his car. He must have been waiting for us, or maybe he followed us."

"Jack Quinn has been following us?" Shame said.

"And now he's taking us to Collins, I think."

"Or a trap," Shame said.

"He's a Hound, Shame."

"My statement stands."

"You still don't get it, do you?" I turned left, following the car. "Hounds are loyal. Jack and Bea told me they'd help me if they could. They're not going to turn against me while I'm in trouble."

"What happens when you're not in trouble?" Shame asked.

"Don't know. It's never happened."

Jack slowed again to a complete stop and flicked on the left blinker.

I looked left. There was a narrow alley between two buildings and what looked to be an open garage door. Since there was also a water tower nearby, that must be where Collins had Davy.

"Nice hiding place." I turned left while Jack continued on forward and drove away.

"Nice place for a trap too," Shame said.

"And I worry too much?" I pulled into a garage next to a car that had a cover pulled over it. It was the kind of shop people probably used to use for metalwork of some sort. A repair shop. There was one door to the left that appeared to lead into the main building.

We got out of the car. I strode over to the door and tried it. It opened, revealing a brick hallway that led to a rusted yellow metal wall at one end. Halfway down the hall was an old white and dust-redbrick arch. Faint gray light filtered through that arch.

We went that way. I heard Shame pull a weapon, his gun, I thought, and Zayvion drew his blade. Since I was in the front of this exploration, I felt a little dumb not arming myself, so I carefully drew the gun out of the holster.

The gun was warm and heavy in my hand, having retained the heat of my body under my coat. It was strange. And uncomfortable.

I stepped through the archway into a huge, open room. There must have been some renovations done to the place since the structure was originally built. Metal beams crisscrossed the ceiling like someone had gone a little crazy with giant Tinkertoys. A huge square skylight filtered dirty gray light down to wash the wide, scarred plank wood floors with a watery patina.

More brick walls lined the place, more white and rusty red arches opened to spaces that were too dark to make out. Steel girders that looked like they were once railroad tracks ran down the center of the floor, plumb with the wood.

The room was empty, except for an old hunting trophy—a huge moose head—mounted on the wall to the right.

I didn't want to call out, but I sure as hell wasn't going to play what's-waiting-to-kill-you-behind-door-number-two either.

Zayvion and Shame stood on either side of me. I could literally feel the heat of pain rising off Shame from all the magic he'd thrown, though he wasn't acting like he was in agony.

I pointed at the arches on either end of the room, indicating they should each take one, and strode off toward the arch directly across from us.

Zayvion caught my arm, and jerked me back toward him.

"We do not split up," he whispered.

"We don't have time for this," I whispered back.

"Ah," a man's voice echoed out among the timbers and steel. "I see you've finally stopped by. So good to have company."

And then Eli Collins strolled through the archway to our left.

Collins was probably no more than ten years older than me, and knew how to work the intellectual, shy-with-a-side-of-crazy look. But his short sandy hair was a little messier than usual and he was sporting dark circles behind those wire-rimmed glasses.

He had on his usual button-down white shirt, with a charcoal pin-striped vest and slacks. His sleeves were rolled up, revealing his right forearm wrapped in gauze, the left burned red. He also had an impressive bruise spreading from his hairline down the right side of his face and neck.

He smiled, and opened his hands wide. I noted his right thumb and two fingers were also wrapped in gauze, as was the palm of his left hand.

Looked like something had chewed him up and spit him out. If I had to guess, I'd say that something was magic.

"You have come by to see Davy?" he asked when none of us moved.

"Yes," I said, pulling my arm out of Zayvion's grasp. "We have."

"Please." His eyes roved over Zay, Shame, and then stopped on me. He slowly and pointedly looked me up from boot to gun, short jacket, chest, neck, lips, eyes, where his eyes narrowed just a moment from my icy stare, then to my hair, and finally back to my lips again, as if they fascinated him. "Allie," he breathed. "You look stunning."

Zayvion pushed past me and was across the floor in four strides. He grabbed Collins by the shirt and shoved him up against the wall.

"Keep your hands," he growled, "and eyes to yourself. Or I'll hang them on my walls for trophies."

Whoa. I'd never seen Zayvion lose control like that.

"Zay, don't," I started.

Collins tried a brief smile, but lost that when Zay tightened his grip on his collar. "I meant no harm, Zayvion," he wheezed, "and intended no slight. Accept my apology."

"Zay," I said again.

Shame walked over to Zay and patted him on the shoulder. "Let him go, Jones. You promised I'd get first blood. No first blood, no neck breaking."

Shame started off toward the archway. "You're welcome, Collins."

Zayvion showed no intention of backing off.

Collins just held very still, and honestly, I was pretty sure there was more curiosity in his eyes than any sane man in his current predicament should possess. He was either used to getting roughed up or too stupid to know that he was teetering on the edge of a beating.

"Are you sure I'm the person you want to hurt?" he finally said.

Zayvion released his shirt, but didn't step back.

Collins nodded. "It's been a challenging day for us all, I think."

"Is there booze in this place?" Shame's voice drifted back from beyond the arch.

"Yes." Collins slid sideways to get out from between Zayvion and the brick wall. "Let me pour us drinks."

He rubbed at his throat and headed through the archway. I stuck my gun back in the holster and walked up behind Zayvion.

"Done defending my honor?" I asked.

He didn't say anything. Didn't move. Just stared at the wall.

"Zay?" I walked around to stand beside him. "Love?"

He punched the wall, and at the last second opened

his palm. I rocked back half a step as dust shifted down between the bricks to powder Zay's boots.

I waited while he breathed, his fingers digging into the edges of the brick. Hard, too hard, as if he was trying to dig his way through something, or dig his way out of something.

And then I knew what it was. Minds. The memories of the men he'd killed. Shame had said he could go through flashbacks.

I shifted so I could see his eyes. Hard and gold with dizzying emotions clashing through him. Too many memories, lives that were not his. He was sorting, sifting, claiming and reclaiming his center, his mind, his life, over and over again, pushing away the lives of the other men, but he wasn't getting ahead of those images faster than they were piling up.

"Zayvion. I'm right here. And so are you." I placed my hand gently on his cheek.

The contact was like lightning. Forget Grounding. Forget meditation. Forget sorting and sifting. Zay came back to himself, back to me, like a lightning bolt seeking iron.

He twisted and pulled me against him so quickly, I didn't even have time to catch my breath. He pressed me back to the wall where Collins had been.

Then he was kissing me, hard, searching, hungry, needing this, needing us, needing me.

Desperate.

I opened my mouth, licking him gently, matching his hunger with patience, with gentle sliding strokes of my tongue, until he seemed to finally feel me, really feel me, there, against him, there, touching him, there, kissing him, breathing him as my own breath.

His heartbeat settled, the desperate hunger eased, and his mouth softened into the familiar caresses of the man I loved.

I pulled away from him, and looked up into his eyes.

Brown. Deep and warm. With only a glint of gold dusting them.

"Welcome home," I said.

He leaned back enough that he could drag one thumb down my cheek.

"Did I kill him?" he asked.

"No," I said, trying not to be surprised that he didn't remember the details of what had just happened. "Shame wouldn't let you."

"Hm. Probably for the better. We're not alone here, are we?"

I shook my head. "We came to see Davy."

Zayvion closed his eyes, gathering himself, then pushed back. The absence of his body left me painfully tingly.

"I remember that," he said. "Which way?"

I started off toward the arch. "Apparently, there's booze."

The darkness of the hallway was interrupted by pools of gold that made the scars and divots of the old wood plank floor glow like stripes of tigereye. The room opened up into a living area with chairs set in a nice sitting space along with tables and reading lamps. The brick walls were covered by heavy shelves made of girders and I-beams in rusted orange.

An arch at the far side opened onto a functioning kitchen, and I expected a bathroom might be back that way. From the layer of grime covering half of everything, the place looked more like a storage unit that had been turned out into a place to live than like a place to live that had storage in the corners.

Collins poured scotch into four glasses, while Shame mooched around the room, probably looking for something to steal.

"Where's Davy?" I asked.

"He's quite well," Collins said. "Don't worry yourself. But he's resting right now. Here." He strolled over and offered a glass to Shame, then two to Zayvion, who handed one to me. Collins kept his gaze carefully on Zayvion's face, not mine. He, apparently, didn't want to have his neck broken today.

I didn't like scotch. And right now, I didn't care.

"To your health." Collins lifted his glass. We all shot it back. Yeah, it had been that kind of day.

The scotch burned a hot line down my throat to the soles of my feet, and my eyes watered. I managed to be a grown-up about it and didn't make the "icky" face as I put the glass down on the shelf behind me.

"So, Ms. Beckstrom," Collins asked with overt civility, his gaze properly fixed about two inches above my left ear. "How is it I may be of assistance?"

I rubbed at my eyes, ran into the damn glasses again. More finger smudges. Great. I took the glasses off and pulled the hem of my T-shirt, cleaning them.

"I'm here to check on Davy's progress," I said. "And I want—" I looked at Zayvion and Shame. "Maybe we all need to stay a while."

"At least until the booze runs out," Shame said.

Zayvion nodded once. Good. We agreed this would work as a place to regroup with everyone. At least temporarily.

"Is this your property?" I asked.

"Belongs to a friend of mine," Collins said. "He's out of the country right now. Uses it mostly for storage."

"Do you think anyone would expect you to be here?" I asked.

Collins walked back to the bar and placed his glass there before turning and leaning his hip against the bar. "Which anyone are you asking about, Allison? The Authority? The Hounds? The police?" He was making eye contact again, his gaze slipping to my lips. It was like an old habit that couldn't be choked out of him.

"Not the Hounds," I said. "I know they know you're here."

He nodded. "I think they're keeping an eye on the place, though they haven't been in to check on Davy."

"I told them to stay low."

"Well, they are indeed doing that." He shifted so he could pour himself another drink. "As far as I know, the Authority doesn't monitor this building or block. It's one of the reasons why I chose it. As for the police, I haven't seen many drive by. I keep the lights low and an eye on the doors, just in case."

"Can we can stay here for a bit?" I asked.

"Too long, and I suppose someone will notice the comings and goings. But there is ample space for beds, and plenty of linens. Food enough for a few days, I'd think. I will, of course, have to add room and board onto the bill you'll be paying for Davy's medical care."

"Of course," I drawled. I'd hired Collins to give Davy magic and medical care. If Dr. Fisher and every other physician I knew who dealt with magic weren't also involved with the Authority, and therefore pretty much out to get me, I would have much preferred to take Davy to a hospital.

But Collins was all I had.

For now.

"Shame, would you let your mom, Terric, and Victor know we're here? Tell her to bring the magic with her tonight, if she can."

"So many," Collins said, a hard edge in his voice. "I didn't realize you'd be inviting so many people for company."

"Problem with that?" I asked.

"Oh, no. Not at all. I'm sure we'll all get along just

fine." And then he smiled, which meant we probably would not.

Terrific. Just.

"So," Shame said. "The bathroom? I need to take a leak."

Collins nodded to the narrow greenish hall. "Down there, second door on the left."

Shame clunked his glass on the shelf. "Don't kill anybody while I'm gone, you two."

"Anything else you'll need?" Collins asked as Shame stalked off. "Food? Supplies? Tranquilizers maybe?" He looked up at Zayvion instead of me. Zayvion hadn't moved since we stepped into the room. He looked like a bouncer who was waiting for the signal to kick Collins down an elevator shaft.

"Where's Davy?" Zay asked.

Collins immediately became interested in adjusting the bandages on his hands. "Resting," he said. "Resting."

That might not be a lie, but it wasn't exactly the truth either.

"Take me to him," I said.

"I'd rather not," he said. "He needs the rest."

"Take me to him or I'll make you wish you had." I put my hand on the gun under my jacket and managed not to flinch at that contact. He looked at my eyes, my hand, then at the gun.

"That is not the gun I gave you," he said, a little offended.

"Davy," I repeated.

He inhaled, as if weighing a difficult choice. "Tell me you didn't lose my gun."

I just glared at him.

"He *is* doing well, Allison."

"Heard that. Now I want to see it."

The shuffling of footsteps from beyond the darkened arch made me turn.

"Yes," Collins said. "He's in there. But I don't think now is the time to see him. He's still . . . recovering."

"Recovering from what? The infection?" I asked.

"I had to make some choices," Collins said. "Things to save his life."

"What kind of choices?" I asked. "What did you do to him?"

A sick dread twisted my stomach. We didn't know how to cure Davy. We didn't know what would happen if the poisoned magic he'd been infected with wasn't stopped.

Well, that wasn't entirely true. Anthony Bell, who had been possessed by a Veiled and then bit Davy, had died from it. Pretty safe bet Davy would die from it too.

"I saved him," Collins said, holding his bandaged hands out and down. "I saved his life."

I pulled my gun, and didn't care how it made me feel. "Then show me how you saved his life."

"Put the gun away," Collins said. "He's fine. He's not a danger. And he's not in danger."

I wasn't listening. I was striding toward the shadows, toward the sound that was not quite footsteps beyond the arch. Toward the room Collins had said Davy was in.

"Allison, stop." Collins somehow managed to outpace me and stood between me and the archway. His eyes were bright, clear. Sober and very, very sane. "He is fine," he said. "You have my word on that. But I can't let you in there with a gun in your hand. Give me the gun."

"Like hell."

"Then put it away. I don't want you to do something stupid. I don't want you to accidentally hurt him."

I felt the presence of Zayvion loom huge behind me, the heat of his body burning like a fire across my nerves.

"Stand aside, Cutter," he rumbled.

"I didn't hurt him, Zayvion," Collins said, reasoning or bargaining; I didn't know which.

I pushed past him and into the darkened room. "Davy?" I called softly.

A shadow moved in the far corner.

I fumbled for a light switch on the wall. "What did you do?" I said to Collins. "What did you do to him?"

I found a whole bank of switches and flipped them all on, flooding the room with light.

The shadow in the corner, the thing that was Davy, flinched, and turned away from the light. But not before I saw him. Saw what he was.

He looked like a Veiled—a ghostly man-shaped shadow made of watercolor hues.

"What did you do?" I whispered.

Collins stepped into the room, and turned off half the bank of lights. "I told you what I did. I saved him."

I didn't know what to say. I didn't know what to do. Collins walked toward Davy.

"The light bothers his eyes," he said softly. "Which is why you caught him . . . surprised. He is learning to control the shift between solid and incorporeal—"

"Get away from him," I said.

Collins stopped, turned toward me, calm. "Come see him for yourself."

I heard a gun cock from behind me. "You're bothering my friends, mate," Shame said from the door. "Why don't you get over to that wall, and keep your hands where I can see them."

Collins did as he was told.

I walked across the room, but stopped short of where Davy was still huddling in the corner. "Davy?"

My eyes were pretty good in the dark. But there was a lot of magic surrounding Davy, like he was wearing a shadow made of thin flashes of black and silver and weird green threads that formed a not exactly human-shaped suit of armor around him.

"It's Allie," I said. "Davy?"

He tipped his head up and I squinted to see through the magic to the Davy beneath.

His eyes flashed red in the darkness.

Holy shit.

Davy was there, the Davy I knew, thin, smiling, yellow hair stuck up with a bad case of bed head, smelling of cedar and lemons and wearing a pair of sweatpants and a loose T-shirt. But he was something else too, something else that surrounded him.

I'd thought he was a Veiled—a ghost—but that wasn't quite right either.

"Are you okay?" I asked him. I held my hand out for him. "I don't think you should be on your feet right now. Let me get you to a bed, okay?"

He hesitated, then took a step forward, but it was like his feet weren't working. He buckled, caught himself with one hand on the wall, his other hand falling into mine.

No. His hand didn't fall into mine. His hand fell right *through* mine.

Somehow he caught himself, pulled his hand back from me and out of the wall. Then he pulled his feet up out of the floor, one by one, and stood there, mostly solid and mostly just Davy again.

"You're tired, Davy," Collins said, with quiet encouragement. "Keep calm and try not to strain. You are fine. You are alive."

"Shut it," Shame snapped.

"Davy?" I said again.

"I'm," he said in a voice that sounded far, far away, "trying." He took another step, and then another. His feet stayed on top of the floor instead of inside it, and with one last step he was out into the light of the room.

"Fuck me," Shame breathed.

"Shame," I said, keeping my voice low and my eyes steady on Davy's face. His eyes were wide with fear. "You're fine. You're going to be just fine."

Davy's gaze searched my face, looking for the lie. He didn't find it, though. Because I believed it, had to believe it with all my heart. Everything might not be right at this very moment—Davy might be flickering between looking like a Veiled ghost and looking like a man—but he was going to be fine. Because I'd make sure he was fine. I'd twist Collins' guts until he made Davy fine.

"Think you can walk over here to the bed?" I asked.

"Is there beer?" His voice was still faint but growing stronger.

I smiled at him. "There better be a beer in it for both of us," I said. I held my hand out, and Davy stared straight in my eyes and took a breath. He lowered his hand to mine.

And it stopped against my skin, warm, a little sweaty. Davy was solid, just Davy again, though he was sweating, trembling, and working hard to stay calm and solid.

Boy was freaked the hell out.

I didn't blame him.

"Don't like that bed much," he said. "Bad dreams."

"Then I'll get you another one." I didn't look away from Davy; I didn't move. "Collins. I need a place for Davy to rest."

"He can use my bedroom," Collins said. "I offered it to him once before. He didn't want to move from this room."

"Show me," I said.

I heard Shame and Zayvion shift behind me. "Don't need your hands to walk," Shame said to Collins. "Keep them up. Let's go."

"Really," Collins sighed. "Under gunpoint in my own house? After all I've done for you? I am not your enemy."

"Lucky for you, we haven't decided what you are yet," Shame said cheerily. "And until we do, I'm not putting this gun down. Probably not even after that, you vengeful bastard," he added.

"Vengeful?" Collins said. "Wherever do you get such ideas, Mr. Flynn?"

"I've heard the stories. I've seen the obits."

They walked out of the room, and Zayvion paced toward me slowly, quietly, but heavy enough Davy and I could hear his footsteps.

Davy was tensing up the closer Zayvion came toward us, like an animal ready to bolt.

"He's your friend, Davy. He's worried about you too, and he's not going to hurt you," I said. "Can you let him stand on the other side of you so we can help you walk?"

Davy nodded.

I risked breaking eye contact long enough to look up at Zayvion. "Be careful—he's still sick."

"We can do careful," Zay said in a gentle voice. "We got you, Davy. Now let's get you in bed so you can rest and we can figure this out."

Davy shifted his look from me to Zayvion, searching Zayvion's face as if he was having a hard time focusing on him. Finally, his eyes cleared. "Hey, Zay."

"Evening," Zay said smoothly. "Ready to sit down for a bit?"

"Sure," Davy said. "Sure. Allie?"

"Right here." I stood next to him and put my arm around his back, gently lifting his arm up and around my shoulder. He was solid; he felt solid. He smelled like Davy should smell, and strangely, the magic that covered his skin like a gauzy veil of color didn't stink. He was the shape Davy should be.

He didn't look like what Anthony had looked like at the end before he'd died—rabid, out of control, desperate. But the weave of magic around him did not go away even though I was touching him, touching his flesh. I could not shake the reality of what I had seen. Davy had been a ghost, a Veiled, just a moment ago. He'd put his hand through a wall.

I was going to tear Collins' heart out through his throat for this.

# Chapter Eight

"That okay?" I asked after I got Davy's arm settled over my shoulder.

"Like I'd complain?" he said.

I smiled. "Like you wouldn't."

Zayvion got situated on his other side and we started walking. Got as far as the door, Davy breathing pretty heavily as if he were dragging an impossible weight behind him, instead of like he was practically being carried by Zayvion and me.

"Need to rest?" I asked.

"Need bed," he panted.

We kept walking. Through the door, down the hall to a room behind another door—this time a wooden door with iron bracers, hinges, and locks that gave it a medieval look.

This was a bedroom. Huge, but a bedroom. There was a potbelly stove in the corner and dressers built into the walls, and an iron four-poster king-sized bed. Collins stood to one side of the room, looking bored.

Shame held the gun level with his chest, looking content as a cat.

"This must be the bed," I said. "Good enough for you, Silvers?"

"It. Will do," he panted.

"Almost there," I said, knowing he was wearing out.

Davy took another step and tripped. I braced to keep him from falling. So did Zayvion.

Something cold slid up my left arm, sticking and grabbing to keep hold of me as Davy's arm slipped from my grasp. I glanced at my arm.

A lash of magic—black with flecks of colors, the same colors that lay over Davy's skin—wrapped around my arm like a vine, like a whip.

No, like a tentacle. I'd seen lines of black like that before. It was what the tainted magic looked like under Anthony's skin. It was what the tainted magic looked like under Davy's skin.

It was the tentacles of poisoned magic that were trying to kill Davy.

"Concentrate," Collins said firmly. "You are alive, Davy. Flesh and bone. Refuse the magic."

Collins' voice snapped me back to reality, and I realized Davy was falling, still falling, Zayvion bracing to catch and hold him, but there was nothing to catch or hold.

Davy fell through Zay's grasp, his feet and shins already sinking into the floor.

"Davy," I said. "Knock it off."

The tentacle let go of me, and Davy landed on the floor. Hard. Solid. His feet and legs weren't in the floor anymore. He was, all of him, on the floor.

"Sure, boss," he whispered. "Whatever you say." He panted, covered in sweat and pain and fear.

I reached for him, but Zayvion brushed me aside and bent. He picked him up, then carried him to the bed.

Davy was so out of it, he didn't even protest the damsel-in-distress treatment.

I pulled the covers back and Zay got Davy in the bed; then I covered him up, except for his chest.

Davy was already asleep, or maybe passed out. His

face was slick with sweat, his hair stuck against his forehead. But his breathing was already settling some. He remained solid. That was something, right?

His pale arms were corded with muscle and marks of magic that inked a hard, thick black line under his skin, wrapping like a vine and splitting at his wrist to send thinner tendrils up each finger all the way to his fingernails.

The tainted magic had spread. Was that what had scraped across my arm while Davy fell? Was the tainted magic inside him trying to get out? But it didn't smell bad. Didn't smell like the taint.

My arm was still sore from that touch, as if fingers had dug in hard, leaving slightly bruised lines behind.

"What did you do?" I turned to Collins.

He inhaled, caught his breath as if gauging what he should tell me that would keep me—well, Shame—from shooting him.

"Everything," I said. "Tell me everything."

"He was dying," he started. "Transporting him here from the den made his condition worse. Much worse. The poisoned magic was spreading faster. The Syphons I set up on him couldn't keep up with it. He was . . . suffocating as it consumed him. I'd done everything I could to keep the taint from spreading through his body, to pull magic out of him."

He tipped his head up, looked over at Davy. "I thought I'd lose him. My skills . . . well, they aren't what they used to be since the Authority Closed me, are they?" He gave Zayvion a sardonic smile.

Zayvion cracked his knuckles, a promise to bruise up the other side of Collins' face if he didn't get on with the explanation.

"This warehouse is built to focus magic," he said.

That would explain the girders and ornate crisscrossed metal rafters.

"And that was something I could work with to help Davy. So I made a decision."

"Without me," I said.

"I couldn't find you. And even if I had told your Hounds to find you, it would have been too late for Davy. I had a matter of minutes to do what needed to be done, Allison, not a matter of hours. It was because of you that I did what I did. You were my inspiration. The magic that marks you"—he pointed toward my right arm, to the ribbons of color, of magic, there—"suggested I could do this."

"Do what? Turn Davy into a . . . into a . . ."

"Living Veiled?" Collins suggested.

Shame exhaled a curse. I just nodded. "Is that what he is now? A dead man? Half ghost, half alive?"

"No. Not exactly." Collins took a step toward me.

"Stay where you are," Shame said.

Collins glanced at Shame's gun, then crossed his arms over his chest and leaned against the wall. "I created a Containment spell, drew magic into it, filtered through several layers of spells and tech, and cast it around Davy and myself. I also reconfigured the equipment, drawing upon several delicate spells at once. Dozens," he added quietly. "Dozens of spells."

I suddenly realized he was more than just bruised up—he was exhausted. He had paid the price of pain for each of those spells he'd used on Davy. I was actually impressed. When the Authority had Closed him, they'd taken away his memories of how to use magic. Everything he did with magic now, he had had to learn from scratch. And I had to admit some of it was pretty genius.

"I had to reroute the paths the magic was already burning through his body. Draw it out of his vital systems, and give it a place to flow. It had to have a place to complete its task, and I needed to give it that place." He paused, staring at the bed. I didn't think he saw Davy there. Or maybe he saw him in a way none of the rest of us ever would.

"Feed a fever," he said.

"What?" I asked.

"Fever," he said. "Extinguish it with ice, or burn it out with fire. Ice wasn't working; stopping the magic wasn't working. So I poured magic into Davy, forced it to burn, to run its course as hot and quick as it could. But not the course it had been choosing to sear through his body, his organs. I forced it to follow pathways of my making. Pathways I carved *into* him."

Okay, crazy man was freaking me out now. "You carved spells into him?" I asked.

His gaze pulled away from some far distance and he studied my face, my mouth, my forehead, and finally met my eyes. "Yes."

I turned and pulled Davy's shirt up. The black tentacles of tainted magic still traced beneath his skin, just like they had since Anthony bit him and infected him. They began on his shoulder in a solid black-and-blue bruise and snaked out from there, across his back, then around his ribs and up over his shoulder, digging down along his collarbones, and his chest.

They had been reaching for his heart. I knew that. They had been reaching for his stomach, his liver, his lungs. But not anymore.

Scars decorated his chest. Thin, morbidly beautiful strokes and lines, some wide and still red, some thin, glossy pink, others white and crinkled. All the lines, the scars, created a design that reached from just beneath his collarbones and tapered down to the edge of his waistband. Through those scars, and trapped between those scars, magic flowed.

I just stood there, staring, trying to get my head

around the reality of this. Of what this was. Of what it meant.

Dad pushed forward in my head, looking through my eyes.

*Ah,* he said in a tone filled with wonder. *Magnificent.*

I didn't think it was magnificent. I thought it was horrible. I couldn't even tell what spells he had carved into Davy, nor how Davy had survived it. People can't hold magic in their bodies—it killed them. And now Davy had it permanently pulsing through him.

Collins had sentenced Davy to death.

"Shame," Zayvion said from so near me, I jumped. "Put the gun away. Collins," he continued, "tell us what you used."

I heard Shame holster his gun. Collins walked across the room and stood on the opposite side of the bed. Shame strolled over to the foot of the bed.

"Well, shit," Shame said. "Better talk fast and talk sweet, Eli."

Collins sighed. "I cannot tell you how tired I am of being treated like an enemy and prisoner. I saved his life. Which is what you hired me for, Allison. To keep him alive, using any means at my disposal."

"I know," I said quietly. "And he's still breathing. He was conscious too. That's something. Just tell me what the spells are. Please."

"It's . . . technical," he said. "I cast Containment, Flow, Passage, Shield, more. Many more. I thought I'd need only a few—Containment, Transference, Flow—but each spell I cast opened up new routes the magic tried to take. His life . . ." He paused, then nodded. "His life was unraveling stitch by stitch like a string pulled on a sweater. But I managed to stay one step ahead, one heartbeat ahead of it all. And when I saw my chance to close it off, to block magic from spreading through him, I cast Lock."

"And End," Zayvion added.

Collins swallowed. "A version of it, yes."

I remembered that spell. My dad had cast it when I was first learning how to use magic with Maeve. Maeve had said it was an old and very difficult spell to use.

"It's brilliant," Zayvion said simply. He looked up at me. "He saved his life, Allie."

"So what does this mean for Davy?" I asked. "Will he have to carry magic like this forever? Will the spells break? Will they kill him? Why is he ghosting out on us?"

Davy jerked in his sleep, then exhaled, the magic pulsing through the lines and the scars in a wash of crystalline hues similar to the colors on my arm. It was almost pretty.

"Let's talk of this in the other room, shall we?" Collins asked. "He does need his rest."

I pulled Davy's shirt back down and covered him with the blanket. "Will he be all right alone?" I asked. "He won't get sucked into the bed and smother or anything, right?"

"When he's sleeping or unconscious, he seems to default to a physical state," Collins said. "So, no, he won't suffocate. It's just when he's awake that things seem to get confusing for him."

We walked out into the living room and I sat on the couch. I didn't know about anyone else, but I was suddenly exhausted.

Collins lowered down into one of the chairs, and was silent for a bit. He really did look tired. The bruises and bandages made some sense. Using that much magic carried a hell of a price. He was probably lucky to still be alive.

"What, exactly, is Davy?" I asked. There was probably a better way to ask that question, but I'd be damned if I knew how.

"He's still human, still a man," Collins said. "But the spells carved into him and the magic flowing through those spells seem to allow him to shift closer to death without losing his life. When he's awake, he struggles to remain flesh and blood, to not become only the embodiment of the spells and magic coursing through him.

"I had not anticipated the incorporeal state he slides into," Collins said. "It is fascinating, and I've documented it, but I certainly hadn't expected it. I did combine Death magic spells with Life magic spells, but there are plenty of studies in the viability of that approach that suggest it should not have made him lose his solidity."

"It's not Death magic that's the problem, mate," Shame said as he poured himself another whiskey—a lot of whiskey. "It's the taint in the magic you're using. Throws off the spells."

"That could be," Collins said. "Have you done any investigation into the wells yet?"

I nodded. "We were able to reach the Life well for a sample."

"You have a sample?" He suddenly perked up. "That's wonderful. Where is it?"

"In Stone."

"What stone?"

"Stone is my gargoyle. It's in him."

Collins caught his breath and held it, thinking. "You have a stone gargoyle?"

"He's an Animate," I said. "Followed me home one day."

"Isn't that . . . convenient?" Collins mused. "An Animate gargoyle who can contain magic. A lucky break you had him at your disposal."

"Not lucky enough unless we get samples from the other wells."

"What are you hoping to discover?" he asked.

"If the wells are tainted," Zayvion said. "If the poison is spreading to them or if one of them is the source of the taint. And if we can make an antidote from tainted magic."

"So far," I said, "all we know is that there seems to be some contamination in the Life well, but not much."

"You'll need samples from each well if you can," he said. "At least three to test. And if we want to try to filter the wells, we'll need a sample from all four." He looked up at Zayvion. "That is the eventual outcome you're looking for, isn't it? To cleanse the wells if they are tainted?"

"Yes. And to use whatever information we can for a cure, a real cure," he added, "for this epidemic."

"Well then." Collins stared at the wall for a bit, sorting through things. Finally, "There are theories. The same sorts of filters that were laid in place in the man-made cisterns that hold magic could be modified for the natural wells of magic. But we'd have to know what kind of contamination we were trying to filter. Tests." He nodded, agreeing with himself. "A lot of tests. The quicker, the better."

"Can you do that?" I asked.

"For the right price."

Shame just chuckled. "Seeing that you get paid for every damn thing is always on your mind, isn't it?"

"A man has need to keep his investments secure."

"A philosophy near and dear to my little black heart," Shame agreed. "But what say we just beat you until you give us what we want?"

"You still wouldn't know what to do with the information I give you. I assume none of you have been studying and experimenting with magic and tech advancements for the last decade?"

"We know people," Zayvion said.

I didn't know whom Zayvion was talking about, but if it was Violet, I was adamantly against getting her involved in this. We were on the wrong side of the Authority right now. Hell, the police were looking for me for the embezzlement charges Bartholomew had trumped up. I didn't want her hurt, and everything about my life right now added up to trouble. "How much?" I asked.

"It isn't money I want, Allison," Collins said. "I want to be Unclosed."

# *Chapter Nine*

"Oh, hell no," Shame said. "There was a reason you were Closed, Cutter."

Zayvion didn't say anything. Neither did I. If I were in Collins' position, that's exactly what I would have asked for too.

Collins just opened his bandaged hands and then folded them carefully together. "That is my price. If you think finding a way to cleanse or filter the magic is worth me having my abilities back, then I will be happy to help."

"And if we decide not to risk it?" I asked. "What happens then?"

"I will honor my current agreements with you, Allison. I will monitor Davy until he is fully able to care for himself for the price you and I already negotiated. But that is all I will do."

I heard a knock at the door, and then it swung open.

"I thought you said you lock your door," I said.

Collins shrugged. "I said I take precautions."

"What kind of precautions?"

"I have cameras. I know who's approaching."

"So who's approaching?"

"Mrs. Flynn and Mr. Kellerman."

Maeve and Hayden. I hoped they got the message from Shame and were able to get a sample from the Blood well.

Zayvion walked out into the other room to greet them.

"All this blackmail is making me hungry," Shame said. "Do you have any food in this joint?"

"The kitchen is just off to your left," Collins said.

"Get you something, Allie?" Shame asked as he walked off that way.

"Sure."

Once Shame was out of earshot, Collins asked, "How much did your father talk to you about his plans?"

"Not much," I said honestly. "More now, but back when he was alive, we never spoke."

"More now?" Collins asked. "Now that he's dead?"

Ah, hell. I forgot he didn't know my dad was possessing me. And I wondered if I should tell him.

*Dad?* I asked.

*It may be . . . useful for him to know,* he said. *But it is your choice.*

I tried to think it through. Would knowing my dad was in my brain change how Collins treated me? Would it change our deal of him looking after Davy? Would it open up a can of worms I didn't have time to unwriggle?

Maybe half a truth would work better.

"He's not completely dead," I said. "There was a magic user who tried to raise him from the dead. Things didn't go right."

Collins' puzzled look shifted over to disbelief and took the corner straightaway to laughter. "That son of a bitch," he managed to get out. "He's alive?"

"In a manner of speaking."

"Where is he? How do you know he's alive?"

"I'm not going to tell you that. But trust me when I say I can get messages to him."

He wiped at his mouth, but was still smiling. "And he can get messages to you too, can't he? He is an amazing man, your father. Even death didn't get in his way. I assume he has some set ideas of what he wants you to do for him?"

"For him?" I asked. "Want to be a little more specific about that?"

"Oh, not really." He bit down on his grin. "I think it's something you and I could discuss in a more . . . private setting." He was looking at my lips again. Like he'd seen me naked, and was more than happy to repeat that circumstance.

I wished I didn't have holes in my memories. Most of my college years were gone. For all I knew, I'd met him and dated him back then, even though he told me we had met for the first time when I'd asked him to take care of Davy.

I gave him a bored stare. "I wouldn't go somewhere 'private' with you if the world depended on it. Got that?"

"I suppose that might be up to discussion if the world actually depended on it."

"No," I said. "It wouldn't."

"Never know what a person would do when *everything* is on the line."

"I know one thing I wouldn't do. You."

"Problem?" Zay asked, walking into the room.

"Not yet," I said.

Maeve was behind Zay, and Hayden rumbled up behind her. They didn't look any worse for the wear. The tightness in my chest released a little. I'd been worried for them. Was still worried for Victor, Terric, Violet and Kevin, and a whole slew of other people. And that reminded me. We needed to check in with everyone.

"Didn't think any of these old warehouses had been rigged for focals," Hayden said. "Thought they were all torn down in the old days."

"They were," Collins said. "A friend of mine likes to do historical renovations."

"Hell of a fine job." Hayden stared up at the weave of metal rafters.

"Thank you," Collins said, surprised at the compliment. "You should see the center. It's inspired."

"Thing would trip the networks all to hell and back again if it was used, though," Hayden said as he helped Maeve sit in a chair.

"Not so. It's very well insulated and has its own storage of magic to pull from."

"I'll be damned," Hayden said. "Your friend really does do it old-school."

Okay, I didn't have the faintest clue what they were talking about. The only focal I knew about was when Dad had said it would take a Focal, a person who could contain dark and light magic long enough, for magic to be brought back together again. And that was assuming dark and light magic could ever be joined again, since the Authority had broken it hundreds of years ago to try to stop Isabelle and Leander's killing rampage.

A rampage they seemed more than happy to pick up where they'd left off.

I wondered if Roman was having any luck convincing the Overseer that Leander and Isabelle were in this world, and trying to find a body to host them so they could destroy the Authority and rule magic as they saw fit. I wondered whether he had convinced her that poisoned magic, not a strange virus or a breakdown in the technology that supported magic, was causing the epidemic. We really needed someone on our side, someone with global reach.

"Have you heard from Victor?" Maeve asked me quietly while Hayden and Collins argued about accessibility to bleed lines and other things I had never heard of before.

"No. Wait," I amended. "Once. Shame said Victor reported that Violet and Kevin are safe. But we need to get a message out to him. To let him know to find us here."

"Ah," Maeve said. "He knows. When any of us send information on the cuffs, it goes out to all of us." She leaned her head back against the chair. "It has been a long day, hasn't it?" she said. "And it's not half-done, I suspect."

"How did it go at the Blood well? Did you have any trouble getting a sample of magic? Was anyone from the Authority there?"

"No one was there guarding the well, which means they still think I'm Closed and without my memories from the last several years. Still, we were careful to open the well very quickly and under blocking spells, and leave immediately after. Getting the sample wasn't easy, but I did have a container with the proper holding spells to put it in."

"You brought it?"

"Yes."

"Good. The more samples we have to test, the better. I think we should try to get one from each well."

She nodded. "Have you been listening to the news?"

"No."

"The epidemic is getting worse. They're telling people to stay off the streets, stay home, unless absolutely necessary. They're telling people to wash their hands and wear masks. If we don't come up with a solution to this . . ." She shook her head.

She was right. None of those precautions would keep people safe from being possessed by the Veiled, bitten by the Veiled, or poisoned by their everyday use of magic—tainted magic.

"The streets looked pretty empty," I said. "But plenty of people were still out at the falls. Has anyone in the media suggested the possibility of magic being the cause of the sickness? Has the Authority sent out warnings for people to keep their magic use to a minimum?"

"Not that I've heard," she said. "The sales of protection and health spells have grown ten times, and Proxy dens are overloaded from people using magic to try to keep themselves safe from the virus they think is going around."

My stomach dropped. If all magic was tainted, and we knew for sure one cistern was filled with poison, and that at least one well was tainted, then that meant every spell someone used to try to keep safe was only causing further risk. By trying to protect themselves, people were increasing their exposure to the very thing that could kill them.

"We have to stop this," I said. "We have to make someone understand what's really going on. Someone who has the resources to deal with this problem. Have we heard from Terric yet on who is taking over the Authority?"

I didn't really care who it was, just so long as he or she was reasonable enough to listen to one of us when we explained what was going on.

Once we tested what was tainting the wells, we might have something solid to give someone. Might have something solid enough that we could make an antidote.

"I haven't heard from him, no," Maeve said. "I'm sure he'll check in when he has information."

"How about food?" Shame walked out of the kitchen with a pile of sandwiches, chips, and a bowl of freshly washed grapes.

"You made food?" Maeve asked, feigning shock. "Did you do it all by yourself, Shamus? With your own two hands? Why, that could almost be considered work."

"And you wonder why I rebel." He handed her a sandwich and offered the bowl of grapes. She plucked out a cluster.

"Oh, I know why. You have too much of your father in you."

"Has nothing to do with that," Shame said. "It's the neglectful upbringing I've had to suffer through."

Maeve just made a dismissive sound and ate her sandwich.

I wasn't sure if this was lunch or dinner. I wasn't really sure that I was hungry. But I didn't know when my next chance for a meal might be, so when he offered me a sandwich, I took one. Peanut butter and jelly. That would do. Everyone else helped themselves to the food too, including Collins.

"Could you tell if the Blood well was different?" I asked. "Did the magic seem tainted to you?"

"Hayden cast the Sight spell." Maeve looked over at him. He had already finished off his sandwich and was popping grapes into his mouth.

"So we're all fine with Eli hearing everything we have to say?" he asked.

"Yes," I said. I didn't have time to deal with who could or should know what, and Collins already knew too much and had done too much for us for it to matter. If he had wanted us dead, if he wanted to turn us in to the Authority, he already would have.

Plus, we had something he wanted—my money and his memories of how to use magic. As long as he still wanted either of those things, I thought we had a fair chance that he would stay on our side.

Hayden picked his teeth with his pinkie. "All right, then. The magic in the well didn't look right. It was darker than it should be. But I didn't see anything that looked like poison and didn't smell anything strange."

And that was the difference between a trained Hound and a trained magic user. Hounds knew not only what we were looking for, but also how to dig until we found it. Anyone could cast Sight, but Hounds knew how to interpret everything they saw, smelled, tasted, and felt.

"Where's the sample?" Zayvion asked.

"I have it here." Maeve pointed to her purse beside the chair. "How are we going to test it?"

"We were just deciding on that," I said.

"And?" she asked.

"We were going to ask Collins to do it."

Maeve brushed back the stray tendrils of her hair and looked over at Collins. "And what price are you asking for your assistance, Mr. Collins?"

If she'd leveled that tone at me, I would have felt guilty. But Collins just gave her a tight smile. "I'll take that up with Mr. Forsythe."

Victor? Then it hit me. He wanted to talk to Victor because Victor was the one who Closed him. And only the person who Closed you could undo that spell.

But Victor had Closed him years ago. I didn't even know if such a thing could be reversed from so long ago.

*There are risks,* Dad said. *But it can be done.*

Collins was a man unafraid of those risks. He'd probably do anything to get back what had been taken from him. I understood that desire. Understood it very well. But I wouldn't hold the lives of thousands hostage to get what I wanted.

"He wants Victor to undo the Close he put on him," Shame said. "And we all know what Victor's answer will be. So I say we might as well come up with a plan B now. Victor doesn't let people bully or blackmail. Not when he's done something under orders."

"But whose orders?" Zayvion said quietly. "Sedra's? She's been possessed by Isabelle for years. Maybe it was Isabelle who wanted Collins Closed."

"She was still the head of the Authority," Hayden said. "And, Collins, you really did do some terrible things that earned you being Closed. Victor was doing his job and following the rules. I say Shamus is right. Victor won't agree to do this. You'll have to name a new price."

"Why don't we let Victor decide what he will and won't do?" Collins said. "He is here now."

Okay, I still didn't know where the cameras were stashed so he could see who was approaching, but I heard the door open.

Zayvion once again walked out of the room. Only this time, Zayvion and Victor took a lot longer before walking back into the room. I ate my grapes and ignored the fact that everyone was straining to hear what they were saying. I didn't have to strain. I had good ears.

Zayvion warned him about Collins' offer. He also told Victor that if Collins didn't give us the tech for testing the magic, we were clearly out of options, since I didn't want to get Violet involved, and he didn't even think Violet would have technology suited for this specific purpose. Victor didn't say anything. Not a single word. That wasn't a good sign. When Victor didn't say anything, the answer was usually no.

I didn't know what we were going to do if we couldn't talk him into this.

*We will find a way,* Dad said. *We could ask Violet—*

*No,* I thought. *We keep her out of this.*

*I was suggesting we ask Violet for names of her peers. There were some people she worked with out of England. A lab that might be convinced to help us.*

*No.*

Victor walked into the room. He was not happy. "You and I will talk this over, Eli," he said. "Not here."

Collins spread his hands. "I hope you don't think me rude, Victor, but I'd rather talk right here, where there are plenty of witnesses."

"Like we'd take your side," Shame said.

"You forget that there is more at risk than just the wells and magic," Collins said. "There are Veiled out there, on the streets now, biting people, infecting people, possessing people, killing people. And I may be the only man in the world who has come up with a solution to slow that process."

"You have?" Victor asked, surprised.

Shame just scoffed. "You mean that spell you carved into Davy? That's not a solution; it's a death sentence."

"Enough," I said. I could not hear him talk about Davy like that, could not bring myself to face that truth. Not yet.

"Allie," Zayvion started.

"No." I stood. "This is how it's going to go down, people, and I'm going to say it only once, so you better shut up"—I pointed at Shame, who had already opened his mouth, but snapped it closed—"and listen to me. Davy's still breathing. He talked to me. He recognized me. He's still Davy.

"But even though Collins' actions may have saved Davy's life, he has also done him a lot of damage. Maybe it's irrevocable damage. We don't know that yet. And if it is permanent, I know Davy can find a way to deal with it. We all deal with the crappy things magic does to us every day.

"But I will not just sit here arguing while we let the city, and everyone else walking those streets—innocent people who didn't sign up to get screwed over by magic—get hurt and die. If Collins has to be an ass and make us pay in blood, then I'll be the first damn person in line to give a pint. Right now he's all we've got and all we have time for.

"We'll listen to his terms; he'll listen to ours. We will get one more sample from the Death well to complete the tests and we will damn well get that done. And as soon as we have enough data, we will come up with a plan to stop this. To stop the poison. No matter what it costs.

"So," I said turning on Collins. "You want Victor to Unclose you. We want tech and fast, accurate information on what the poison is, where it's coming from, and how we can stop it. And we want an antidote, a filter, a cure. Not what you did to Davy. Because that's not ever going to happen to anyone ever again, understand? But something we can give to doctors so that people can survive this.

"Victor," I said, asking him a question I had no doubt he did not want to answer, "will you Unclose Collins so we can do this before there isn't anyone left to save?"

"Yes."

I blinked. I hadn't really expected he would agree. I thought I'd have to argue, plead, hell, threaten him into this.

"But not everything," he said. "There is knowledge Collins had that no man with his . . . morals . . . should retain."

"Oh, I think not." Collins stood. "I won't let you cherry-pick what I will and won't be able to remember about magic. About using it. About the experiments I spent *years* of my life conducting. You will give me my full abilities back, all my memories back, my *life* back, or this discussion is over. No matter how pretty a speech Beckstrom gives."

Victor looked over my shoulder at Collins. "Do you even know what level I Closed you at, Eli?"

"I've read the reports," he said.

"That's illegal," Hayden noted. "How did you even get your hands on them? Those are under lock and key."

"There's not a lock I can't pick," Collins said. "And there is always someone who will do a man a favor for the right price. Even broken down to this . . . state, I have many, many talents to offer."

"I Closed you at a level twelve," Victor said quietly. "I took away from you more memories and more abilities to use magic than the Authority asked me to take."

Collins blinked. "The reports said it was at an eight. That you only Closed me at an eight."

"That's what they wanted me to Close you at," Victor said. "But you were too dangerous. Far too dangerous with your knowledge."

"You forged the reports?"

"I didn't have to. As you said, there is always someone who will do a man a favor for the right price."

Holy crap. Victor had gone against Authority rules years ago. I wasn't sure how to take that.

*Collins was a very dangerous man,* Dad said. *And Victor has always had a strong sense of right and wrong,* he added with a strange note of respect. *I've always wondered how many decisions he has "guided" to his way of thinking.*

"Well," Collins said, trying to swallow that revelation down. "My terms are simple. Unclose me so that I regain my abilities. All of them. Or I will not give you the technology you need to test magic, and find a cure."

Shame raised his finger. "Can I say something, teach?" he asked me.

"No."

"Too bad. Listen," he said to Collins. "If Victor Uncloses you at that level, you are going to be a brain-rattled idiot for at least a couple days, if not weeks. You know that. You know it's true."

"What are you getting at, Mr. Flynn?"

"You won't be able to show us technology or do any tests in that state. Which means Victor Uncloses you *after* we test the magic."

Collins looked at Victor. "Is that the game, then?"

"There is no game," Victor said. "I can Unclose you. I can give you back half of what I took before you show us the technology. After you run the tests, I can give you the other half."

"Edited, no doubt, to your approval?" he asked.

"It is the only offer you are going to get from me," Victor said. "And I am the only man who can restore your mind."

Collins held Victor's gaze, considering.

"I'm just to take your word on this?" he asked.

"As we are to take yours."

Collins flicked his gaze to each of us in turn. "Done," he said. "If you agree to a Seal."

Victor pulled a small, mother-of-pearl-handled switchblade out of the cuff of his jacket and nicked his thumb.

Collins got out of the chair and strode over to him. He unbandaged the thumb on his right hand. It was raw. He pressed his bandaged index finger against it, freeing the blood to flow.

"Zayvion?" Victor said.

Zay walked over. Victor and Collins pressed their bleeding thumbs together. "Agree to your terms," Zayvion said.

Victor and Collins repeated the deal.

Zayvion spoke a word, and I could feel the heat of that spell like a quick flash that washed through the room.

Neither Victor nor Collins flinched, but I knew that had to have hurt. And when they pulled their hands apart, I could see that neither of their thumbs was still bleeding.

Okay, so the boys had spit and shaken on it. Swell. Time to get some work done.

"Show us the equipment," I said.

"First the Unclosing," Collins reminded me.

For cripes' sake. We were running out of time here. "Before even that," Collins said as he rebandaged his thumb, "I'd like to show everyone else Davy's condition."

"Why?" I asked.

"If, for some reason, the Unclosing goes poorly, someone here will need to take over his care. There are ... specific things that can be done to assist him. Things I believe the Flynns might be best suited for."

"Why us?" Shame asked.

"Because you are efficient with Death magic, and your mother is efficient with Blood magic. I believe both of those specific disciplines are needed to help Davy recover."

Which meant Collins was also efficient with those disciplines.

Maeve stood up. "Then let's get this done, gentlemen," she said. "Quickly, now."

Collins walked off to the bedroom where Davy was sleeping. Maeve, Shame, and Hayden followed.

"You might want to see that too," Zayvion said to Victor.

Victor raised his eyebrows, then nodded. He started after them.

"Victor?" Zay asked before he'd gone too far. "Do you think you can do it?"

"Unclose Eli?" he asked.

Zay nodded.

One corner of Victor's mouth quirked up. "We'll find out, won't we?" He turned and left.

"What was that all about?" I asked.

Zayvion was still looking after Victor. "Victor has been recently Closed and Unclosed himself," he said. "One of the things I took away from him was his ability to Close. And to Unclose."

"But you gave it back, right? When you Unclosed him?"

"Yes."

"There's a chance he'll totally screw this up, isn't there?"

Zayvion glanced down at the floor, then back up at me. "There's always that chance. If Victor thinks he can do it, he will." At my look, he added, "He was my teacher, Allie. He was the best Closer I've ever known. Still is."

I nodded. I hoped he was right. For all our sakes.

## Chapter Ten

Maeve looked a little pale and flushed when she came out of the room that held Davy. But she took my hands and assured me she could help him if things went wrong with Collins.

I didn't believe her, but I hugged her and thanked her anyway.

Hayden just looked disgusted by it all and stomped off to lean against a wall so he could glower at Collins.

Victor looked thoughtful. And when he glanced at me, his eyes wandered from the whorls of magic that caught at the edge of my right eye and then flowered down along my jaw and throat, down my arm to my fingertips.

Collins had said my marks were what gave him the idea to work magic literally *in* Davy's skin. It might have saved his life. It might have sentenced him to a slow death. But it looked like Victor found that idea fascinating too.

Which was fine and all, but we had work to do.

"So now, Victor," Collins said. "The sooner you fulfill your part of the bargain, the sooner we can put the samples to the test."

Victor nodded. "I understand that. Where are the other samples, Allie?"

"Maeve has one from the Blood well. Stone is carrying a sample of magic from the Life well."

"Really?" he said. "Stone? Who managed that?"

"Me," Shame said. "And I'd rather not have to do it again. That spell won't last forever."

"How long?" I asked.

"I don't know what being inside an Animate will do to it," Shame said, "but I'd say we have about eight hours left before it fades."

"And by 'fades,' you mean the spell breaks and we lose our sample?" I asked.

"Yes."

I turned to Maeve. "How long does your sample have?"

"Maybe sixteen hours."

"You used the flask, didn't you?" Shame asked.

She nodded.

"Show-off," he said.

"Then we need to get Stone," I said. "I'll take care of that while you Unclose Collins. Maeve, will you keep an eye on Davy for me?"

"Of course," she said. And the way she said it, I knew she also planned on keeping an eye on Victor and Collins too.

"Hayden—," I started.

"I'm staying here."

"That's what I'd hoped you'd do. Shame, you're going."

"Damn right I am."

I walked toward the other room, toward the outside door. He followed like I knew he would.

"You're not going with us," I said.

"Where else would I be going? Think I'll leave you and Zay out there summoning a gargoyle on your own? And why can't you just do that here, anyway?"

"I do not want to summon Stone to the warehouse

because if he is being followed, I don't know that he'd be smart enough to know it."

"Who would follow Stone?" Shame asked. "Hell, who even knows he exists?"

"Nola. Cody. Detective Stotts," I said.

"Ah." Shame nodded. "Didn't think of that. Must be the lack of fun numbing my brain. So, you going to summon him, magic girl?"

"No. Zay is. And you"—I zipped up my coat and pushed my glasses back on my face—"are going to try to get a sample from the Death well. If, for any reason, it looks dangerous, I want you to back out. Repeat what I just said."

"Allie doesn't think you can handle yourself, Shamus," he mimicked in a high voice. "Not only that, she thinks you'd walk stupidly to your death."

"Would you?" I asked.

"Not stupidly." He gave me a grin. "I'm not one of your puppies. You don't have to worry about me. And by the way, when I walk to my death? You will fall on your knees in awe."

"We don't have time for awe," I said. "We have time for careful, quick, and come back here immediately."

"Shouldn't be a problem."

We stepped out into the garage area. I heard the door behind me lock, and a bolt slide into place. Good.

"Later, lovelies," Shame said. He got into Maeve's car and rolled out of the garage.

"Zay," I said. "Can you tell Terric he needs to go to the Death well and help Shame?"

"I can tell him to go to the well. I think it'd be better not to mention Shame." He adjusted his cuff and tapped at the bracelet.

"Ready for this?" he asked.

"Sure," I said. "It's just one little gargoyle. How hard can it be to find him?"

An hour later, sitting as close to my apartment as we dared to park, with Zayvion casting a third Summon spell, I had decided it was damn near impossible to find one little gargoyle if he didn't want to be found.

"Nothing?" I asked Zay, who had cast a short tracer on the Summon to see if he could at least track down which side of town Stone might be clambering around in.

He shook his head. "I think I need to throw a Tracking spell."

"Tracking spells are too easy to follow back to the caster," I said.

"And?"

"And it's too dangerous. You cast that and any Hound in the city working with the cops or the Authority will see your signature and point to you from half a city away."

"Three Summon spells will do the same," he said.

"No. Summon has a way of screwing up its trajectory. They're notoriously difficult to follow back if you aren't the person who's being summoned." I rubbed at my hair, tucking it behind my ears even though there was nothing really to tuck anymore. I felt twitchy, trapped.

It didn't help that I could see the Veiled walking the streets, more of them—a lot more—than real, living people. The Veiled were searching for magic to eat, stopping at permanent spells to open their wide, black-hole mouths and drink down the magic until the spell broke. And then moving on to another spell.

Zayvion had been very careful to cast only when I'd told him I didn't see any Veiled in our vicinity. But we were running out of time.

For all I knew, Roman had made it to the Overseer, and she'd decided we were the dangerous ones. She might be sending forces to Portland right now to make sure we were taken in, or taken out.

Shame said there were only eight hours left on the spell Stone held. And I had no idea how long it would take to actually test the purity of the magic.

It was getting dark, which was probably good as far as cover went. Every time a cop car cruised by, it took everything I had not to hide my face.

"Sorry, babe," Zay said. "It's time to track Stone. At least to which quarter of Portland he's in. Or if he's not."

"Wait, what? You think he's not in town? Of course he's here."

"It wasn't just Detective Stotts. People in the Authority knew about Stone too," Zay said. "They could have taken him."

Hells. He was right.

"Something light and fast," I said. "What Tracking spell do you do best?"

"All of them," he said, and I knew he was not bragging. "Ping is the most subtle."

I liked Ping. It was a little unreliable, but usually got the job done. And it was almost traceless. "Okay," I said.

"Tell me when it's clear." Zay drew the multilegged glyph for Ping, and it spun there in his hand, not yet holding magic, looking like a ball of twine with twelve legs wriggling off it, giving it a cartoonish, excited, wavy look.

A Veiled walked in front of the car, and I shivered a little. It was weird to know I could see them plain as daylight, but Zayvion wouldn't be able to see a Veiled unless he drew a Sight spell. And if he drew a spell, the Veiled would be all over him to get at the magic.

"Hold on—Veiled man walking down the street. He just turned the corner," I said. "Okay, you can cast it."

I loved to watch Zayvion cast magic, but right now I

loved even more that he could do it quickly and with minimal draw on the networks. He knew exactly how much magic it would take to power a spell, and didn't waste any time doing it.

Magic filled the Ping and Zay threw it out through the car window. The spell rose, then hit a building, paused, and pinged off to another building, leaving very little trace behind.

"Impressive," I said.

"Be more impressed if it finds Stone." Zayvion started the car and we followed the spell.

"How long will it last?" I asked.

"Fifteen minutes, tops," Zay said.

Which was smart. Short spells were harder for Hounds to track. Hopefully this spell was short enough to disappear before anyone got a read on us, but long enough to point out where Stone might be.

"Think it would be easier to just go back to the Life well and get a new sample?" I asked.

"No," he said. "But if this doesn't work, we might have to."

Walking back to a crime scene where we'd left five men dead was not my idea of a fun way to spend the evening. Of course, neither was hunting a gargoyle.

Zayvion glanced down at his wrist.

"Pooh-gram?" I asked.

"Yes. Do you still have the book?"

I dug in my back pocket. "I thought you had the entire thing memorized."

"I do. I'm just a little busy."

Oh. Right. Driving a car, following a spell, and reading secret codes. "What's the numbers?"

"Three, one, sixteen. Three, one, twenty-one. Shit." Zay slammed on the brakes and the car skidded out into the intersection on a red light, traffic coming at us. He put it in reverse, and glanced up at the buildings around us. "Do you see it?"

I bent so I could get a better look. "It's headed west."

"Got it," he said. He glanced at his wrist. "Forty, three, twenty-two, twenty-three."

"Is that all of it?"

"Most. I think I missed a sequence."

I pulled the book out of my pocket and thumbed through it. "Head. Is. Hostile. Intent," I said. "Does that make any sense to you?"

"Must be from Terric," Zay said. "Head of the Authority is hostile intent toward us, probably."

"That's news?" I asked.

"He knows who the head of the Authority is. That's news."

"There," I said, pointing. "I think Ping found him."

The spell settled on the side of a building, then sank into the ground, spent. But it hadn't just faded away to ashes. Good. That meant it stopped because it found something, not because it ran out of energy.

"Do you know this place?" I asked.

Zay circled the block. "No. Offices of some kind?"

"I don't think so. Didn't it used to be an electrical store? Housewares or something?"

"Antique shop," Zay said.

"That's right."

He parked the car up the block. Didn't turn off the engine yet.

"You don't think Stone's alone in there, do you?" I asked.

"Do you?"

I shook my head. "It's not like him to not answer a call, or not to be somewhere around my apartment. He made it all the way to Multnomah Falls when Shame called him. There's no reason he shouldn't answer your Summon in a few minutes, max."

"Which means he's trapped," Zay said.

I nodded. "I have no idea what can trap him."

"We'll find out." Zayvion didn't pull his weapons. Neither did I. Didn't mean we left them behind either.

We got out of the car and strode down the street. I suppose we could have taken the back alleys and tried to find a back entrance. But it was dark. There were no streetlights shining on the building, and very little traffic. Whoever had picked this place wanted it to be out of the way, but not too out of the way.

I wondered how they'd lured Stone in. I wondered what they did to him.

"Anything on the door?" Zay asked as we approached.

"No magic," I said.

"Good." Zayvion rolled his fingers, making it seem incredibly easy to pull a glyph together without looking, then held whatever he'd just drawn in his fist, ready to use it, but without pouring magic in it yet.

He pushed the door. It was unlocked.

I was right on his heels.

The empty room was dark, but light spilled out across the floor from an open door on the other side of the room. The sound of a TV playing quietly reached me, along with the scent of hot rocks—that would be Stone—and a familiar, orange-heavy cologne.

Footsteps from the other room approached us. But only one set. A man. And then that man stood in the doorway, blocking the light. He did not look happy.

"Allie, Zayvion," Detective Paul Stotts said. "Drop the magic, unload your weapons on the other side of the door, and you can come in."

"Do you have Stone?" I asked.

"Yes." He turned and walked back into the other room.

I looked at Zay. "Why don't you stay out here? In case." It wasn't that I didn't trust Paul. Okay, that was a lie. I mostly trusted him, but he was a police officer, and I was currently up on embezzlement charges, and if anyone had found Bartholomew's smoking corpse, I was also up on murder.

I'd tried to tell him before about the Authority, about dark and light magic, the Veiled, and everything else, but he'd wanted proof. And that was the one thing I was short on.

"Come in, Allie," he said. "We have a lot to talk about."

"Don't," Zay started.

I pulled my gun out of the holster and pressed it in his hand. I also unpacked the clips and the knives.

Zayvion's eyes were glowing gold in the low light of the room.

"You'll know if I'm in trouble," I said. "Just try not to kill my best friend's police officer boyfriend if you come riding to my rescue, okay?"

I turned and walked into the light, leaving Zayvion behind. I didn't have any magic on me, and I couldn't use it even if I did have a spell planned.

I'd just given Zayvion all the weapons I owned. And I was walking into a room with at least one police officer who was armed and skilled with magic.

Not my smartest moment.

"Like hell," Zayvion said behind me. He strode up, and was thrown off his feet from the barrier over the door. I hadn't even felt it when I passed through. Hadn't seen it. It must be some kind of Ward that activated only when someone with magic, or weapons, crossed the threshold.

Holy shit.

"Listen, Stotts," I said as I turned back to the room.

To find him standing against the far wall, a gun in his hand, pointed at me. Stone was chained at the wrists, ankles, and neck to a metal loop in the wall, his big mouth duct-taped closed, his fingers also duct-taped together, his big round eyes glowing with anger.

"Have a seat, Allie," Stotts said. "The Ward has a Knockout spell on it. Zay will be unconscious for plenty long enough."

"Long enough for what?" I asked.

"For us to have a little chat."

# Chapter Eleven

I crossed my arms over my chest. "I didn't bring any weapons in here. I can't use magic. So I'd really appreciate it if you put the gun away."

He considered me. I'd known Paul for a pretty long time now. Long enough to know he was a decent man, and in love with my best friend. I'd never seen that hard look in his eyes. I'd never seen him behind a gun. I'd never seen him look at me like he was looking at a criminal.

"Do you know you have been implicated in a crime, Allie?"

I nodded.

"Embezzlement from your own business. And then we get a tip about one of your investors—a man who recently made a deal with Violet Beckstrom for part ownership in your father's company. We find that man dead. Killed. By magic."

He must be talking about Bartholomew. I didn't know how public Bartholomew had gone with his intent to screw over everything my father had ever planned and built. Public enough Stotts had found out about it. Which meant whoever was running the Authority had wanted him to find out about it.

"Just shortly after his death there was a spike on the grid. The mid cistern is blown like an old fuse. Someone reported seeing a rock creature climbing up a building right after the cistern went out."

He waited. Waited for me to say something.

"What?" I asked quietly. "What do you want me to say, Paul? I tried to tell you what was going on before, but you wanted proof. What I had to say wasn't enough for you."

He pressed his lips together, then holstered his gun. "Talk. I'm listening."

I didn't know where his crew was, didn't know if he had already called in police, FBI, hell, maybe even a SWAT team.

"I've already gone over this," I said. "There are a group of magic users who use five disciplines of magic, and have been doing so for centuries. They call themselves the Authority and are in charge of how much information the general public knows about magic. They have infiltrated into every level of society worldwide. They have the ability to wipe memories—they have many abilities.

"I got involved with them because my dad was involved with them. At that time the organization was breaking apart and each faction wanted magic in their hands. The right to say who could use it, and how it could be used.

"But they opened a door into death, and something—someone—got through. Now those someones want to rule magic in this world. The . . . things they released from death are soulless, heartless, insane. They're called the Veiled.

"Some people have sided with them. Some people are trying to tear the Authority apart from the inside out. Some of us left the group and are trying to take care of the real problem."

"And what is the real problem?" he asked. I couldn't

tell by his tone of voice if he believed anything I was saying.

"The real problem is that the people who came through from death have poisoned magic—at least that's what we think has happened. And now the walking dead—the Veiled—are spreading that poison. It's why people are getting sick. It's why people are dying. It's why Anthony Bell died.

"And I'm doing everything I can to find out how magic has been poisoned, what has poisoned it, and how to stop it."

"Alone. Without the police. Without going through any of the proper channels," he said. "What you're doing is illegal, Allie."

"What I'm doing is the only chance we have to make this right. If I go to the police, to the proper channels, they won't believe me. And they'll want proof too. The members of the Authority inside those departments will make sure I'm dead long before anyone gets the proof they want.

"I've been framed, Paul. I didn't embezzle from the company."

"What about the cistern?" he asked. "Were you involved in destroying it?"

"Yes. But the cistern was booby-trapped, set to spread the poison as fast as it could through the network. I was trying to stop that."

He was silent for a moment. Then, finally, "You told me you would name names."

"And I will. But I don't have time to fill out paperwork."

He sighed. "I think you do. I think you have to."

I did not want to fight him—hell, I didn't think I could and come out on top. I couldn't even cast the simplest Block spell. I was tired, weaponless. He was a trained man of the law who had all the equipment he needed to put me down.

And Stone was tied and taped.

"Paul," I said. "I'm telling you the truth."

"Doorways into death? Monsters on the loose? Secret societies?" He shook his head. "Until I get names, dates, specifics, Allie, those are all just stories to me."

"If I don't get Stone in for testing, those stories are going to become nightmares," I said. "The poison will spread unchecked. It won't just stop at the edges of Portland—it will follow all the natural lines of magic through the world.

"Are you going to stand here arguing with me when we could be finding out how to save the people dying out there?"

Stotts hesitated, then glanced over my shoulder.

Zayvion walked up behind me. Man could be quiet when he wanted to be. Looked like he wanted to be. I didn't know how he'd gotten through the Ward. From the look on Paul's face, he didn't know either.

"I can give you proof," Zayvion said. Then he threw a spell at Paul.

"Zay," I said, "no!"

Paul staggered back, his hand reaching for his gun as the spell wrapped around his wrists and throat.

Zayvion stormed over to him, just as angry as when he'd pinned Collins to the wall.

Was he having another flashback?

"Don't hurt him," I said. "Zay, don't hurt him."

Zay lifted his hand, fingers spread, and cast another spell. This one wrapped around Paul's head, then pulled into a burning red glyph in the center of his forehead.

Paul had stopped moving. He was staring straight at Zayvion. He didn't look like he was in pain, but he didn't look like he was exactly conscious either.

Zayvion whispered a mantra, a litany, while he slowly, slowly closed the fingers of his right hand together, until the tips of each finger were touching and the glyph in the center of Paul's forehead was a small red light.

"Don't take his memories, Zay," I said, touching Zay's arm. "Don't kill him."

Zay took a deep breath, then said one word. "Open." He opened his hand and the glyph spun like neon knot work, growing bigger, spreading over Paul's head, face, and down to his heart.

Paul's eyes went wide and he slumped forward. Zayvion caught him as his knees gave out.

"What did you do?" I said. "What did you do to him?"

"I gave him back his memories," Zay said. He carefully lowered Paul to the ground and made sure he was lying in a fairly comfortable position.

"You Unclosed him?" I asked. Yes, I was a little stunned about that. I'd fought for the Authority to give Paul back his memories. And I'd been told Victor had Closed him. "How can you do that? Victor Closed him."

"He did. Last time."

Oh sweet hells.

"How many times has Stotts been Closed?" I asked.

Zay just shook his head. "Several. I think. He's a good detective, Allie. He's been on our heels for years. I Closed him only once, if that's what you're worried about."

Zayvion rubbed his hand over his face, resting the heel of his palm on his forehead as if pressing against a headache. Which was probably a doozy since he was paying the price for the magic he used. He hadn't set a Disbursement—no time—so that meant magic could just pummel him however it wanted to.

"He stumbled on me Closing a Gate and fighting the Hungers a few years ago," he said. "Pulled a gun on me.

I'd told him a lot of things, took him back to see Victor. And Closed him."

"So Unclosing him will give him back all those memories?"

"Yes. I put a Sleep spell in with it to give his mind time to sort it out. He'll be down for a couple hours, I think." Zay lowered his hand away from his eyes and winced even though the room was only dimly lit. "Let's get Stone."

I nodded, trying to decide whether I should do something more for Paul. Nola would kill me if she found out I left him unconscious and alone in an abandoned building. I still had my journal in my pocket. I tugged it out, wrote: "I'm with Zayvion. Find the Hounds. Show them this note. They'll take you to me if they know where I am." And then I signed it and drew the glyph for Truth at the bottom.

I didn't know if the Hounds would believe it, but they would know by the way I drew the glyph that it was really my signature and not some kind of forged note. I hoped it was enough to let Paul know I wasn't trying to ditch him.

Well, not permanently.

I turned to help Zayvion with Stone. Zay was standing far enough away from Stone, Stone's arms and wings couldn't touch him. Stone's eyes were narrowed slits, and he was growling.

Not a happy rock. "Is he hurt?" I asked.

Zayvion gave me a placid look. "I don't know. He's your pet. Does he look hurt?"

"He looks angry," I said. "Hey, Stone," I said, using a soft voice. "Are you okay, boy?"

I didn't see any spells on him, didn't see any nicks or scratches on him. Didn't see anything missing or leaking. Still, he growled.

A whole lot of my common sense was telling me not to pull the tape off his mouth until he calmed down.

"Stone," I said. "I'm going to fix it, okay?" I walked over to him and crouched down close enough to touch him. Close enough he could touch me too. He pulled against the chains, trying to reach me, his wings arching up over his back, the prehensile tips tugging and clipping at my short hair.

Oh. I didn't look a whole lot like myself. I wondered whether Stone was so freaked-out from being trapped that he couldn't tell it was me. I pulled off my glasses and my gloves. "Look, Stoney," I said, showing him my magic-marked hands. "It's me. Allie." I held out my hands and he sniffed, then tipped his head to one side, his eyes still narrow. He woofed out air, puffing up his cheeks. One ear perked up. Which made him look like a doofus. A doofus who could tear me apart with one swipe.

"I'm going to fix your mouth," I said. I caught hold of the duct tape and pulled it off.

He tipped his head back to center and opened and closed his big jaws like he was trying to get his ears to pop. Then his lips drew away from his teeth in a huge grin. He sat on his haunches and held out his duct-taped hands for me, his eyes wide and expectant, his ears pointed up.

"You're going to come with us, boy," I said as I tugged on the tape and unwound it from his right hand.

He wiggled his fingers and burbled at them like he was greeting long-lost friends.

I untaped his other hand. Stone reacquainted himself with those fingers too.

The bindings around his ankles, wrists, and neck were leather straps that buckled. It took me only a minute to get him out of them. I didn't know how Stotts had talked him into the things in the first place, but Stone did not seem harmed in any way.

"That's it, buddy," I said. "You're free. C'mon, boy. Let's go for a ride."

Stone stomped around me in a wide circle, burbling at his hands and feet in what sounded suspiciously like complaining. Then he stopped and looked at Stotts. His ears tucked back and he showed more teeth. He growled. Took a step.

"No, Stone. He's a good guy. He's a friend. He's just a little mixed-up. Want to go for a ride?"

Stone growled again.

"In the car, buddy?" I said.

Stone wasn't budging.

"Go for a ride?" I tried.

"Stone," Zay said. "It's time to go." Stone looked up at Zayvion and then trotted over to him like a well-trained dog.

"Fine, listen to the man," I muttered. "Next time you get taped up, see who comes to your rescue."

We walked through the door and I still didn't feel the Ward or any other indication that we had passed through magic. "How'd you get through the Ward Stotts put up?" I asked as we picked up our weapons and strapped them back on.

"I canceled it. It's not something he'd know to guard against."

Zay strode over to the door, and looked outside. "Allie?"

I looked out the door too. "Clear. I don't see anyone or any magic."

We left in a hurry. Zayvion snapped his fingers several times to keep Stone with us. For some reason the stupid rock was really distracted and looked like he wanted to fly away. Maybe because he'd spent who knew how much time tied up in a room. Stone didn't like being tied up, chained up, stuck to the earth.

I couldn't think of anything he would hate more than not being able to fly.

We crossed the street, the shadows keeping us hidden.

"Back to Collins, right?" I said.

Zayvion nodded. "Before the spell wears off and we lose the sample."

"We still don't have the Death well sample," I said.

"Shame and Terric might have it by now."

"We could go out to the Death well and see if they need help. The graveyard's public property. It would be easy to get in."

"Too risky," Zay said.

"We need that last sample, Zay. And they haven't sent any sign that they have it."

"Don't you think the Authority will be waiting for us there?" he asked. "They've had enough time, Allie. Enough time to know their men are dead."

"Those were Bartholomew's men," I said quietly. "The Authority—whoever is running it now—might not know. Might not know what Bartholomew wanted them to do. Might not know that they're missing."

"They'll know," he said. "Whoever is the head will know. And they'll know we did it. Our signatures are all over the place. So they'll be looking for us. And if we went to one well, they'll expect us at the other wells. The graveyard. The gardens. The inn."

"They didn't stop Maeve at the inn." But even as I said it, I knew that was a different matter altogether. One, Maeve lived there. Two, she hadn't just been out at the Life well killing people.

"They might not think we'd be stupid enough to do it," I said.

He half turned to me, shaking his head. "Don't count

on it. Everything we've been doing lately is ... insane. We've broken from the Authority. People who do that are hunted down and Closed or killed. Always. No matter how long it takes."

Stone growled.

I looked away from Zayvion and searched the shadows. Something shifted between the buildings.

"Veiled," I said. "Zay, we've got Veiled." The slide of watercolor light slipped at the edges of shadows. Men and women with black holes where their eyes should be, mouths filled with too many teeth, shifted forward, lining the street behind us. Not just one person or two. A lot. Way too many.

They paused.

Then rushed.

"Run!"

We ran.

They were closing in on us. Fast. Too fast.

The car was just a few yards away. The Veiled were gaining on us.

We'd never make it to the car before they swarmed over us.

Shit, shit, shit. My gun wouldn't stop them. My knife wouldn't cut them. The only thing that worked on Veiled was magic. And I couldn't use magic.

About fifty yards from the car, Stone stopped. He growled, his head down, his fangs bared. He wasn't running. He wasn't flying. He was just standing there in the middle of the street, growling at the Veiled.

"Stone!" I called. "Come on, boy. Run. Get in the damn car!"

But Stone did not move.

The Veiled shot past us. I smelled the rotted-meat stink of them. Their fingers scraped and slapped as they crashed in a wave and streamed past me.

Aiming straight for Stone.

"They want his magic," I said. "Zay, they want the magic in him. In Stone. The sample!"

Stone tore into the Veiled, ripping off arms, heads, and leaving wet, shredded ribbons of colored magic to scatter the ground. But there were too many. They latched on with wide, wide mouths and sucked the magic out of him, draining him down.

Zay cast a quick Sight to see the Veiled and dropped it like a struck match. "Fuck," he said, wiping his foot over the ashes of the spell to muddle his signature.

"Witnesses?" he asked.

I turned a full three-sixty. "No."

"Get back!"

I got out of the way. Zayvion pulled his sword and muttered a Disbursement spell that crawled down his spine and bit deep at his low back. Then he traced Impact. It skittered and sparked like lightning down the blade of his sword.

He strode into the mob of Veiled and swung. Hard, clean strokes cleaved through half a dozen Veiled. The Veiled screeched and fell, clawing at him, clawing at Stone, even as they were pulverized into a liquid magic mess.

The Veiled turned on Zay like wild animals. They bit, tore, clawed at him.

"No!" I ran toward the fight, unable to just stand by and watch. I didn't have a weapon, but I wasn't going to let them tear him apart.

Before I could even reach Zay, he threw Hold. The mass of Veiled around him froze. He swung his blade again and the undead shattered like glass beneath his blow.

But for every Veiled that fell, more swarmed toward us from the shadows. Stone was still fighting, tearing them apart. So many more were still coming. Too many.

I pulled my knife and slashed at the Veiled, but my

blade slid right through their faces as they pushed past me toward Stone.

Stone roared out, a painful rusty screech I'd never heard before. The Veiled grabbed him by wings, arms, and legs and forced him to the ground. They piled on him, burying him in a heaving, sucking heap.

"Zay!" I yelled. I slashed and hit the Veiled, trying to get them off Stone, but it was like punching fog. I hated this. Hated being so damn helpless.

Stone was slowing, the magic in him fading. The light in his eyes was growing dim, and even the rusty screech was down to a whisper.

He was dying.

"We have to save Stone. Zay, we have to get him out of here."

Zayvion took three steps back, and called on magic. And magic answered. He slammed his sword, tip first, into the concrete. Magic crackled across the buildings, scrambled down the street, licked arcs from storm rod to storm rod across the night sky.

And then magic poured into his sword and blasted through the concrete. The street fissured into a glyph, a spell: Grounding.

The Veiled were sucked toward that spell like smoke to a chimney.

They flew, to Zay, to his sword, swirling around him in gruesome, tattered shambles of the once-living, then lost all form.

Watery hues of magic, of the dead, washed down the glyphs of his blade and spread out into the fissured spell broken into the concrete. Then the Veiled were gone, like rain sluiced down the drain.

Zayvion crackled with sparks of magic that wove silver and burned copper over his skin.

He said a single word and pulled the sword out of the

concrete. He took a step back, wavered a little, and caught his balance with his arms spread slightly.

"Are you okay?" I asked.

He didn't say anything. Was still staring at the massive pothole he'd just carved into the street.

That was when I realized the magic sparking around him wasn't leftovers from the spell. It was the Disbursement — the price he was paying for throwing that massive Grounding spell.

Holy hells, he must be on fire.

"Where are your keys?" He still didn't move, maybe couldn't move. I patted his jeans, found the keys in his front pocket. I jogged to the car, got in, and started the engine. That spell Zayvion pulled down from the heavens was going to call attention to us from every magic user in the city. Especially the ones who were looking for him, for me.

I turned the car around and stopped next to Zay. I got out, leaving the engine idling. "Can you walk?" I hurried around the passenger's side of the car and opened the door.

"Zayvion. Jones. Can you walk?"

He shifted slightly and inhaled, then groaned. Somehow that man lifted his feet. Somehow he turned around.

Then I was next to him, my arm around his waist.

His pain shot through me, bit so deep I wanted to let go. But I gritted my teeth and helped him get to the car. He slumped into the passenger side and closed his eyes. I shut the door behind him and looked at Stone.

"Stone?" Far off, I heard the wail of a siren, then two. Another joined in. Maybe coming our way to check what the big explosion and spike in magic had been.

Definitely coming our way.

Stone was frozen midstride, his right hand lifted. The light in his eyes was very, very dim.

I jogged to him and put my hand on his head. "Stoney?"

He rumbled, a sigh of his usual bag-of-marbles sound.

"You're going to be okay," I said. "I'm going to help you, boy. It's going to be okay. Everything's going to be okay."

Sure, the mouth was promising, but the brain had no idea how to deliver.

Stone was doing what he could. He managed to get his hand to the ground, shift his weight, and take another underwater slow-motion step forward.

I needed to get the car closer to him. Otherwise we wouldn't be out of here before dawn.

I scrambled back to the car, got in, pulled up so the back door could open right in front of Stone.

Then I got out, opened the door, and put my shoulder to Stone's hind end, helping shove him into the car, even though he weighed a ton or two.

The sirens were louder. Flashes of blue snapped in the distance. The police were coming. Probably the Authority too. Time to make scarce.

I ran around to the driver's side again, got in, and hit the gas. Screw the speed limit. I needed to get us out of there as quickly as I could. I wondered if I should backtrack and do something sneaky so they wouldn't follow us, but the best way to stay out of sight was to look like every other car out there.

There were no spells on this car, which wasn't that unusual, and Stone and Zay and I weren't leaking magic, so that was good. After several blocks, I brought it back down to the speed limit, took the first corner, then navigated a long, meandering route to the warehouse, heading toward it from the opposite direction than the last time I'd been there.

I didn't know what the Veiled had done to Stone. I

didn't know what they'd done to the magic he held. Zay-vion was hurting, and too damn quiet.

"Zay, are you hurt?" Dumb question. I'd felt his pain from the Disbursement. I knew he was more than hurt. Nothing but slightly ragged breathing from the passenger's seat answered me. I glanced over at him. He had his eyes closed. Sweat covered his face.

"Zayvion?" I said a little softer. "Are you okay?"

He swallowed. "Fine. The spell . . ."

And that was all he had to say. The cost of casting a spell that damn huge was crazy. "Pretty dramatic," I said, trying to keep him talking and conscious. "Think you could have maybe pulled on more magic to Ground them? I think most of Washington still has power."

"Could have," he managed. "But we were in a hurry."

He shifted, and pressed his hand against the dash to push himself more upright in his seat. He left a thick smear of blood behind. He had been injured. Injured by the Veiled.

"Zayvion," I said. "You're bleeding."

He shook his head, though his eyes still weren't open. "No, I'm fine. Fine."

And then he passed out.

# *Chapter Twelve*

Shame was pacing in the garage area of the warehouse smoking a cigarette. He didn't even wait for me to get out of the car before he started in on me.

"Where the hell were you? It's been hours."

"We got hit by the Veiled."

"Jesus, Beckstrom. You leave to call in one little gargoyle and end up tangling with the undead?"

"Zay's hurt."

That shut Shame up, which was what I had hoped it would do. He circled the car with me. I opened the passenger-side door, and Zayvion opened his eyes.

Relief washed over me. At least he was conscious.

He was sweating, his face covered in finger burns and bruises, blood flowing from his forehead and nose. His eyes were slits of molten gold. I don't think he saw either of us.

"We're going to get you inside," I said, calm and matter-of-fact. "Shame's here to help. Can you stand up out of the car, or do you want me to drag you out on a gurney?"

Zay closed his eyes. Swallowed. I could feel the mustering of energy he pulled inward. Not magic, just a steeling of will before the effort.

And then he swung both feet out of the car, held on to the doorframe, and pushed up on his own two feet.

"Bravo, hero," Shame said around the cigarette in his mouth. "If you put one arm over my shoulder and don't fall down before we get inside, I'll give you a cookie."

I put my arm around his waist on one side, and Shame did the same on the other. I didn't expect Shame to actually be much help, but I was wrong. Shame might not be up to full power, but he was plenty strong enough, or at least stubborn enough, to help me get Zayvion inside.

Lucky for us, the door was unlocked.

"Where's Stone?" Shame asked as we navigated the first room.

"Backseat. He's not moving very well."

By the time we'd hit the arched doorway to the next room, I could hear people moving.

"Let me trade places with you, Allie," Hayden said. And even though I was doing just fine, I slipped out from beside Zay. "What happened to him?" he asked.

"Fought the Veiled," I said. "Grounded everything in a ten-mile radius."

"Good lord, boy," Hayden said. "You should know better."

"Go get Stone," Shame said. "We got him."

"I could use some help," I said.

Terric walked over. "Let me."

I nodded.

Terric looked good. No bruises, burns, or blood. "What did you find out?" I asked.

"I sent a message to Zay," he said.

"We missed part of it. Who's the head of the Authority?"

"Jingo Jingo."

"Hells," I said. "Just what I didn't want to hear. Does he know about you defecting? Or are you a double agent now?"

Terric shrugged. "He has a small group of people he

trusts. I'm not one of them. Neither is Violet, if that helps any."

"It does. Did you see Violet? Is she okay?"

"I didn't see her. But Victor said he contacted Kevin. He'll keep her safe."

"I hope so," I said. "She can be strong willed sometimes."

"Stubbornness seems to run in Beckstrom women," he said.

We were at the car now. Terric bent down and looked through the window at Stone. "Is he moving at all?"

"Some. But the Veiled sucked the magic out of him. They piled up on him. Hundreds. I couldn't get them off him. I couldn't do a damn thing to help."

"Well, he's here now," Terric said. "If we have to, we can try transferring magic into him. Maybe give him a jump start. I don't know if it will work, but if he's not moving, it might be worth a try."

I opened the car door. "Hey, Stone. You awake?"

Since he always slept with his eyes open, it was sort of hard to tell if he was even conscious.

Stone tipped his head to one side, slowly, but faster than he'd been moving before. Maybe the rest had helped. Maybe the warehouse would help too. Collins said it was built to channel magic, to focus. And Stone looked like he could use a little of both.

"Good boy," I said. "Time to go inside. We have stuff for you to stack in there, buddy." I stepped back and waited. For a moment, I didn't think he was going to follow. Then he lifted one hand and one foot, and eased out of the car.

"This way." I put my hand on his back and walked with him, slowly, into the building.

"How did it go out at the Life well?" Terric asked.

"Didn't Shame tell you?"

He gave me a look. "You know how he is."

"There were men waiting for us there," I said. "They tried to kill us. We killed them back."

"Zay didn't Close them?" he asked.

"He took their memories. Then he killed them."

Terric nodded. He didn't seem surprised. "Did he get any information out of them?"

I stopped walking. "Enough to know they were Bartholomew's men. I didn't ask about anything else. He can do that?"

"Sometimes. It's like standing under a waterfall with your mouth open. The memories hit so hard and fast, it isn't easy to focus on any of them. But Zayvion's always been good at it. Better than most."

He gave me a soft smile. "Better than me, even before I lost the ability to use dark and light magic." His smile turned wry. "And Blood magic. And Death magic."

Not being able to use those disciplines had ended Terric's chance to become Guardian of the gates, a job both he and Zayvion had vied for.

"I've been meaning to ask you," I said. "A while ago when we were all at the Life well, fighting Leander and Isabelle. After the fight, Shame asked Mikhail to heal you so you could use all those magics again."

"Mikhail said he couldn't heal me, remember?" Terric said.

"I remember. I just wondered . . . what did he do when he touched you?"

Terric took in a breath and looked down at the floor. "He gave me this." He tipped his right hand out toward me. In the center of his palm was a symbol—no, a glyph. It was just the faintest outline, and could be mistaken for the lines of his hand except for one thing. A very, very thin thread of magic pulled through it, like the finest stitches holding it to his skin.

"I don't understand," I said. "It looks like—what is it?"

"I think it's a Renewal of some kind, a Binding. I've never seen the glyph before, and lately there hasn't really been time to ask anyone—"

"There's been some time," I said. "Enough time. Why haven't you asked Maeve or Victor or Hayden about it?"

"I just—" He shook his head. "It's over my Lifeline."

"So?"

"I've always had two breaks in my Lifeline, here"—he pointed to a skip in the line that arced down his palm closest to his thumb—"and here." This break was a little farther down the line.

The glyph not only bridged those gaps; it also reached out with thin lines to wrap around other lines, and create the symbol in his palm.

"I'm not following you," I said.

"A friend once told me that if you have a break in your Lifeline, you're going to die young."

"You believe in palmistry?" I asked.

"No. Maybe. I don't know." He sighed. "It's just strange that a powerful undead Death magic user decided to mark my Lifeline. To patch the break. And it's annoying that it is all he gave me for Shame's begging. For Shame almost dying. A useless scar."

"There's magic running through it."

"What?"

"Not much. I mean I can see magic all the time now, and I can barely see it."

He stared at his hand, then rubbed his thumb over it. "I don't feel it."

"Maybe it's not in your body, Terric," I said. "Maybe it's just on your body."

"Difference?"

"Only one of those things will kill you?"

"Okay." He nodded and tipped his hand to better see

it. "Still looks like a thin pink scar to me. Tell me what you were going to say."

"About?"

"What it looks like," he said. "To you."

"Like an infinity symbol. A figure eight. Kind of. Or a knot. Or both maybe. A knotted figure eight. Might be a hell of a tie to life."

"Infinity, huh? So you're telling me Mikhail made me immortal?"

I grinned. That was one thing I liked about Terric. He recovered his footing quickly, no matter the situation.

"Maybe." I started walking again. Stone had gotten a good way ahead of us. "I can think of worse people to let live forever."

"Like?"

"My dad."

Terric made a little *hm* sound. "Or Shame."

I laughed. "Can you imagine him living forever?"

Terric grimaced. "Yes. All the world would be in ruin. But there'd be plenty of whiskey."

"Did you get the sample from the Death well?" I asked.

"We did. Just cost us a little pain. We didn't see anyone there guarding the well."

As well they wouldn't. Shame and Terric had closed that well. If anyone in the Authority was even paying attention to it in the last couple weeks, they would have thought it secure. I didn't know if it took the same magic users who had shut a well down to uncap it, but even if not, there had been enough chaos going on that it was possible the well was being watched.

"Are you sure you weren't followed?"

"Fairly certain." He paused. "Strange, right?"

"No stranger than anything else lately."

"I couldn't tell if the well was tainted," he said. "We

were in and out so fast, uncapped it, unlocked it, stole the magic—that was a lot of no fun at all—then lock and cap. There wasn't time to see if there was a taint. But there weren't any Veiled coming out of it, which is something. Did you get a look at the Life well?"

I nodded. "We think it's poisoned. We're not sure. Stone has a sample from it. Maeve has a sample of the Blood well. I think Victor got a sample from the Faith well. And I hope all of it is enough to get a read on this problem."

Terric glanced down at Stone. "Where is he holding it?"

"In a spell Shame cast—Passage—that he smashed down so Stone could hold it in his chest. Don't ask me," I said to his look. "I don't understand it. It was Dad's idea and Shame's execution. Of the idea," I amended. "Shame executed the idea, not Shame, you know." I pulled my finger across my throat.

"So you're going to test the magic samples?" he asked.

"If Collins has the equipment to do it like he says he does. Did Victor Unclose him?"

We'd made it inside the warehouse and halfway across the room by now. "He did. But I don't think—" He shook his head.

"What?"

"I don't think Collins was a good choice as an ally when he was less crazy. To put more information, more power, into his hands now is a bad idea. I think you should cut ties with him as soon as possible, Allie. We all should."

"I don't have anyone who can look after Davy," I said. "Especially now."

"Shame told me about what Collins did," he said. "It's not right. It's against everything the Authority stands for."

"What would the Authority have stood for, Terric? Letting Davy die?"

He pressed his lips together, then, "Yes. They would have let him die, rather than turn him into that . . . I don't even know what to call it. Necromorph, I guess, since he's half between life and death."

"Isn't that what they called Greyson?" I said. "But Greyson had been changed by one of my dad's magic disks being implanted in his neck. He was very solid, either as a beast or a man."

"Greyson was caught in a form of living and dying by the dark and Death magic worked through that disk implanted in him. It wasn't the shape that made him a Necromorph. It was that his soul and body were caught between life and death. When magic changes someone to the point that he is only half alive, he's a Necromorph. And Davy isn't fully alive or dead."

What Terric didn't say, what he didn't have to say, was what had happened to Greyson. He'd gone insane, tried to kill me, been caught, escaped, joined with Chase to try to kill us all, and then been imprisoned. And even in the prison where magical criminals are kept, he'd been possessed by Leander, who was looking for a body that was caught between life and death. Leander had forced Greyson to kill Chase, his own Soul Complement, with his own hands.

We killed Greyson, but Leander went free.

Not exactly the bright future I was hoping for Davy.

"Davy's going to get better," I said. "Once we get magic cleansed, we'll find a way to heal him, undo the spells Collins put on him. We'll find a way to heal everyone."

"Allie." Terric stopped and turned toward me. Stone just kept going in his slow-motion straight line toward the main room. "What if we can't cleanse magic? What if there is no cure? No antidote? We need to make plans for that. Get better people with better minds working on this."

"Which is why Roman went to talk to the Overseer," I said. "If this is something that we can't fix, then she'll have to decide what to do."

"Unless she decides the best thing to do isn't letting us win," he said.

"Why would she do that?" I asked.

"There's only one sure way to guarantee magic won't harm anyone," he said. "Close off all access to magic in Portland, lock it down from the rest of the world, quarantine it, and make sure magic can't be used until we find a cure."

"One, we aren't the ones who are going to make that decision. And two, if that's what needs to happen to keep people alive, we'll do it. But first we try to fix what's gone wrong. And the only way to do that is to test the magic to see if we can find the source and cause of the poison."

"I'm not saying I disagree with the steps we're taking," Terric said. "I just . . . don't want you to get your hopes up. Even testing the magic may not give us the answers we need."

"Don't worry," I said. "My hopes have been pretty down most of my life."

Shame walked through the doorway. "There you are. Get on with it, will you? We're waiting for the sample. Plus, Zay's asking for you, Allie."

"Is he okay?" I asked.

"No, but he isn't any worse than when you brought him here."

"Does Collins have the tech set up?" I asked.

"As much as." Shame paced over to Stone, who was still walking incredibly slowly. "Hey, Stone. How's my buddy?"

Stone gurgled. It was a little louder than last time.

"Looks like you could use a recharge," he said, scrubbing at Stone's ears.

"Think you could do it?" Terric asked.

"What do you mean?"

"Give him a jump."

Shame stared at Terric, then at Stone. "Don't know. Ever since you sank this damn rock in my chest, things haven't rolled off my fingers in quite the same way. You thinking a Transference?"

"Maybe. Like back a few years ago, when we used to . . ."

Shame gave him a look.

"Okay, more than a few years ago," Terric said. "You were pretty good arcing the storm rods and hacking Refresh spells. Do much of that in the last couple years?"

"Wait," I said. "You found a way to hack the storm rods?"

"Just took a nip or two now and then," Shame said.

"But that's my dad's tech—my company's tech. And you're hacking into it? I didn't think they could be accessed like that."

Shame doused his smile and gave me wide, innocent eyes. "They can't. I have no idea what Terric's talking about, the delinquent. Your da's handiwork is above the genius of all other men and will never be soiled."

I pointed at my face. "This is me not believing you. Think you can help Stone?"

Shame shrugged and stuffed his hands in his front pockets. "Or hurt him. Dunno. Want to risk it?"

I thought about it. This was a fairly safe place. Maybe the safest in town. For now.

"Not yet. Not until we get the sample out of him. That might be the thing that's wrong with him."

"Or it could be the undead that were trying to suck him dry," Terric said.

"The hell you say," Shame said.

"So Beckstrom tells me."

"Is that what you two have been out here gabbing about?" Shame asked.

"Pretty much," Terric said while closing his right hand and tucking it into the pocket of the jacket he was wearing. Hiding it. Hiding his hand from Shame.

He hadn't told Shame that mark was all he'd gotten out of the hideous pain Mikhail had put Shame through when he'd possessed him. I'm sure Terric had let Shame believe Mikhail had given him some kind of blessing on a much larger scale.

Shame looked at Terric, then at me. "Either of you going to tell me what else you were talking about?"

"Swatches for my living room," I said.

Terric's eyes twinkled. "I think she should go for a strong maroon, but leaning toward fuchsia so she doesn't overdo the masculine energy. Better than that drab rent-me-cheap and leave-me-dirty white walls you currently have."

"Hey," I said. "Rental property. Not my fault."

"You asked for my opinion," he said. "And by the way, cute haircut."

Shame just shook his head. "Fine, don't tell me. We have bigger problems to solve."

"Like what?" I asked. We were in the main room, and everyone was there, Maeve, Hayden, Zay, Victor. And Collins, who was passed out on the couch.

"Like that."

# Chapter Thirteen

"What happened?" I asked.

"Victor Unclosed him," Maeve said. "He was fine for a bit"—she glanced over at Victor, who stood against one wall, arms crossed over his chest—"...and then he wasn't."

What I wanted to do was panic. Instead, I assessed our situation. Zay was in a chair, not moving much, his eyes still half-lidded from pain. I walked over to him and put my hand on his shoulder. He was hot with pain, tight. But I think me being there helped some, so that's where I stayed.

Hayden was pacing toward the hall and back. Maeve stood behind Collins' couch, keeping an eye on Victor and Hayden.

"I assume there's been a disagreement?" I asked.

"He wouldn't listen to sense," Hayden said.

"It's done," Maeve interrupted. "Let it be."

"No, Maeve. I won't." Hayden came toward me and I once again was reminded that I never wanted to get in a fight with the man.

"Victor did this." He pointed at Collins. "Intentionally."

"What's wrong with Collins?"

"He's in a coma. Likely just as broken-brained as Cody. That man won't be worth squat to anyone once he wakes up. If he wakes up."

"He'll wake up," Victor said softly, his voice a little rough as if he'd been running hard.

"Maybe in a year," Hayden said. "You didn't Unclose him, Victor. You brutalized his mind."

"Is this true?" I looked at Victor, who gave me a steady gaze. Then I looked at Maeve.

"It was . . . harsh," she agreed. "But I am not a Closer. The complexities are beyond me."

I couldn't believe what I was hearing. That Victor, whom I'd always counted on, who always went into any situation with levelheaded thinking, had let his anger destroy our chance of finding out how to cleanse magic.

"Tell me you didn't do that," I said as I paced over to Victor. "Tell me you didn't just destroy the one man who knows enough about magic technology to cleanse the wells, to find a cure, to save us."

"I didn't destroy him. He'll wake up," Victor said. "He will have enough use of his mind to be advantageous to us. To serve our needs."

This near, I could see that Victor's eyes were bloodshot, and he was a sick sort of pale. Pain radiated off him in a hot, nauseating wave.

"Did you brutalize his mind?"

"You don't know what he once was, Allie. I refuse to restore him to that again. Refuse to let loose another monster in our midst. I made . . . choices."

"Did you brutalize his mind? Break him like Cody has been broken?"

"You know I'm better than that." He drew his hand up to pinch the bridge of his nose, and I noted it was shaking.

He noticed it too, caught my gaze, and folded his arms again. More than just paying the price for a spell, he was emptied out from the effort of doing magic at all. His knees were locked to keep him leaning against the wall, and even so, his entire body was trembling slightly.

"I know you *were* better than that," I said.

"And I still am. Hayden may not think so. Apparently"—he flicked a glace at Maeve, then looked back to me—"neither does Maeve."

"Don't put words in my mouth," Maeve said. "It was harsh. I didn't say it wasn't effective."

"Can you wake him up?" I asked.

"He needs time. It was . . . harder on him than I expected."

"We're running a little short on time," I said. "How long does he need?"

"Several hours."

I closed my eyes and took a step back. We didn't have several hours. I wasn't even sure if we had an hour left. Stone was winding down and we had no idea what that would do to the Life well sample. We needed to go to wherever Collins had stashed the tech and then, I assumed, set it up, run tests, wait for results, check our accuracy, and try to come up with ideas of how to make a cure.

"We don't have several hours," I said. "I don't even have—Jesus, Victor. Wasn't there an easier way?"

He just gave me a calm Zen look and said nothing.

I took that as, no, there wasn't an easier way.

That wasn't getting us anywhere. I needed a new option. "Are there any spells that can test the sample magics? Magic that can test magic's purity?"

Maeve shook her head. "Not that I know of. Magic isn't supposed to be able to be poisoned in the first place."

"So we just went to all this work, wasted all this time, and we have nothing we can do with what we have?"

*Stone,* Dad said hesitantly.

*What about him?*

*He might be something we can use to test the magic.*

*Might even be something that could give us a basic set of data we can use to filter the magic.*

*Stone's a magic filtration device? I'm not buying that.*

*I'm unsure. However . . .* He paused, and I could feel him poring through a hundred possibilities.

Images of tech, experiments, theories, flashed behind my eyes—his memories that were too fleeting for me to catch. What I did get from them was more than a little boggling. I hadn't really realized just how many things my father had tried to do with magic and technology, nor how many outcomes that had resulted in.

*I think that Stone being an Animate—a device that runs on magic—might be something we can . . . modify. We would just need some basic equipment. Things that might be here. Things Collins may have used on Davy. Medical instruments,* he added.

*Who can run the tests?*

*I could.*

He didn't add any more to that statement. Didn't beg me to trust him, didn't order me to believe. Just waited for my decision.

Since I couldn't think of any way this plague was to Dad's advantage—

*It's not,* he said.

—I decided.

"Fine. New plan. We test the magic ourselves using the tech Collins has here, and Stone."

Stone, who had sat himself down next to Zayvion, huffed at the sound of his name.

"Is it strange," Shame asked, "if I'm the one who has to tell you you've lost your mind?"

"Dad said he can do it. Might be able to do it," I corrected. "And unless someone has a better idea?" I waited, but no one said anything. "Then this is what we've got, and we're going to use it. Maeve, how's Davy?"

"Sleeping last I checked." She glanced at her watch. "About half an hour ago."

"Terric, Shame, help me gather the equipment," I said. "Medical things Collins might have used on Davy. Has anyone done a thorough search of this place?"

"I have," Hayden said.

"I need a room to set up in, something we can Block in case what we do triggers a spike in magic."

*Or an explosion,* Dad added matter-of-factly.

"Or an explosion," I passed along.

"He has a lab," Hayden said.

"Who?"

"Collins. Here. Don't think he wanted us to see it, but while Victor was tearing through his brain, I took a stroll."

"Hayden," Maeve said. "Enough." And this time she was clearly as annoyed by the bickering as I was. "Leave this be. When you next Unclose someone, you can do it the way you see fit. Now show Allie the lab. Allie, I'll check on Davy and make sure he's comfortable."

She turned and, with her cane, walked down the hall to Davy's room.

Hayden watched her go, and frowned. "This way."

I brushed my hand down Zayvion's back. "I'll be right back."

Zay didn't say anything, but his hand caught mine at the last moment, our fingers linking, before he let me go.

Hayden strode through the arched doorway at the far end of the room, and then to a hallway, with a metal door at the end—a metal door he opened.

Below us spread the bulk of the warehouse. I just gave it a cursory glance. Concrete floor, scaffolding and empty shelves at one side; large equipment that maybe had something to do with repairing ships, or maybe cutting lumber, cluttered up the other half of the place. It all looked long unused, stuck in storage, just like Collins had said.

I didn't know why Hayden thought this was such a great place to do magic.

*Look up,* Dad said.

I did so. "Oh," I said. The ceiling was pitched by iron- and glasswork in a gothic spiderweb that was breath catching.

Hayden was in front of me, Shame and Terric behind me. They paused, glanced up.

"Don't make them like they used to," Hayden noted as he continued to another door.

"Did they always make buildings this beautiful?" I asked. "I mean, this was just a warehouse."

Hayden swiveled his head to look down at me over his big shoulder. "Do you know what kind of magic you can do in a warehouse like this? A lot. And this was back in the days when there was still a lot of crazy experimenting being done. Thanks to your dad and things like this"—he nodded up toward the ceiling—"the Authority was balls out to keep people from frying themselves into steaming piles of dust."

*He's exaggerating,* Dad said. *Warehouses like this were very useful in finding out what level of magical information was most beneficial to the populace.*

"I don't think my dad agrees with you," I said.

"He never did. Had a thing about letting people push the limit of what they could do with magic. Didn't care if it went too far. Said it made for good data. I think it just got people killed."

Hayden shouldered the door open, stepped in, and flipped on a light. "Will this do you?"

I walked in behind him. "Well, so much for Collins' story about this being a temporary setup."

The room was big enough to park half a dozen cars in,

but sterile white, the walls worked with glyphs fed by sophisticated and high-yield Refresh spells. Tables of equipment marched off down the center filled with lots of medical, and not-so-medical-looking, devices.

Shelves, check. Computer screens and monitors, check. A couple white-sheet hospital beds with restraints primly folded on top, roger that.

And the place stank of magic, the cloying, rotted-meat smell. Collins had been doing magic in here, running experiments, very recently.

I walked between tables and saw iron, lead, glass, and plastics, put together into shapes both familiar and strange, some of which I could see the use for, and others I wish I hadn't.

*Did he really used to torture people?* I asked Dad. Not that I had to. These devices made it clear just what Dr. Collins' specialty was.

*Yes.*

*Do you see anything here you can use?*

*I believe so. I'll still need Stone. And a clear table for equipment.*

"This will do," I said. "Shame, could you go get Stone for me? Terric, Hayden, let's see if we can clear a place for what we need to do."

"What do we need to do, exactly?" Terric asked.

"Follow what my dad says."

"And then what?" Terric asked.

"And then I'll let Dad use my hands and see if we can't come up with ideas for how to filter or cleanse magic."

Terric loaded his arms with something that looked like a miniature engine made out of stained glass, Tiffany-style.

"Don't think Zayvion would think that's a great idea," he said.

"Zayvion isn't on his feet yet," I said. "Which is why

you, Shame, and Hayden will be here. If anything goes wrong, you can take me down and take care of it."

"Think letting your dad use magic through you might knock you out?" he asked.

"I don't think he's going to use magic," I said. "I think he's going to use this tech."

*Magic through the tech. You should be all right. I should be able to insulate you from it.*

"He doesn't think it will be a problem," I said.

"Did I ever mention," Hayden asked as he swept several small, delicate amulets off the table and into his palm, "that I've never trusted your father?"

"I can't see how our failure would help him in any way; do you?" I asked.

Hayden placed the amulets on a shelf, gently and carefully arranging them. He shrugged. "No. Doesn't mean he doesn't have a plan."

"He always has a plan," I said. "Besides, I can take him."

He gave me an appreciative nod. "There, I agree with you. You're tougher than your dad ever was."

Dad didn't say anything. But there was a strange feeling of . . . I don't know—amusement? pride? confusion?—from him.

*Cat got your tongue?* I asked.

*I don't have a tongue,* he said as he modified his emotions to cool and calm.

"Can you check and see how it's going with the gargoyle roundup?" I asked Hayden.

Hayden headed toward the door. But he didn't have to bother.

Stone clomped into the room, moving much better than when I'd last seen him.

"I think the shock of getting bitten is wearing off," Shame said. "And what did I tell you, Stoney? Look at all the cool things you can stack in here."

Stone paused just inside the door and looked around the room. When his gaze landed on me, I saw a spark of fear in his eyes.

"It's okay, Stone," I said. "Come over here, boy. I won't let you get hurt."

He padded over to me, cautious, his ears back. I rubbed his head, then knelt down and rubbed his muzzle. "We need to get this magic out of you." I touched the Passage spell. "And we need you to help us with some other magic. I promise to buy you a new set of blocks when this is done. You want blocks, boy?"

For the first time since I'd met Stone, his ears did not perk up at the sound of the word "blocks." He just growled softly. He sounded worried, and wary.

Yeah, well, that made two of us.

"Let's get this done," I said.

I stood, and looked up as Zayvion, Victor, and Maeve all stepped into the room.

## Chapter Fourteen

I was a little surprised to see Zayvion walking, but he slowly strolled over to a bare part of the wall, where he leaned, his arms crossed over his chest, his head resting against the wall. At least someone had helped him clean up the blood on his face.

"We're all still on the same side, right?" I asked.

Victor paced through the room, his hand resting on shelves, tables, countertops, taking in all the instruments and devices. "And you ask me why I won't give Collins back all of his memories. Can you see what he has done with the memories and the skill he currently has? Giving him more of what he once was would be putting deadly weapons into the hands of a madman."

"This isn't about Collins," I said.

"I agree," Victor said. "This is about protecting the city, protecting the innocent from the ways of magic that will harm them, kill them, cause them pain. Which has always been our vows as members of the Authority. That has everything to do with Collins."

"I don't care what you did to him right now. He's done what I've asked him to do, and I'll cut him a check for it. This"—I opened my hand to indicate the room—"is a terrifying stash of tech to have stockpiled in the middle of the city. And right now, I don't even care what he was doing with it. All I care about is testing the magic and hoping to hell that information gives us something to go on to save Davy and all those people dying in the hospitals. I will do damn near anything to see that it gets done right now.

"So if you want to talk me out of using all the resources at my disposal," I said, "including Collins, then you better leave the room. Because so help me, I will call on the devil himself if that's what it takes to save this town."

Victor pressed his lips together and considered me, as if calculating how well I had learned a lesson.

I did not have time for school. Or arguments, or men who wouldn't listen. I turned back to the empty table.

*What do you need, Dad?* I asked.

*I wouldn't let Victor hurt you,* Dad said with the kind of quiet power that gave me chills.

*So not what I need to hear from you now. Do not hurt Victor—for that matter, don't hurt anyone in this room. Understand? Now tell me how to test the magic.*

*It would be faster if you let me speak through you.*

We'd done that before. Still, old habits of not trusting him made me hesitant.

*Allison,* he said. *I promise not to harm your friends.*

That wasn't what I was really worried about.

I didn't want him to shove me into the back of my brain again and make it so I couldn't see or feel my body. I didn't want to be trapped, boxed up, hidden away. I hated small spaces, and hated feeling helpless.

And since he could still use magic, and I couldn't, letting go of the control of my own body seemed a hundred times more dangerous this time around.

I said I'd call on the devil himself. I wondered whether I already had.

"Dad is going to run this experiment. I'm going to let him share my mouth with me," I said. Wait. That sounded wrong. "I mean, he and I will both be talking and I gave him permission, so don't throw magic at me, okay?"

"For Christsake, Beckstrom," Shame said. "It's your show. We got that. Put wheels on it and get it on the road."

I didn't look over at Zayvion. I was pretty sure I knew what he thought about me letting Dad control my body.

I mentally stepped to one side of my mind, and felt my dad's presence rise beside me, then take a step in front of me.

I could still see out of my eyes, could still feel my body, my hands. Could still hear. But there was sort of a fog, just the lightest haze over all my senses.

*I have added a barrier between you and magic so you won't be harmed by what I do. I will strive to only touch magic in the briefest of ways, and not draw it through your body. Does the haziness of the barrier bother you?* Dad asked.

It didn't. Not really. *It's just annoying. Are you sure your working magic in my body will be different from if I worked it?*

*You and I cast magic in very different ways. We come from different teaching. I think I can keep the actual contact with magic to a minimum.*

*Want to teach me that trick?*

*It wouldn't work. You will always draw upon magic your way. I believe my style will lessen the impact on your reaction, that is all.*

*Fine. Let's do this.*

"Very well, then," Dad said through me. Everyone in the room straightened just a little. It was weird. Even though it was my voice, the rhythm, the emphasis, the tone, was all Dad. He shone through clear and strong. Maybe too clear and strong.

"Please place the samples of magic here on the table, but do not let them touch."

Maeve walked forward and placed a metal flask scrolled with glyphwork and glass on the table. "The Blood well," she said.

Terric tugged a clay urn out from his coat pocket and set it down directly across from the flask. "Death well," he said.

Victor came forward next. "Hello, Daniel," he said. "What, exactly, do you plan to do with all this magic?"

"Find a solution to our problem, Victor. An antidote to whatever poison it is that is spreading through the city."

"How will you do that?"

I felt my eyes narrow. "Blending the magic, and filtering it through technology to separate the poison from the magic. I will be doing it right here in front of all of you," he said. "If you see anything you disagree with, you are welcome to tell me. But time is of the essence. Do you have the sample from the Faith well?"

Victor drew an amulet out from under his shirt, and pulled it off. He held it for a moment against the palm of his hand, then placed it on the table reluctantly. He stepped back.

"Mr. Flynn," Dad said.

"Yo."

I felt Dad fight back an annoyed sigh. "Please retrieve the sample of Life magic."

"Get it yourself. It's in Stone. You want it, it's right there."

"You locked it in a Passage spell—is that correct?"

Shame just looked at him. "You were there."

"Then the magic is held in the Passage spell in the Animate."

"And I care because?"

Dad ignored him and instead walked down along the shelves. "We'll need something to hold it in. Something clean."

He bent—well, I bent. It was a weird sort of feeling that made me want to hold my arms out to the sides to keep from tipping over. I could tell he wasn't used to moving a body that wasn't his, but he got the hang of it pretty quickly. He looked at the bottom shelf and finally pulled out a black glass bowl.

"This will do."

I thought the metal swirling through the bowl was looped in a glyph, but couldn't tell which one. Dad didn't seem concerned about it.

"Have you removed that spell, Mr. Flynn?" he asked.

Shame strolled over to Stone. "I hope you take a nice long look and enjoy it, Mr. Beckstrom," he said.

"Enjoy what?"

"The one and only time I'll ever do anything you ask me to do."

"Shame," I said as I or Dad, or maybe both of us, put the bowl down on a clear spot on the table.

"Wasn't talking to you, Allie." He looked down at Stone. "Okay, bud. Time to give me the magic." He put his hand down for Stone and wove a sort of haphazard symbol of Life in the air. It wasn't strong enough to actually carry magic, but Stone somehow got the idea.

He burbled and stood up.

Shame set a Disbursement. I could still see it even with Dad hazing up my eyesight. He was opting for something slow this time, and it appeared as oozing black smoke that pressed against his chest, right over his lungs, and then seeped in deeper and spread out.

Then he pulled on magic. The lights flickered as Shame pulled the magic through the ironwork of the warehouse and then focused it into the glyph he was drawing.

He said a single word, and sent that spell into Stone's chest—but he didn't let go of all the spell. He held a tendril of it between his thumb and middle finger. Stone held very still, and didn't look like he was in any kind of discomfort. Shame exhaled, inhaled, then tugged on the string while he was drawing a second spell with his left hand.

The Celtic knot picture-frame-like spell lifted out of Stone's chest, and I could once again see the Life well magic flickering there. Shame inhaled through his nose and exhaled a hard stream through his lips, as he pushed the spell to open, to grow bigger.

He pivoted, the spell still in his hands.

I grabbed the bowl and stood in front of him. "It's right here," I said. "There's a glyph on the bowl; pour it in here."

Shame tipped the fingers of both hands down over the bowl and the magic stopped spinning. The knot-work spell also tipped, and Shame ran a finger across the corner of the spell, breaking it, but keeping enough of the spell intact to still hold.

Holy crap. I'd never seen anyone manipulate magic like that.

And from the startled response I felt from my father, he hadn't seen it handled that way before either.

*Just not for a very long time,* he thought to me.

The magic poured out into the bowl, a stream of silver and white with golden threads running through it, and flecks of tar black.

Once it was all poured out, Shame broke the spell completely, and I took the bowl and placed it back on the table.

"These are the four wells in Portland," Dad said. "Four wells in one city is powerful. Unusual. If there is a chance of cleansing magic, we'll find it here. Now, Stone," he said. "Come."

Stone pulled his lip back from his teeth and growled.

Shame laughed. "I don't think he likes you."

*Allie?* Dad asked.

"Come here, Stone," I said. I patted my leg. "Come on over. . . . Where do you want him?"

"Here," I said to myself, or rather Dad answered. "We'll want a little space in case there is a backlash of any kind."

"All right. Come here, Stoney," I said.

"Weird," Shame said. "Just fricking creepy. I can tell when it's you and when it's your dad. Everything about you changes, even your . . . I don't know . . ."

"Soul," Zay said softly. The first word he'd spoken since he came into the room. He was sitting on the foot of one of the cots now, his elbows resting on his knees, his hands folded lightly together. Gold eyes burned, weighed, judged.

"I was going to go with 'body language,'" Shame said. "But I suppose you're closer to the thing of it."

"Don't worry," I said. "This isn't permanent. I'm sub-letting out of necessity."

Stone finally walked over toward me, sniffed at my foot, then sat.

"Good," Dad said. "This will do nicely. I would suggest that you all leave the room, but I know that you won't. Step back, please, and have a Block spell at the ready. This might flash a bit."

Everyone moved to stand closer to the walls, creating a circle around the open area between tables where Stone and I stood. The samples from the well were in easy reach.

Dad waited until each person had drawn some kind of Block. There was no magic in any of the glyphs, but if they each decided to throw those spells, we'd all proba-bly pass out from the concussion.

Well, I knew I would.

*Don't reach outward, Allison,* Dad thought. *I'll shield you as much as I can, but you might want to step back as far into your mind as you feel comfortable.*

*I'm comfortable here,* I said, standing my ground.

*Very well.*

Dad sang a soft song, a lullaby I thought I'd heard before, while he wove a pattern in the air in front of Stone. Stone stood, and tipped his head sideways, his ears perked up, his wings lifted off his back.

Then Dad cast a Disbursement. Looked like I was going to be running a hard line of body aches and bruises by the end of this.

He cast a spell that was a variation of Unlock. But there were strange dark lines echoing through it. The glyph filled with magic, and a shadow of magic traced behind it. That wasn't how magic was supposed to work.

I tried to blink to clear my vision, but Dad was in full control of my eyes.

*What are you doing?* I asked. *Dad?*

*Hush,* he thought softly. It was taking every ounce of his energy and concentration to do what he was doing. And I wasn't sure if what he was doing was magic, in the strictest sense.

I wanted to say something to Maeve, or Shame, or Zay, but Dad had the mouth too. I could fight him for it, but if I got control of my body right now while working with that much magic, I'd just pass out.

Or worse. Dad had said it might flash. Which meant it was a pretty safe bet whatever he was doing was explosive as hell.

Shit.

The best thing I could do, the only thing I could do right now, was try not to distract him and hope that he knew what he was doing.

Dad picked up the Faith well amulet, and held it over Stone's head. Stone, for his part, straightened his head and locked his legs, standing on all fours, ears up, mouth slightly open, showing his teeth.

Whatever song Dad had sung him, Stone responded to it like he had been trained to obey. Weird.

Dad said a few words in a language that sounded like Latin, then pressed his palm over the amulet and twisted, opening it.

He poured the magic out of the amulet on top of Stone's head, right between his ears. Stone lit up, lines of neon pulsing through the concrete gray of him as the glyphs carved under his skin suddenly flared to life.

Stone was an amazing piece of sculpture, but this changed him, made him look even more beautiful, otherworldly.

And I wasn't the only one who noticed. "Beautiful," Shame whispered.

"Savant," Victor said softly. "There has never been another like him. Before, or since."

He wasn't talking about Stone. He was talking about Cody. Before Cody had been Closed, he'd been an amazing artist with magic. A savant. A Hand. Someone who could turn magic into art, and make it do things never before imagined. Things like Stone.

Dad reached over for the flask of Blood magic, spoke a short phrase, then ran my left thumb over the flask stopper, which was razor sharp.

*Ouch,* I said even though I couldn't feel it.

Dad rubbed blood into the spell on the flask, triggering the spell to open it. He poured the magic on the same place on Stone's head. The glyphs carved into Stone shifted and flowed into new glyphs that burned bloodred.

No one said anything this time, but I could feel the

press of magic in the room. Heavy, charged. It was like standing in the middle of a lightning storm that was about to break.

Dad placed the empty flask back on the table and picked up the clay urn.

No soft song this time. He just smashed the urn on the edge of the table, scooped up the dust and ashes, and poured it on Stone's head. The dust soaked into Stone's head and the glyphs shifted again, gray and cracking through him like fissures in concrete.

Stone grumbled a little but didn't back away.

Dad reached for the last container of magic. The bowl from the Life well. He picked it up, and even though I couldn't feel much sensation right now, I could tell my hands were shaking, my arms, fatigued. Even my voice sounded rough as I ran my fingers along the outside of the bowl. The bowl shivered with the sound of bells, and glyphs spun open along the inside of the bowl. He then spoke three words, and poured the magic out of the bowl, magic that was a lot darker than it had been just moments ago, rushing down over Stone's head.

The Life well's magic never looked dark. Was it the taint changing it? Or was I seeing something else? Something like dark magic?

Stone's glyphs took on a vinelike appearance, green and growing, stretching, curling, blooming.

And then the glyph in the bowl folded in on itself, like a flower closing, and a single, black drop of magic fell to Stone's head.

No, that magic wasn't black—it was dark. Dark magic. Holy shit.

Working dark and light magic made people crazy. You had to be trained to use them together for even a short amount of time. And people died who tried to contain light and dark magic to become Focals. I had no idea what it would do to pour even a drop of dark magic into a gargoyle filled with light magic.

I suppose my dad's mental stability had been in question before, but using dark magic now, when we were trying to cure magic, didn't make any sense.

Stone didn't like it either. He shuddered and growled. Then he howled as the whorls of magic flashed between each of the forms they had taken, spreading, cracking, webbing through him like a net of fire, ash, vines, blood.

*Stone,* I said. *He's hurt. You're hurting him.*

Dad was holding fast, holding a wall between me and my own body, between me and magic, between me and me.

Fuck that.

I shoved at the wall, shoved at him, pounded against the barriers until they cracked and I fell through and was once again very much me.

Magic was so thick in the room, I could feel it brushing hot against my skin, tugging at my hair, prickling my nose and eyes.

But it wasn't making me pass out. Somehow Dad was still there with me, beside me, equal in my body and mind. And his entire focus was on Stone. He didn't want me to pass out. He didn't want me to be hurt by magic because he didn't want to miss seeing this.

This was important to him. Very important.

Well, it was important to me too, but I didn't want it to hurt Stone.

The single drop of dark magic on Stone's head flattened.

Stone lifted his wings, as if to fly.

The drop burned like a flash, joining all the glyphs of magic, fusing them together in one solid pulse of pure, whole magic.

Stone froze.

A sound rang out like a gong, so loud I slapped my hands over my ears. I couldn't block it out.

The sound came from my bones, from the floor beneath, the walls, the ceiling, and beyond that. The sound came from the world, from everything magic touched, from everyone magic touched, from everywhere magic touched.

And magic filled the world.

For that moment, everything seemed to lift, to grow brighter. Then the world wavered, blurring and bending in ways my mind could not comprehend.

I reached for Zayvion, yelled his name, knew he was reaching for me, calling for me, but we could not find each other, the distance between us worlds away, even though we were standing in the same room.

I heard Maeve screaming, Shame yelling, Victor praying.

And then there was silence.

## *Chapter Fifteen*

"That son of a *bitch*!" Dad said through me. "The bastard. Locked it. Put in a fail-safe."

I pressed my palm over my mouth to make Dad shut up, though he just kept right on cursing in my brain. I didn't understand what he was saying. Well, I understood the swearwords—the ones in English, anyway.

I was still standing. All of us were in the exact same place we'd been before that hellacious sound had turned the world inside out.

"Did the world just snap in half and come back together again?" I asked.

I hurt from the roots of my hair to the bottoms of my feet.

Zayvion walked up to me. He looked like I felt. But he wrapped his arms around me. I shuddered from the relief in that contact and leaned against him, needing to be reminded that I was alive, real, breathing, and me. Needing to be reminded that he was alive, real, breathing, and mine.

We stood there for three heartbeats, and for those three heartbeats, everything was right in my world.

Man had a way of making me feel like there wasn't anything I couldn't take. Made me feel like there wasn't anything I went up against that he wouldn't be right there at my side, taking it on with me, hit for hit.

I stepped back. "What the hell happened?"

"You used dark magic," Victor said with a flat sort of numbness. "Or your father did. Used it on Stone. With all the other magic."

"Is that what roller-coastered reality?"

No one said anything. Except Dad.

*Yes. It was the one way I could think of cleansing magic, putting it all back together again in a small enough sample it wouldn't completely destroy the world as we know it. But the backstabbing bastard put a fucking fail-safe on it.*

"How about less swearing, more specifics?" I said.

*Cody Miller made Stone—made this Animate that can house magic. In theory, it can contain all magics, even light and dark. He put a lock on it I cannot pick. He set a fail-safe to shut it down if ever all magics are combined within it.*

"I don't even know why he would think of putting in that kind of safety catch," I said. "It doesn't make sense."

"Crazy girl?" Shame said a little hoarsely, "You're talking to ghosts."

"My dad," I said. "He said Stone's locked. That Cody put a fail-safe on him in case he's ever used for magic this way. Ever used to join magic, light and dark."

"He used dark magic?" Hayden asked. "Where? How?"

"I think it was worked in a glyph in the bowl."

"Well, fantastic," Shame whispered.

I looked around the room.

We did not look good. Correction, we looked great for just having been through a magical meat grinder. At least everyone was breathing, moving, alive.

Except for Stone. He stood stock-still, half crouched, one hand raised, his face tipped up to a sky his eyes could not see, wings unfurled.

He was silent, unmoving, a strange sort of quiet I'd never seen in him before.

"No," I said. "Stone? You okay? Stoney?"

I touched his face. He was cold. Unbreathing. Nothing but a statue now. That spell hadn't locked him. It had killed him.

"Fix this," I said out loud, even though I was talking to my dad. "Unlock him."

*I can't unlock him,* Dad said, *which means I can't unlock the magic in him.*

"No. You put the magic in him. Undo the spell."

"I can't," Dad said through my mouth.

Okay, I wasn't getting anywhere with this. I took a couple calming breaths and tried to look at this problem through reasonable eyes.

Stone was a statue. All the glyphs that I'd seen on him before were gone, faded. He really did just look like a piece of garden decor.

"Allie," Maeve said softly. She cleared her throat. "Allie, dear. Tell us what your father is saying."

"Stone's locked," I said. "All the magic in him is locked too. Dad doesn't know how to open him up. He said Cody made it so he would lock up and do this. Turn into a statue."

Stone looked sad. He looked afraid. He looked like when I'd first met him, chained down by magic that would not let him touch the sky.

I hated this, hated that he was trapped. Yes, also trapped in him was all the magic we'd just gone to so much trouble to secure. But he was my buddy. My gargoyle. My Stone. I didn't want to lose him. Not like this.

"Cody made him. Cody put this lock on him. We can't get to the magic, to see if it can be used for a cure, until we find a way to unlock Stone."

"At least we know what the problem is," Terric said. "That's something."

"Not damn much," Hayden said.

The door to the room burst in. And six hands raised six different spells that could cause six different versions of pain.

Bea and Jack, two of my Hounds whom I had told to stay away, stay safe, stay out of this, strode into the room.

"Hi, Allie," Bea said with her customary perky smile. "The police will be here in less than ten minutes. Don't know what you all are doing, but it's time to run."

# Chapter Sixteen

"How many?" I asked.

Bea shrugged. "I think they emptied out the entire department."

Shame pushed off the wall he was leaning on. "I say we get the hell out of here."

"We can't," I said.

"Can't?" Shame raised one eyebrow. "I don't see why not."

"We have two unconscious men we need to look after and a two-ton gargoyle who's frozen solid and happens to be our only chance to cleanse magic."

"The van's here," Terric said. "We could probably get Davy and Collins loaded in it. Maybe Stone too."

"In ten minutes?" I said.

"Nine now," Jack noted, his restless gaze taking in all the technology and implements lining the room. His gaze rested the longest at the restraints on the bed, and his mouth pressed a hard line.

Hounds weren't dumb—he knew what kinds of things happened here, even if he didn't know exactly how those things happened.

"Are you sure they're coming here?" Victor asked.

Bea nodded. "We have our ear to the ground on this. Hounds don't get these kinds of things wrong." Then to me, "Allie, you *really* need to run now."

"Where are we even going to run to?" Hayden asked. "Split up? Try to regroup?"

"Hell," Shame said. "Maybe we don't run at all. We can take them. Take them here. Look at all this." He waved his hand toward the equipment that filled the room. Most of it looked like it could do a lot of harm.

"No," I said. "We will not get in a standoff or shootout with the police. They're just doing their job. They don't know what's really going on with magic, and they don't deserve to die for it."

"Some of them work for the Authority," Victor noted.

"I don't care. We protect the innocent."

He nodded, his approval clear. "So we run."

"Where?" Hayden said again.

I didn't know. Didn't know if splitting up was a better option or if staying together would be safer. "Anywhere away from here, for the moment, will do. Hayden, Maeve, get Collins, see if you can wake him. If not—"

"I'll carry him," Hayden said. He and Maeve hurried out of the room.

"I'll get Davy," I said. "Terric, can you help me with him?"

"What about Stone?" Shame asked.

"He'll have to stay here," I said reluctantly.

*No,* Dad said. *He's the only chance to cure magic. He has the samples.*

"We can't carry him," I said. "And he can't move."

"And we're running out of time," Bea said again.

"Gate," Zayvion said.

I stopped halfway across the room. I hadn't thought of that. "Can you do it?"

Zayvion turned to me. His eyes burned with molten gold and there was no warmth in his smile. He was burning hard, hot. Asking him to throw such a massive spell after all that he'd been doing, with no recovery time, might just push him too far into a killing insanity.

"Easy as breathing," he said with an unconvincing smile.

That was a lie. The possibilities of what opening this Gate might do to him—physically, mentally, magically— washed over me with sticky, cold fear. His fear, my fear. Same thing.

"Maybe Terric or Victor?"

"They can't hit this jump," Zay said.

"Maybe—"

He walked over to me and gripped my upper arm. "Go get Davy." Fear pushed through that contact. So did anger and determination. We had to get out of here, all of us, now, alive.

"Can't do anything until you let go of me, Zay," I said evenly.

He let go of my arm and began drawing a Disbursement.

"Terric?" I said.

"I'll stay here," he said.

I ran out the door, with Shame, Bea, and Jack jogging to keep up.

"Anything else we can help with the . . . Gate thing?" Bea asked.

"No. You two need to disappear. I don't want to see you, hear you, or so much as catch a scent of you. The police have a lot of powerful magic users behind them right now who want a bunch of us dead. I don't want you hurt."

"We could help—," Bea started.

"No," I said again. "I'll call you when we land."

"If we land," Shame added as we hit the main room. Maeve and Hayden already had Collins, who was semiconscious, off the couch and on his feet.

"We could leave him," Hayden noted.

"No. He comes with us. Take him to the room. Zay's going to open a Gate."

"You let him talk you into that?" Hayden asked.

"No choice. We'll deal."

They started off and we hurried down to Davy's room. Bea and Jack were still behind me. I understood why they hadn't left yet. Davy was one of them, one of us, a Hound. Last they'd seen him, he was on death's door.

But they were about to find out that he'd walked right over death's threshold.

"Davy?" I said as I strode to the bed.

Davy opened his eyes, and thankfully, he was solid. "Hey, boss," he whispered.

"We have to move. Cops are closing in. Think you can walk?"

He swallowed, nodded. "I think. So."

"C'mon, now, mate," Shame said. "You could dance if a pretty girl asked you. Someone like Sunny, maybe. Am I right?"

That got half a smile out of him. "Sure."

Shame and I helped him to his feet. Davy was breathing hard. I wrapped his arm over my shoulder, and Shame did the same.

We took a step, and Davy lost hold on his physical self, fading to watercolor magic, his feet slipping into the floor.

"Jesus," Jack whispered.

Bea gasped. "What did he do to him? What did Collins do to him?"

"No time," I said, giving her a hard look. "Get the hell out of here." Then to Davy, "Keep your mind on your feet. We can move faster if you're solid."

Bea tugged on Jack's sleeve. "Let's go."

"This isn't right, Beckstrom," Jack said.

"I know," I said. "Working on it."

Jack and Bea jogged down the hall, and were out the front door by the time Shame and I had half carried, half dragged Davy through the front room toward the back of the warehouse.

"You're doing fine," I said as Davy concentrated on his feet, lifting them and putting them down a little gingerly as if unsure that the floor would be there for each step.

"Freaks," Davy breathed. "Me. Out."

"Collins did this to keep you alive," I said. "We're working on a way to reverse it. You're going to be back to your old self soon."

Shame spoke up. "You're just a temporary sort of ghost. Although I, for one, could see the advantages of being able to slip through walls." Shame sounded calm, happy even. Our doom was closing in around us and Shame didn't seem a bit flustered.

Then, I'd always wondered if Shame didn't have a little too much of a death wish.

We made it to the walkway overlooking the warehouse. The sound of sirens I'd been ignoring was growing louder. The police were almost here. Maybe some were already here, outside, with guns drawn.

I hoped Jack and Bea had made it out safely.

The entire warehouse shook like a bomb had just gone off.

"What was that?" I asked.

"That," Shame said, "is our gate. Davy, if you can walk any faster, now's the time to do it."

Amazingly, Davy picked up the pace.

I pushed the door open.

The room stank of magic and the hot salt and sulfur of the Gate spell.

Zay had opened the thing right in the middle of the room where Stone was frozen.

Correction. He opened the Gate *around* Stone so that Stone was already inside it. If Zay could push the Gate, he'd be able to close it behind Stone. I didn't know a lot about Gates, but I thought that might make it so Stone ended up not so much going through to the other side, but having the other side pull him there.

Zayvion stood several paces in front of the gate, his arms out to both sides, feet spread, as if by will alone he physically held the gate open.

Hayden walked through the gate with Collins. There was no one else in the room, which I hoped meant everyone else had gone through.

"What is. That?" Davy asked.

"Our way out," I said. "Shame—you got him?"

"No." Shame helped me get Davy to the edge of the gate. "You take him. I'll knock out Z and drag him through behind me."

"We all go," I said.

"Look at him. Allie," Shame said, urgently, "look at him."

I looked at Zayvion.

He burned with gold light. Black fingers of smoke curled around him, feeding magic into the Gate. His eyes were pure gold, no white, no pupils. He looked like a pillar of magic, a grounding wire, a storm rod.

"You touch him, and you're going to get swept up in that. I'm just going to hit him over the back of the head," Shame said. "Go!"

He let go of Davy, who slumped against me.

"Don't hit him," I said as I took the three steps needed to get to the gate. "And do not make me turn around and come back here after you two."

God. I sounded like a den mother.

"Hang on, Davy," I said. "This might be a little rough."

I stepped into the gate.

Magic hit me like a truck. I screamed and fell as if I'd just stepped off a cliff. Magic poured through me, burning, slicing, taking me apart and fusing me back together with lashes of pain. I couldn't breathe; I couldn't see. And then I couldn't even scream.

I hit. Hard. Shoulder, hip. Something landed on top of me. Someone. Davy. Damp grass beneath me, darkness around. Then hands helping me up.

"You'll need to back away a bit," Hayden said as he pulled me away from the Gate to where everyone else was gathered.

"Davy?" I couldn't think. I was supposed to do something. Help someone. Where the hell was I?

"We have him," Hayden said. "Terric and Maeve are walking with him right behind you. But you"—he pressed down on my shoulder—"need to sit before you pass out."

Hayden stopped walking and I sat, unable to put more than two words together in my brain before they slipped away like a poorly tied knot. Collins sat on the grass next to me, mumbling. Talking, talking. To himself, I thought. Maybe to voices in his head. I didn't think he was entirely sane.

But then, I didn't think I was exactly up to par right now either.

Terric and Maeve helped Davy walk toward me. He looked a little better. Certainly looked more solid. I think the Gate hadn't been as bad for him as it was for me.

They eased him down to sit next to Collins, and Davy bent his knees, folded his arms across them, and then rested his head against his arms. He was breathing heavily. But he was still solid. That was good. I thought it was good.

I didn't know what everyone was standing around looking worried about.

Then it hit me. The Gate. Shame and Zayvion were supposed to be walking through that right about now.

I stared at the opening in space that hovered there in the . . . Where the hell were we?

A park. No, not just a park. A very familiar park.

"You're kidding me," I whispered. I glanced over my shoulder. Yep. There was the St. Johns Bridge, stretching down the hill we sat upon, and pushing out across the river.

Why here? I didn't know if this was where Zay had intended to take us, but if it was, I didn't know why.

Where was he?

"Zay?" I said, though I don't think anyone was in earshot to hear me.

I stared at the gate. It wavered there, flickering. Two shadows filled the hole in the air, filled the gate, and then the entire thing imploded. The shadows were thrown to the ground, and gray ashes rained down from where the gate used to be.

I knew who those shadows were—Shame and Zayvion.

I pushed myself up onto my feet and ran for them.

Terric was on his feet, running right beside me, reaching for Shame, fear hard in his eyes, on his lips, as I reached for Zayvion, my heart pounding too fast, fear caught in my breath, slick and hard in my chest.

We pulled them from each other, Shame having fallen beneath Zayvion.

"Zay?" I touched his face, his neck. Breathing, heartbeat, he was alive, covered in ash, knocked out. Relief flooded me, and was swallowed down by fear.

Terric swore. "You fucking kill me, Flynn. That's the way you go through a gate? What were you trying to do? Burn all the clothes off your back?"

He paused. "Breathe, you idiot." Terric placed his right hand over the crystal that lay within Shame's breast. Then, softer, "Breathe." He exhaled, and it was almost like he dimmed just the smallest amount, that light filtering into Shame.

Shame coughed, groaned, and elbowed up. "Goddamn." He turned his head and spit, then wiped blood off his mouth. "Forget what I said. Next time *you* can drag him through the gate, Beckstrom."

Terric stood, and helped Shame up onto his feet, something Shame did not argue with.

I shook Zayvion, but he didn't open his eyes. His skin was cold, which seemed really weird since the last time I'd seen him, he was surrounded by gold fire. I kept my hand on his chest. I needed to feel him breathing, and each rise and fall of his chest assured me that he was still alive.

"Allie?" Victor walked up beside me.

"He's unconscious," I said. "We need to get out of the park, somewhere safe. Do you have any contacts we can use in St. Johns?"

He shook his head, then crouched down and felt for Zayvion's pulse. He looked as tired as I felt.

"We'll need to do something with Stone too," he said.

I glanced over. Stone stood there, where the Gate had been, his face tipped up to the sky, one hand reaching out, wings angled as if he could take flight. But he was stuck, frozen. Cold. Dead.

No, not dead. Locked. We'd find a way to unlock him. We'd find a way to fix him and fix magic.

We just needed a place to catch our breath and make a plan. Before the police showed up.

Or the Authority.

"Mama's," I said.

"Your mother?" Victor asked, startled.

"No. Mama owns a restaurant here. I used to Hound for her. She took me in once, when I needed a place to stay. She might take us all in. Might take Davy and the other injured at least."

"None of us has a phone," Victor said.

"I have a phone," Collins mumbled weakly. He dug in his pocket and handed it to Hayden, who was standing over him.

Hayden brought it to me.

I turned it on, dialed Mama's number.

"We're closed," her familiar voice said, with the buzz of the crappy landline rattling in the background.

"Mama," I said. "This is Allie. I'm in trouble."

Silence on the other end. Silence and the buzz of electricity.

"How much trouble?" she asked.

"More than I can handle. My friends and I need a place to land for just a few hours. Some of us are hurt. There's magic involved. A lot of magic."

Silence again while she considered. Then, "Come to the back door. Boy will let you in."

"I don't have a car."

"You want me to do everything?" she snapped. "Fine. I send Boy with car. Where are you?"

"Cathedral Park," I said.

Mama hung up.

I thumbed off the phone, hoping I hadn't just given our location away to someone who would call the police. I didn't think Mama would. She'd had too many run-ins with the law to turn to them in times of crisis. She hadn't

even called for an ambulance when her youngest Boy
was hurt. Zay had called it for him. And it had probably
saved his life.

"Is she coming?" Maeve asked.

I looked up into her worried face. "I hope so," I said.
"I really hope so."

# Chapter Seventeen

It didn't take long, maybe fifteen minutes, before we heard a car rumble into the parking lot. Zayvion was still out, still breathing evenly. I knew that because I hadn't left him and my hand was still resting on his chest. Shame sat next to his mother, looking singed and sick. Davy was still sitting with his head bowed forward, and Collins had decided lying on the grass and staring at the sky was the best option.

Victor and Hayden were standing, and Terric was trying not to hover over Shame, though every time he paced near Shame, he slowed a bit.

Stone was stuck. Still a statue, still not moving.

Someone needed to go check to see if the car that had just pulled up in the parking area was our ride or not. Even though I didn't want to leave Zayvion, the longer I sat here, the more restless I became.

I stood and started across the damp grass.

"Where are you going?" Hayden asked.

"To see if our ride is here."

Hayden walked beside me, and I was fine with that. Better to have backup. Even though there was no magic in this neighborhood, that didn't mean there were no guns.

We made the slight uphill climb and finally caught a view of the lot. An old pickup truck idled in the empty parking lot, lights off. Two people in the cab. The passenger stepped out of the truck and into a bit of light.

Mama had gotten her name from taking in boys off the street and raising them up as her own. She didn't legally adopt them, but she'd done a lot of good for kids who fell through the cracks. When they were old enough to make it on their own, some of her boys stayed on and worked her restaurant, which had living quarters above it. All of them went by the same name: Boy. Loyal and gun-toting, Mama's Boys were pretty easy to pick out in a crowd.

And the thirty-something man with his hair pulled back in a ponytail and the shotgun in his hand was one of her Boys.

"Hey," I said with just enough air to carry my voice to him.

He glanced our way, not lifting the gun, which I appreciated.

"It's Allie," I said.

He nodded. "Truck's ready."

"Wait. I'll get the others."

He walked back to the truck and Hayden and I turned around and headed back to where everyone was waiting.

"They're here," I said. "It's a truck, so we'll have to ride in the back. Hayden, can you help me with Zay?"

"What about Stone?" Victor asked.

"We'll have to leave him here for now. Let's get all the wounded to Mama's first; then we can come back for him."

"Shouldn't someone guard him?" Maeve asked.

"Yes," Collins said as he sat up. "It's too dangerous to let that fall into the wrong hands."

Interesting. I didn't even know Collins had noticed Stone. And now he had an opinion about not only what he was, but also how dangerous he might be?

"Who wants to stay with him?" I asked. It wasn't go-

ing to be me, even though I felt guilty about it. I didn't
think Stone could get any worse—I mean, unless someone took after him with a hammer. But Davy, Shame,
and Zayvion were all hurt and needed a bed to lie on. I
had to make sure they were okay first; then I'd come
back for Stone if I needed to.

Collins opened his mouth.

"Not you," I said.

I didn't trust him much before, and I wasn't sure how
much I could trust him now that he had even more of his
memories back.

He shrugged.

"I'll stay," Victor said.

"Maybe I should," Maeve said.

"No, I'll be fine," he said. "If anyone comes by, I can
keep Stone and myself hidden."

Terric paused in his pacing. "It should be me, Victor,"
he said. "The Authority doesn't even know that I'm not
a part of them. They probably wouldn't question me sitting in a park with a gargoyle."

Victor shook his head. "You need to go with them."
He glanced over at Shame, who was groaning as he got
his feet under himself and stood.

"How far is this car-topia?" Shame asked.

"Not far," I said.

Terric took a step toward Shame, one hand stretched
out for him. Shame had his back turned and didn't see
the gesture. But Terric seemed to realize what he was
doing and let his hand drop.

"Fan-freaking-tastic," Shame panted. "Mum? Shall we?"

He held his arm out for her. She gave Terric a soft
look, then took Shame's arm. "Careful, now, son. It's a bit
uneven."

Terric watched them for a minute, then walked over
to Davy. "Hey," he said. "Need any help?"

Davy nodded. Terric helped him up, and wonder of wonders, Davy remained solid. They started across the grass, Terric talking quietly to him.

I glanced at Collins and at the unconscious Zayvion. "Think you can walk?" I asked Collins.

"I'll manage." He heaved up onto his feet, and swayed a little. Then looked over at Victor. "It's been so wonderful seeing you again, Forsythe. These little meetings of ours are so . . . informational. Please do be careful out here. I'd prefer that you not get killed, as I don't believe you've fully restored my memories."

"Give it time," Victor said. "I'm sure you are concerned over nothing."

"Doesn't feel like nothing." Collins began walking, and after a few steps looked pretty steady.

Hayden and I bent, and lifted Zayvion into a sitting position. Hayden was a big man, but there was no way we were going to carry Zay the entire way to the parking lot.

"Come on, Zay," I said. "Wake up. I really need you to be awake."

He inhaled, and lifted his head.

"That's it," I said. "Wake up. Zay, wake up."

His lids fluttered open, and he blinked, wincing like he was fighting the mother of all migraines. Which I assumed he was. The Disbursement spell wrapped red-hot bands around his head, burning lines down the sides of his neck, and running beneath his shirt. I didn't know how he had decided on paying the price of pain, but there didn't appear to be an inch on the man that wasn't on fire.

"Allie?" he said softly.

"You need to walk," I said. "Hayden and I can help."

He did what he could to support his own weight, but from the first step I could tell he was barely on the upside of conscious. Still, he put one foot in front of the other, every step sending a flare of pain through the Disbursement glyph pulsing on his skin. He was breathing hard, heavy, and was covered in sweat by the time we made it to the truck.

I didn't know how he was going to crawl up into the back of the truck, nor how we were going to lift him. One of the Boys showed up, and somehow between me, Hayden, Boy, and Terric, who reached out from the truck and helped pull, we got Zay into the vehicle.

I was so glad it was dark.

The night was cold, quiet, and damp and we all rode in the open bed at the back of the truck, jostling along in silence.

The truck came to a stop in the rutted parking lot behind Mama's place. It had been a long time since I'd been here. A few months at least. It felt like a lifetime.

I got out of the back of the truck. As soon as my boots touched the concrete, I shivered. Dread washed over me and settled heavy in my stomach. Something bad had happened to me here. Something bad enough my body remembered this place as a danger, as pain.

Even though I couldn't remember it, I knew what it was—I'd channeled a wild magic storm here. I'd been shot here. I'd saved Zayvion's life here. But I knew those things only because Nola had told me about them.

I'd lost days of my memory. Days of my life for those things.

And I'd been told not to come back here. Ever.

Yeah, well, that hadn't lasted, had it?

I reached up to help Zayvion down out of the truck. Hayden had shifted to get Zay to the edge of the pickup bed, and kept one hand on his back, helping him stay sitting.

Zay pushed forward onto his feet and stood.

"Careful, there," Hayden said. "You got him, Allie?"

"I think so. Yes."

Zay leaned on me, but stayed standing with only my arm around him. He wasn't better yet, but he was getting stronger.

"Why here?" he asked me.

"It seemed like our best option."

"Best?"

"Only," I amended.

"Don't think. It's such a good idea."

"Better than where we were. Let's get you inside. Then I can help the others."

"I can walk," he said.

"Good, because there is no way I'm gonna carry you."

We headed toward the back of Mama's restaurant, and the door swung open.

A woman, barely five feet tall, dark hair pulled back in a messy bun, stepped into view.

"Allie girl," she said, "come in. Come in, now."

She stepped outside and held the door open for me while Zayvion and I walked past her.

"Thank you," I said. "The others might need some help too."

We walked through a storage room, filled with the things one would need to run a restaurant, and then we entered the kitchen.

I froze. Every nerve in my body told me not to go forward, not to step out there. Panic set my heart beating faster, soured my mouth, and made my knees week. I wanted to run.

I had been hurt here. Zay had been hurt here. This was not a good place to have come to.

But I didn't leave. Instead I walked forward, keeping my eye on the door that led to the dining room.

One memory and one memory only, of this room, of being here, burbled up out of my brain and flashed behind my eyes. Blood. Too much blood. Zayvion's blood. My blood. We had died here.

I didn't know how long it took before we exited the kitchen. Logic said just a minute at most, but emotion said it took months, years, aeons to walk from one door out through the other.

This door opened onto the dining room area.

Quiet now, dark. I could count on the fingers of one hand how many times I'd been to Mama's when Boy wasn't standing behind the counter. But tonight the room was empty, with only the light at the top of the stairs at the back of the room lending it warmth. I knew Mama lived at the top of those stairs.

There were beds up there. At least one. And if that was where the bed was, that was where I intended to take Zayvion.

"How do you feel about stairs?" I asked him.

"Not happening," he rumbled. He was sweating, breathing too hard for such a short walk.

"How about a chair?" I offered.

"More my speed."

I guided him to a chair and pulled it out. He lowered himself gratefully into it with a grunt.

By the time I looked up, everyone else had wandered into the room.

What a vision we all made. Zombies would have looked more spry.

Except for Mama. She strode in and wove her way between people like a stage director prepping for opening night.

"You. Help that one up the stairs to the bed." She pointed at Davy and one of her Boys hopped to it and helped Terric get him upstairs.

"You," she said, giving Collins a nod. "Over there at the table."

He followed the direction of her finger, while she looked at Shame. "Stay out of my liquor."

Shame gave her a grin. "Yes, ma'am."

Shame walked over and took the chair next to Zayvion.

"Do you know her?" I asked.

He shrugged. "I've eaten here once or twice."

"And left an impression, obviously."

"Of course. I make an impression everywhere I go. You should know. Once someone sets eyes on me, they'll never forget I was in their life." And that roguish smile he gave me would have worked better if he wasn't both pale and singed.

Well, at least he wasn't feeling as bad as Zayvion.

Maeve and Hayden sat at one of the empty tables, and Mama got busy telling another Boy to brew coffee and fetch us water.

I didn't know why she was suddenly feeling so generous toward me and my friends. She and I hadn't exactly left on the best of terms. Her son, James, had gotten mixed up with people, people who I now knew were members of the Authority, and specifically the head of the Authority, Sedra. James had helped kill my father.

Mama knew it. Her son had pulled a gun on Zayvion and me in her kitchen too, and I'd gotten him thrown in jail.

It hadn't made us the best of buddies.

And yet, here she was, tough loving on us.

Maybe it was our down-on-the-luckness that softened her stance. Maybe things were worse than I knew. She told us all to sit and stay that way while she stormed off to the kitchen and yelled for the remainder of her Boys to fire up the stove and get something more than hot coffee cooking.

Something at the corner of my eye caught my attention, a blur of color, a shadow shaped like a man. A Veiled?

I jerked and looked across the room.

At a ghost. No, not just any ghost, a nice-looking young boy. Blue eyes the color of summer skies, hair so yellow it might as well be white.

Cody Miller. His dead self, his broken spirit, the part of him that Zayvion had permanently Closed away. It was a little confusing, but the best way I'd been able to think of Cody the ghost and Cody the alive was that when Cody had been Closed the second time—an order given by Sedra, who was possessed by Isabelle at the time—his mind and soul had snapped.

Because of that break, the living Cody had a childlike intelligence and half a soul, and the dead Cody was a ghost who had an adult intelligence and was the other half of his soul.

This ghostly part of him I'd last seen taking Mama's hand and walking away with her to St. Johns when we were trying to deal with the wild magic storm.

"Hey," I said.

He smiled and drifted over to me.

"I thought you were going to fix it," he said.

I bit my lip and shook my head. I didn't know what he was talking about. "Fix what?"

He very gently pressed one finger into my left hand. His finger was cool, but not frost-cold. It was a nice touch, a soothing touch.

I opened my hand and turned it to look down at it.

Cody placed his finger on the circle of black, the mark Mikhail had placed in my palm.

"This," he said. "You haven't fixed it. Not yet. Not even after my father . . ." His voice faded, and when he spoke again, it was with great sadness. "He marked you.

Gave this to you, so he could save my mother. Save her from *them*."

I knew whom he was talking about. Mikhail and Sedra were his parents. They were both dead now. Very much dead. Because Mikhail had saved Sedra from Leander and Isabelle possessing her. But the only way he'd been able to save her was to kill her, and release the rest of her soul Isabelle had kept trapped in her body.

"I don't know what to do," I said. "I don't know what this mark in my hand does."

He nodded, and looked thoughtful, as if he wasn't quite sure what I should do either.

"Something," he said. Then he looked up at me, his eyes so blue, I was caught by their beauty. And their intelligence. He might look younger than the living Cody Miller, but he had a wisdom and sorrow that belied his years.

"It's important," he said. "And if you don't do it, people will die."

"People?" I repeated. "Who? Who will die?"

He looked away, at a great distance, as if he could see to the end of a far horizon. And when he looked back at me, his eyes were dark with sorrow.

"Everyone."

# Chapter Eighteen

Shame sighed loudly. "Really, Beckstrom? The crazy talk. Still? You do know you're talking to air, right? Or is this one of your teatimes with Daddy in the gray matter café?"

"Cody's here," I said, not taking my eyes off Cody. "His spirit. His ghost."

"Yeah?" Shame shifted in his chair. "I don't see anything."

"If you used Sight, you'd see him," I said.

"And since that ain't happening," Shame said, "why not just ask him if he knows how to unlock Stone?"

Holy shit. I'd forgotten. It wasn't just the alive Cody that had made Stone. This broken, Closed, dead part of him had still just been him, a whole soul, when he made Stone.

"Stone?" Cody said. "Who has Stone?" He said it cautiously, like it mattered a great deal whose hands Stone fell into.

"Right now, he's in the park. Victor's watching him."

Cody nodded. "Oh."

*Ask him if he'll help us,* Dad said quietly.

"Will you help us?" I asked. "Stone's locked. We tried to put samples of magic in him to see if we could cleanse it, but all it did was lock him down. He's just a statue now and we can't access the magic in him, which we think might be the antidote to the spread of poison."

"Who put the magic in him?" Cody asked.

"We did," I said.

"Who? Exactly who?"

"My dad," I said quietly enough I hoped Collins didn't hear. "In me." I lifted my hands. "We did."

He shook his head. "He's not supposed to do that."

"We didn't have any other choice," I said. "Magic has been poisoned. You know that, don't you?"

"I can feel it," he said. "I can feel the Veiled rising. Gathering. Getting stronger. Feeding. Being fed upon. A lot of people are dying."

"We want to help those people and cleanse magic," I said. "But we need your help with unlocking Stone. Can you help us?"

He thought about it for a long while. Long enough Mama, who had gone into the kitchen and left only one Boy to stand watch over us—the Boy with the shotgun—came back into the room.

"How long are you staying?" Mama asked. "Long enough to eat?"

I nodded. I didn't know about everyone else, but I was hungry. And the smells coming out of the kitchen would stir anyone's appetite.

Terric and the Boy who had helped Davy upstairs came down into the room.

I glanced at Terric and he gave me a slight nod. Davy was settled. That was good.

Cody drifted away from me, glanced at the stairs, and then walked up them, making no sound at all, his hand sliding along the old banister, his face tipped upward toward the light. I guessed he was going to see Davy, though I didn't know why.

Leaving without an answer. Not okay.

"I'm going to check on Davy," I said.

"Wait," Zay said.

"I could help," Collins offered.

"I'm just going to make sure he's settled," I said to both of them. I put my hand on Zay's hand and added, "I'll be right back."

Collins shrugged, but Shame gave me a hard look. "Not getting into trouble without us, are you, love?"

"No." And just in case he didn't believe me: "I promise. Eat. Make sure Zay eats or drinks something, okay?"

"Want me to feed you with a spoon airplane, Zay?" Shame asked.

"Shut up, Shame," Zay said.

I headed up the stairs. Terric passed me, caught my gaze, then made his way to the table I'd been sitting at. He started talking quietly with Shame and Zayvion, who, I was relieved to hear, was answering Terric's questions in a voice that was a little steadier.

We were all recovering fairly quickly, considering everything we'd just done. St. Johns always had a way of making me feel better, making me feel good, safe, when magic was making me pay the price. I didn't know why—maybe because there was no magic in St. Johns. Or maybe because, even broken-down and neglected by the rest of the city, it had always been one of my favorite neighborhoods.

I just liked it here.

The hall at the top of the stairs was well lit. It wasn't hard to find the room I'd stayed in before, even though I'd lost most of that memory channeling the wild magic storm. Luckily Zay and Nola had filled me in on what they knew. I paused outside the door, which was half open.

I pressed my fingertips against the old wood that had been darkened by years of hands pressing against it. The old door swung inward silently.

The room didn't seem familiar to me. Not even the

smells. And seeing Davy there, solid in the bed, with Cody sitting beside him, one hand on his upper arm, really wasn't familiar. A soft pink light spread out in a glow around Cody's hand. The light whisked across Davy's arm, and curled up toward his heart.

It was like the light that Cody—the alive Cody—had used on Davy back at the den when he'd first been bitten by Anthony. Back before Collins had carved the halfway-to-death spells into him. The pink light also looked a hell of a lot like the crystal in Shame's chest. I knew my dad had found that crystal in St. Johns. I wondered if the pink glow had anything to do with St. Johns or with the crystal.

"He's in between," Cody said. "Like me, but not like me."

I walked into the room, stopped next to the bed. "Yes. Collins scarred those spells into him to try to save him from the poison the magic carries."

"The magic is bad," Cody noted.

"Is there anything you can do for him? To help him?"

Cody stared at Davy for a moment or two. "No." Then he looked up at me. "You're right. Magic is poisoned. Even though that shouldn't happen. Magic can't go bad."

"But it has. And the poison is spreading and making people sick."

"Not here," Cody said. "Here at Mama's. Magic doesn't make anyone sick here."

"There is no magic in St. Johns, Cody."

"But I thought—" He frowned. "Maybe you're right."

I didn't know what it was like to exist as a ghost, but Pike had told me the living world was confusing through the eyes of the undead. He said magic pushed and pulled at you, and twisted and turned in rivers of darkness and light that made the living world difficult to navigate.

Cody seemed to navigate it pretty well, but I figured that was mostly owing to the lack of magic in St. Johns.

"Outside of this part of town, all the magic is like that." I pointed at Davy. "Poisoned. People are dying. The Veiled are rising, just like you said they were. Magic is poisoning them too, and they are biting people, possessing people, and that's how the poison is spreading."

"It kills them," he finished for me. "The people?"

"Yes."

He looked out the narrow window. Out at the night and the street. No magic here in St. Johns meant nothing but electric lights burning in the darkness. No spells, no neon glyphs, no crayon Illusions. Just a broken-down neighborhood in a broken-down part of town.

"I'll help you," he said. "I'll try to help you. But I can't do it without all of me."

"You mean you want the living you here too?" I asked.

"Yes." He looked away from the window. "The . . . spells I carved into Stone will unlock only if I'm whole. The living me won't remember it all. They're hard spells to break, to . . . untangle. And I'll need to be in his mind—I mean my mind—and use my hands to make it work."

"Why did you put those spells on Stone? Is he important in some way?"

"Has Daniel told you anything about Stone?" he asked.

"Only that he is an Animate and might be able to help us isolate and filter the poison from magic. Is there something more he should have told me?"

"Maybe not," Cody said with what might have been a sigh if he could breathe. "When I was alive . . ." He shook his head. "Everything made more sense. I made Stone to hold magic. No one else had made an Animate for . . . years." He smiled. "And he can hold magic. That was the experiment. I didn't want . . . anyone to use him for something bad."

Shame had told me the art and skill for casting the kind of spells it took to make an inanimate object alive, or at least lifelike, was thought to have been long lost. But Cody had managed to do it.

Shame had also told me Cody was a real hell-raiser when he was younger and had gotten in with the wrong crowd, and then fallen into the wrong kind of debt with them. Maybe this spell, this walking, burbling, almost-alive gargoyle had been his proprietary intellectual property, and the chip he was going to use to bargain his way out of trouble.

Whatever the reason, I was beginning to believe fixing Stone was going to take more than just putting Cody the ghost and Cody the living in the same room with the gargoyle.

"When you said you couldn't help us without all of you, what, exactly, do you need?" I asked.

"I need to be fixed."

"Fixed?"

"Zayvion has to Unclose me so I can be whole again."

He didn't say it like he was sad, or worried, or particularly unhappy about being Closed. Still, it was something that had always bothered me.

"Zay told me he didn't mean to break your mind when he Closed you."

That got a small smile out of him. "He didn't. I mean, he Closed me. Twice." Here the smile slipped up to a grin. "I had that coming. Both times, really. This might be a shock, but I haven't always played on the right side of the law."

"The Authority's law, or the law of the land?"

"Both."

"But Closing you twice broke your mind and your spirit," I said. "Didn't it?"

He shook his head. "Zayvion didn't break me."

"Who did?"

"Jingo Jingo."

Well, now I had another reason to hate the man. "Do you know why?"

"He didn't tell me. And I was in too much pain. I think he was under orders. He wanted me to . . . stay with him. To hold on to him like I'm holding on to this place, to Mama, but I wouldn't do it. I held on to myself instead."

"You haunted yourself?"

He shrugged. "That sounds silly, doesn't it?"

"No, I think that was a good choice. Will Cody be able to hear you if you talk to him?"

"If he's here, it will be easier, I think. I could try to talk to him now, but it wouldn't be easy."

"I'll call Nola and ask her to bring him. You're going to have to help us talk him into this. Talk him into being Unclosed."

"He doesn't always listen to me, even when he can hear me." He stood up—well, kind of floated up. "We've been apart for so long, we are almost different people now."

An image, a memory, flashed through my mind. Of my dad, but not the father I had known, the father who was still in my head. No, it was the image of a younger him, a kinder him, the ghost and soul part of him that had been in death all these years, the part of him I had seen when I crossed into death. He had seemed kinder than the father who shared my head. He had seemed capable of love. Of loving me.

I wondered again why Dad had a broken soul and now, looking at Cody, I wondered if someone had broken Dad's mind, like Cody was broken.

But before I could ask, Dad said, *No*. Then he turned away, far enough I could not feel him in my mind.

Cody tipped his head to the side. "Does your father talk to you a lot?"

"Sometimes," I said. "You can hear him?"

He nodded. "Does he bother you?"

"Endlessly." I walked over to the door. "I'll call Nola. Will I see you again?"

He glanced back at Davy, then nodded. "I'll come downstairs. Mama's there. I like her."

I stepped out into the hall, and stopped short. There was a man standing there, near enough I could make out his military-cropped hair and pale eyes. No, not a man, or at least not anymore. A ghost.

"Pike?" I said, sorrow catching in my chest at seeing my friend and Hound mentor again.

"Thought I'd check on Davy," he said. "Took me a while to find him. How goes the war?"

"Not great," I said. "We—I lost Anthony. I'm so sorry, Pike. I tried."

"I know," he said. "I've seen him. He doesn't blame you, if that's any help."

I nodded. It did help, but it didn't make me regret his death any less. "Davy's hurt and changed. We had to use magic on him to keep him alive. Mostly alive. I'm looking for a way to reverse what happened to him. I'll find a way to fix it."

Pike walked toward me. "Some things can't be fixed, Allie," he said. "I'd tell you to stop worrying, but you never listen."

"I listen," I said as he paused, then pushed his hand through the closed door. "I've always listened to you."

He looked over his shoulder, most of him already halfway through the door, and gave me a smile. "Then stop worrying. And eat something. You'll be no use to anyone exhausted."

He walked the rest of the way through the door. In a

second or two, Cody stepped out of the room. "Pike's a nice man," he said.

"You know him?"

Cody shrugged. "I've seen him. Not while I was alive. He tries to look after Davy. I'm glad he's here."

"Me too," I said. And I meant that. Davy had always looked up to Pike. It meant a lot to me, and I think to Davy, to know Pike still had his back.

I headed down the stairs, half a dead guy in my head, and half a ghost following on my heels.

"What were you doing to Davy?" I asked as my shoes made a soft shuffle against the old wooden stairs.

"Just sitting with him," Cody said. "He's . . . lost."

"What do you mean?"

"Not dead. Not all the way alive. It can be scary. I thought he might like some company."

"And the pink light?"

We had made it to the bottom of the stairs. I turned and looked at him.

"What pink light?" He really looked confused.

"In your hands?"

Still the blank look.

"When you were touching him. There was pink light around your hands."

"Really?" He looked down at his hands. "Are you sure?"

I shook my head. "No. I've been seeing a lot of things I don't usually see."

"Oh, don't feel bad," Shame said as he walked over to me. "Seeing things isn't nearly as crazy as talking to things no one else can see." He handed me a cup of coffee and glanced over my shoulder, his gaze resting eerily close to where Cody was standing. "How's it going, Cody?"

"Tell him he still owes me money," Cody said.

"He said you owe him money."

Shame blinked, and the smile faded. "How much?" he asked me, his eyes bright and sharp. He was obviously feeling better.

"Tell him he knows how much," Cody said. "I wrote it on the wall so he'd never forget."

"He said he wrote it on the wall so you wouldn't forget."

Shame drew his head back a bit and searched the empty space over my shoulder again. A smile slowly crept over his face.

"And that," I said, taking a sip of coffee, savoring the warmth and deep, rich flavor, "is the end of me being your private ghost whisperer."

"Hold on, now," Shame said. "I think you're on to something, Beckstrom. We could make money with that little talent of yours."

I groaned and walked toward Zayvion, who nudged a chair with his foot away from the table he and Terric were sitting at.

"I will not charge money to talk to dead people," I said, taking the chair.

"Not just *talk* to dead people. It could be so much more."

"No."

"You haven't thought this through." Shame followed me to the table. "Besides, I'd be the one doing all the work. I'd set up the jobs, maybe send the ghost to look in on something, maybe a friendly hand of cards, or the combination to a safe, or maybe who's sleeping with who—some such thing—and all you'd have to do is tell me what he saw. Then"—he snapped his fingers—"easy money."

"Shame, I will not blackmail people with the dead." I sat and took another drink of coffee.

"It's not like the ghosts would be losing any money.

Come on, now," Shame coaxed. "For the good of others? We could investigate criminal activity—like private detectives. Bet we could find out who's embezzling from your company."

"No."

"Zayvion, tell her this is the opportunity of a lifetime," Shame said. "If I were a ghost, I'd be proud to be serving on the side of the alive-and-wells."

"Shame," Zayvion said, low but even, "we're not even sure if you're on the side of the alive-and-wells now. I don't think your death would do a lot to realign your moral compass."

"Hey," Shame said. "We all have a bit of darkness in our souls, don't we? It's what makes us family."

"It's what makes us able to tolerate you," Terric said.

"So funny." Shame punched Terric in the arm.

"Ow!" Terric rubbed his arm. "Maybe you ought to try dying so we can find out."

"You'd miss me if I were dead," Shame said. "Wouldn't you, Ter?" He plunked down in the empty chair, staring straight into Terric's glare.

They sat there for a second. I wondered if they could tell what the other was thinking. I knew they felt what the other felt, so that punch in the arm must have also hurt Shame. Not that it looked like it bothered him.

"With every damn beat of my heart," Terric ground out. I noted he had his right hand closed, and out of the way of Shame's sight.

Shame blinked. He hadn't expected that answer. "Liar," he said.

Terric just stared at him. "Think so?"

Shame frowned. Terric didn't look away.

Finally, Shame scowled. "You used to be fun to be around, Terric," he said, breaking eye contact, and scowling down at his coffee instead. "What happened to you?"

"You, Flynn," Terric said. "You happened to me." He looked away, and sat back, taking a drink out of his coffee cup at the exact same time, with the exact same motion, as Shame.

Neither of them seemed to notice that they were practically mirror images of each other. And I wasn't going to be the person who pointed that out.

"Does anyone have a phone I can use?" I asked loud enough everyone in the room could hear me.

"I think we left Collins' phone with Victor," Maeve said.

"Who are you calling?" Zay asked.

"Nola. We need her to bring Cody here so he can help us with Stone. Mama," I said. "Is there a pay phone in the neighborhood?"

Mama had been standing at the counter, wiping down water glasses that didn't need any wiping. She obviously just needed something to keep her hands busy while she, and three of her Boys—who all had guns—kept an eye on us.

"My phone," she said.

"What?" She didn't like anyone using her phone. Certainly didn't like me using her phone.

"You use it, Allie girl." She nodded toward the phone. "No one follows that line. No one hears it."

Well, maybe that explained the crappy buzzy landline. I'd always thought it had something to do with St. Johns being the only place in Portland without magic. Mama had once been involved with Perry Hoskil—my father's business partner before my dad had forced him out of the company and into bankruptcy. It was whispered that Perry had more than just a small part in inventing the Beckstrom storm rods and many of the initial magical technologies. Technologies that had made my father rich.

It was possible he would have known how to set up an untraceable landline.

Or maybe I was reaching. Maybe one of her Boys was handy with espionage and had jimmied an easy line blocker.

"Thank you." I walked over to the phone hung on the wall by the doors to the kitchen, picked up the receiver, and hesitated with my fingers above the keys.

I was pretty sure Nola was still staying with Detective Stotts. I was pretty sure that if he had been found, if he was awake, if he'd gotten over Zay Unclosing him, he'd be with her. He wasn't a stupid man. He'd expect me to call her and he'd monitor those calls. He might even talk her into doing something "for my own good."

Which meant I was very likely about to bring Detective Stotts, his crew, and, hells, the rest of the police force down on us.

There had to be a better way.

I dialed a different number.

It rang once. Then, "This is Sid."

One of my Hounds.

"It's me," I said.

"Bad line," he said.

"I know. Can you tell Nola I need to see her and Cody in St. Johns? You know Mama's place?"

"Want them there now?"

"Back door. Faster the better. Police are looking for me. And she's been staying with—"

"I know where she is. Give me twenty minutes." He hung up.

God, I loved Hounds.

# Chapter Nineteen

One of Mama's Boys pushed through the kitchen door and almost ran into me. He had both hands full with plates. On those plates were piles of delicious things that should be wrapped in a tortilla and devoured.

My stomach rumbled.

Mama stepped closer to the counter in a practiced, unconscious movement that made me realize they must have been avoiding these kinds of collisions for years. I followed her lead and stepped inward so he could press past us and take the food to the tables. A couple of the other Boys went back in the kitchen and helped bring out the rest of the food.

Even though I was suddenly starving, I didn't head over to the table yet.

"Why are you helping us?" I asked.

Mama just lifted one shoulder, and put the glass back on the shelf, drawing another into her hand to be wiped down. "You came when Boy was hurt. I never paid. This makes us even."

She wasn't looking at me. There was a reason why she never paid me for coming to look at her youngest Boy, who was only five years old or so, and probably asleep somewhere upstairs. It had turned out her son, James, had been involved in my father's murder, and in framing me for it.

"How is Boy?" I asked. Last time I'd seen him, he was dying from a heavy Offload spell. I'd traced that spell back to my father. I was wrong. It hadn't been my father who had cast that spell to kill Boy; it had been James.

She looked up at me. "He's good. Very good. School. Soccer. Good."

I wanted to tell her I was sorry for what had happened between us, but the time for that talk was long past. She and I had never been close, but I'd always thought we might be friends. I thought now, maybe the best we could hope for was not enemies.

"I'm really happy to hear that. He's a good kid."

That got a small smile out of her that she quickly tucked away. "You go eat now. We open in a few hours. You will be out of here by then, yes?"

I glanced over at the room. "I think so. Sooner, if we can."

All we had to do was convince Nola to let Cody unlock Stone for us; then, I hoped, we'd have an idea of what we could really do to cure magic.

"I might need a place for Davy to stay, though," I said. "I don't think he's going to be out of bed for a while."

"You mean him?" She pointed her dish towel at the stairs.

Davy stood there, one hand on the banister, looking a little confused, a little sleep-rumpled, and a lot more solid and steady on his feet. The pale image of Pike lingered on the landing behind him.

"Davy?" I headed across the floor. Pike nodded once to me, like he was handing off the duty of watching after Davy. Then he faded from sight.

Collins was already up and moving. He stopped before actually touching Davy. "How are you feeling?" he asked.

Davy frowned. "I don't know you."

"Eli Collins," he said with a slight bow. Yes, bow. "Allie hired me to help with your medical condition."

I walked up and put my hand on Davy's arm, but he pulled away gently.

"I think I'm getting the hang of this." He started down the stairs and seemed to have the falling-through-the-floor thing under control.

"Do you remember what happened?" I asked as I followed him.

"Some of it. Anthony. He bit me, right? Then he died. And . . . and someone said magic was poisoned?"

"That's right. And the bite infected you with poisoned magic. You've been very, very sick."

"Which explains why I feel like death warmed over." He sat in the chair Zayvion had vacated for him. "And why I'm starved."

Shame shoved an untouched plate of food over to him. "Welcome back to the land of the living, mate," he said. "We have fajitas."

Davy carefully picked up a fork. Then, when that didn't fall through his hands or do anything un-fork-like, he began eating.

Yes, we were all staring at him. Yes, I was wondering if food would, you know, stay in his stomach, which was dumb because he was as real and solid as anyone else in the room and nothing had fallen out of him when he'd gone ghost before. If I couldn't constantly see magic, and see the pulsing ribbons of light and dark that shone through the thin material of his T-shirt, I'd think he was just a normal guy.

A normal, hungry guy. He inhaled that food in about ten seconds flat.

Apparently, being half dead gave you an appetite.

Boy came over with another plate of food and silently handed it to me. I really was hungry.

"Thanks." I glanced at Zayvion. He nodded toward the empty chair at the table, and paced across the floor to the windows so he could look out at the street.

Zayvion wasn't all better yet, his pace shortened, a little stiff, but I could tell moving helped some.

I sat. "Shame, could you let Victor know Nola's coming?"

"Sure. I could use a smoke anyway." He got up and headed toward the back door. I didn't know if there was Pooh code for that, but figured Shame could get the idea across.

Terric watched him walk off, then rubbed his left thumb over his right palm, where the mark, the blessing, from Mikhail rested.

Cody, the ghost, had been sitting on the bottom step, making one of those bouncy balls slowly roll from one side of the step to the other. But once Shame was out of the room, he stood up and drifted over to stand near Terric.

"He has a mark?" he asked me.

I had to chew for a minute before answering. I was not shy about getting my chow on, and Mama and her Boys knew how to cook.

"Do you know what it is?" I asked.

"What?" Davy and Terric asked at the same time.

"Cody," I said.

"She can see the ghost of Cody Miller," Terric explained.

Davy just frowned. "Like Pike?"

"Yes," I said.

Cody was bent over and staring at Terric's hand, which was on the table, curled slightly. His palm wasn't visible. That didn't seem to stop Cody from seeing the magic Mikhail had worked there.

"I think it's a Binding spell," Cody finally said. "Very

specific. I don't know what it's a Binding for. Maybe magic? For life? Health? No, that doesn't seem quite right. I don't know. It isn't a spell I know. It's beautiful, though," he said longingly.

"He says it's a Binding of some kind, Terric," I said with a slight nod toward his hand.

Terric's eyebrows raised and he tipped his hand so he could see his own palm. "To what? Death?"

I shrugged. "He doesn't know."

"Thank him for me, okay?" Terric said.

"He's welcome," Cody said, looking pleased to have done something to help him.

By the time I was mopping the last bit of sauce off the plate with my tortilla, I heard a familiar voice coming this way from the kitchen area.

Cody heard it too. He turned, an expectant, nervous look on his face.

It was weird to think that he probably hadn't seen himself for a long time.

Nola walked into the room. Her blond hair was pulled back in a braid, and she had on a flannel jacket, work boots, and jeans. She looked like she'd wished she'd brought her shotgun too.

I stood and walked over to her. "Hey, Nola," I said. "Really good to see you."

She wasn't smiling as she looked around the room and took in the situation. A situation that included three Boys still holding guns. Her gaze finally rested on me and she took a long moment before she said anything. Finally, "Are you okay?"

"I'm fine. It's been a rough night or two, but I'm okay. I'm sorry I couldn't call you. I was worried I'd get you in trouble with Paul. Have you seen him?"

"Not since this morning. Is something wrong? No,"

she said, "let me try that again. What's wrong? How can I help?"

I hadn't heard sweeter words in days. "A lot has happened. Let me bring you up to speed. How about we sit down? This will take a couple minutes."

"All right." She looked over her shoulder.

As Cody, the living, breathing Cody, walked into the room. He looked surprisingly different from ghost Cody. Ghost Cody seemed younger, slighter of build. His face still retained an edge of childhood that alive Cody no longer carried. But their eyes were the same extraordinary blue, and when they smiled—which they both did—it was the exact same smile.

"Hi, Cody," ghost Cody said.

"I'm Cody," the alive Cody said. "Me? Are you me?"

Nola walked over to the living Cody and took his hand. "Yes, you are Cody. And everything is fine. Do you want to sit down? You could have something to drink if you want."

"No, thank you, Nola," he said nicely. "Me? Are you me?" he called out.

The ghost Cody walked over to him. "I'm you," he said. "Everything's okay, but you should probably be quiet now. Let's sit down together."

Cody smiled and walked over to an empty table and sat. "Hi," he whispered. "I can't find monster."

Nola looked at Cody, and then at me. "That isn't like him," she said. "He hasn't done that for a long time."

"It's okay. Really," I said. "Let me explain."

I guided her over to a quieter corner of the room. Maeve and Hayden had been silent for so long, I'd almost forgotten they were there.

"What is going on?" Nola asked quietly. "They have guns. And your friend, Sid? He didn't even stay, just dropped us off. If I hadn't seen Shamus outside, I wouldn't have come in."

"It's such a long story," I said. "You know about Stone, right?"

"You mean the half ton of statuary that found us not too far from here a few days ago, followed us home, and keeps sneaking into the house and making fortresses out of books?"

I smiled. "At least he's staying out of your ice-cream sandwiches. Those make a hell of a mess when they melt. You know he's an Animate—a magical construct—but you might not know who made him."

"Who made him?"

"Cody."

One of Nola's eyebrows hitched up. She glanced at Cody, who appeared to be talking to thin air. "All right," she said slowly.

"Cody was really good with magic. He worked some spells into Stone that would make him shut down if someone decided to use him to blend magic."

She shook her head. "I don't understand. Isn't all magic just magic? All of it the same?"

Nola didn't use magic. She lived on a very nonmagical farm out in Burns, growing very nonmagical alfalfa, which sold through the racing circuit. She'd taken in Cody back when he'd been hurt and I'd been accused of murdering my father.

Nola was like that. She took in strays and helped them get on their feet. In many ways, I was one of her strays, even though we were the same age. She just had an over-active motherly streak.

"There are really only two different kinds of magic," I said. "Light magic and dark magic. It's been kept un-der wraps, but magic was broken a long time ago—

hundreds of years ago—into those two things. Both can be used with the same spells, and you have to know one of the five disciplines to use magic. The disciplines are Faith, Blood, Life, Death, and Flux, but using the same spell with light magic or with dark magic will vary the results. For one thing, dark magic kills most people who touch it or use it for more than very short and infrequent times."

"I've never heard of Death or Flux magic. And isn't Blood magic just magic mixed with drugs?"

"No. There's been a lot of misinformation circulated. On purpose so people wouldn't hurt themselves using magic."

"Okay."

"So here's the thing," I said. "We're not exactly sure how, but magic has been poisoned."

A glass shattered against the floor.

I looked over. Mama was standing there, staring my way, her hands empty, the glass a spray of shards at her feet.

Her Boys sprang into action, two at her side, another bringing over a broom and dustpan.

"I'm fine, I'm fine," she said, brushing them off and taking the broom. "So I drop a glass. Just a glass."

She swept the floor in short, hard strokes, her gaze riveted on the glass, a flush of scarlet pouring down her cheeks. I'd never seen her this flustered before. Not even when her littlest Boy had been dying in her arms.

A couple of months ago I would have tried to keep this all secret, even from Mama. But right now I didn't care who knew about this stuff, just as long as we could fix magic.

"What poisoned magic?" Nola asked.

I turned back to our conversation. "We don't know.

We went to one of the cisterns that holds magic beneath the city and tried to filter it to cleanse it. That failed. Explosively."

I swallowed. What I didn't say, what I couldn't bring myself to tell her, was that it had failed because of Bartholomew Wray.

Whom I'd shot and killed.

"Allie?"

"Sorry," I said, pulling myself away from grim memories. "Since we didn't know where the poison was coming from, we had to tap the wells."

"What wells?"

"That's another secret. There are four wells beneath the Portland area. Ancient natural wells of magic. No one knows about them except a certain group of people who keep a lot of magical secrets. The amount of magic in those wells is immense and each well is glyphed so if you wanted to access the magic, you'd have to use a certain discipline of magic."

"Why? I'm not following."

It was hard to explain the subtleties of magic to someone who never used it. "Think of magic as music. Everyone's using the same notes, but how you put them together works better for a rock song, or classical piece, or jazz.

"To try to find out how magic has been poisoned, we had to get a sample of magic from each well and combine them in Stone, because we thought he'd have a way to contain magic and maybe even filter it. When we did that, it made Stone lock down. He's out in the middle of Cathedral Park, unable to move. He's nothing but a statue now, but he's holding the one thing that might help us figure out how to cure magic."

"Do we have to cure magic?" she asked. "Are you sure it isn't something that can naturally purify itself if we give it some time? Like a muddy river getting back into shape after a hard rain?"

"We don't have time to find out," I said. "The flu epidemic isn't a flu. It's caused by poisoned magic and it's making people sick. Nola, if we don't find an antidote, if we don't use the magic in Stone to cleanse magic, a lot of people are going to die."

She shook her head, and I could tell I'd crossed the line and just told her more than she wanted to believe.

"I don't understand why we have to do anything," she said. "There are police, doctors, scientists, who know more about magic than we do. They should be working on this. I'm sure they *are* working on it. None of us is an expert at magic. I think you're overreacting, Allie."

"I'm not an expert. But these people, well, everyone except Mama and her Boys, are."

She didn't glance around the room, which would have been my first instinct. She just stared straight at me.

"You want Cody to use magic, don't you?"

That was the rub. Part of why Nola had taken Cody in was to protect him from people trying to make him use magic for them. Even broken-minded and broken-souled, Cody was a hell of a magic user.

"Yes, I do. But that's not the biggest problem." I took a breath, trying to figure out how to tell her about Cody's ghost. If she didn't want to believe things about magic, was she going to believe I could see the dead?

"Remember a long time ago when you told me I was a savant with magic?"

She nodded.

"I'm not. But Cody was. And he used his outrageous skills to get in with the wrong crowd. He owed people favors, and money, and probably much more. He was using magic to do a lot of illegal things. So the people who know all the secret things about magic decided to take away his memories. They cast a spell so they could get in his head with magic, and take away his memories of how to use it."

"But he remembers magic."

"Sure. They didn't take away his memories of magic, just of how to use it. He was good, Nola. Amazingly good. And they thought it was kinder to take away his memories than to have him turn into a criminal or something worse."

"Is that why he's . . . Did someone hurt him to make him the way he is?"

I didn't think telling her it had been his own mother, Sedra, who had been possessed by Isabelle, a dead magic user, would be a good idea. So I kept it simple.

"Yes. Someone hurt him and broke him mentally. That someone is dead, but they are the reason why he is mentally challenged."

Tears welled up in her eyes and she shook her head. "Allie. I don't think I can believe you. I think . . . I think you've been listening to people, and they've told you things that seem real, but they aren't. You've been so different lately, and I heard about the money you stole from your company. Paul is looking for you. He's going to arrest you."

Well, she'd been keeping up with the headlines. "I can prove that I'm innocent. And I can prove all the things I just said are true. But we need Cody to unlock the spell on Stone."

She shook her head again and wiped at one eye. "I called him," she said.

"Called who?"

"Paul. Before I left with Sid, I sent him a text. He knows I'm here. He knows I'm meeting you. He should be here any minute. With the police."

"That's fine. We'll deal with them when he shows up. But I'm not done telling you what we need to do."

"I can't," she said. "Allie, I can't listen to all this. I can't believe you believe what you're telling me. You've always asked me to look after you—to look after your memories and to tell you if you're not acting like yourself. Have you looked in the mirror?" Her gaze searched my face.

"You aren't acting like yourself. You don't even look like yourself. What did you do to your hair? And your clothes? I'm going to get you help. Help you've relied on me to give you, even if you didn't know you needed it."

"Please, Nola." I closed my eyes for a second, trying to think of what would make her believe, what would turn her around.

"You're right. You are my best friend. You have always been my best friend. And you've helped me so many times. But in all the times I've come to you, licking my wounds, not even remembering who I was, you never once told me I was crazy. I'm still not crazy. I need you to trust me just a little longer. Please do me just one favor."

"What favor?" she asked quietly.

"Cody's mind was broken—that wasn't supposed to happen—but when I say he was good at magic, I mean it. He found a way to hold on to the part of himself that broke. Found a way to hold on to his mind, his soul, the personality that he used to be. And he found a way to keep his higher-reasoning skills viable. That part of him, his soul, mind, self, is here, in this room with us."

"What does that even mean?" She didn't believe me. But at least she wasn't walking away. Yet.

"I know you can't use magic," I said. "Right now, I can't either—it's making me sick. So I'm going to ask someone to draw a Sight spell for you. You should be able to see Cody's ghost—the part of him that was broken when his memories were taken away. And Cody should be able to see him too.

"I want you to talk to Cody. If he wants to help us unlock Stone, or not, I'll stand by your decision of what you think is right."

"Just a Sight spell?"

"Just a Sight spell."

She hesitated, then nodded. "I'll look through a Sight spell."

"Who do you trust to cast it for you?"

She didn't know any of us here very well. Maybe she knew Zayvion the best, since he'd stayed a while with her at the farm when I was in a coma.

"Zayvion," she said.

I walked over to where he was standing, holding back part of the blind so he could see the city beyond.

"She doesn't believe me," I said.

"I know."

"She called Stotts. She says he'll be here soon and she needs someone she trusts to draw Sight so she can see Cody's ghost."

"I can do that."

I nodded. I hadn't told him that I talked to Cody and that he wanted to be Unclosed. I needed to take this fire one frying pan at a time.

He walked over to Nola.

"How are you?" he asked.

"I'm fine," she said. "A little worried about . . . well, everything."

Somehow, Zayvion pulled out a smile and a calm tone. "It's going to work out. We just need Cody's help to unlock a spell. That's all." He wasn't using Influence, which got me thinking. We probably could cast Influence on Nola and force her to let us do this with Cody.

Except I hated Influence and would never let anyone use it on my best friend.

"That's what you said last time," she said.

Zay nodded. "We needed his help with the medical equipment. He didn't do any magic at all then. But this time we are asking him to use magic."

"Magic?" Cody said. He got up and walked over to us, his hand out to the side, as if he were dragging a suitcase or wagon behind him. Only it wasn't either of those things. He was holding hands with his ghost self, who floated behind him.

"Where do you want us to stand?" Nola asked.

Zay looked at me. "Can you see him?"

"He's next to Cody."

"I'll stand over here," ghost Cody said to alive Cody. "And you can stand next to Nola, okay?"

"Okay." Cody walked over to Nola, a smile on his face. "He said stand here with you."

He did just that, and took Nola's hand.

Zayvion stood between the ghost of Cody and Nola. He set a Disbursement, something that came out black and slick like a snake and burrowed into his gut.

I winced, but he didn't even flinch. He calmly drew a wall-sized Sight.

Nola gasped.

I didn't have to look through Zay's Sight spell to see ghost Cody wave to Nola. "Hi," he said.

"Can you hear him?" I asked.

She shook her head.

"He said hi," Cody said helpfully. "That's me. Hi, me!"

Ghost Cody smiled. "Hi, Cody," he said. "Hi, Nola." He looked at me. "Can you tell her thank you for me?"

"He wants me to tell you thank you," I said.

"What for?" she asked a little breathlessly.

He looked at her. "For giving me such a great life." He pointed at Cody.

"He said for giving him such a great life."

"Oh. You're welcome. Allie"—she glanced at me—"could you tell him that for me?"

"He can hear you," I said. "But I'm the only one besides Cody who can hear him. I think." I looked around the room. Davy raised a finger.

"You can hear him too?" I asked.

He nodded. "I didn't realize he was a ghost."

Well, that meant he could also see him.

"So, Nola, would it be okay if Zay dropped the Sight?" I asked.

"Wait." She looked at ghost Cody. "Do you want this? Do you want to unlock the spell Allie was talking about?"

"Yes," he said. And for good measure, he nodded.

"Cody," she said to alive Cody. "Do you want to help with magic? Help Allie unlock something with your . . . with him?" She pointed at ghost Cody.

"Uh-huh. I like us."

"Okay," she said. "Wave good-bye for now."

"Bye, me." He waved. "I like me. Older me is smart."

"Older you," Nola echoed. "So that's who you've been talking to?"

"Yes. He's been away for a long time. Monster too."

Ghost Cody waved back and then Zayvion canceled the spell. There was the slightest scent of pear blossoms, and then the room was just a room again.

Zayvion, however, was sweating pretty hard. He wiped his forehead on the shoulder of his shirt. It took a lot of concentration and effort to pull magic all the way into St. Johns. There were no networks, storm rods, or natural wells out here, which meant pulling on magic was like hauling in a barge by hand.

That little spell had been a hell of a lot harder than it looked.

Everyone was quiet for a moment. Then Nola turned to me. "Tell me exactly what you want to do with Cody."

Shame strode into the room. "Yes, do. And tell her damn fast. The cops are coming."

# *Chapter Twenty*

"How many, and from where?" I asked.

"Don't know, and everywhere," Shame said. "Time to be moving, people."

The front door opened. And Detective Paul Stotts stepped into the room, gun drawn.

Six Boys pulled guns, and every magic user in the joint drew a glyph while pulling weapons.

No. This was crazy. I was not going to get into a shoot-out with my best friend's boyfriend.

"Stop it," I said. "All of you. Boys, Paul, put your guns down. No one is shooting anyone. Got that?"

Since no one put their guns, or for that matter spells, down, apparently the answer to that was no.

"Nola, Cody," Paul said. "I want you both to come with me."

Nola looked at me, then at Paul. "I'm not going anywhere with anyone until everyone puts down their guns and spells," she said.

"Detective Stotts," I said, walking toward him.

"Allie," Zay warned. "Don't."

"You might not want to come any closer, Ms. Beckstrom," Paul said.

I just kept walking. "Did you get my note?"

Paul's gaze flicked from Zayvion to me. "Yes. Jack Quinn brought me here."

"Did Jack tell you why we're here?"

"No."

"We're trying to find a way to filter the poison out of magic. Shooting us isn't going to help matters any."

"What will help matters?" he asked. "Taking away people's memories?"

"No," I said, ignoring the look Hayden shot my way. "That's a problem. The thing that helps is giving memories back. Just like we gave your memories back. So you could make a choice. An informed choice about what we're doing."

"I'm not sure I see it that way," he said. "And I see no reason to involve Nola or Cody in this."

"There is a reason," I said. "Nola is my best friend and we stick together. She's looking after Cody right now and we need Cody to unlock a spell so we can hopefully come up with an antidote to the poison that's spreading through this city and killing people."

"Cody?" he asked. "Why do you need him to cast magic?"

"Because he's a savant with magic."

"Magic is pretty," Cody added.

So not helping.

"Cody can do things with magic none of the rest of us can do," I said. "Like create Stone. And like putting a Lock spell on Stone that we can't undo. Stone might help us find a cure to the epidemic."

"Are you sure about that?"

"Not in the least," I said honestly. "But it's the best chance we've got and we need Cody to unlock him for us so we can find out if we're right or not."

Paul considered me and the other people in the room.

Sure, no one had put their weapons down, but no one had cast any of those spells they were holding either.

"Time, people," Shame said. "We're running out of it."

"Where's Stone?" Paul asked.

"In Cathedral Park."

"What are you going to do to Cody?"

"Zayvion's going to Unclose him," I said. "He's going to give him his memories back, just like he gave yours back. We hope he'll remember how to unlock Stone."

"I will," ghost Cody said.

Alive Cody nodded.

Paul's gun shifted slightly to aim at Zayvion's chest. "Do I have all my memories back?"

"No," Zay said. "Victor can give you the rest."

"Where's Victor?"

"Cathedral Park with Stone."

There were no sirens. But I knew the police were closing in, could feel the tension radiating off Shame. They had to be just a few blocks away. And I didn't even hear engines. They were coming in quiet, and they were coming in hard.

"Then let's go." Paul lowered his gun and so did everyone else. "The MERC van is outside. Someone else can drive." He held up his keys and Hayden came forward and took them.

"The back door," I said. I gave Paul a thankful smile, which he did not return.

I turned and touched Nola's shoulder. "Thank you."

She nodded. "We'll figure this out."

"Of course we will," I said.

I moved to help Davy, but Terric was already offering him a hand, not that I thought he needed one. Davy looked even stronger.

Maybe the no-magic of St. Johns was helping with that.

Collins stared at me from where he was slouching in a chair, a thoughtful look on his face as if he was trying to find a category to sort me into.

"Coming?" I asked.

"I wouldn't miss this for the world," he said. "You know what you're doing breaks every rule of every law that there is, both in the common and uncommon world."

"Oh, I don't know," I said, picking up my coat. "I'm sure there's a few I missed. After all, the night's young."

Zay was waiting for me, holding open the kitchen door. I hurried his way.

"Wait!" Mama called out. I looked over my shoulder. She hustled down the stairs, a blanket in her arms. "Here," she said. "For the Boy."

She pressed the soft old quilt into my arms. "Thank you," I said. I would have hugged her, but there was no time. "Don't get in a shoot-out with the police."

She scoffed. "You. Run. I know my business."

I ran, past the Boy in the kitchen who was holding the pantry door open, and who locked it behind us. Then out the outside door, and into the familiar white box van that Stotts' crew always used for cleaning up messy, il legal spells. I caught the burly profile of Hayden at the wheel.

I jogged to the back of the box van and jumped up inside. Terric waited just a second while Shame pressed a message on his wrist. Terric shut the van door, plunging us all in darkness. The van started off. I sat on the cold metal floor, braced against the wall, rocking as the van rattled over the old streets.

There were no lights in the van, no windows. But the glow of magic on and around people revealed a few things to me.

The crystal in Shame's chest gave off a slight pink-going-bloody light, showing him and Maeve sitting next to Nola. Next to Nola sat Cody. Neither of them seemed to have any magic around them.

The webbing of magic wrapped around Davy shone with an amber light. Zay stood next to him, and closest to the door. Stotts leaned on the other side of the door, across from Zayvion, who I could only assume he had decided was the most dangerous.

Stotts shifted, pulling something out of his pocket.

Every nerve in my body tightened. If that was his gun and he was going to shoot—

"Wait!" I said.

A click echoed in the metal van.

And the light of a flashlight hit the floor.

"What?" Paul asked, shining the beam up on the ceiling so it gave a better ambient light—just enough that we could actually see one another.

I swallowed hard, more than once, trying to choke my heart back down out of my throat. Sweet hells, I thought he was going to shoot him. Shoot Zay.

"Nothing," I said a little shakily. "I thought." I looked over at Zayvion, who closed his eyes a little too long and shook his head.

He knew exactly what I thought was going to happen. Could probably feel the echo of my heart beating in his chest.

"Nothing," I said again.

Paul glanced over at Zayvion, who gave him a don't-fuck-with-me glare.

Stotts' expression changed, softened. "I wouldn't do that, Allie. Not that way. And not now. I'm not your enemy."

"Might be a bit more convincing on that if you weren't just waving a gun around at us, mate," Shame said.

"Would you have walked unarmed into a room full of armed magic users?" Stotts asked.

"Probably," Shame and Terric said at the same time.

"Death wish," Terric supplied helpfully.

Paul nodded, his gaze on Shame. "That explains some things about you, Mr. Flynn."

"Oh, piss off, Ter," Shame said. "It's not a damn death wish. I just know how much my pain is worth."

The van took a sharp right and we all braced. I hoped that meant we were near the park.

We'd need to get Cody across the park to Stone before the police closed in on us—if they were closing in on us. I hadn't heard from Victor this entire time. I hoped everything was okay with him.

Wait. Cody! I'd forgotten about his ghost self. I squinted against the light in the van, looking for the ghost.

"I'm right here," he said softly at my elbow. I jumped and glanced at him. He was right next to me, but little more than a shade in the darkness. I realized he had one hand clutching the quilt in my arms.

"Are you okay?" I whispered.

"Yes. But I've been holding on to Mama for a long time. It's hard to let go and haunt something else."

The quilt was not only Mama's—it looked handmade. I was sure it had covered and comforted many of her Boys she had brought in off the street. Just as it was comforting Cody.

"Can I help any?" I asked.

"You could tell Zayvion to Unclose me so we can be together," he said. "Alive Cody and me. That's what I need. That's all I need."

Yeah, about that. I hadn't even asked Zayvion if he

would do it. And I wasn't sure if he was going to be able to do it. Unclosing someone wasn't an easy spell. To do it right, Zayvion had said the person needed to have some time to recover. Which meant the faster we could get to the Unclosing, the quicker Cody would be able to get his wits together, and then, hopefully, be able to unlock that spell.

And all of this had to be done in the hardest place in Portland from which to draw on magic.

A lot was hanging on this.

No, everything was hanging on this. I looked over at Zayvion. He was still standing, holding on to a loading strap, resting his head against the wall of the truck and watching Stotts through lowered lids.

And that was when I knew it wouldn't matter. Zayvion would do this, no matter how much it hurt, no matter how hard it was. Because it was the only way to protect the innocent, and to save magic. It was the only way to uphold the vows he still held true.

The van finally rolled to a stop and the engine went silent. I could hear Hayden shut the cab door, then jog back toward us, his boots loud on the pavement. He lifted the latch and opened the door.

The smells of the river, recently mowed grass, and the cool dew of night rolled into the van. We were here. We were somewhere beneath the big arch of St. Johns Bridge.

"Everyone out." Hayden held his hand up for Zayvion, who took it, and jumped down out of the van.

It didn't take us long to unload onto the grass, and start walking toward the middle of the park.

Electric lights lined the concrete path and gave off enough illumination that Paul pocketed his flashlight. He was walking with Nola, talking quietly. Cody strolled along with them, taking in the park like he was on some great adventure in a strange land.

Maeve and Hayden were in the lead not too far ahead of them, and Terric, Shame, Davy, and Collins were all walking not too far behind them.

Which left the ghost Cody and Zayvion and me to bring up the rear.

Zay reached out and wrapped his arm across my back, and I shifted the quilt to slide my arm across his back too.

He was hurting. A lot. Enough that I hissed and then opened my mouth a little more to try to breathe away the pain coming off him.

"You're hurting."

"Yes," he said.

There was no use for us to hide it from each other, but there wasn't anything we could do about it either. No one but Zay could Unclose Cody.

"Give you a back rub," I said.

"Mmm. Now?"

"After this is all done. I'll get you naked, I'll get me naked, and I'll warm the oil."

I could feel the flush of pleasure that rolled down his spine.

"Then what?" he asked.

"I'll lay you down on the bed, pour some of the oil in my hands, then start here." I slid my hand down and rubbed it up his ass, slowly. "Of course since I'll be straddling you, I'm bound to get some of that oil on me. Might get messy."

"I like where this is going." He glanced over at me. "I can handle this."

He didn't mean the back-rub fantasy—he meant magic. "I know you can," I said. But what I didn't say was how much it killed me not to be able to use magic. Not to be able to help him bear this cost I was telling him he had to pay. I hated having my hands tied. Hated not being able to carry my own weight in this fight.

"We're going to get through this," he said.

I nodded. "Sure we are." But that didn't even sound convincing to me.

# Chapter Twenty-one

"Oh!" Cody squealed from ahead of us. "Monster! Monster is here." He took off running toward Stone and Victor.

Nola called his name, but he didn't listen.

Ghost Cody, drifting next to me, pulled in a little closer to the quilt, as if uncomfortable to be out in the open. "Have you asked him?" he said.

"Who?"

"Zayvion. Have you asked him to Unclose me?"

No time like the present. I took a deep breath.

"Cody wants you to Unclose him."

"I'm going to," Zay said. "But it's going to take a little time. I Closed him twice, so we'll need to do it in stages."

"Will it hurt, do you think?" Cody didn't sound worried, just curious.

I passed the question along to Zayvion.

"It will be disorienting," he said. "But not painful. Not painful for him."

"I can Proxy," I said.

"No."

"Zay—"

"No."

"Really?" I said. "Because the knight-in-shining-armor thing you have going is a nice look, but it is so last season, Jones. Just because I can't use magic doesn't mean I've forgotten how to deal with pain. You Unclose Cody; I'll Proxy."

Zayvion stopped and swung his arm forward. Since my arm was still locked around his back, I had to take an extra couple steps and turn toward him.

He pulled me close. "Listen to me." He dragged his thumb along the whorls of magic that ran from my temple down the side of my face, his golden gaze burning into me. He cupped my jaw and brushed his thumb over my lips, his mouth opening slightly as if hungry to taste me.

"What—"

"Listen." He bent his head, just enough that his eyes were even with mine. He looked away from my eyes, his gaze falling to my lips. And then he kissed me.

I melted against him, opening my mouth and savoring the flavor of peppers mixed with the taste of him. His shoulders rolled as he shifted around me, holding me as if he could guard us from prying eyes, from the world.

As if his body alone could shelter me from the night.

I shivered with the want of that, to find myself lying warm and safe in his arms, far away from this fear, this pain.

I pushed my hands under his coat, palms pressing up his sides, wanting the heat of his body against more than just my hands. I shifted closer, pressing my hips against his.

Zay made a soft sound deep in the back of his throat and drew his hands up my back, his fingers sliding up into my hair and clenching there.

Then his pain rolled though him, rolled through me, washing over us like a wave. We endured it, caught on exhalation, caught in his pain and so much more. His fear for me, his love for me, his need for me, all wrapped around us, blending with that pain, thickening it with an aching sweetness. It was heady. Intoxicating. Overwhelming.

I was drowning, breathless in the heat of his emotions. Breathless in the heat of him.

Zayvion gently pulled away, breaking our kiss, but not our connection.

"No," he whispered.

And I understood. It was going to take a lot of his strength to Unclose Cody. He knew he could do it, but after that, the pain might be more than he could bear and remain conscious or sane. If he used me as Proxy, I'd be in pain too. I might even be unconscious. We were too close together to work Proxy.

Soul Complements meant we could make magic do things no one else could make it do. But I couldn't use magic right now. And if I were bearing Zay's Proxy price, it was entirely possible neither of us would be worth anything to anyone.

Soul Complements or not.

"I want," Zay began, then, "I *need* you to watch over me. And Cody. The only thing that matters right now is unlocking Stone."

He stepped back and held me at arm's length, pausing a moment as if trying to get his footing that far away from me. "You have to make sure we win this." His gaze searched mine and he smiled. "Because I want that back rub."

The heat he had planted in me bloomed across my stomach and pooled at the base of my spine. Lord, the man could get under my skin. I licked my bottom lip, savoring the taste of him that lingered there.

"Let's do this," I said.

"Let's," he agreed.

We turned, holding hands now, just holding hands, and crossed the park to where everyone was standing around Stone in a circle.

As we got closer, I heard Paul talking to Victor.

". . . all of them," Paul was saying.

Victor didn't look convinced. "If I do that, and at this point I don't see why I wouldn't, you have to understand it will take you time—hours, if not a few days—to recover from it."

"You let me worry about that," Paul said. "Just give me back my memories."

Victor shifted, tucking his arms across his chest. "Do you want me to do that now? Tonight?"

Paul opened his mouth, then glanced at Stone.

The living Cody knelt next to Stone, his arms thrown around him in a huge hug. He was mumbling to him, and was on the edge of tears, telling Stone it was going to be okay, he was going to be okay.

Paul's mouth turned down. "No. Not now."

Stotts might not know all the rules to the game, but he was smart enough to make sure he wasn't compromised when the action was going down.

"Good choice, Detective," Victor said.

I knew he meant that. Victor respected Paul—hell, all of us did. He'd been fighting the good fight, trying to keep innocent people safe from magic just like we had. He just hadn't been a part of the Authority while doing it—which appeared to have been the better choice the way things were working out.

He wasn't on their hit list, for one thing.

"How are we going to do this, Allison?" Victor asked.

Paul raised one eyebrow and looked from Victor to me. And the realization that I was the one calling the shots here worked a dark blend of surprise and worry across his face.

What? Didn't I look like a leader? Sure, I'd given most of the decision-making powers in my father's business to Violet, but that wasn't because I couldn't run the business. It was because I didn't want to run the business.

Stotts knew I was the head of the Hounds in town.

But he obviously hadn't expected me to be the one calling the shots.

Yes, okay, I hadn't expected it either. Still, a little confidence would have been nice.

"Shame said there are police looking for us in the neighborhood," I said to bring Victor up-to-date. "Paul, do you know how many?"

He shook his head. "I wasn't informed, and it's not on any of the channels."

"Are you sure it was police, Shame?" I asked.

He shrugged one shoulder. "Looked like it to me. Lot of unmarked cars moving through the neighborhood like they had a certain purpose. Could be Authority."

"Either way, we can assume they'll have Hounds, or will be trying to track us," I said. "Zayvion needs to Unclose Cody, which means using magic. And if it is the Authority, they'll know your signature, Zay."

"Illusion?" Maeve offered.

"I think so," I said. "Or Block. But they know all of our signatures too."

"Let me," Terric said. "I still haven't turned in my resignation. They might think I'm on their side."

"They know by now," Victor said. "I'm sure they know very well that we have turned against them."

"Who's them?" Paul asked.

"The Authority," I said.

"Names? People?" Paul ticked on his fingers.

"Jingo Jingo is leading them now," I said.

"He's a piece of work," Paul said. "I ran his record after you gave me his name."

"And?"

"And I don't know why he hasn't been locked away in a cell for the last ten years."

"Did he kill children?"

Paul gave me a sharp look. "You knew about that?"

"Someone told me they thought he'd killed children. I didn't have any proof. Still don't."

"Neither, apparently, do the police in five counties," Paul said. "So he's the one in charge of this secret group who decides how people use magic?"

"Right now he is," I said. "And he'll be the one deciding whether they're going to stop the spread of the poison."

"He wants the poison to spread?" Paul asked.

Terric spoke up. "He doesn't think it's a problem that needs to be dealt with. Said it will just work itself out."

"You talked to him?" Paul asked.

"He called a meeting," Terric said. "I was there."

"I'll want to talk to you, Mr. Conley."

"Not now, but yes," Terric said. "And please, just Terric."

"Still need an Illusion," Shame reminded us. "I'll do it. Don't care if the bastards see me do it. Don't care if Jingo himself comes by." He cracked his knuckles, then dug in his pocket for a cigarette. The crystal in his chest was still burning a bright pink. "Might actually like it a little."

"Can you do it from a distance?" I asked. "Throw a spell, but make it look like it's coming from somewhere else?"

"Maybe." He glanced at Terric.

Terric and Shame were Soul Complements. No, they'd

never taken the test, and no, Shame hadn't outright admitted it. But the way they used magic together, the way they fell into natural sync with each other, made it obvious to everyone—well, everyone but Shame—that those two men could bend magic to their will if they wanted to.

Terric was considering Shame. "It's possible. In theory. We haven't tried it."

"No," Maeve said. "It's too dangerous and difficult. If it isn't done precisely, they'll see it for what it is, and just track it back to Shame. That is, if he's still standing from the backlash."

"We need a solution," I said. "We need to keep the magic Zayvion is using hidden. I'm open to suggestions, people."

"I'll do it," Paul said.

"Paul," Nola said, startled.

"They don't know I'm with you," he said to her, then to me. "They probably know how I cast magic, but they might think I'm looking into something else in the neighborhood. I'm out here fairly often."

It was a good idea, our best bet to buy enough time for Zay to Unclose Cody.

"Yes," I said. "What Illusion can you cast, and how long can you hold it?"

"Solitude is probably the easiest," he said.

"Nice choice," Victor said. "And it will take less magic than some of the others to support it."

Paul nodded. "Which is why I like it."

"Can you pull on magic out here?" I asked.

"I've done it before. Give me a minute."

He strode away a bit, then walked around us, pacing to calm his mind for the spell, and also sort of feeling for where the pull of magic seemed easiest, like an antenna tuning in on a signal.

He finally stopped about three yards away, closer to the river than the city that rose beyond the park's hills and up the streets.

"Cody," Zayvion said. "I need you to let go of Stone for a minute, but you can sit right there next to him."

"Monster is all broken now," Cody said, turning so he was sitting with his back against Stone's side.

Zay crouched down in front of him. "I know. We're going to fix him. And we need you to help us fix him. Do you want to do that? Fix monster?"

"Yes," Cody said, nodding vigorously.

"Allie," Zay said, not looking away from Cody. "Can we have the blanket?"

I handed Zay the quilt and watched as ghost Cody hesitantly stepped forward with it, and then stood next to the living Cody.

"So the first thing I'm going to do is help you get warm and comfortable," Zay said, draping the quilt around Cody's shoulders.

"I don't know how to fix monster," Cody said quietly, as if it were a secret between just him and Zayvion.

"That's okay. The older part of you knows how. And I'm going to help you hear him better. He'll know what to do to help monster."

"Okay," Cody said. "Older me is smart."

"So are you," Zayvion said.

He couldn't have given him better praise. Cody practically beamed. "I try," he said. "But sometimes it's hard."

"You do a good job," Zay said. "Nola's told me you are a lot of help to her."

He smiled over Zayvion's shoulder to where Nola stood.

Nola smiled back.

"Allie?" Zay said. "Is he ready?"

The ghost Cody sat down right next to himself. It was

strange to see the younger version of Cody sitting next to his older version.

"I'm ready," ghost Cody said. He took Cody's hand, and the living Cody smiled.

"He's ready," I said.

"Tell Stotts to cast his Illusion." Zay placed one hand down in the grass and settled, cross-legged, in front of Cody.

The rest of us stepped back, far enough we would be outside the edge of the spell Paul was already drawing.

The Disbursement he had cast hovered near his side, like a blue jellyfish balloon. A string tied the Disbursement to the ground at his feet, not to any part of his body. He was going to Proxy this spell so he didn't have to pay the price of pain for it.

Police officers had access to the Proxy pits.

I'd seen Solitude a few times. In some public places like libraries, coffee shops, churches. Places where people wanted the feeling of being alone in a crowd. But Paul used a modification to the spell.

He finished the glyph, pulled magic into it, and cast. The spell wrapped around Zayvion and the Codys and Stone.

Solitude usually just blocked something from casual notice. It wasn't that it turned anyone invisible; it just made looking straight at something less intriguing.

But this Solitude closed down like a proper Illusion, and where a moment before, I had seen Zayvion drawing a spell, slowly and carefully between him and Cody, now I just saw grass, a few trees, electric lamps, and the dark sky around.

I blinked a couple times and the spell ribboned apart just enough I could see through it to Zay and Cody.

"Does it look solid to you?" I asked Maeve, who was standing next to me.

She nodded. "I can't see them. Hayden?"

"It's tight. You know your magic, Detective Stotts."

"Thank you," Paul said. The glyph for the spell also remained as a black and green netting over the fingers of his right hand. "It should hold for an hour. I can Refresh it if I need to."

"How long do you think it will take Zayvion to Unclose him?" I asked Maeve.

She glanced at Victor. "Maybe an hour or so?"

"Maybe." But Victor didn't sound certain.

"Then I want everyone to stay here," I said. "Shame, I'll need one of the Pooh thingies."

"What you need is to get your head checked," he said. "Where do you think you're going?"

"Out. On the streets. To see who's looking for us. And to see if I can throw them off our trail."

"Oh, you're so very not doing that," Shame said.

"Allie," Maeve said. "I don't think that's a good idea."

"Listen," I said. "I can't do any good here. I'll take only a half hour. Just enough time to see if there are any Hounds in the area who can give me the lay of the land. We can't let anything stop Zay from what he's doing, and after that, we can't let anybody stop Cody from unlocking Stone."

"Allie," Nola said. "Maybe I should go with you."

"No. Cody's probably going to be really disoriented after this, and we'll need you to keep him calm. Terric, you and Shame can set up a perimeter by the parking lots. Anyone heads this way, tell Victor."

"Not going to happen," Terric said. "Shame and I are going with you."

I opened my mouth to argue, but from his bland deal-with-it look, I knew I wasn't going to get anywhere.

I turned to Victor. "I think it's a good idea to have more eyes out there. If you think some of us should set up out a little farther from this"—I pointed at the empty spot where Zayvion was Unclosing Cody—"would you see that it gets done?"

"Yes," he said. "Be careful."

"I'll be back in thirty minutes exactly."

I got walking, and after about six strides, Shame was on my right and Terric was on my left.

"Do we really have to do this together?" I asked.

"Why?" Shame asked. "Don't you like our company?"

"I'm looking for Hounds. I can do it faster alone."

"Alone and without magic," Terric mused, "you will also probably die faster."

"I know plenty of ways to defend myself without magic," I said.

"Right," Shame agreed. "Like with that gun you refuse to shoot."

"If you don't give that a rest, I will make you regret it."

"Or she could try empty threats," Terric suggested.

"What," Shame said, "like 'I'll sic my big scary pet gargoyle on you after my boyfriend and a mentally disabled ghost find the key to start his engine'?"

"It'd make me want to avoid eye contact with her," Terric said. "That's something, right?"

"Sure it is," Shame said. "Almost like being invisible. Was that your plan? Being so crazy no one would come near you?"

"Enough!" I said. "Fine. I can't use magic. But that doesn't mean I can't gag the both of you."

We were headed up the hill now, almost to where the street ran parallel to the park itself.

"Let's gag Terric first," Shame said. "Please? I'll help."

"You'd try," Terric said.

"Let's just all shut up," I said. "I need quiet so I can find a Hound. And so help me, if you say another word, I will use my gun."

And wonder of wonders, they both shut up and did as I said.

If I'd had the time, I would have pulled out my journal and made a note: Shame and Terric actually listened to me for once. Warn hell. There's a freeze coming.

# Chapter Twenty-two

"**D**o you see what I don't see?" I asked.

Terric, Shame, and I were crouched down behind a row of bushes that separated the park from the street. Even in daylight we would have been hard to spot, but since it was night, we were well camouflaged.

Terric turned toward me, his grin beneath that silver white hair obvious even in the dark. "Do you listen to what you're saying?"

"Yes," I said, trying to ignore his smile, but unable to. He was a good-looking man. A nice man, even though I'd seen him kill without pause or regret. But no matter what happened between him and Shame—hell, no matter what happened among all of us—I suddenly knew that I would always count Terric as one of my closest friends.

"I'm saying," I continued, looking back out at the street, "that there is something missing out there."

"Proper sewage treatment?" Shame asked.

"No. Well, yes, but no. The Veiled."

Both men were quiet as they studied the street.

"So," Shame said, "you don't see them?"

"I haven't seen any since we got to St. Johns."

"Probably because there is no magic here," Terric said. "There's nothing for them to feed from."

"Maybe," I agreed, "but that might mean this is a . . .

haven of sorts. Maybe a backup plan. If all else fails, maybe St. Johns can be a safe zone where magic can't hurt people."

"I see where you're going with this," Shame said. "Interesting. Don't know if it would work, or how long it would work. I think magic, and the poison, would find its way across the line eventually."

"The best plan is still for Stone to have some kind of hint for the cure," Terric said. "Though I'm a little fuzzy on how we plan to distribute the cure, if we actually do stumble on how to create a cure."

"One disaster at a time, Terric," I said. "We'll figure it out."

"So how long are we going to squat in the bushes?" Shame asked. "Because my ass is numb."

"You can go back and check on Zay," I suggested sweetly.

"Zay's fine," Shame said. "You'd know if he weren't. Soul Complements." He rolled his eyes.

"Don't start with me about Soul Complements, Flynn," I said. "You don't want to go down that road."

Shame couldn't help it—he glanced at Terric. To Terric's credit, he just scanned the street, as if he hadn't heard us.

"I thought you were looking for a Hound," Shame said.

"Was," I said, standing up. "Not anymore."

I strode around the bushes, doing what I could to stick to the shadows and stay silent. Since I was good at both those things, I did a damn fine job.

"Jack," I whispered.

Jack Quinn stopped, and made it look like he was throwing a cigarette to the sidewalk and rubbing it out with his boot. He did not turn and look at me. "There's trouble coming," he said. "Police. Ten units. On my heels. Make yourself scarce."

And then he was walking again, not hurrying, but I could tell in the brace of his shoulders that he was planning to make it somewhere, probably back to his car, in the shortest amount of time possible.

"That's what you wanted to know?" Shame said quietly next to me as we walked the opposite way from Jack down the street. "Bloody hells, Beckstrom, I told you that an hour ago."

"That's not all I wanted to know," I said. "I wanted to know if it's the police or the Authority after us, and how many. It's police—there's ten cars. Now I want to throw them off our trail."

"Are they even on our trail yet?" Shame asked.

"If they're any good, they are already at Mama's questioning her."

"So how?" Terric asked.

"That's what the police do," I said.

"No, how do we throw them off our trail?"

"They're looking for me. We want them away from the park. I'm going to bet Mama didn't finger us, so that means I just need to call in a favor. Either of you have a phone?"

Terric pulled one of those pay-as-you-go phones out of his pocket.

"Who are you calling?" he asked.

"Grant." I just hoped my friend was at the coffee shop. I dialed his number. It rang twice, then picked up.

"Get Mugged," Grant said.

"You have my credit card number, right?" I asked.

"I do," he said.

"I'd like a large cup of coffee. Black. Run it on my card," I said. "And when the police show up, tell them I took it and walked west."

"Everything okay?"

"It's going to be soon. The stuff you've heard—it isn't true."

"I know."

The knot in my chest loosened a little. Grant was a good guy, and he'd stuck by me through a lot of things, even back in my Hounding days before I tangled with the Authority. If it weren't for him, I'd probably be in jail right now. Or worse.

I hated that he might have thought I really had embezzled from my dad's corporation. And whatever other things the news might be saying about me.

"Thank you," I said. "Be careful. I owe you for this."

"There's a play coming to town. Buy me tickets?"

"For opening night."

And then we hung up.

"That's pretty smart," Shame said. "Think it will do any good?"

"My card was frozen. They'll be watching for me to try to access my accounts. And now I just did. Kind of."

"Do you think Grant can handle it?"

"Without a doubt." Even though I was worried he'd get in trouble lying to the police, he was already in on this with us. He might not know exactly what we were trying to do, but he had let us escape through the Shanghai Tunnels beneath his building.

The sound of sirens started up. We kept walking down the street and were just about to take the corner around the bushes when a police cruiser rolled down the street.

Shame lifted his hand to cast something—probably an Illusion.

"Don't," I said. "No one uses magic out here."

He shifted his motion so that he was digging in his shirt pocket for a cigarette, pulled it out.

"Look happy, children," he said as he lit the cigarette.

"Bar," Terric said. "Casey's. Thought we should walk to the bus stop. Been there since eleven. Headed home."

"You're out of your head," Shame said loudly. "The day the indie music scene is over in Portland is the day the world ends."

"You just can't appreciate the change the Internet has brought about," Terric said without missing a beat. "One, there's a lot more people sitting in front of their screens than there are venues for musicians, and two, nobody wants to see groups live anymore anyway."

"Horseshit." Shame actually sounded offended.

"And we're still arguing about this because?" I asked.

I knew why we were arguing about it. Because if that cruiser rolled down the windows, or decided to check us out, we needed to be acting like three friends out for the night, not three silent, light-avoiding people trying not to be seen by the cops.

Hiding in plain sight. An old Hound trick. Made my palms sweat every time.

"Because," Shame said, "Ter here has some kind of stick up his ass—not that *that's* news—but now he thinks the digital revolution has killed live music."

"Oh, go cry on your grandpa's Gibson," Terric said. "I didn't say it killed live music; it's revolutionized it."

"It—," Shame started.

"Which is a good thing, you idiot," Terric said louder. "Times have changed and they've changed for the better. Grow up and take a look around you at the real world for once. At how real people are living. For that matter, how about you give this 'living' thing a try? Blinding yourself with angst doesn't make you mysterious or broody or strong. It just makes you blind."

"I'm . . . living," Shame said, something like hurt in his eyes.

"No, you're not," Terric said calmly. "Not like you used to, Shame. Not like you used to."

The hurt in Shame's eyes shifted to something else. Looked a little like a moment of clarity.

"Enough," I said so that this didn't go any further. "If you two don't drop this, I swear I'm going to tie your wrists together and make you fight it out."

They both paused, and turned to look at me.

"Do we get weapons?" Shame asked.

I nodded. "Bowling balls."

They both started laughing. I couldn't help it. So did I.

Yes, even though we were in the middle of trying not to get caught, jailed, killed. There had been more than a little truth in Terric's "pretend" outburst. Shame knew it. I knew it. Terric knew it. I think it was something Terric had needed to say to Shame for a long time. Funny how those sorts of things showed up when the end of the world was near.

"Is there a weight limit?" Terric finally asked, wiping at his face.

"Oh, hell, no," Shame said. "If I'm going to bludgeon you to death with a bowling ball, I'm taking a sixteen-pounder into the ring. Get it over with fast."

"Humane of you," Terric noted.

"Straight from my heart." Shame tapped his chest.

The car was almost alongside us now.

We were walking again.

"So it's settled?" I said. "No more arguing . . . over music," I added. "We move on to something more important."

"What's more important than music?" Terric asked.

"Well," Shame said, pointing with his cigarette, "there's sex."

Terric grinned. "I'll give you that. So there's one thing

more important than music. Want to talk about your sex life, girlfriend?"

"No," I said, "I do not."

"Saw you smooching up your man," he pressed. "Hot."

"He means your man," Shame said, "not you. You aren't his . . . type."

"He does have a pair of shoulders on him," Terric mused.

Shame shook his head. "He'd never."

"Oh, I know it," Terric said. "I wouldn't either. Still, gotta appreciate the workmanship."

"It's all gym."

"Are you jealous?" Terric looked Shame up and down. "Would a workout kill you?"

Shame sighed dramatically. "Yes. Deadly allergic to the things."

"Well, no need to worry," Terric said. "I'm sure there are plenty of girls who like scrawny Irishmen."

"Oh, you did not just go there," Shame said.

"And now we are changing *that* subject," I said a little louder. "Let's go back to music."

The car slowed, and we all looked over at it, just like any normal people who were out on the street would do if a cop car pulled up next to them.

I thought, for a brief second, that the car would just keep driving. Instead it stopped.

So did we.

The window lowered. Shame stepped forward, and leaned down toward the policeman.

"Evening," Shame said, keeping his cigarette out to one side so the smoke didn't waft into the car.

"What are you folks doing out tonight?" The officer had a wide, flat mouth, a nose that had been broken more than once, and a buzz cut that left nothing but a dusting of black over his skull. The bags under his eyes were carrying their own luggage.

"Walking home," Shame said. "Thought we'd catch the bus."

"You been in the park?"

Shame glanced over his shoulder at the park as if just noticing it was there. "No. We just closed out Casey's. Why? Is there a problem?"

"We're looking for someone. Woman, about the height of your friend there, about her age."

Shame shrugged. "What's her name?"

"Allison Beckstrom." The cop unbuckled his seat belt and stepped out of the car.

"She's that rich girl, on the news, right?" Shame asked.

"That's right," the policeman said as he walked past Shame. "Miss? Can I have a word with you?"

"Sure." I had both my hands in my jacket pocket and put on my best confused smile. I walked over to him but stopped short of putting my face in the brighter light from the electric lamppost. I squinted at him through my glasses. "What's going on?"

"What's your name?" he asked.

"Amy Smith," I said without hesitation. I wasn't usually any good at lying. But in the dark, this late at night, with, oh, my life and pretty much everyone else's lives on the line, it came easily. Go figure.

"Can I see your ID, please?"

"Sure." I took my hands out of my pocket, and made a show of checking my back pockets and front pockets. "I had it," I said, thinking furiously, trying to come up with a way out of this that wouldn't involve any of us— including the police officer—getting hurt.

"I had it in my hand, and I put it in my pocket." I paused, like I just realized I didn't have it on me. "God, I must have left it back at the bar." I looked up at the police officer. "I could—we could go back and get it. I'm sure someone is still there."

"That won't be necessary," he said. "You are under arrest, Ms. Beckstrom."

This was not the first time in my life I regretted my father being a well-known and very public figure who lived his life in the spotlight. That cop had known all along it was me; he was just stringing me along, and had nicely gotten me to perjure myself.

Damn it all.

"What?" I asked. "I don't understand." Think, Beckstrom, think. Or the nice police officer who was just doing his job might end up dead.

There was no way I was going to let him drag me off to jail.

"Hold on, Officer," Terric said. "I think you made a mistake. Her name's Amy."

He wasn't listening. "You two keep your hands where I can see them. I'm going to take her down to the department and ask her a few questions, that's all." The police officer reached for the handcuffs at his belt.

Terric and Shame kept their hands out in the open, but exchanged a look.

Yes, *that* kind of look. The one that Zay and I probably tossed at each other when we were reading the other's thoughts. Another advantage to being a Soul Complement, though I didn't think I'd ever seen Shame and Terric use it.

I didn't know what they were planning, but would lay money it involved a lot of hurt to the man.

"Wait," I said.

Too late. Terric and Shame both said one guttural word and the cop froze.

"Nice night, isn't it?" Terric said.

The honey overtones of Influence covered those words. I hadn't even seen him draw the glyph for it. Maybe he didn't have to. The Authority had a lot of spells that were triggered off words, though I hadn't had a chance to learn many of them.

What I did know was that Shame was pulling on magic in a hard, even stream, the fingers of his left hand splayed toward the ground where red and black light lifted up out of the soil to his fingertips, and turned pure black as it arced to the hand Terric held behind his back.

Terric's fingers were pointed at the ground, and the black magic he accepted from Shame turned white, then white gold, as it rained like water off his fingers back into the earth where Shame drew it up again.

They were recycling magic, looping it. I'd never seen anyone do that before.

And that was because there were damn few Soul Complements in the world. And the few I had known were dead.

Shame and Terric were using magic together unconsciously, effortlessly. Both of them were outstanding magic users. But together they became something more, something transcendent.

They were beautiful to watch.

Terric traced another spell. I knew that spell. It was Close.

Shame's right hand still held the cigarette, but he was also drawing a spell. Some kind of Illusion or Diversion. Not that it would help. Any Hound worth a paycheck would know who cast these spells. If the cops figured out Shame and Terric were with me, or if the Authority got nosy in the neighborhood, we were leaving a big ol' neon sign announcing we had been here.

Which was pretty much the opposite of our goal.

The police officer still wasn't moving.

"You're feeling calm, for the first time in a long, long while," Terric said as he walked over to him. "And you want to get back into your car and continue looking for Allie Beckstrom, because you haven't seen her. You did get out of your car to take a leak, though."

The police officer nodded, and scratched at his head. Then he walked back to the car, behaving as if he couldn't see us standing there. He got in the car, checked his watch.

Terric twisted his wrist and sent the Close spell racing to the officer's temple.

It struck him. He didn't jerk or show any sign of being hit. It didn't look like it hurt as it sank into his head until it was gone.

Terric didn't move, though he was breathing a little hard, enduring pain.

Shame shifted to stand closer to him, and Terric's breathing evened out some as Shame shared some of his pain.

The magic still coursed between them, from earth to hand to hand to earth. Then they simultaneously placed their right fingers on their left shoulders and drew their hands down in a slash to the right. The magic they both used crackled and broke, a flash of white, a flash of black, and then just wisps of smoke rising into the air.

I blinked, realizing I'd been mesmerized. Without the magic they had been casting, the night felt cold.

Soul Complements. They could make magic break its own rules. And they could do it beautifully.

Shame swayed and took a step backward to steady himself, his eyes wide as he stared at Terric, who was looking a little shell-shocked himself.

That was when I knew it for sure. They had never really cast magic together before. They'd cast it at the same time, but this was different. Just here, just now, they had been connected, a part of the other, just like Zay and I were connected. Well, maybe not exactly the same, but similar.

"Walk," Shame said, doing so. "Now."

Terric took in a deep breath, then exhaled. "Oh," he said, staring at Shame's quickly retreating back.

"Walk," Shame said again.

We did so. I glanced back. The officer put the car in drive and started down the street away from us.

"What did you do to the police officer?" I asked Terric.

"Influence," he said a little distractedly.

Since he hadn't taken the time to cast a Disbursement spell, magic snapped off him like hundreds of electric shocks. I didn't know how long he'd have to pay that price, but I winced in sympathy.

I hated when I forgot to set Disbursements.

"You Closed him too, didn't you?" I asked.

"Just his memory of us. He'll remember stopping to check the bushes and street with his flashlight. He won't remember us."

"You used magic. In St. Johns," I said. "People are going to notice. And they'll see your signature. Shame's signature too."

"No," Shame said.

I glanced back at where we'd been standing.

There were no magical ashes left behind, no mark of a spell. I knew I could see magic with my bare eyes, and I didn't sense a hint that there had been any magic worked there at all.

"How?" I said.

"Death magic," Shame answered. "Transference. I gave back as much, traded for what we used. And then I threw a Cleanup spell after us."

"You gave what? Traded what?"

"My own energy. Mine. Me. Just me." But he sounded less and less certain of that with each word.

"You gave up your energy, your life energy, for that? For an encounter with a police officer? How much? How many years? Days?"

"Allie," Terric said softly.

"No. We could have found a different way. You didn't have to give up your life, Shame." Yes, I was a little panicky. That crystal in Shame's chest was constantly eating away at him. It also could be fed by the life energy of other things, but it didn't draw in as much energy as it took from Shame.

And now, to have him losing even more of his life for this? For one police officer?

"It wasn't just him," Terric said.

"Great. So you gave up some of your life too? It's not bad enough that one of my friends is making stupid decisions, but now it's two?"

Terric placed his hand on my arm.

I stopped, even though Shame was walking forward like a man determined to make it to the finish line.

"We used magic," Terric said. "Shame and I used magic. Together. Each gave a little energy. Each took a little energy, from magic. From each other."

"And? I've seen you cast spells together before."

"Not that way," Terric said. "Not as Soul Complements."

"Oh." I knew that. I just didn't know how that figured into it all. "Are you . . . Is he okay?" I finally managed.

He looked over at Shame, and even at this distance, I could see Shame tug his shoulders back as if he could feel the brush of Terric's gaze and was trying to rid himself of it.

"We're good. Just . . . I didn't expect . . . I don't think he expected it to be . . ." He shrugged.

"To be what?" I asked.

"Nice." He shook his head and smiled down at his shoe. "So nice," he said quietly.

"Was it . . . sexual?"

He looked back up at me, met my gaze. "No. It was . . . intimate. But not in a sexual way."

"Do you think it's going to be a problem?" I asked.

Terric started walking again. "You know how Shame is."

"So, you're saying, yes, it's going to be a problem?"

"Absolutely." Terric smiled. Satisfied. Curious. Content. I'd never seen any of those expressions on his face when he was talking about Shame. "And I wouldn't have it any other way."

# Chapter Twenty-three

Z ayvion was still sitting in front of Cody, the alive
Cody, who still leaned on Stone. And Stone was still
a statue.

But the spell that Paul had cast around them was
gone, which made sense. No one in the group was using
magic, so nothing they were doing needed to be hidden.

I didn't see the ghost Cody anywhere. And if Zayvion
had done his job right, I never would again. Cody wasn't
two people, wasn't dead and living, wasn't broken anymore. Cody was just Cody.

The sirens grew distant, heading out of St. Johns,
heading, I thought, toward Get Mugged.

That didn't mean there weren't police in the area. But
at least now there were fewer units, and a reason to believe I was not in the vicinity. That was something.

If we kept things quiet, tried not to use too much
magic too obviously, we might just get Stone unlocked
enough that he was mobile. Mobile would be good. We
could get him out of the middle of the open park and
somewhere out of sight.

And then Cody could unlock him, and we could see if
putting that magic in him wasn't just a waste of time. See
if he had some kind of filtration device worked into his
inner gears and spells.

Hopefully we could separate the poison from the

magic and provide enough data to better minds, scientific minds. I didn't know what we'd need to do after that. Take it to the hospitals? Throw it in the wells? Tap the main network lines? Whatever it was, we'd see that it got done.

The electric lamps flickered. Shame glanced up, then turned on his heel so he could look down the line of streetlamps to the city.

"That's . . . not good," he said.

And then the lights all went out.

Zayvion stood. So did Davy. Everyone else, Maeve, Victor, Paul, Hayden, was already on their feet. Shame shifted to look south, away from the area where we had parked.

Rising out of the thick blackness, coming from the other parking lot, was a group of people. An army. Walking our way, easy as you please. As if they owned this park. As if they owned this city. As if they owned us.

"Now we have a problem," Terric said quietly.

I didn't need electricity to know who was coming our way. Just enough moonlight off the clouds showed me their faces.

It was the Authority, people I knew. People I didn't know. Marching toward us. Marching to take us down.

"Damn it to hell," Hayden breathed.

My thoughts exactly. We had two choices. Stand here against them, or run and leave Stone for them to use.

And lose our chance to cleanse magic.

"If you want to retreat, do it now," I said. "I'm not going to let them take Stone. We need to get Cody out of here."

"No," Cody said. He stood and placed one hand on top of Stone's head. "I won't go. I need to . . ." He paused, and then, in what sounded like a much younger, frightened voice, "Monster?" He picked up the quilt and draped it over Stone's back, trying to tuck it around his wings.

It took time to sort through the changes of being Unclosed. I was surprised Cody could even talk.

"Nola," I said, "get him out of here. Paul, get her out of here."

"Cody," Nola said. "We need to go now. Come with me."

Cody looked over at her, shook his head. "I'm sorry," he said in a much older voice. "I can't. I need you to hold my hand."

Nola walked over to him and took his hand. "It's going to be okay," she said.

"I know." And then Cody pulled on magic. So much magic.

It leaped to him, dancing, bright. Down from the sky. Up through the ground. A shattering of color that surrounded him and Stone like a glass cathedral, a holy fortress. A spinning, dizzy rush of magic, that twirled and slipped and melted like pieces of the heavens falling into a great design to create a wall, a barrier of magic.

Then the magic went black and flickered with opal fire.

Thunder roared, so loud, my ears cracked with pain. I put my hands over my ears, until the thunder faded.

And when I pulled my hands away, only the softest chime of bells in the wind remained.

We were all looking at Cody. Well, we were all looking at where he had been. Now there was nothing but a spinning curtain of black, cut through with crystal shards of rainbow. That was a lot of magic—a hell of a lot of magic to pull here in magicless St. Johns.

Paul was reaching for Nola. "Nola, no!"

"Wait!" I said. "Don't."

Too late. Paul could not reach her. He slammed into the magic, now as solid as granite, no longer spinning, no

longer shot with color. Nothing but a black obsidian obe-
lisk stood in the dark of night, sober as a grave marker.

"Nola!" Paul yelled again.

I stepped up and pressed my hand against the wall.
Solid, smooth as silk over steel. And warm.

*She is alive,* Dad said in my head. *So is Cody. This is a
very old spell of Guardianship. Nothing will break those
walls until the user has finished his spells.*

"She's okay," I told Paul. "Cody's okay too. When he
finishes the spell, when he unlocks Stone, this will come
down. And I want you right here waiting to catch them.
Can you do that for me? Grab them—take them and
Stone away as soon as this wall goes down?"

He nodded. "You couldn't drag me off this field."

"Good."

I turned back to the crowd approaching us. Holy hells,
there had to be sixty people. "Who's staying?" I asked.

"We're all staying," Zayvion said. He strode over to
me, a looming tower of muscle, anger, and grace. Not a
shred of fear on his face, not a fleck of worry in his burning gold eyes.

His lips curved in a grim smile as he turned to me.
"We've got a world to save, remember. None of us is doing that alone."

He kissed me, and I kissed him back. Hot, deep. Wanting so much more. Promising we'd have more. Promising
we'd have tomorrow.

Then he pulled away and took his place beside me at
my right.

Shame stood at my left, Terric beside him. Maeve and
Hayden stood next to them. On my other side, beyond
Zayvion, were Victor, Collins, Davy, and, near the wall at
our back, Paul.

We were ten strong. Ten standing against the world.

No. We were ten standing for the world. Standing to

protect the world. Standing to uphold our vows and protect the innocent.

"Do we have a plan?" Victor asked.

"Paul's going to watch for that spell to come down and take Cody and Nola somewhere safe," I said. "We're going to make sure Cody has time to unlock Stone."

"Not much of a plan," Shame said. "I like it."

The crowd stopped walking about a hundred yards from us, the line of trees and bridge at their back. They spread out to stand shoulder to shoulder, at least twenty wide, and spaced far enough apart that everyone had room to cast magic.

Movement at the farthest edge of the group caught my eye.

Three women—the Georgia sisters, out of Seattle—pulled magic across the deadline of St. Johns. A punch of air made my ears pop. The sisters cast a bubble of Illusion around the park.

Just as they had done when we had stood in this park while the wild magic storm raged around us. No one would look twice at what was going on down here. No one would step through that wall of Illusion. No one would see the magic we were about to cast, the war we were about to wage.

We were on our own. Completely.

"Allison Beckstrom," a familiar low voice called out from the crowd. "Are you still standing in our way, child?"

The crowd parted, making way for a huge mass of a man to pass through them.

Jingo Jingo.

He was leaning on his cane, but other than a slight limp, he looked as strong—no, stronger than I'd ever seen him.

And no wonder. Where once I had seen the ghosts of children covering him like a robe, now I saw the Veiled.

Hungry, angry, black holes where eyes should be, the Veiled were watercolored visions of dead magic users, swarming around Jingo like his own personal entourage, like a cloud of serrated teeth in mouths that moaned in agony.

Maybe that was where all the Veiled in St. Johns had gone. Haunting Jingo Jingo.

Or maybe Jingo Jingo was keeping these Veiled close to him for a reason. He was a Death magic user. Maybe the plague suited his plans just fine.

He stopped on a slight rise in the middle of the crowd.

Not just a crowd. Those were members of the Authority. People I had fought with, people I had fought for.

I saw the twins Carl and La with their scythes, my dad's accountant, Ethan Katz, who had traded out his briefcase for a halberd. Dr. Fisher wasn't carrying a weapon, but Sunny, who was Davy's girlfriend, though they'd probably taken that memory away from her, had a long knife in each hand.

My heart sank when I saw Kevin, Violet's bodyguard and Zayvion's friend, at one side near the back of the group. I had hoped he could have stayed out of this, and instead been with Violet protecting her and my little brother.

Bartholomew's Truth spell bitch, Melissa Whit, had a shotgun in one hand and an ax at her hip, and was staring straight at me and grinning. There were more unfamiliar faces from Portland, and probably Seattle.

I recognized Paige Iwamoto, the Blood magic user from Seattle, with her knife and a whip; the handsome Nik Pavloski, who carried a sword; the family-man Closer Joshua Romero, who had a gun tucked in his belt, but both his hands free.

Many of those standing against us were people I liked. People I did not want to hurt. People who had had their memories Closed by Bartholomew. People who believed that by following Jingo Jingo, and taking us down, they were doing the right thing.

"Magic has been poisoned," I said, my voice plenty loud enough to carry across to where Jingo Jingo stood. "And it's killing everyone in this city. We think we've found a way to purify it. Bartholomew wouldn't listen to us; he didn't care that people were dying or that the—the epidemic was spreading as more and more innocent people were poisoned by magic—"

"And so you shot him," Jingo said. "Shot a man because he wasn't doing things your way. Do you think you have the knowledge to be the head of the Authority? Do you think you can make the decisions that need to be made to keep magic safe in this town? Do you think you can kill a man just because he's in your way?"

"If you stand between me and my goal tonight, I think we're going to find out," I said.

"Now, now, little angel," Jingo said. "We're not here to hurt you. We've been watching you all along—don't think we haven't. We saw you go to the Life well, then the warehouse. We saw you out Tracking, and we sure as much saw Zayvion Jones throw that Grounding spell that nearly broke a street. We've been holding out hope that you'd turn yourself around and realize you've been used. There's still time for your redemption, Allison. But that time's running short.

"You can see you are outnumbered. But I am a reasonable man. I'm going to give you a chance to listen to reason. To listen to the things I know, things your daddy never wanted you to know. I've been watching him all your life, Allison. Watching you all your life. I know what he's been using you for, know just how much he's been using you. Your memories, your soul. Even your body, God have mercy."

*Don't listen to him,* Dad said in my mind. *He sharpens his lies with an edge of truth so they cut deeper. He doesn't know me, Allison. He doesn't know what I've done, what I've sacrificed to see that you are safe. That magic is safe.*

Jingo put one hand up to his ear. "Is that your daddy I hear talking to you now? Bet he's saying as how I don't know what he's been doing to you all your life. Bet he's saying I don't know him, what he is. But I do. Oh, yes, I do, Daniel. I know you. Know what you've done to your little girl."

*Lies,* Dad said. *He only wants to stop you from doing what you know is right. From cleansing magic.*

"What's he done?" I asked. Frankly, I didn't give a damn what Jingo Jingo thought my dad had done to me. Right now, it was the last thing I wanted to know. But if it would keep Jingo Jingo talking, and give Cody more time to unlock Stone, then we could chat about every crappy day of my crappy daughter-father relationship.

"When you were a child, it was terrible things," Jingo said. "Things the law would have put him away for— things the Authority itself tried to put him away for. Things we might have had to kill him for. But he had his money and he had his Influence and he had no soul. No soul at all."

People were shifting, spreading out to the sides of the Illusion barrier, while Jingo talked. There were so many of them. They could pull on so much more magic than we could. It would take them only one hard rush to bring us down.

"Keep an eye on the edges," I said quietly.

"We got it," Hayden said.

None of us had our weapons drawn. I didn't see any indication that the Authority was going to make a move yet. But it was just a matter of time.

We were severely outnumbered, outpowered. There

was no option of retreat unless we wanted to leave Stone, Nola, and Cody to their mercy. Jingo Jingo's mercy.

And one twitch, one flick of a wrist, one glint of a spell, would set this whole thing off like a powder keg.

"You want to know the saddest thing, Allison Angel?" Jingo Jingo took a step forward and so did the other sixty people surrounding him.

"Sure," I said, reaching out for Zayvion's hand as he was reaching for mine. "What's the saddest thing?"

"Your daddy's pushed himself inside you tight as a man can be. He's made you think he's doing it for your own good. That he's helping you. That he doesn't want to be there, but now that he is, you need him and you need to listen to him. The saddest thing," Jingo said, taking another step, "is you know in your heart he's been using you, treating you like nothing more than a napkin he's going to throw away when he's done wiping his mouth. You won't get rid of him because you think the pain is worth the good he's promising. The good he says he can help you do for the world."

"You're wrong," I said. But my heart was pounding, my mouth dry. There was truth in his words, but I didn't know how much.

"You think that Boy of Mama's would have almost died if it weren't for enemies your father made? You think those disks Violet invented would have been stolen and used to turn Greyson into a beast if your daddy hadn't wanted them to? You think your daddy didn't know Zayvion, the one man you ever loved, would stand up and be killed fighting Greyson? You think it was your idea to go clear on over into death to save Mr. Jones? No. It was your father's idea, Daniel's idea. Because he needed a way to fulfill his dealings with Mikhail. He needed to give to him that little bit of magic you used to hold inside you—magic he stole from you, his baby girl.

And when you came back into life, he made sure you opened the way for Leander and Isabelle to come on over into this living world so they could possess Greyson, and kill Chase."

Collins nodded, and Victor was frowning. Even Maeve seemed to know some of this was true. She glanced down the line at me, though I don't think she was looking for my reaction. I think she was looking for Dad's reaction.

He remained silent in my mind. Didn't say a single word to refute what Jingo Jingo was saying. It was terrifying.

"Your daddy wanted all this," Jingo Jingo said, holding his arms out wide. "Your daddy planned all this. He bargained away Shamus Flynn—the son of the man he killed—to let Mikhail get up inside him and use him, like he's using you. Even your friend Davy is half alive and dying fast because of your daddy and his driving need to take over the world, take over magic, light and dark, and rule it all for himself.

"And you, Allison. His own daughter. You think you've been making your own choices all your life? Making up your own mind? He owns your mind. He took your memories, so many memories, it's a wonder you have a mind left at all. He stole away anything he didn't want you to know and fed you full of the things he wanted you to believe. Made up memories for you that suited his needs. And when you had nothing of your own left, he moved into you, into those places he'd made for himself.

"So he could use you. So he could get what he wanted—no matter what price you would have to pay. And you know what price you're paying? Your life. You've paid your life for his ambition.

"He's left you poor. Put that vile man Collins into

your life to give you the gun he told you to take so you could kill his enemy Bartholomew Wray. You are a killer now, Allison Beckstrom. He made you that. And it don't matter whose law you're trying to follow—you know it's wrong. You know it's a sin to walk up to a man and shoot him in the head. But your daddy don't care. Your daddy wanted you to take Bartholomew down. To turn against the Authority and take anyone in your path—in your daddy's path—out of the way. So he could rule magic. So he could wrest it from the Authority's hands and use it for what he wants. Eternal life."

Hayden swore softly. I knew what he was thinking. This made sense. This all made sense.

And still, my father was silent.

"And you've been a good little girl and did just what he wanted you to do. All this time. All your life. You know your daddy don't ever do a single thing without thinking out the ways it will work to his advantage. He didn't want you born, but he's turned you to his advantage. You've been a fine tool for him. Fine. But he's near worn you out.

"Now's the time for you to walk away from that devil of a father. Step away, Allison. We'll help you. We'll get him out of you for good. Then you can let the Authority take care of magic the right way, the proper way. Then you can let the Authority take care of the world. That hasn't ever been your place, to try to save the world. A sweet little Hound like you? No, you weren't meant for that. Not at all. No matter what your daddy tells you."

I was trembling, sweating. Angry, confused, and, yes, frightened. Why didn't Dad defend himself? Why didn't he tell me these were all lies?

Zayvion squeezed my hand, and I held on to him, focusing on that contact to pull me away from the fear, the doubt, the horror of a lifetime of being used by my father. Even if Jingo Jingo wasn't right about everything, it was easy to believe he could be. Could be right about it all.

"Interesting theory," I said. "But I think you haven't considered one thing. Maybe I've been using him."

Jingo's head snapped up and he stared at me for a long moment. Apparently he hadn't wondered if I was the upper hand in this creep-a-thon my dad and I had going.

And from the sudden still focus from my father, he hadn't ever considered it either.

Then Jingo Jingo smiled, a big wide grin that glowed like a flash of moonlight against his dark skin, against the dark of the night.

"Oh, I don't think so, girl," Jingo said. "You don't have it in you to be that kind of cruel. Not like your daddy."

I smiled back. "Maybe I don't have to. My father and I see eye to eye on a lot of things right now. Maybe he and I have made deals. Contracts that cancel any kind of deal you negotiated with him. Deals that cut you out, and expose you for what you are, Jingo. A rapist. An abuser. A murderer. A monster who's not fit to breathe."

"You gonna throw your lot in with your daddy?" Jingo Jingo asked. "You going to do that now? Can't you see who's holding the power on this field?"

He spread his hands, the left still holding his cane, to include the masses around him, behind him. Masses willing to follow his orders. Willing to kill us.

"You know your life, the life of your pretty friend Nola, your boy Davy there, and even your man Zayvion, are all in your hands right now. You make the wrong choice and they're gonna die, Allison. Gonna die real hard."

"You could leave," I said. "We don't have to do this. If you take your people and leave St. Johns, we can all walk out of this alive."

Jingo Jingo chuckled. "You think you got any chips

left to bargain with? You've lived this long only because of the goodness of my heart, Allison. Because I believe you got steered wrong by your father. But at just a flick of my fingers"—he flicked his fingers, and I flinched—"this whole town, you and all your friends, are gonna fall beneath me."

"We won't follow you," I said. "We won't let innocent people die because of the decisions Bartholomew made. And we won't let innocent people die because of the decisions you make."

"I never said I wanted innocent people to die," Jingo Jingo said. "Not ever once did I say so. There will be casualties. Always is in a war. But you tell me where the simulacrum is, and I let you walk out of this park still breathing."

*Don't trust him,* Dad said.

So now he wanted to talk?

"What simulacrum?" I asked. I had no idea what he was talking about.

"That's the question, now, isn't it?" Jingo Jingo said. "That's the thing I want to know. You ask your daddy for me. Tell him if he gives me the simulacrum, I'll let you live."

*He wants Stone,* Dad said.

*Stone's a simulacrum?*

*Stone is an Animate. Jingo thinks I have a simulacrum hidden away. Some legendary thing that will promise the user power over all magic. I don't have anything like that, but if he sees Stone holding dark and light magic and filtering it, he'll think that's what he is. He'll take him. He'll destroy him. And he'll destroy our only chance to stop the spread of poison.*

"He doesn't have a simulacrum," I said to Jingo Jingo. "He lied to you."

Jingo Jingo chuckled. "That what he told you, child?"

"That's the truth."

"Well, then. We just might need to see what you've got hid behind that wall at your back."

I drew my sword. As if we were one, we all drew our weapons.

"That's not going to happen," I said. "Turn and leave. Or die."

Jingo Jingo laughed. "There's ten of you. There's sixty of us. I'm not going to be the one dying this day."

And just then there was a movement behind us. I wondered, briefly, if Cody had finished unlocking Stone, wondered if the wall had fallen, wondered if Nola was stepping through, unprotected, unguarded.

Everyone in front of us noticed the movement too.

As well they should.

Because it wasn't the wall falling. Stone wasn't unlocked and free.

I glanced over my shoulder and saw the Hounds, my Hounds, forty at least, men and women, people I knew well, like Jack and Bea and Sid, and people I'd worked with only briefly over the years, fading out of the shadows, and storming this way. They carried baseball bats, guns, rifles, knives, axes. They were ragged, hard-edged, grim. And they came to stand behind me, at my back, ready to take my fight on as their fight.

Because Hounds never abandoned their own.

My people. I had never felt so fiercely proud of who I was, who I had chosen to be. Had never been so proud of whom I counted as my friends.

"Go to hell," I said to Jingo Jingo.

Jingo Jingo shook his big head. "Such a shame." He turned and walked away, toward the back of the crowd.

A low murmur of chanting from the Authority built to a chorus of voices. Voices raised against us, voices raising magic to kill us.

"They don't touch the wall," I said to the Hounds as we spread out and took our stand. "They don't touch anything or anyone inside that wall. We kill anyone who gets too close. Understand?"

"We understand," Jack said, his voice low, but carrying on the still night air. "Kill anyone who gets too close."

I heard the snick of a lighter catching flame. "This ought to be fun," Shame said, lighting a cigarette. "I call dibs on that piece of shit Jingo Jingo." He unzipped his coat and pulled out a long knife and a gun.

"Do you care how we kill them?" Davy asked. His voice was even, strong.

But I knew he had to see Sunny out there in the crowd. Yes, she was a member of the Authority who was standing against us. She was also the woman he loved.

Just like the others gathered were my friends, and friends of all of us.

Or at least they used to be.

"Unless they are breaking down that wall, wound; don't kill," I said. "Knock them out, stop them, hamstring them. Some of those people are my friends. Our friends. Good people. They just don't understand that they're following a madman."

"But if they touch the wall?" Bea asked from where she stood next to Jack.

"We're going to make sure they don't get that far."

# Chapter Twenty-four

We stood, fifty strong against the Authority, city to our left, the river to our right, the empty parking lot behind us. The Authority was holding about eighty yards in front of us, each of them with one hand free to use magic, the other around his or her weapon of choice. There was a lot of manicured grass between us, a few trees at the edges, and the St. Johns Bridge spiraling up to the night sky behind them. No one was moving. No one was throwing magic, other than the Georgia sisters, who stood at the rear of their group, holding the bubble of Illusion around us all.

It was like teetering on the edge of a fall, breathless, calm, knowing the storm was about to hit and swallow us whole. I didn't want this to happen. But there was nothing I could do to stop it.

The ground beneath my feet shook. Hayden swung his broadsword, the shotgun in his other hand, and yelled, casting a spell I'd never seen before. It rose up like a huge wave, a barrier that grew and grew, then crested, falling, rushing toward the mob in front of us.

And when it fell, it sucked down all the sound. All the chanting, all the air. At least twenty people fell. But the rest, all of them, came rushing across the field toward us, throwing magic, so much, so fast, my throat burned from the heat of it; my eyes watered from the sparks; my skin seared with the acid of spells.

No magic for me. If I cast, I'd pass out. And then I'd be killed.

"Stay back," Zayvion said to me. "Behind us."

"This is my fight," I said. "I can handle it."

He turned to me, grabbed my arm. "It's all of our fight. We need you to keep us together, Allie. The Hounds won't listen to my commands or follow anyone else. Hell, you're the only one all of us will listen to. We need you behind us, directing, keeping us alive."

Sweet hells. He was right. I hated it, but he was right.

"Don't you go hero and die on me," I said.

He smiled. "Never that."

And then he waded into the fray, sword in one hand, spells in the other, running across the field to meet the mass, mowing people down as he went. I didn't look to see if the people who fell at his feet were alive or just knocked out. I didn't have time to count, to wonder, to worry. Mike Barham, a magic user from Seattle, and a man Shame hated, came at Zayvion with magic wrapping both his hands like gold gauntlets.

Zay Blocked his first attack, then swung his sword, cleaving through the gold fire burning in the air between them. He countered with a black glyph that spun a net to tangle Mike's hands, and then Zay stepped in, and clubbed him with the hilt of his sword. Mike crumpled to the ground.

Hayden charged into the crowd and fought, sword and magic, and sheer brute force. Lesser magic users were tossed aside as he held our left flank. Maeve and Victor stood ground just a few yards ahead of me. They worked Shields and Blocks holding our line and pushing the Authority back, while Terric and Shame launched spells high overhead to batter the Shields the Authority held in place, and give Zay, Hayden, and the Hounds some breathing room.

The Hounds were everywhere, fighting in pairs. Bats, crowbars, rifles, and magic were doing a hell of a lot of damage as they wove in and out of the Authority's forces. I caught a glimpse of Collins diving into the fray and disappearing in the press of people.

Davy ran straight into the crowd, and my heart stuttered. He wasn't using magic. He wasn't even drawing a weapon. He was running, calling a name as if there weren't a battle being waged around him. Calling for Sunny.

"Davy," I yelled, "no!"

He couldn't hear me, or didn't want to hear me. He phased from solid to ghost, as magic struck him. Each time he was struck by magic, he went ghost and sucked the magic in. He used that magic, like tentacles lashing out from his hands, grabbing and holding his attackers, throwing them aside. And then he became solid again.

People were screaming. People were writhing. And still Davy ran, calling Sunny's name.

Sunny heard him. Found him. Stood in front of him as a pressing crowd of Hounds swarmed around them, rolled past them like surf over ragged stones.

Davy and Sunny were in their own world, silent, still. They stood close enough they could touch each other, but remained untouching.

Until Davy raised his hand, and gently brushed her dark braid away from her face. She searched his eyes, frowning, as if trying to remember something and unable to do so.

A man—I didn't know his name, had never seen him before—threw a spell the size of a tank at Sunny.

Davy grabbed Sunny around the waist, shielding her

with his body. He lifted one hand, his arm straight and high, like a lightning rod, and the magic poured into him. He faded, became nothing but an outline of who he was. Davy fell to his knees as he whipped the spell back at the caster.

That man went down, and didn't stand up again.

Sunny reached for Davy, but her hand went straight through him. She was trying to help him to his feet, trying to fight off the people coming toward them, trying to get him away, safe. Trying to stay alive.

I started toward them and nearly fell.

Even though I wasn't casting magic, so much poured around me, contained in the Illusion bubble, it made me sick, dizzy. I took a few deep breaths, trying to hold it together.

Jack Quinn appeared beside me, caught my elbow, and made sure I was steady on my feet before jogging off to stick that bowie knife of his into the side of a man who had Bea pinned.

I glanced at the field. Davy was on his feet, his arm around Sunny as they worked their way out of the worst of the fight.

Maybe three-quarters of the magic users were still on their feet. We were fighting, but we were falling just as quickly as they were.

Dr. Fisher knelt beside one of the Authority, a woman. She cast a healing spell, then stood, and walked over to one of the Hounds who was trying to stanch a gut wound. For a second, I thought she might end him, but she gently moved his hands away and healed him too.

Looked like the good doctor wasn't taking sides. That was something, at least.

Still, it wouldn't take much more for them to break past our Shields. There were still more of them than us. And if they reached the wall where Cody and Stone and

Nola were trapped, they would destroy everything we were fighting for.

"Maeve," I yelled, "can you hold alone?"

She nodded.

"Victor, to Hayden."

Victor dropped his Shield spell, and drew his sword as he ran toward Hayden. Hayden had sheathed his shotgun down his back and was holding off his attackers with broadsword and magic. But he seemed to have become the main target for half the remaining Authority, and I didn't know how long he could hold.

Then from the middle of the Authority, I heard a broken yell. Two goons who had worked for Bartholomew heaved a massive spell across the field. A roll of blue fire caught and poured across the grass, burning and electrocuting everyone who couldn't throw a Block, a Break, or a Protection spell.

Nothing could stop it. It was too fast. I couldn't stop it. I couldn't throw magic. And it was headed right for me.

I turned to run, and a hand gripped my arm, pulled me up off my feet. Yanked me away.

Not Zayvion. Not Shame.

"Run, Allie." It was Kevin, Violet's bodyguard. He pushed me forward as he spun and spread his stance. He threw a Block spell that could extinguish the sun. The blue fire hit it, hissed and blistered, and was snuffed out.

Count one more fighter on the good guys' side.

I ran. To open ground, back toward the wall, where Paul stood defending magic that licked and crackled past Maeve's Shields. There was still no sign of Nola or Cody or Stone. I pivoted to look out over the fight again.

Melissa Whit broke free from the crowd. She was running my way. Even at this distance, I could see the glint of her teeth, bared in hatred.

She wasn't headed to the wall. She was after me, out

to kill me. She pulled her shotgun up to her hip as she ran, then fired.

Maeve's Shield stopped magic, not bullets.

I fumbled for my gun, pulled it free from the holster. I raised the gun. But couldn't fire.

My finger was on the trigger. I couldn't force myself to squeeze, couldn't fire the shot.

Melissa didn't pause. Melissa didn't stop. She fired again.

A hand reached around from behind me. A hand wrapped warm and strong over my hand on the gun. A finger slipped on top of mine and a man pressed tight against my back. I could feel his heat and arousal.

"Just relax," Collins said, his voice an intimate exhalation in my ear. "And let me show you how to kill someone."

"No," I said, "don't."

He pulled his finger and my finger down on the trigger.

The kick of six shots in rapid succession shook through me, through him.

Melissa Whit shuddered with each bullet that buried into her flesh in a clean circle over her heart. She staggered. Fell.

"Was it good for you?" Collins said.

I turned to punch him in the face, but he was already ripping the gun from my hand and backpedaling fast. Then he took off running.

That son of a bitch.

The horror of what I'd done raced through me and froze me in place. I hadn't fired the shots, but I hadn't stopped Collins either. I'd killed a woman. I'd shot someone until that person was dead. Again.

*She was not an innocent in this, Allison. She wanted everything Bartholomew wanted.*

My dad's voice snapped hard and sharp in my mind. I blinked several times, trying to get my bearings.

*Defend yourself,* Dad said. *Defend your friends.*

I hated taking orders from him, but he was right. I couldn't fall apart now. Plenty of people were going to die today. Some of them by my hand.

But not with a gun. I drew my sword, the rightness of it doing more good to clear my head than anything else, and scanned the field.

Victor was holding his own against at least half a dozen magic users, canceling and breaking each spell they threw at him, while Hounds took out knees with baseball bats, threw dirt in eyes, and fought dirty with weapons and magic.

Collins had given up on the gun and produced a crowbar from somewhere, probably from one of the Hounds who was down. He used it with a vicious sort of glee, a wide smile on his blood-spattered face. He swung it like a bat, then with surgical precision, cracking bones, breaking limbs. And carving out great hunks of flesh with the hooked end of it.

Davy and Sunny defended our right flank. Out in the fray I caught the mesmerizing power of Shame and Terric. They fought side by side, light and dark, wielding magic and weapons in perfect sync. They fought with a single mind and single purpose. To kill Jingo Jingo.

Jingo Jingo had been Shame's teacher, probably Terric's too. Jingo Jingo had also betrayed us all and tried to kill Shame's mother, Maeve. He'd left her with injuries she still hadn't recovered from.

Shamus Flynn was not a man who held forgiveness in his heart. There wasn't room for it with all the hatred caged there.

Terric fought with an ax in each hand, and I could hear his voice over the roar of the fight. He was chanting magic, using so much he glowed with gold and white light.

Shame's voice was lost to the battle, a low hiss of curses, vile and sharp, falling from his lips as he knocked out man after man, the grass dying away to dust beneath his feet with each step he took. He was sucking energy out of grass, the bushes, the trees, calling ribbons of magic to rush to him and feed his anger. The trees might never be the same again, but I did not see him draw the energy or life from a single person.

He didn't need to. He was a burning column of controlled hatred, magic whipping around him, black as death, crackling with hungry red flames.

And then I didn't have any time to watch. A wide, dark-haired man swung a sword at my head. I ducked, and stayed low, sweeping his feet just as he reached the extension of his swing.

He stumbled, pushed up, chanting a spell. I couldn't block magic. I had no defense against it. But it took a lot of concentration to cast magic.

I lunged, the tip of my katana brushing dangerously close to his face. He parried the move, but stopped chanting to engage my blade. He moved backward, and I was forced to follow, darting in fast, driving him so he didn't have time to think of another spell. I needed to stay close to stop him, stab him, make him shut up.

He drew a very quick Freeze spell.

Holy shit, that was going to hurt.

I pulled a knife out of my belt and threw it at his head.

He jerked. The knife sank into his shoulder and the spell he was casting shattered.

Now!

I rushed, slammed him in the injured shoulder, and silenced his scream with a punch in the face. He folded to the ground unconscious.

I spun, ready for a second attacker.

No one else was near me, the fight still a few yards off.

Fewer Hounds and fewer Authority members were still standing. But no one was laying down arms.

Zayvion, Hayden, and Victor were positioned at the front of the onslaught. From the graceful, unconscious way they all seemed to know who was going to throw magic, and who was fighting hand to hand, in a flowing exchange, I suddenly realized that this was not the first bloody battle they had fought in together. They were brutal. Efficient. And worked as a unit.

But so did our enemies.

I heard a yell and turned. Shame and Terric were almost on Jingo Jingo. Twenty yards, ten. I could see the fear on Jingo Jingo's face as he raised his hand.

The world shook. Thunder rolled beneath our feet, shuddered through the arc of Illusion that covered the park.

Four women and three men stood in a circle near Jingo Jingo and cast a massive Shield around him.

The backwash from the huge Shield spell almost blew Shame and Terric off their feet. Shame leaned into it, walking forward as if through fire. Spells in black and red leaped from his hands, spiral gouts that could sear through metal. But they did not touch Jingo Jingo. Did not harm the Shield.

Terric walked shoulder to shoulder with Shame. Just like on the street with the cop, they pulled magic in a loop between them, black fire dancing in Shame's hands, white gold liquid pouring from Terric's. Two hands traced the same spell; two men poured magic into those spells. Magic arced, overlapped, twisted, until there was only one glyph hovering in the air in front of them.

Death.

Sweet hells.

Magic comes with a price. If you kill with magic, you must bear an equal price. To cast Death meant you had to die.

Or so the common magic user believed. There were ways to defer that price, ways to Proxy it, to Offload it on others, that most people did not know about.

But Shame knew. Terric knew too.

Terric threw a Proxy, tied to an Offload, and then cast Ground.

The spell would kill.

The price for that killing would flush through the three spells, spreading the price like a net over the ground, over the trees, over the bushes, over the river. A lot of living things were about to die when that spell hit its mark. But none of those living things were people.

Except for Jingo Jingo.

Jingo Jingo yelled, "To me! All to me!" The Authority turned, retreated, fighting their way to Jingo Jingo's side.

Except the Hounds wouldn't let them.

Jamar swung a metal bat like he'd been street brawling all his life, and took out Joshua Romero's knees. Just to his right, Theresa cast a Sleep spell that knocked six people flat. Ahead of her, Sid cast a Hold spell, locking the twins Carl and La in midstep. The new Hound, Karl, was using some kind of Taser that had a frighteningly quick recharge. But he was not quick enough to stop one of Bartholomew's goons from aiming a gun at Sid, and shooting him.

Sid crumpled to the ground.

"No! Get the wounded out of there," I yelled.

Jack and Bea pounded across the distance to where Sid lay and pulled him out of the fray.

Terric and Shame didn't seem to notice any of this. They drew their hands in perfect, mirrored strokes and threw Death at Jingo's protectors, at the Shield, at Jingo Jingo.

Then Shame pulled a gun from his coat and aimed at Jingo Jingo's heart.

He fired shot after shot, emptying out the cartridge, cursing as each bullet flew, wrapping the bullets in bloody black spells.

Still the Shield held.

Terric pulled one of his remaining knives. It glowed white-hot with magic. He threw it at the nearest person holding Jingo Jingo's Shield.

The woman screamed and buckled as the knife buried in her leg.

And Jingo Jingo's Shield fell.

The Death spell hit Jingo Jingo square in his massive chest, and riding with it was bullet after bullet. He shuddered, stumbled back, his eyes wide with shock.

Then he smiled. He lifted one wide hand and placed it gently on the injured woman's head. He stroked her hair, and looking straight at Shame, he drank her life down until she was nothing but bones.

"No!" Shame yelled.

Gasps and cries of shock rose from other people on the field, including members of the Authority. The fighting slowed.

Jingo was bigger now. Stronger. The ghost of the woman he had just killed clung to him, black holes where her eyes should be, serrated teeth hungry for magic. Hungry for death. She was now nothing but a Veiled.

Jingo pointed one thick finger at Shame. A black, electric arc of magic shot out and dug into Shame's chest.

Shame yelled, but didn't fall.

Then the electric arc ran bloody as Jingo Jingo drank Shamus' life down.

I wanted to run. Run to save Shame. Run to save Terric, who fought alone at his side. Run to save my Hounds who were falling, my friends who were dying.

But I could not use magic.

"Zay!" I yelled. "Shame."

Zay looked across the field. He ran, and even at a dead sprint, he commanded magic to do his bidding, wielded it to cripple, maim, end. Anything, everything, to speed his flight to Shame and Terric.

The battle slowed to an unworldly rhythm. I heard Maeve yell, saw her fall beside an already unconscious Hayden. When had Hayden fallen?

There was blood everywhere.

Paul unloaded his gun into the wave of men, a dozen at least, too many, far too many, who were almost at the wall. Men who threw Unlock, Impact, Implosion, and half a dozen other spells to break the wall. Men who would kill Cody and Nola without a second thought. Men who would destroy Stone.

We were losing. Dying.

"Allie!" Paul yelled.

The wall buckled, magic thinning.

I saw Cody on his knees in front of Stone, Nola standing beside him.

The wall crumbled. Magic tore apart like sand beneath a hurricane.

I couldn't stop it. I desperately looked for who could. Victor was down, clutching one hand over his bloody eyes, holding a Shield spell in the other. Maeve was on her knees, maintaining a Protection over Hayden's unconscious form.

Davy and Sunny fought alongside Kevin, barely holding off their attackers. And Collins was nowhere to be seen. That left Zay and me.

We weren't losing. We had lost.

But I refused to let Nola and Cody die for our failure.

"Zay!" I reached for his soul.

He risked a look, and saw beyond me to the wall that

was falling, to the men who were waiting with swords and magic and knives for Nola and Cody.

And then Paul went down, struck by a bolt of magic that lashed a whip of pure copper fire down his spine.

Zay gave one last look at Shame and Terric, who were fighting against a mob of bodies that pressed in on them, deflecting magic and blows with the unconsciousness of two minds locked between two bodies, using magic in ways no one else could.

Making magic bend to their will.

Soul Complements.

Zay had to choose. Help Shame and Terric kill Jingo Jingo, or save Cody, Nola, and Stone.

Desperation crossed his face as he realized he couldn't get to either side of the field fast enough. Not without magic.

Zay sheathed his sword and cast Gate.

The explosion of the spell opening in front of him, closing, and instantly opening in front of the wall rocked the park.

And when he stepped through to the wall, he had his sword in his hand again. He wielded so much magic, half the men waiting to kill Cody went down.

And so did the wall.

Zayvion turned and stood with his back to Stone and Cody and Nola, standing between them and me, facing the Authority. He cut another glyph into the air, then spread his arms, his feet braced wide as if ready to bear a great weight.

He spoke three words and magic arched across his body, licking like silver fire, painting glyphs against his skin, against the air. Magic shot out, pouring from his left hand to encircle the boundary of where Cody and Stone and Nola stood, then returned to his right hand. Magic created a barrier, a protection around them.

And Zayvion was that barrier.

The pain of it crawled across my skin and set fire to my nerves. I screamed. Even though I wasn't touching him, I felt magic devouring him, killing him, burning him alive.

The wall he created was a Grounding, a Shield, a Closing. It was a protection that was powered as much by his body, his will, and his ability to endure pain as by anything else.

I couldn't move, couldn't feel my own body beyond his pain.

But I heard Shame yell.

I looked up.

As Terric threw himself between Jingo and Shame. He swung his ax, wielding a Cleave spell. And sliced through Jingo Jingo's spell that was killing Shame. The spells collided and an explosion poured over him like acid. Terric stiffened.

Terric stood there for a second, a heartbeat, as blood bloomed in patches across his skin and poured free. And then his ax slipped from his bloody hand.

He severed the hold Jingo Jingo had on Shame. But at a cost. At a high cost.

Shame, weak, winded, somehow managed to catch Terric as he fell and lowered his bloody body to the ground. He pulled a Block spell around them, a spell so strong it ate into the ground and sent up tendrils of smoke.

Even at this distance I could read Terric's lips as he looked up, searching Shame's face.

"Last thing ... we do," Terric said, his eyes clear though his breathing was ragged and blood poured a river around him. "If it's the only ... thing. We do ... together. Kill. That. Bastard."

"No." Shame shook his head, dark bangs wet with

blood and sweat. "We're going to get you to a doctor," he said. "We're going to fix you."

"I know . . . what my pain's worth too," Terric said. "I give you my . . . life . . . and soul, Shamus Flynn. Make it worth it. No mercy. Kill Jingo Jingo."

Terric dragged his hand to the crystal in Shame's chest and pressed his palm there.

Shame leaned over him, pressing his forehead against Terric's forehead as if by doing so he could make him hear him, make him listen to him, make him live.

"This isn't how it happens," Shame said raggedly. "This isn't how it ends. Not for you."

Terric mouthed one last word. I couldn't tell what it was. It might have been *love*; it might have been *liar*.

Then Terric exhaled, and Shame suddenly breathed in, taking down Terric's soul, green like growing things, brilliant gold like sunlight, and silver shot with moonlight that poured pure, living energy into the crystal in Shame's chest, into the air in his lungs. Terric gave Shame his life, his energy, his soul.

And then Terric Conley died and lay still.

# *Chapter Twenty-five*

Shame paused, not breathing, holding himself even more still than Terric. Then he gently laid Terric down on the grass. Head low, eyes burning white and silver through the dark swing of his bangs, Shame stood and smashed apart the Block spell.

His back was toward Jingo Jingo, yet he stood there, unguarded. He pulled his chin up and gazed at Zayvion, keeping Cody and Nola and Stone safe, looked at Maeve and Hayden beneath the Shield she held, looked at Davy and Sunny, and Victor and Kevin, all who were still fighting, still breathing, still living.

Even though there was no chance we would win this battle.

And then he looked at me. He knew we couldn't win. But he made his decision anyway.

"No," I said, little more than a whisper. "Shame, don't."

Shame smiled, and tipped his face to the sky, closing his eyes as if in prayer, as if savoring the last breath he would breathe. He lifted his hands palms up at his sides, welcoming the wind and the rain to wash away his sins.

There was no wind. There was no rain. There was only blood, his blood, Terric's blood, falling from his fingers.

Collins appeared at his side, the crowbar a tool of destruction in his hand. He kept the members of the Authority at bay, protecting Shame as he tried to talk sense to him, talk him down out of his rage.

But when Shamus drew his gaze back from the heavens, his eyes burned silver. The golden white light of Terric's soul flickered out from the crystal in his chest, and slipped down into his hands, his fingers, giving him the life he needed, giving him the strength he needed to kill Jingo Jingo.

The last thing Terric had asked of him. The one thing Terric had given up his life, his soul, for.

Jingo's death.

Collins' words fell upon deaf ears.

Shame pulled all that magic into his hands, and more. He drank down the energy of the earth so far away I heard trees crack and groan in the distance.

Then he hurled magic, raw, blasting, burning, jagged flames that needed nothing more than hatred to guide it, lashing, cutting, toward Jingo's head.

With no Shield to protect him, the spell struck Jingo Jingo right in the middle of his forehead. Jingo rocked back on his feet, clutching at his throat. He fell.

His hand landed on the woman nearest him. And he drank down her life. Using that to bolster him, he pushed up onto his knees, the gaping hole in his head from Shame's attack closing as he drank down the life of the man next to her, and the next, and the next, a line of people falling to their knees, falling to their deaths to feed him.

Jingo grew larger and larger, fattening himself with each death, growing stronger as he created more and more dead—Veiled who clung to him like a writhing coat of souls.

Hounds screamed and fell; Authority members screamed and fell. Still Jingo drank. Still Jingo destroyed, the circle of death growing and spreading.

The Hounds hustled out of the way, grabbing any wounded people they could, whether Hound or Authority, and dragging them with them. The Authority was doing the same. Repulsed by the monster Jingo Jingo had become, they picked up wounded, dead, friend and foe, and stumbled away in shock, in horror.

Collins walked slowly backward, watching Jingo Jingo, and staying just one step out of the range of Jingo's hunger.

But Shamus still stood.

"They'll never be enough," Shame said, his voice carrying across the distance between them. "Not all the magic in the world will be enough for you. Not all the children's souls, not all the people you've killed and drunk down to the grave."

Jingo Jingo chuckled. "Think I don't know that, boy?" His words were sloppy. He was drunk on the lives, drunk on the deaths. "You think you're the big Death magic user in town? Think you know what living is? Know what dying is? Think you got it in you to use Death magic like it can be used? 'Cause it's powerful stuff. More powerful than anyone ever dared tell you.

"Your own daddy begged me to kill you. Said he saw the demon inside you. Knew what you could become, and begged me to burn it out of you. He sobbed on his knees in front of me, afraid and ashamed of what he'd brought into the world. He was willing to trade his life for yours. And I suppose he did, didn't he?

"Look at you now. Nothing but a scrawny piss-poor disappointment. And all this screaming—" He pointed his hand at a man who wasn't any older than twenty, and pulled so much life, so much energy out of him, he fell, dead.

"—all this dying's just sugar frosting I'm gonna lick off my fingers. What I want is the simulacrum. What I want is magic. All the magic."

He took a step, his cane in one hand.

The incredible bulk of him made the ground shake. "If you stand in my way, I'm gonna eat you down, drink up that fag lover of yours, then use your mama's bones to pick my teeth."

"Are you?" Shame said quietly. "Then you'd better get on with it now, big man. Kill me." He held his hands out. There were no weapons in them. He was not tracing a spell. He just stood there, staring at Jingo with dead silver eyes.

Jingo licked his lips and smiled. "It's gonna be my pleasure." He drew on magic, a great gob of it, pulling it out of the Veiled who winged around him, catching up their magic and crumpling them like empty shells between his fingers. He twisted the magic and carved it into one spell: Death.

Shame tucked his hand against the crystal in his chest. He pulled the energy Terric had given him, Terric's life, his soul, out of the crystal, like a man yanking a knife out of his gut.

People cannot see magic with their bare eyes. But I could. And I saw Terric's soul hovering in Shame's palm, white and gold and the soft green of growing things. If Shame were nothing but darkness and death, Terric was his exact opposite: life and light.

Shame suddenly went gaunt, pale. He swayed as if just keeping his feet took more strength than he had. He was so injured by Jingo Jingo that Terric's soul was all that had kept him alive.

He whispered something against his bloody fist where he clutched Terric's soul. Maybe he said "love"—maybe he said "live"—but his words carried a soft spell. And then he threw Terric's soul, Terric's life.

Not at Jingo Jingo, but back at Terric.

The soul, the life, the magic, flew true, and struck Terric in the chest, resting there for a moment like water waiting for parched soil to drink it down.

Terric inhaled on a yell.

And Jingo Jingo's spell hit Shame. Death tore through Shame like a beast made of fangs and claws. It bit the back of Shame's neck, ripped through the side of his throat, and crushed the crystal in his chest.

Shame made not a single sound. His eyes glazed. Blood poured from his mouth. He fell, the spell, the beast, devouring him. Jingo fattened and grew, slurping down Shame's life through that spell, growing strong as Shame faded.

"No!" I screamed, Maeve screamed, Zay yelled. I pushed onto my feet, every step burning through me, the taste of blood and hot copper slick on my throat. Moving, any movement, was agony, my agony, Zay's agony.

But I wasn't going to let Shame die. He couldn't die.

*Save him,* Zayvion whispered in my mind. *Save Shame.*

Every step I took shot through me, through Zayvion. Too much pain. Zayvion fell to one knee. I stumbled, as darkness curtained my vision.

I refused to fall. I forced myself to move, forced myself to walk, to keep walking until I could touch Shame. Touch Terric. Hounds were good at enduring pain. The best. And I was a hell of a Hound.

Terric rolled up onto his hands and knees. Head hanging, he was calling for Shame, crawling to Shame.

Crawling to his fallen body. Empty now. Jingo had sucked the life out of him, leaving him a hollow husk.

Shamus Flynn, my friend, Zayvion's brother. Shamus Flynn, who had fought with us, laughed with us, bled with us, was dead.

I didn't see another Veiled around Jingo Jingo. Didn't see Shamus' ghost.

Then magic exploded out of Shame, smashing into the bubble of Illusion surrounding the park and making it ring like an angel's scream.

The magic gathered together, pouring down to re-form into a spirit, a soul, a magic user's ghost with silver white eyes.

Shame.

I fell to my knees in awe. "Shame?"

Shame watched me, his face calm. And even though he was no longer alive, I could see the fire of hatred burning through him. Could see that he wasn't nearly done with this fight yet.

A single black line of magic wrapped around Shame's neck like a leash. A leash that Jingo held in his hand.

Terric couldn't see him unless he cast Sight, and Terric was in no condition to stand, much less pull on magic.

"Don't," I said to Shame. "Shamus, please. Don't do this. Don't let him do this to you."

Jingo was laughing. Big, lungy guffaws. "He won't listen to you, Allison Angel. I own him now. Just like I own all the dead." He gestured to the Veiled who circled him, feeding him their magic, their energy. Draining out to making him stronger. And I saw that they were attached to Jingo by lines of magic too.

"He is a part of death now, a part of Death magic," Jingo said. "And I am Death magic's ruler. Come to me, boy," Jingo commanded, yanking on the leash of magic. "Sit at my feet."

Shame pulled against him, pulled against the line that connected them.

"Oh, we can do this hard, if you want," Jingo Jingo crooned.

He flicked his fingers and the Veiled lashed out. They attacked Shame, digging fingers and teeth into him and pulling him toward Jingo Jingo.

Shame leaned back, fought to hold his ground. But there were too many of them. He was dragged closer and closer to the man.

*The mark,* Dad said in my head. He had been quiet for so long, I jumped at the sound of his voice.

*What mark?*

*Your palm. The death mark Mikhail gave you. Use it against the Veiled. Break their ties to Jingo Jingo, so he no longer has their strength.*

Using magic would knock me out. But if it gave Shame a chance, I didn't care. I lifted my left hand. Even though Dad had always been the one who used this mark before, I knew that circle of Death magic in my palm was mine to wield.

I traced a glyph: Sever.

Cold fire washed down my left arm, but I focused, refusing to lose the spell. My right arm burned hot, hotter. I guided magic as it whipped out from the mark in my palm, filling the Sever glyph with raw power.

Then I threw it at the Veiled.

The Death magic spell shattered the bindings between Jingo and the Veiled. I teetered on the edge of unconsciousness, blinking in and out of awareness. Jingo Jingo's yell was the sweet song that called me back.

The Veiled pulled away from him, free, running fast, faster than any living thing could, returning to the bodies of the fallen. Some of the Veiled stepped back into their own bodies. Some ran through the streets, toward the city, toward the hospitals, in a flash.

And those that had no body left to return to simply faded away.

Except for one.

Shamus Flynn.

He did not run away from Jingo. He ran to him.

Jingo Jingo never had a chance.

Shame was on top of him in an instant. He drove his fist into Jingo's chest. Then Shame wrapped his hands around Jingo Jingo's heart.

"Rule this, you fucked-up son of a bitch," Shame growled.

Jingo Jingo shuddered, his mouth popping open and shut, gasping for air. There was no life left to him, no air left to him.

Shame drank him down, first his heart, which smoldered until it was nothing but dust, then his body. Shame plunged his hands into Jingo Jingo's head and took from him all the lives, all the magic, all the souls, Jingo Jingo had feasted upon.

Jingo collapsed in on himself, smaller and smaller, until he was nothing but bones with globs of flesh hung upon them.

Empty, burned. Jingo Jingo was dead. Not even enough of a soul left to rise as a Veiled.

Shame stood and exhaled. The souls, the magic, the death, he had breathed in from Jingo Jingo slipped from between his lips in silver smoke that faded into the night.

Just as Shame was fading.

"No," Terric growled. "You will not die, Shamus. You will not leave me alone."

Terric placed his bloody palm over the physical Shame's chest, cutting his hand on the jagged edges of the shattered crystal there. Even though it felt like forever, it had been only moments, no more than a minute, since Shame had fallen. Terric's hand glowed white and gold and green, and the mark Mikhail had placed in his palm—the blessing, the Binding, he had given him—pulsed silver-hot.

Terric glowed with that light as if his skin were stretched over moonlight.

"Where are you?" he asked. He looked over at me. "Where is he?"

I pushed up to cross the remaining distance between us and took Terric's hand. Somehow he got to his feet, and I guided him over to where Shame stood.

"He's in front of you," I said. "He's right there."

Terric's gaze fell on Shame, even though I knew he couldn't see him.

"Death can't have you," Terric said. "Not all of you. I still have some of you, here." He pounded his chest. "I'm not going to let you get out of it this easy. If I have to live, you have to live." He limped forward, and occupied the exact same space where Shame stood.

The mark on his palm grew into a silver and white thread that bound his wrist, and bound Shame's wrist. Terric cast that magic, weaving it into a glyph for Life. At the center of the Life glyph was the infinity symbol, the symbol Terric carried on his palm.

He threw that spell, that Binding, out to wrap around Shame's body.

Shame was caught by the thread, fueled by Terric's life energy and magic. And even though the ghostly form of Shame shook his head and tried to step back, he was thrown back into his body, ghost, soul, and all.

Shame inhaled, and a hoarse, broken heave of air escaped through tortured lungs. He swore, once, then started coughing weakly.

Alive.

Terric passed out. I couldn't even move to catch him.

I looked around me. No one was fighting anymore. The Authority, the Hounds, my friends. A lot of people had Sight spells in their hands. They had seen what happened. They had seen what Jingo Jingo had done, had seen the monster he had always been.

Dr. Fisher moved through the people, her voice distant against the ringing in my ears, directing people to help the fallen, taking care of everyone still breathing, or breathing again as the case might be.

I looked for my own. Victor sat near Zayvion, holding a cloth over his eyes, blood staining his sleeve down to the elbow. Hayden was flat on his back, unconscious; Maeve next to him held a Blood spell to cauterize the stump of his arm.

Oh, God. He had lost his hand.

I needed to get to them, to help them, to help Dr. Fisher help them.

But before I could move, the air filled with the sound of a gong. Not just the air, and not just a sound. It was that bone-deep ringing of magic, all magic, light and dark, joined, reverberating out through the soil, the world, and everyone within it.

I'd heard a sound like that just once before.

Cody had unlocked Stone.

The Barrier spell Zayvion held broke, and he dropped, catching himself with one hand. He didn't stay down for more than a second. He tipped his head up, met my gaze across the field, then pushed to his feet, standing strong, standing like every breath, every nerve in his body, wasn't on fire.

Beyond him, Stone sneezed and shook his head. He flexed his wings and rubbed at his face with one hand. He burbled, first looking at Cody, then at Nola, who both looked well and alive.

I hoped to hell Stone still had the blending of magic stored inside.

*He does,* Dad said. *He should.*

That meant we won. That the price we had paid would be worth it. We could test this magic, see if Stone could filter it, find a cure.

But at such a cost. I was exhausted, reeling with pain,

shock, sorrow. I glanced at Shame. He was still breathing. I glanced at Terric. He was still breathing too. Both of them were unconscious.

I didn't know what to do next.

"Such a mess you make in my neighborhood." I knew that voice. I turned to look up toward the city. Mama walked down from the edge of the Illusion spell toward us.

Mama wasn't a tall woman. She wasn't a big woman. But she moved like she owned the world. A dozen of her Boys walked behind her, shotguns in their hands.

Behind the Boys were dozens and dozens of other people who called St. Johns their home. Business owners. Neighbors. Community. Family.

"It's time for everyone to go home now," Mama said. "The park is closed. You leave our neighborhood. Now."

The click of guns being loaded filled the air. The Boys' guns, and more, many more, as the people of St. Johns fanned out and leveled their weapons at us.

Magic is fast. Bullets are faster.

I didn't need a second invitation. If I was going to get me and my people out of here, this was my chance.

But instead, I said, "We need doctors. All of us need medical care."

At least twenty people stepped forward out of the crowd behind Mama, and spread out on the field, helping to tend the wounded. I saw Dr. Fisher on her way toward Hayden and Victor. I wanted to move, I wanted to do something to help, but it was taking all my energy just to remain conscious.

A man knelt beside me. Hair and beard just going gray, he had a round face and wide brown eyes. "Hello," he said. "I'm Dr. Ed Tullis. Can you tell me what happened to him?" He wasn't looking at me. His hands were moving over Shame, checking for things doctors checked for.

"Magic," I said. "A lot of bad magic."

"Let's get a stretcher," he called, then looked over at Terric before adding: "Two."

People showed up with stretchers. And then there were a lot of well-meaning strangers helping Terric and Shame onto those stretchers.

Maeve had made it across the field. She stood beside me, even though I had managed to do only one thing: remain standing.

I had no idea what the price to pay would be for dying, then killing someone while in a magical state, then living again. I didn't know if what Terric had done—made Shame live—was a gift or a curse, but right now, since Shame was still breathing, I counted it in the gift category.

I knew Maeve did too.

"He's alive," I told Maeve.

"Stubborn, foolish son of mine," she said, gently touching Shame's face. "Why is your heart so gold?"

"We need to go, ma'am," one of the men who was carrying the stretcher said.

"Wait." She looked over at me. "Where, Allie? Where do we go?"

I had no idea. We had the van, but walking all the way to the parking lot felt pretty impossible right now. I didn't think a hospital was the best choice, but maybe it was. It was going to be dawn soon. We couldn't stay in the park forever.

"Who wants to speak for the Authority?" I called out, not caring if civilians heard me talking about a secret group.

To my surprise, the twins Carl and La walked up. "We'll take it," Carl said. "For now. What do you want us to do, Allie?"

"Promise me you're not going to order someone to hunt us down and kill us."

Carl shook his head. "You're safe. We're calling an emergency halt on all orders and will get in touch with the Overseer. No one's going to do anything more until we get this straightened out. After what Jingo Jingo did . . ." He looked at the lumpy burned mess of his corpse and swallowed.

"We'll follow your recommendations, right now," La said. "We know you must be doing something right to force Jingo Jingo to show his hand . . . to show what he really is. Was," she amended.

I would have been giddy with relief, but I was just too numb. "Take care of the wounded. Take care of the dead. The plague spreading through the city is caused by tainted magic. So if you can somehow tell people not to use magic as much, that might help some. We think we have a way to cleanse magic, but it's going to take us a little more time to figure it out."

"We can do that," Carl said. "We'll get the word out."

Then he and his sister headed off to talk to the other members of the Authority, none of whom looked like they were willing to argue about anything.

Good.

"This way," a man said at my elbow. I would have jerked in surprise but I was pretty out of it. Between my pain, Zay's pain, and sheer exhaustion, I was amazed I was still on my feet, much less thinking in coherent sentences.

The man was one of Mama's Boys. This one was redheaded and maybe sixteen. He nodded, reassuringly. "We have a car for all of you and a place for you to recover. Let me help."

"Go," Mama said to me. "Boy will help. It is all arranged."

I was too tired to argue. "The Hounds? My friends?"

"We have doctors here and we've called 911," Boy

said. "We'll get anyone who needs medical care to a hospital. Ambulances are on the way."

"Zay?" I said, a little dazed.

And then I saw him, walking my way, with Cody and Stone at his side. Nola was with him too, her arm around Paul, who was limping badly.

I wanted to run to him, knew I'd get only a few steps before passing out. So instead, I waited, studying his face, locked in a calm expression, watching his body, moving smoothly and strong even though I knew he was in god-awful pain.

I smiled, because I had never seen anyone so beautiful in all my life.

Davy and Sunny were walking our way too. Davy was solid as any living man, and looked a little singed, but otherwise was saying something softly to Sunny, who kept her arm tight around him.

Collins was wandering through the fallen, whistling and rolling up his bloody sleeves. He occasionally stared at the sky as if expecting rain, then gave me a raised eyebrow and a smile before executing a sweeping, formal bow. "Well played," he said. "Very well executed indeed, Beckstrom."

Hayden wasn't walking. They'd put him on a stretcher with an IV and were taking him to a waiting ambulance. Victor was on a stretcher too, though he seemed to be talking, his eyes wrapped in clean gauze and padding.

I did a quick count of how many Hounds were still standing, and couldn't help but grin.

There were only six Hounds sitting in the grass, surrounded by the other Hounds, who were making sure no one, other than the doctors, touched them.

Jack looked up, caught me staring, and raised a hand. He was bruised and cut, but had his arm over Bea's shoulder. She handed him back his cigarette, and exhaled smoke before giving me a big smile.

Hounds. They were all crazy. Loyal. I loved them for it.

Sid was one of the injured they were guarding. A woman tended what looked like a gunshot wound to the shoulder.

I held up my hand and mouthed, *Thank you.*

Jack nodded, and said something to the Hounds. Half of them gave the park one last look, nodded toward me, or gave a wave, then faded off into the shadows of the night.

They had survived. We had survived. Maybe not without pain. Maybe not without injury. But we were alive and Stone was unlocked. Magic had a chance. The people in Portland had a chance to be okay again.

That was something, right? Maybe that was even more than something.

And then Zay was there, in front of me, taking up my world, taking up my senses. He wrapped his arms around me and pressed his mouth against mine, kissing me as if we'd just survived the world's end. I kissed him back, because I thought maybe we had. And I didn't care if I saw or felt anything or anyone else ever again.

# Chapter Twenty-six

Mama's Boys took us to a church that had long ago been converted into a house. The house belonged to an artist friend of Mama's, who'd filled the walls with paintings and found objects and some remarkable metal art.

She had the place set up like a minihospital at Mama's request, with plenty of equipment and supplies.

But there was no magic here—none at all, just a lingering sacred hush that seemed to cling to the bare rafters and floor and soothed my rattled nerves.

It didn't take us long to get settled in the large room that had half a dozen couches, a few cots, and plenty of chairs. I suggested Davy take one of the rooms to sleep in, but he just gave me a look from my head to my feet, and told me I looked worse than he did.

I would have argued, but he was right.

However, our most wounded were Victor, Hayden, Shame, and Terric. They each got their own beds, monitors, IVs, and painkillers in the main room. Dr. Tullis had come with us as a favor to Mama and brought two nurses with him. It didn't take them long to get everyone comfortable.

We all had a long way to go to recover from our injuries. But we were as settled, tended, and safe as we could be.

It was agreed we'd stay here through the remainder of the night. Dr. Tullis said he'd stay until morning to keep an eye on everyone. Depending on how well the next few hours went, he might recommend one or all be moved to a hospital for better care.

I was on a couch, leaning against Zayvion. He had his head back, eyes closed. The thought of sleep rolled through me like a sensual promise, just as I could feel it roll through Zayvion. I was dog-tired. But we weren't quite done with this fight yet.

"Yes, we are," Zayvion said. He shifted his arm around me, holding me closer. I rested my head on his shoulder, my knees tucked up on the couch.

"No fair listening to me think," I said.

He grunted. "Stop thinking so loud."

"We have to get Stone, have to get the information . . . somewhere for someone to start formulating a cure," I said.

"We have to sleep," Zay said.

"But—"

"Allie," he said with a sigh. "We can't take another fight right now." Zay picked up one leg. I could feel the ragged agony of just that much motion rattle down his spine. He rested his leg on the footstool. "I can't. You can't. None of us can. Whatever it is we need to do with Stone—whether it's taking him to a scientist, or door-to-door for personal inoculations—it's going to take a hell of a lot more energy than I have right now. Than any of us have right now."

"Think it can wait until tomorrow?" I asked.

"It's damn well going to have to."

Shame moaned in his sleep, and Maeve, who sat in a chair at the head of his bed, reached over and gently brushed his bangs away from his forehead, hushing him.

The doctor said he and Terric were stable, but he didn't expect them to be conscious anytime soon.

Collins sat at the head of Terric's bed, his shirt half unbuttoned, and the white of a bandage covering a wound across his ribs. A second, massive bruise bloomed down the other side of his face. He had his hands clasped, his fingers steepled against his lips, as he stared, blearily, into the middle distance.

Victor was sleeping. The doctor didn't know how much permanent damage had been done to his eyes. He couldn't use them right now, maybe wouldn't ever be able to see again. Or maybe the magic burn would heal, slowly. And Hayden, well, there was nothing that could be done about the loss of his hand.

We might have won, but we had paid a heavy price.

Not all of us were broken, though. Davy and Sunny were spooned up on a couch together, and Nola had taken Cody off to a room of his own, Stone following him like a big, stupid puppy. Paul had gone with them. Limping, but not permanently damaged.

I believed Carl and La when they said they'd keep things quiet, but Mama had told me she left several of her Boys in the neighborhood just in case, and they'd keep a lookout for trouble and drive by the place to make sure no one showed up unannounced.

We were as safe as we could be.

The way I looked at it, I had two choices. Stay up and argue with that very stubborn man of mine, who was not going to budge off this couch or change his mind anyway, or go to sleep so we could take care of magic tomorrow.

How many people would die if we didn't get the cure to them? How many would be hurt because we needed sleep?

*It will take time,* Dad said quietly in my mind. *To unravel the poison and create the cure. None of us has the strength to take on that task right now. None of us has the clarity of thought and will to do what must be done.*

Hells, even my dead dad wanted to throw in the towel.

*Do you know how to do any of that?* I asked.

He paused, thinking. *This has never happened before, so even my best guess is still just a guess.*

*And?* I thought.

*And you know how much I deplore making guesses. I don't want to cause the further spread of the poison. I don't want to damage Stone.*

*Wait,* I thought. *Why don't you want to damage Stone? What does he mean to you?*

Okay, yes. A little of what Jingo Jingo had said about my dad sort of sank in. Dad might be working all of this, working me, all of us, to his advantage. Maybe he wanted Stone for something important.

*Stone means nothing to me,* Dad said. *If I were alive, I would find him a fascinating tool of magic, but since that is not the case, I care that he isn't damaged only because you seem fond of him.*

*I am,* I said. *When he isn't stacking everything in my apartment.*

Dad paused again, and I could tell he was working calculations, but slowly, as if they were figures he'd worked over many times and always arrived at different answers. *Give me some time to think this through,* he said.

"Just a few hours," I said out loud.

Zay rumbled in agreement, though he was already sliding off to sleep assisted by painkillers.

*Sleep while you can,* Dad said. *I'll wake you at dawn.*

Well, there was one thing I hadn't ever thought to use my undead dad for—an alarm clock. Who knew he was such a multifunctional ghost?

I looked around the room one last time. Everyone had their eyes closed except for Dr. Tullis, who was tapping information into a computer on the far side of the room. I closed my eyes, and followed Zayvion into sleep.

I didn't remember my dreams. What I did remember was someone placing a bowling ball on my thigh. A bowling ball that moved. And made a sound sort of like a cross between a vacuum cleaner and a pipe organ.

I opened my eyes. Stone was scrunched up on the end of the couch, his hands propped under his chin, which also happened to be propped on my hip. Even though I didn't recall moving, Zay and I had somehow rearranged ourselves on the couch so that he was stretched out on his back, his left arm over the back of the couch, and I was lying, more or less, on top of him, on my side.

Stone must have decided my hip was a good chin rest.

He noticed my eyes opening and burbled at me.

"What?" I whispered.

Stone burbled again, his wings lifting and sending a wash of cooler air over me.

I pushed at his snout with my palm. "Off, so I can get up."

Stone seemed to understand some of that and lifted his head. I disengaged myself as carefully as I could from Zayvion and stood.

Ow. An awful lot of me hurt. And the majority of the parts of me that didn't hurt wanted coffee. There was just enough light coming in through the curtains, I knew it must almost be dawn. In the low light of the room, everyone appeared to be sleeping soundly.

Even Shame and Terric.

I tiptoed over to look down at each of them in turn. Both breathing, both sleeping without lines of pain at their eyes, or on their lips. There were still smudges of blood here and there, and they each had bandages over wounds, but they didn't seem to be in distress. Amazing what a few hours' sleep and really good painkillers could do for a person. Even a person as wounded as they were.

Stone burbled again, one hand on the couch, looking like he was considering curling up with Zayvion. I doubted Zay wanted a half ton of rock for a blanket.

"Come on, Stone," I whispered. "Let's go find breakfast."

Stone slunk down off the couch and did so with so little noise it was a bit surprising. He followed at my side as I tried to remember which way led to the food and coffee.

After the first hallway, I didn't have to wonder. The smell of hot oats and something buttery like pancakes filled the air. As I neared the kitchen, the heavenly scent of fresh-brewed coffee mixed with the others and made my mouth water.

I pushed open the door to the kitchen. It was large enough that between the chairs surrounding the island and the actual dining table, all of us could have sat and had a meal along with an extra twenty friends.

Nola was at the stove, stirring a pot, a waffle iron to the side.

"Do you always have to get up before dawn?" I asked.

"Yes," she said. "Good morning, Allie. Did you get some sleep?"

I walked across the room and started opening cupboards, looking for a cup. "Not enough," I said. "But some."

"Last one the right," she said. "Stone wouldn't sleep and I didn't want to let him outside. I've spent the last hour trying to keep him occupied so he didn't wake you."

I found a mug, filled it with coffee, took a sip. Oh, good God, that was sweet, sweet heaven.

"Where's Mrs., um . . . Mrs. . . . ?"

"Stanley?" she asked. "The owner of the house? She

works the morning shift at the barge company. She told me to feel free to use her kitchen. How's oatmeal and waffles sound?"

She opened the waffle iron, pulled out the golden brown cake, and slipped it into the oven to keep it warm. Then she poured more batter on the iron and closed it again.

"If you're cooking? Delicious." I leaned against the counter and watched while Stone nosed around until he found a cupboard of canned goods, and started sorting through them, stacking them on their round side, instead of upright on their flat ends.

"Are you okay?" I asked.

She was quiet for a minute, then sighed. "I think so. It's just . . . a lot. Overwhelming. Coming out of that circle with Cody and Stone and seeing all those people injured. I don't know how you've been handling it for so long."

"I haven't. Not really." I shifted to sit at the table, because my feet hurt. "It's not usually this bad." I decided now was not the time to give her the list of fights and magical scrapes I'd been in over the last few months. We'd have time, later, to catch up on all of that, because I intended to tell her everything.

She turned around, her mouth tucked down in a worried line. "Should I apologize? For thinking you were crazy?"

I smiled. "Absolutely not. I'm glad you were looking out for me. And the day I do go crazy, because hey, look at the odds, you better be right there, making sure I know it."

She walked over and gave me a quick and gentle hug before walking back to the stove. "You know I will be." She checked the waffles, then walked over to the freezer, searching through the contents.

"What time is it?" I asked.

"Just after six," she said, taking sausage out of the freezer.

"We'll need to make some decisions soon."

"About Stone?" she asked.

"Yes. About Stone, the magic inside him. About Shame and Terric. About Cody." I watched Stone carefully balance a second layer of cans on top of the first. So far, so good.

"Well, if the smell of coffee didn't make them stir, I promise this will do the trick." Nola put the sausages on a griddle and popped the waffle in the oven.

And she was right. Within the next fifteen minutes or so, Maeve walked into the kitchen. "Good morning, ladies," she said. "Breakfast smells heavenly."

"Morning, Maeve," I said. "Think we should haul this out for everyone?"

"I believe if we don't, we may have a riot on our hands."

Between the three of us, we gathered breakfast, extra plates, bowls, cups, and cutlery, and took it all out into the main room, spreading it across two of the coffee tables by the couches. Since the cots were along the wall, we shifted the couches a little and created an area where we could all sit together and still help the wounded with their meals.

To my surprise, everyone was awake, including Victor and Hayden, and Stotts and Cody, who had wandered in from the spare bedrooms. Only Shame and Terric were still out.

I didn't know about anyone else, but I was starving. I practically inhaled a waffle, and was digging into a bowl of oatmeal—with fresh blueberries—when Paul finally spoke.

"So how does this work now?" he asked.

"Which part of it?" I asked.

"The magic. Stone. The Authority."

"Carl and La told me the Authority is going to listen to us, to what we need to get the cure distributed, as soon as we formulate a cure."

"Carl and La?" Victor asked, his voice a little hoarse. His eyes were still bandaged, but he was doing a remarkably good job of eating his oatmeal without seeing.

"They stood up at the end of the fight," I said. "Told me they're calling a state of emergency, and contacting the Overseer."

"Practical of them," he said with an approving smile.

"So that's one thing not to worry about right now," Hayden said. I could tell he was still heavily medicated, his eyes a glassy sort of yellow. But he'd apparently taken the news of losing his hand with stoic acceptance.

Still, it was hard for me to hold eye contact, knowing he'd been damaged because of my plans, my orders.

"What are we going to do about magic?" he asked.

"We need someone to test it. Maybe Collins or Violet or . . . I don't know, really."

Zay gave me an odd look, then put his hand on my thigh. I knew he felt my shame, my guilt, for other people bearing the cost of my fight.

"Anyone in this room regret what we've done so far?" Zay asked.

I snapped my head up and looked at him with horror. I couldn't believe he'd just asked that.

"Why?" Victor asked. He might be blind, but he wasn't unaware of what was going on around him.

"Allie's worried she made the wrong choices," Zay said.

"Zay. Stop—," I started.

"Worried that we regret our wounds," he continued. "Worried about you, Hayden, and you, Victor."

Hayden scoffed. "The hand?" he asked, raising the stump of his arm. "Rather lose it than my life. And I've vowed to give up my life if that's what it takes to keep the innocent, and magic, safe. You told us where the battle was going to be," he said. "It has always been our choice whether to fight."

"This isn't just your fight, Allison," Victor said. "It's always been ours too. And it always will be. Until the day we die."

"Ditto, boss," Davy said around a mouthful of waffle.

"You suck," I said quietly to Zayvion.

He smiled. "I'm just tired of you worrying so much," he said. "Why not just clear the air between us and give you a little peace of mind?" He leaned back, looking satisfied with himself, then grunted at the pain and drank his coffee.

"So who are you going to task with running the magic and poison through its paces to find a cure?" Collins said.

"I don't know," I said. "I think that's part of what you promised to do."

"I did," he said. "And I still could. I might need some things, though. A lab to run tests, for example. Do you think your father would let me use his lab?" he asked.

"Maybe. He said we'd need fail-safes. He said he was thinking about how it might best be done."

"We may need you to ask him for his help, Allison," Victor said. "Your father knows Flux magic, and the integration of magic with technology, better than anyone else in the city. Perhaps, the world."

That didn't sound good. But then, Dad hadn't been working against us lately. He'd been helpful—hell, he'd been vital to our cause and done things none of the rest of us could do when the chips were down.

"I think he'll do it."

*Won't you?* I asked.

*I'll be of any assistance I can be. But give me a few hours to rest.* Then I got the distinct feeling he was sleeping, or in a deep meditation—the closest to sleep that I'd ever felt from him.

"He said he'll be of any assistance he can be," I said. "But he needs a few hours of rest."

Paul put down his coffee cup. "You're telling me your father, Daniel Beckstrom, isn't dead?" he asked.

Oh, right. He didn't know that part. Neither did Nola. I looked over at her.

"He's dead. But he's a ghost."

Nola's eyes went wide.

"So you can talk to him?" Paul asked.

"Yes."

"Is he here now?" Nola asked.

"Yes, Allie," Collins prompted. "Is he?"

It was too late trying to keep this information away from Collins, and I didn't want to keep it from Nola any longer. "He's in my head. Someone tried to raise him from the grave and he's kind of been possessing a part of my mind and body for a few months."

Nola looked like she was about to cry. "Oh, Allie. I'm so sorry."

I shrugged and managed a smile. "It wasn't my idea for him to possess me, and it wasn't his idea either. But in some ways it's sort of worked out for the better. I think he'll help us. Help us with Stone."

"Oh, I'm sure he will at that," Collins said over the edge of his coffee.

"It's a good start," Maeve said, giving Zayvion a wink. A wink?

But before I could ask, she stood. "Do you think there's any tea in that kitchen, Nola?"

"Yes, let me help you with that." Nola looked like she

needed a moment to pull herself together. It was sweet of Maeve to help her out. I think if I'd offered to go with her, she and I would just end up sitting on the floor crying. And I couldn't do that. Yet.

They walked off and Paul got up to pace, working his knee to move more fluidly. His back looked like it was killing him. Plus, he was probably trying to swallow down the whole ghost-on-the-brain revelation.

"Before we go anywhere or do anything, or decide who's going to try to cook up the cure," Zay said, "I want a hot shower." He plucked at his sweaty, bloody shirt. "And all the rest of you could all use a change of clothes too."

"I'll see if there's anything here," Davy said. "If not, I'll hit up a thrift store."

"I'll help," Sunny said.

He smiled, and they left the room, hand in hand.

"You," Zay said. "Woman. Shower." He heaved up off the couch, and I could tell it took everything he had to straighten. But he did straighten, and then sniffed, as if dismissing the pain.

"You don't really think you can boss me around like that, do you?" I asked.

He licked his lips and I could see the sweat on his forehead. "Just wanted to make sure I'd caught your attention. Shower?"

I glanced around the room, my gaze lingering on Shame and Terric. "Do you think they're going to wake up?"

"Not for a while. And if they do, everyone is here to look after them." He started across the room. The hitch in his hip was worse. Bad enough he couldn't cover it with his usual swagger.

I followed after him. I did want a shower and clean clothes.

Zay stepped into the bathroom, except it wasn't a

bathroom. It was a bedroom. A big bowl of popcorn waited on the nightstand with two cups of tea. That would be Maeve's doing and must have been what all the winking was about. A flat-screen was paused on the opening credits of a movie.

"This isn't the shower," I said.

"No, it isn't. That comes after this."

"And what's this?"

He started toward the huge bed, then reached up to pull off his shirt. He groaned and pulled it over his head, swearing under his breath.

And no wonder. He was covered in bruises and several shallow cuts that Dr. Tullis, or maybe one of the nurses, had cleaned and spread some kind of cream over. His right shoulder was noticeably swollen, and his left arm was burned down to his wrist. He wadded up the shirt and dropped it on the floor.

"This is what you and I are going to do for the next two hours." He crawled across the patchwork quilt, snagging up three pillows on his way.

"Popcorn and a movie?" I asked.

"I believe that was the deal. When this was done, and we were still standing."

"This isn't done. We haven't cured magic. All we've done is poured a bunch of magic—both light and dark, which is very dangerous together—in Stone, Unclosed a madman, put Cody's soul back together, and dragged the rest of my friends into a fight that we almost lost.

"And we killed the head of Portland's Authority. Again."

"True," he said. "We also sent Roman to give the Overseer word about what's going on here, about Leander and Isabelle, did the world a service by removing Jingo Jingo from it, and possibly, for the first time in months, have a chance for the Authority to be working as it should. We'll talk to your dad, Collins, and Violet soon. We'll find a way to stop the sickness. But the world is going to wait for two hours. Two," he said to my inhalation. "Because we're still standing, aren't we?"

He stretched his legs out with a grunt, positioned the pillows behind his back and head, then gave me a smile. "Well, one of us is anyway." He patted the side of the bed next to him. "Come here."

I shook my head, but couldn't hide my smile. "I can't believe you."

"How amazing I am?"

"This. All this. It's ridiculous you remembered I wanted this."

"Ridiculous? A man should always remember the important things."

I strolled to the bed and crawled over the quilt to settle beside him. "I get only two pillows?"

"That was also the deal. Good pillows are mine," he said. "But you can hold the popcorn." He handed it to me and picked up the remote.

I settled beside him, leaning on his chest, not even needing a pillow. Zay was right. We all needed showers, fresh clothes, and more than four hours of sleep. Dad wasn't responding, and Collins was half asleep over his coffee. We couldn't do anything until we were rested.

In a few hours, by afternoon at the latest, we'd pull our plan of action together. Right now, we needed all the downtime we could get.

"So what are we watching?" I asked, stuffing popcorn in my mouth.

Zay had already hit play on the remote and was munching on a handful of popcorn. He pointed at the screen, which revealed a close-up of a bookshelf.

Bright yellow letters appeared.

"*Winnie the Pooh and the Blustery Day*?" I asked. "You have got to be joking."

Zay chuckled. "I couldn't believe Mrs. Stanley had it in her library. I guess she has a grandson who loves it."

"We're watching *Winnie the Pooh*?" I asked again.

"Shh. This is the good part."

"Your idea of a romantic movie is *Winnie the Pooh*?"

"She didn't have *RoboCop*." He took another scoop of popcorn, chewed, and then as the music faded, he recited, right along with the narrator: "This could be the room of any small boy."

I started laughing. "You do not have this movie memorized."

"Of course I do. It's a classic."

We watched the entire thing, and Zayvion proved his attention to storybook detail by pointing out the differences between the book and the movie. The movie was nowhere near two hours long and after it, we were going to raid Mrs. Stanley's other shows, but instead fell asleep.

I woke to a sudden cold numbing in my left palm.

Zayvion woke up too, and turned my hand, expecting, as I was expecting, to see a knife sticking out of it. But there was no knife there. Only the black mark, the seal of death Mikhail had left in my hand.

"Why is it hurting?" I asked. And then I knew—we knew. Someone was homing in on it to open a Gate.

We were off that bed in a flash, running to the living room.

Light. Sound. An explosion of magic tore through the room, tore through the house, shaking it on its foundation.

Thunder cracked and rolled.

The hot concrete and salt smell of a Gate opening burned my nose, my mouth, my lungs. This wasn't any

Gate. This was something huge, something more powerful than I'd ever seen before.

*Ezekiel's Hands*, Dad said.

The Gate that could open across any distance, no matter how far. The Gate even Zayvion couldn't cast. Opening here, in the center of an old church in St. Johns.

The explosion of light and sound blasted outward, then hammered inward, striking the center of the room with painful precision I could feel ringing down to my core.

Magic cut through the middle of the room, and a golden orb hovered in midair. An orb made of pure magic. Like a lock turning, the orb opened, spiraling wide like a flower blooming, spinning in flashes of magic that burned the air, the space, the reality of the place.

It melted through the distance between here and wherever it had been cast from, creating an archway that flickered, as magic welded the two spaces, the two great distances, together.

And through that doorway staggered a man.

Not just any man. Roman Grimshaw, the ex–Guardian of the gates.

He was bloody, burned, his coat missing. His exposed skin smoked and blistered as if he had bathed in acid. And as soon as he was through the gate, he was on his knees.

"Roman!" I said.

Zayvion and I rushed to him.

"They are coming," he gasped.

We caught him in our arms. Maeve and Paul brought blankets and made a place for us to lay him down. We did so, propping up his head.

He was bleeding. Badly. From so many places, I couldn't tell where I should apply pressure.

"Isabelle," he whispered. "Leander."

"How?" Zayvion asked.

"They have taken." Roman inhaled, exhaled with far too little air, and far too much rattling in his lungs.

"Get the doctor!" I yelled.

Davy was already running down the hall to get him.

"You're going to be okay," I said. "Just rest."

"Tell us," Zayvion said. "How are Leander and Isabelle coming?"

"They possessed the Overseer," he whispered. "Killed her. Raised her from the dead. And now they are her. And now they are . . ."

The doctor rushed in, and I got out of the way.

Zayvion didn't move. "They're what?" he asked. "What are Leander and Isabelle doing?"

Roman's eyes unfocused. He had stopped moving. Every breath seemed more shallow than the last.

The doctor pulled his burned shirt aside and revealed a gaping wound. A deadly wound. I could see bone and muscle and veins and organs. And then Roman stopped breathing.

"Roman," Zayvion said. "No."

I watched as Roman stepped out of his own body. The ghost of Roman, the soul of him, the Veiled, since he had been a powerful magic user. A very powerful magic user. He looked like Roman, only unburned and sad-eyed.

"More's the pity," he rasped, his voice scratching at my mind, just as Shame's voice had done.

"What are Leander and Isabelle doing, Roman?" I stood, faced him.

Zay looked up at me. The doctor and everyone else looked over at me too. At the crazy woman who could see magic and hear dead people.

Two pretty handy skills at the moment, thank you.

"They are coming to kill you, Allie. They are coming

to kill Zayvion. They will eradicate the Soul Complements in this world. Starting with you. So they can rule magic. So they can rule the world."

"How?" I said. "Are they using Gates? Are they coming now?"

"The possession of the Overseer has tired them. They cannot use magic yet. But they will, and once that is so, they will come for you. They will bend all the world, and all the minds they need, to destroy you. You, and Zayvion."

"Just because we're Soul Complements?" My heart was pounding. Pounding too fast.

"No. Because it is within you both to stop them. Here, on this hallowed ground. They know what you are, Allison Angel Beckstrom. They know what you have been made to be. And they mean to unmake you."

"Do we have days?" I asked. "Hours?"

"Three days at the most. They will try the gates. If they are locked, they will try to travel by conventional means. I will give you all the time that I can."

"How?" I asked.

Roman turned and walked into the gate that was still open in the middle of the room. He stood, arms to his side, stance set wide. Even though he was no longer alive, I could see pain wash over his face. He tipped his head down, bearing the pain and holding the Gate open, as if by sheer will alone.

I had ever seen only one other person, one other soul, stand like that in a gate. Cody's spirit, when he had leaped into the gate, not to open it, but to hold it closed so that nothing could get through. And nothing had; not a single gate had opened until Cody finally stepped out, exhausted, and had been tied to Mama.

"You will know their weakness," Roman said. "For it is their strength."

And then he spoke one hard word. The gate closed with a roar.

I stood there, shaking, sweating. Burning with cold. Roman was dead, the kind of dead you didn't come back from. I could not bear to turn and see his bloody, lifeless body behind me.

But I did.

Zayvion was still on his knees, holding Roman's hand even though the doctor had already leaned away and was no longer touching him. Zay bowed his head and whispered, "To keep magic safe, and the lives of the innocent. You have upheld your vows with honor. Safe journey, Guardian." Then he folded Roman's hands on his chest, and stood, the sorrow all too clear in his eyes.

"Hell of a way to wake a man," Shame said, his voice barely more than a whisper.

"Is it the end of the world already?" Terric whispered.

We all turned to look at them.

Collins, Dr. Tullis, and Maeve all rushed to their side.

I studied Shame's face from where I stood. Too pale, too gaunt. There was a darkness to him that I had never seen before, as if a deep shadow covered him in a shroud. Then I looked at Terric, who was glossy with sweat and running a hell of a fever. He almost glowed with a silver white edging, as if there were light trapped inside him. They had changed. But they were alive.

"I didn't expect you gentlemen to be awake," the doctor said. "Not with the beating you took. And the blood loss, the magic overload, the . . . well, everything. This is a good sign." He looked at Maeve, then Zayvion, then me. "A very good sign. Let me wash my hands." He left to do so.

I glanced at Zayvion. The sorrow was still bare on his face.

"I'll help you with Roman," I said. "We can talk to Shame and Terric after the doctor's checked on them."

Zay nodded, and Paul came over to help. Then I spent the next few minutes trying not to think too hard about helping them pick up a dead man and take him to one of the back rooms. We lowered him onto a cot, where the nurse who had stayed the night drew a sheet over him, and told us she'd make a phone call.

No more waiting. No more resting. We had a lot to take care of and very little time to do it all. Leander and Isabelle were coming. And we were in no shape to stop them.

Yet.

As we walked back into the living room, a plan was beginning to form in my mind, even though I was shaken, frightened.

Zayvion had pulled his calm Zen mask back into place. "It's not the end of the world yet," he said. "We still have time."

"And we're still standing," I said. "Davy, would you call in the Hounds? Any who are still on their feet. Any who still want to help our fight. We'll need to let them know everything that's been going on."

"Will do, boss," Davy said.

"Sunny, could you contact Carl and La and tell them we need to talk to them and any member of the Authority they trust who might be in a decision-making position? We'll need to meet. Later today would be best. Tomorrow, at the latest."

"Sure," she said.

Sunny paused halfway out of the room. "What should I tell them the meeting is about?"

I looked up. "Tell them now we have a real war to wage." I stood where the gate had opened, staring down at Roman's blood on the floor. Zayvion moved beside me, his hand wrapped around my waist, gripping my hip tight. He was still hurting. So was I. We all were. But there was only option left to us. Take out Leander and Isabelle. Hit them before they hit us. Or we'd all be dead.

Read on for an exciting excerpt from the
new novel in Devon Monk's
Age of Steam series,

## *TIN SWIFT*

Coming July 2012 from Roc

Stump Station wasn't much more than a collection of shacks built precariously into the pockets and wedges east side of the Bitterroot Range. So barren and out of the way, even the vultures risked starvation. It was the perfect sort of place to attract those members of society who preferred to remain unnoticed by others. Hard men and rangy women who spent most of their days waiting for the right wind to carry them up to the glim grounds, where they could harvest their fortune.

Glim, more precious than diamonds or gold, used to power ships on air, water, or land. Used to heal the sick, cure the blights, turn the tides in wars, and make anything and everything stronger and longer lasting. Glim was even rumored to extend a man's life well beyond his years.

Rare and desired, glim. And as hard to locate as Hades' back door.

Some said glim could be found underground or out at sea. But the only place glim was known to occur was up in the sky, high above the storm clouds, floating like nets of soft lightning. Difficult to find. Deadly to harvest. Most ships couldn't launch that high, last those storms, or lash and land without killing those who flew them.

So it was no wonder glim fetched a high price in the legitimate markets and a king's ransom in those markets less savory.

Captain Hink counted himself among his own kind out here in the rocks. Outlaws, prospectors, glim pirates, soldiers of luck, fools, and the foolhardy—brothers all.

Not that he wouldn't drop a brother at a thousand paces if he jumped his claim, stole his boots, or touched his airship, the *Swift*.

But then, he supposed any of the rock rats who ported, docked, or launched at Stump Station would do him the same.

"Problem, Mr. Seldom?" Captain Hink asked as his second-in-command ducked through the canvas tarp that hung in place of a door in the tumbledown Hink called home.

Seldom was a wiry-built redheaded Irish who looked like he'd snap in half if he sneezed too hard. Most people thought he got his name from how often he spoke. But Captain Hink knew he went by Seldom for how many times he'd lost a fight.

Hink figured he and Seldom didn't much resemble each other. Hink scraped up a full six foot, three inches, and had shoulders that took the sides off doorways if he wasn't mindful. Yellow hair, skin prone to tanning, and eyes the gray of a broody sky set in a face that women had never complained about, Hink might have been considered a catch if he'd grown up in the social circles of the old states instead of the bastard child of a soiled dove.

And whereas Seldom looked old for his thirty years, Hink looked like a man in his twenties, and that was no lie.

Seldom stabbed one thumb over his shoulder, stirring the wool scarves around his neck and jostling his breathing gear, which hung at the wait near his collarbone. "Mullins."

Captain Hink put the cup of boiled beans that passed

for coffee up here in the stones down on the edge of the map spread across the buckboard that served as his desk. He leaned back in his chair, enough so his Colt was in easy reach. He wasn't expecting Les Mullins to come in and shoot him dead. But he wouldn't be surprised if that's what the captain of the big—and recently crashed and burned—*Iron Draught* hoped to accomplish.

Especially since Mullins had to patch up that old mule of a steamer the *Powderback* to get around.

Mr. Seldom stepped to the corner of the room and faded into the woodwork like a stick in a stack.

The canvas tarp whipped aside and in strode Les Mullins. Big man. High forehead under stringy black hair and a face permanently burned red from flying too long in the cold upper. He looked mad enough to chew coils.

"Just because I don't have a door," Captain Hink said, "doesn't mean a man shouldn't knock."

Les Mullins smiled—well, more like sneered—showing tobacco stumps where his teeth ought to have been.

"Here's the deal, Hink," he said. "You give me that tin devil of yours, and I won't tie you up like a hog, throw you off this cliff, and drag your broken bits in to the people, who will shower me with gold for my trouble."

"Deal?" Captain Hink said. "Why, we haven't even cut the deck yet. How about you get the hell out of my house, Mullins?"

"How about you explain this?" Mullins tossed something that landed and rattled like a tin can on Hink's desk.

Hink made a big production of leaning forward and picking up the item, even though he knew exactly what it was. "It's a tin star," he said.

"It's a badge," Mullins said.

"So it is."

"Says U.S. Marshal."

"I see that, Mullins," Captain Hink said. "You thinking of wearing this around so folk respect you? 'Cause it's going to take a damn bit more than a tin star to make people stand up and take notice of the bluster that comes out of your yap."

"What I think," Mullins said, advancing toward the desk, "is that you've been spying on us since you set up nest last spring. Weaseling out our stakes, claims, and buyers. What I think, *Captain*, is that you're the president's man, or near enough it don't make no matter otherwise. You come to shut our operation down and to haul us in to the law."

"Shut it down?" Hink brought his hand, star and all, back casual-like toward his holster. "Why would I want to shut down an enterprise in which I make so much money?"

"Don't know the mind of a turncoat dog like you."

Captain Hink weighed that remark for one second. He had a reputation of a bad temper and a quick trigger. Something his mother had told him would get him killed, God rest her soul. So he always gave every statement a full-up two seconds of consideration before he acted upon it.

Then he pulled the knife from his belt and threw it straight and true into Mullins' throat.

Mullins stumbled back. He clutched at the knife with one hand and clawed for his gun with the other. Wasn't much successful with either attempt.

"I sure hope I haven't damaged your talker." Captain Hink stood and sauntered over to the big man, who had stumbled to brace his back against the wall. Not that it'd do him any good. Walls couldn't save men who rode the skies. "Because your story was just getting interesting."

"There's a thing I have a powerful need to know, Mr.

Mullins," Hink said. "Where in the world did you get this from?" He held up the badge. "You been sniffing down around the townies? Catch up some poor land lizard with a knack for a tall tale?"

Mullins leveled him a glare and finally got hold of the knife hilt. He pulled it free with a yell and fell to one knee. Didn't much matter, Captain Hink thought. There was no chance this traitor to the states was walking out of his house alive.

"Found me a yellowbelly who knew you, Captain Hink Cage," Mullins rasped. "Said his name was Rucker."

"Rucker?" Captain Hink said. "Name doesn't jostle the memory."

"He knew you," Mullins said. "Knew what you did at the battle of Flatstand. Knew you took more than half your regiment and turned on General Alabaster Saint. Disobeyed orders. Refused to fight. Walked away. Left them all to die. You cost the Saint his eye, you traitor snake bastard."

"He tell you any other stories, this Rucker you jawed with?" Hink asked.

"Not after I shot him dead, he didn't."

Hink didn't even wait a second. He clocked Mullins straight across the chin and dropped down over him so he could continue with the beating, as he was the sort of fellow who didn't mind getting his hands dirty to see that a job was well done. Got in one more hit before Mullins pulled his gun.

The cold click of the hammer cocking back soaked through the anger Captain Hink was enjoying and put him right away into a most reasonable and sober mind.

"Don't matter if you're alive or dead," Mullins said. "Just so long as I bring you in."

Mr. Seldom seemed to appear out of the walls themselves. And just like that was standing above Mr. Mullins.

Then, just like that, Seldom swung the oversized iron marlin spike, slamming the gun out of Mullins' hand. Likely broke up a few of the man's fingers in the process, seeing as how loud he screamed.

"Thought you'd know better than to upset my second, Mullins. You know how he doesn't take well to people trying to plug me." Hink rolled back on his heels and stood, staring down at the bleeding man.

Seldom retrieved the gun from where it had landed, wiped the blood off with one of the scarves hanging to his waist, and tossed the gun to Hink.

Captain Hink caught the weapon, gave it a glance, then tossed it back to Seldom, who pocketed it.

"Won't matter if you kill me," Mullins gasped. "Word's already out. This whole town's coming for your neck, Hink Cage."

Seldom lifted the marlin spike again.

"Name's Hink," Captain Hink said. "Captain, if you can't remember that much. Don't go on and kill him yet, Mr. Seldom. I've still a question or two I want answered."

Hink rolled the tin star between his fingers like a poker chip, then held it between the tips of his index and middle finger.

"What's this matter to you, Mullins?" he asked as the star caught a shine of light. "Some lander giving you guff about me being a Marshal don't exactly stand that it's true. And if so, what do you have to hide you wouldn't want a marshal to know?"

Mullins closed his mouth and didn't do much more than glare and bleed.

"I think this isn't just your business you've got yourself hitched up to, Mr. Mullins," Captain Hink said. "I think you're working for someone. Someone who don't cozen to the law. Makes a certain sense seeing as how we straddle the border of legality, shooting the sky for glim. But more than all that, I think there's a spy in this house who ain't me."

Hink glanced over at Mr. Seldom. "You don't suppose Mr. Mullins knows old Alabaster Saint himself, do you?"

Mullins caught his breath. Not a dead giveaway, but a giveaway nonetheless.

Hink rubbed at his chin. "Let me take a shot and tell you a story, Mr. Mullins. I say there was once a man named Les Mullins. Came from out Kentucky way. Signed up to serve beneath the hardest, bloodthirstiest monster that ever put on a uniform. Followed that monster—oh, let's give him a name . . . say, General Alabaster Saint—through hell and worse. Les Mullins saw nine out of ten of his fellow soldiers die obeying the Saint's bloody command.

"Thought himself damn lucky to have survived. Maybe even thought himself blessed, anointed, and appointed to continue following General Alabaster Saint's orders long after the battles this United States were engaged in were done and gone.

"So Les Mullins wants to make himself useful to that general he worships. But a leader needs more than loyal dogs. He needs power. And it takes riches to get power. Luckily for Les Mullins, he knows there's one thing in this world that can get a man filthy with riches and power—glim."

Hink paused and nodded toward Seldom. "It's a good story so far—don't you think?"

Mr. Seldom shrugged, focused mostly on flipping the marlin spike—*slap, slap, slap*, as if his palms were restless determined to use it again.

"Let's see," Hink said. "How does this story end? I'd say it ends with General Saint's spy Les Mullins getting killed on the floor of a shack in the Bitterroots unless he tells a man named Captain Hink just who, exactly, he's working for and what, exactly, that man wants."

Mullins had gone from bleeding to wheezing. His good hand was pressed over the neck wound as if he could hold the blood inside. Looked like he thought he could hold the words inside too. But Hink would get them out of him. He'd done worse to better men.

"I'll give you a moment to consider my request, Mr. Mullins," Hink said. "Because that's the last time I'm asking you to give me answers. From here on out, I'll just be doing an awful lot of painful taking them from you."

Hink turned back to his desk and took a drink of coffee. His hands shook from a hard anger.

George Rucker had been a friend. The younger brother of William Rucker, a man Hink served with and had been unable to save from Alabaster Saint's bloodthirsty loyalists.

Hink had come too late to stop William's hanging, but he'd found young George Rucker and taken him in. Looked after him as best he could, even while carrying out the president's orders. Because Mullins was right about that. That tin star was his. He was Marshal Hink Cage when he wasn't wedged up here with glim pirates, trying to suss out the kingpin of their black-market trade.

He'd given that star to George Rucker for safekeeping and as a promise that he'd return from this mission to retrieve it from him.

A promise he couldn't keep now because of Les Mullins. A promise that had gotten George Rucker killed.

A shot rang out and the high steam whine of engines catching hot pounded the air. Not just engines. The *Swift*'s engines.

"Captain Hink!" A woman yelled from a good ways off. "The ship. They're on her!"

The gunshot boomed out again, louder. That was the *Swift*'s cannon.

Hink grabbed the map off the table and his shotgun, which had been leaning against the wall. Seldom already had one foot out the door. Hink gave half a second's thought about taking the time, and wasting the bullet, to kill Mullins.

Decided the man wasn't near enough worth either and was on the road to dead anyhow.

He pushed through the canvas and squinted at the onslaught of harsh afternoon light.

There was enough of a tumble of rock and scree on this outcropping that the *Swift* could land and lash, but not so much that any ship bigger than her—and that meant every other ship in the range—could catch hold.

He'd chosen this spot for just that reason.

Mr. Seldom ran quick as a gangly jackrabbit over rock and around wind-twisted scrub toward where the *Swift* hovered just so high above the ground that a man couldn't catch her ropes with a jump. Not that she had any of her ropes dangling.

Built like a bullet, the *Swift* was one of the smallest airships that carved the sky. Outfitted with the biggest boilers she could bear, she had more power per pound than the North's battle cruisers. She carried a crew of twelve, if needed, and enough water, coal, wood, and glim to get her an eight-hundred-mile range.

But the thing that gave her the edge over bigger, more powerful ships was her skeleton. She was made of tin, which lightened her load considerably and made her sing like a crystal glass tapped by a spoon when she hit the cold upper.

All who heard that siren song knew it was the *Swift*. Wasn't a ship that could launch into the storm as quick as her, wasn't a ship that could ride it out better, wasn't a ship that could fly as fast and true.

Which was all that was saving her tin hide at the moment.

The *Swift* hovered above the heads of two dozen men and women who were unloading shotguns at her belly.

"Get her up, get her up!" Hink yelled. "Who's at the helm?"

He ran up alongside Molly Gregor, his boilerman, who had just a moment before hollered him out of the shack.

Molly was a solidly built woman with curves in the right places and a crop of straight black hair shaved short at the temples so as not to queer her breathing gear. He'd never seen her wear a dress a single day in the three years they'd been running glim together.

But even with boots, breeches, and a hell of a hand at steam tinkering, there wasn't a man who'd disrespect her. Not if they wanted to wake up breathing the next day.

"It's Guffin," she said, pounding across the rocks beside him. "He was on watch. Checking on that squall headed in from the north."

They were almost upon the mob beneath the ship now.

Molly pulled the nozzle of the flamethrower she had strapped across her back around to the front and struck a match. The slow-burning wick spring-hinged below the tip of the nozzle caught fire. Molly twisted the valve at her belt, readying the mix of oils she'd rigged up to throw a burn a hundred feet.

"Don't set her aflame," Captain Hink said. "And don't burn me neither." He pulled his gun and rushed into the crowd, headed for Jonas Hamilton, the highbinder who was yelling orders to take the *Swift* down.

"Hamilton, you horse's ass!" Hink yelled. "Get away from my ship."

Hamilton turned. He had a goosed-up Sharps carbine tucked at his shoulder and took aim straight at Hink's chest.

"Damn it all." Hink raised his pistol and shot Hamilton in the shoulder, just above the butt of the carbine.

Hamilton reeled back, his shot clipping high, but still close enough Hink heard the buzz of it as it passed his ear.

An explosion pounded rock walls and eardrums alike and damn near threw Hink to the ground. He stumbled, kept hold of the pistol, trying to see his way through the thick black smoke that filled the air. That smoke better not be the *Swift* going down, or he'd be skinning these rock rats until doomsday.

A hand reached down out of the smoke and caught hold of his arm and yanked him up hard.

"Rope!" Seldom hollered. The Irish was dangling from the *Swift*'s ladder by one foot and two fingers, looking like a squirrel ready to jump a limb. Since his other hand was helping drag Hink up to catch hold of the ladder, Hink was more than happy to see him.

The smoke was still thick enough it burned his eyes, but the *Swift* was already climbing again. Hink could just make out ragged shadows of those below him picking themselves up from that blast. It wouldn't be long before those guns in their hands were aimed at his head.

"Where's Molly?" Hink yelled over the roar of the ship's fans.

"At the boiler," Seldom said as he scurried uncommonly quick up the last of the rope.

Captain Hink put one hand over the other and hauled up the ladder as fast as he could. His crewmen heaved on the ladder while he climbed. Just as he breached the hold and pulled himself into the solid interior of the *Swift*, he heard Molly call out, "Get her up, Mr. Guffin! Get her up fast and hard!"

"He don't know any other way," Seldom muttered.

Hink laughed as the floor tipped alarmingly to one side. He pushed up off his hands and knees and staggered toward the helm.

The *Swift*'s engines popped three hard thumps of steam and power, the awe-inspiring noise of that beautiful steam engine drowning out the crowd and gunfire below, as she took aim for the clouds and let fly.